A STRANGER IN THEIR MIDST

By the same author

FRANK DELANEY

A STRANGER IN THEIR MIDST

HarperCollins*Publishers*

HarperCollins*Publishers*
77–85 Fulham Palace Road,
Hammersmith, London W6 8JB

Published by HarperCollins*Publishers* 1995
1 3 5 7 9 8 6 4 2

Copyright © Frank Delaney 1995

Frank Delaney asserts the moral right to
be identified as the author of this work

A catalogue record for this book is
available from the British Library

ISBN 0 00 224189 7

Photoset in Linotron Caledonia by
Rowland Phototypesetting Ltd, Bury St Edmunds, Suffolk

Printed in Great Britain by
HarperCollinsManufacturing Glasgow

TO MICHAEL SHAW

When he smiled the room grew warm. His brown eyes welcomed all. In any business deal, nobody ever felt that he alone had won, and they alone had lost, because, in commerce's most humanitarian dictum, he 'left room for the other man'. Within this company of ours, he forged and devised and invented and strove. He made, in the very fullest sense – he made the careers of many of us.

These words come from the funeral eulogy given in 1989 for Dennis Sykes by his successor. The Chairman also said, 'None of you at this memorial service will take offence when I say that we have never worked with – or for – anyone as clever, anyone as *intelligent* as the man for whose life we here give thanks today. He was our leader, our inspiration, our dear friend.'

The eulogy rose and grew into a hailing piece of praise-singing. Some jokes, the poignant recollection of a kind deed, his prodigious memory for family enquiries and the thoughtfulness shown towards everyone – typists, drivers, cleaners. The eulogy contained no original words, perhaps, but no unnecessary lies. Apparently. The Chairman delivered it beside a twinkling photograph of the departed, who wore a silver tie.

Nobody mentioned, nobody knew, Dennis Sykes the emotional criminal, the sexual psychopath. Who practised seduction, manipulation, destruction of the heart. He dreamed up, organized and executed, crimes against the spirit, against trust. Like a hired killer, a lone gun (he always referred to his penis as 'my Weapon') he reconnoitred, spied, assessed: he measured his booty in units of female vulnerability: he struck, and he vanished. With no regrets. All this he did with as much secrecy as possible. He understood secrecy, saw it as a kind of hidden energy source.

=

9

Dennis Sykes was one of the first of what came to be called a 'clear-desk executive'. In the interests of perceived efficiency, he had nothing in front of him except the file he was working on at that moment, and a large and beautiful blotting pad, with leather corners. This blotter remained perpetually snow-blank: no doodles. In 1984, at the age of seventy, he retired, wealthy and distinguished, from the chairmanship of Consolidated. His last company days show the warm-smiled, humane business leader, photographed bright and dapper in side-by-side handshakes, giving diligence awards to young graduate engineers in their first year with the company.

Nowhere do the photographs or the house magazines reveal a depressed man, his imagination full of revenge fantasies. Nor did anyone record that during seventeen years at Consolidated, Dennis Sykes never hired for his own office even one pretty secretary or female assistant. As part of his life-scheme, he kept his secret 'exercises' fanatically remote from his public activities, and therefore he chose to work with sober and restrained, untempting women.

Outside Consolidated, he golfed, and led the usual accompanying social life. People invited to his home for cocktails or less frequently dinner, teased him over not having a wife: how a woman would have loved that house: how a wife would have untidied that fastidiousness and had rose petals falling on his shining mahogany.

In other circumstances – were he perhaps a less clever or educated man, but just as depressed – Dennis Sykes would probably have killed. He might simply have gone out and seduced women in a systematic pattern in order to take them somewhere safe, and then attack them. His wish to destroy women had all the hallmarks of a killer, and it was restrained by the white-collar society in which he moved. In Scotland and Ireland, he was also curtailed by the parochial size of the communities in which he lived and worked. Yet, in their secrecies he flourished, with his hidden life full of duplicitousness. And his destructiveness caused damage from which people never recovered.

1

llen Kane released the handbrake abruptly, and the green, glossy car jerked forward. Men of the parish standing in their gossipy line outside the gate doffed their caps and stared hard. In the passenger's seat, Thomas Kane sat upright, rigid and dignified, with bleak eyes. An unbarking dog chased the wheels, and skidded in the summer's dust. Slowly, with her chin raised so that she could peer over the steering-wheel, Ellen negotiated the sharp right-angled turn of the high churchyard wall. Straight as an arrow now, the car at last departed, and birds fled the trees at the noise.

On the steep descent to Hogan's Bend, neither spoke, and the sunlight disappeared when they entered the black nave of overhanging trees. When they emerged, Ellen indicated the plunging mare in the field on their left: her commentary began.

'Can you believe he paid three hundred guineas for her? Three hundred guineas!'

Outside one of the cottages, a young wet-lipped adult went 'Uuuhmmmnrh!' in delighted fright, and pranced awry as the car gleamed past.

'Poor creature,' murmured Ellen, 'but they say the new baby is normal. Thanks be to God.'

Up in the fields to the left, by that famous copse of the best hazelnut trees in the county, a horseman looked down at them against the sun, his hand shading his eyes. Ellen with her amazingly good sight, said, 'Look, look! There's Cyril Stephenson, and they're saying he will, that he really will, marry her.'

Thomas Kane nodded.

'Thomas, are you able for a big breakfast?'

They drove past the dispensary. Ellen chattered on; 'The Hogans aren't up yet. I s'pose they'll go to last Mass in Mooreville.'

She had worked out a method of reminding him how the parish lived. With never a direct statement, she made oblique references only, and spoke of many things as if he automatically understood the references. 'I *knew* Mrs Greege paid too little for that paint on the haybarn last year. Look, the paint is all blistering.'

Up to their right, she pointed happily to the ruin of Deanstown Castle. The turrets and casements shone golden in the morning sun, a place fit for the streamers and flags of a jousting tournament.

'What are you thinking, Thomas?'

He shook his head, and folded his hands again.

They passed the Greege boy who stood at a field gate preparing to take cows across the road. He saluted. Thomas even tried to turn his head to look back at him.

'Easy, Thomas. You'll see him again.'

She yawned: Ellen had conceived three weeks ago.

This August Sunday morning was their first outing, his re-entry into their small community. Up to eight weeks ago, Thomas Kane had lived in a coma. For thirteen and a half months, he had lain stretched on a day-bed in his own home, with his wife living out a frantic, but powerfully-directed life aimed at his recovery. Mid-morning, Friday, 17 June 1927 – she later wrote the date in violet ink in her housekeeping book – a carter rapped at the school window and said, 'Essie says you're to go up home, Ma'am. Yes, Ma'am, *now*. She looks a bit urgent.'

Out of breath after her short run from the school, Ellen forced herself to stand still, to make no movement. She did not raise Thomas's heavy head, whatever the temptation; she did not take his pulse or his temperature. If anything, she pressed back a little, withdrawing the child. Right behind her, Essie, the big, mottled servant-girl, breathed as she always did when agitated: a little hissed moaning: 'Gu-nnnhhh-sss, gu-nnnhhh-sss.'

Helena, thirteen months and walking early for her age, sensed the stillness in the room and made whispering, conspiratorial noises. Ellen stood poised, suspended. No gambler ever eyed a dice closer: no sailor ever surveyed a threatening rock so watchfully. The death-faced, supine man closed his filamented eyes again.

Ellen said, quite sharply, 'Thomas?' in that tone of voice that has lost patience with someone feigning sleep. '*Thomas?*'

Nothing happened. She turned to Essie with an enquiring and

disappointed shrug, but the servant-girl pointed again. He had reopened his eyes, and they blinked as lazily as a lizard's. Then he looked at her, but did not focus.

Day after day, week after week, Ellen had wondered – and she said it to several – 'What will his first words be?'

She never voiced the 'If . . . *if*'; she could not afford to; had invested everything in 'when', not 'if'; she kept two calendars side by side on the kitchen wall, last year's and this year's.

In the novels she read, an unconscious hero or swooned heroine always asked, 'Where am I?' Her husband Thomas Kane, his mind and spirit absent from her for over a year, said nothing at all.

As his eyelids found the strength to stay open, she stepped forward and took his hand. She turned the palm upwards, and rubbed his fingers as if attacking frostbite.

'If you can hear me, love, grip me, would you?'

His eyes focused on her and he coughed, releasing a little saliva; she wiped it with her finger.

'Thomas, do you know me? Do you know who I am?'

He blinked, once, then once more, then sighed, then closed his eyes again for a second or two, and when he reopened them, she said, 'Your eyes – they're a bit sharper now.'

She leaned towards his face, smiling as she did when picking Helena from the cot in the morning.

'Thomas, you're Thomas Kane. That is your name. I'm Ellen, your wife, Ellen. You've been hurt, you've been hurt for a long time.'

She straightened up and turned to Essie: 'I don't know what to do.'

'Bathe his forehead, Ma'am,' and the servant-girl hurried once more, this time to the back-kitchen to get a basin of water and flannel. As Ellen began to apply them, Thomas closed his eyes again. He put out his tongue, and licked the wet towelling of the facecloth. She looked down to see him make a flicking gesture with his fingers.

'I'll stop, will I?' she asked him, leaning back – and he spoke his first word in fifty-eight weeks.

'Do.'

=

In a wide circle, Ellen turned the car gingerly through the gate and saw its brass headlamps reflect golden sunlight on the bay-windows. At the front door stood Essie, holding up wriggling Helena.

With imperious hand, he did not permit Ellen to help him from the car; he even reached back inside, fetched his hat, and, holding it like a president, walked unaided to the house. She followed, removing the pin from her brown cloche and shaking her hair. Briefly she checked whether she had put a dinge in the car when she hit the church wall on the way in to Mass.

Sunday always meant a fresh tablecloth, but Essie had laid the white Belfast linen, the best. The servant-girl hung about waiting for a little praise, and Ellen smiled and nodded. Thomas smoothed the cloth as he sat; his clean, rounded fingernails traced the sheen of the damasked shamrocks.

'Couldn't Helena go down for her sleep now?' Ellen asked Essie. The child was held forth generally for kissing purposes.

Alone together, as they started breakfast, Ellen smiled at him. Both hands smoothed down her bosom in excitement.

'You see. You see! You did it! Your first outing! Oh, dear man, I'm proud of you.'

Thomas looked at her, then without a word turned to gaze out of the window.

Wildfire had carried the word of Thomas Kane's recovery. In an hour the news had spread. Mrs Hand in the public house said she knew something would happen because that morning, with not a puff anywhere, 'Lovely summer's day, a day like you'd write away for, we had a fairy wind here, didn't it run down through the village and rip a slate off the roof of the pub?'

Miriam Hogan found a fossil in the quarry the previous evening, and put it aside knowing Thomas Kane would have a view on it – when he could.

By six o'clock all knew everywhere in 'Deanstown and District', as officialdom called the place. By nine, after milking-time and supper, forum after forum opened up: the cross-roads; Hand's pub; the tree below the Canon's house where they played cards; Ryan's gate.

No two oracles bore the same tale. The Master was up and walking. He'd asked for potatoes, sick of that bread-and-milk, could you blame him? No, he was not up at all, not by any long chalk, he was only after opening his eyes and his speech wasn't working yet. Someone that someone spoke to heard from somebody else that someone saw him at the window. No. How could he be up at the window this quick?

As to his first words – what did they speculate? What did they actually insist that he said?

Easy to guess his first question: a hard man would want revenge, so he asked – 'Who did it?'

So they said.

By eleven o'clock on that balmy night of big summer stars, that was an established fact: 'Who did it?' – with variations such as, 'Who fired the shot?' and 'How many shots?'

Their comments had to remain speculative. Nobody got near the recovering man, and nobody would until this morning, his first reappearance at Mass. When Ellen Kane struck crisis, this soft and protected city girl abandoned her convent piety. She quarried ferociously for resources within herself, and discovered that privacy made her strong in that small, invasive community.

Therefore, for that crucial eight weeks after his awakening, from June to August, she kept them out. His dignity had to be guarded. To nobody could she, or would she, show his changing face, his staggering steps, his anger at his own debility. Even inside the house, she had to rush and hide from Essie his desperate, rock-hard erections each morning. This unanticipated embarrassment led to her moving Thomas back into their own bed sooner than she had expected.

Besides, Ellen needed all her concentration: she had to make adjustment after rapid adjustment. He panted with anxiety as she left to go to school each morning. When she returned he would not let go of her hand. In that first week, he once tried to slap her face in anger as she said her afternoon 'Hallo'.

As each twilight fell, she closed and locked the gate, and when he developed sufficient mobility, took him into the warm dusk and walked him up and down the gravel path, into the garden, back again, around to the garage, back again. He staggered often; he stopped and started. A hidden onlooker would have reckoned this was someone trying to sober up a drunk.

=

15

'What will I do about all he has missed?' Ellen asked the doctors, who arrived some weeks after she had sent them her telegram: 'THOMAS KANE RECOVERED FROM COMA TODAY. THANK YOU. THANK YOU. ELLEN KANE.'

They considered, looking one to the other.

'Don't overload him.'

One said quickly, 'He may feel odd.'

'Odd?'

'People who have bad illnesses, and who recover from them, especially *accidents* –' how he chose the word – 'they sometimes feel they themselves are to blame.'

'But he wasn't.' She never lost that childhood quickness.

'Now, Mr Kane,' they asked him, 'how have you been?'

A letter gave notice of their arrival via Liverpool and Dublin. She dressed Thomas in the suit of his wedding. The couple stood by the door as the surgeons from London, gleaming in this country-side like Martians in pressed grey suits, walked to meet him.

Thomas had the presence of a senile ambassador, as he slowly ushered these metal figures into the house.

They asked him ungushingly, 'Have you had any regressions?'

Thomas looked a little puzzled, and they amplified, 'Meaning, is all life normal? No blackouts or dizziness, no ailments associated with the head?'

Ellen again interposed. 'Not really, have you Thomas? Not that I've noticed anyway.'

'Your trauma was acute,' they continued.

Thomas looked slowly from one sleek, relaxed man to the other. Ellen said, 'He wanted to know a few days ago, he asked me – which of you did the actual operating, the surgery?'

The answer came with a smile attached. 'There were five pellets, and a fragment of another. Three of those were close enough to the surface, two were farther in, one very much so. It became a question of, well, lightness of touch, really.'

Her lips sucked in, Ellen nodded.

Thomas began to speak: then stopped.

He stared straight ahead between the two men. Tears flowed unimpeded towards his mouth. He gazed at *The Monarch of the Glen* print in its gilded long frame, a wedding present. Nobody said a word, not even Ellen.

One man remarked, after a moment, 'Well, here we are. Here we are. You seem to me as if you're going to be right as rain.'

The other looked down into his empty cup. 'Yes, I will, please, Mrs Kane,' he said, when Ellen held the teapot aloft.

Thomas allowed his tears to dry, and sat motionless during the rest of the visit. In due course the surgeons prepared to leave. Still, Thomas sat: eventually he stood to shake hands, and by the window watched them walk to the gate. He had red patches on his cheeks, bright as the dots of a clown. Ellen accompanied the Englishmen to their car and waiting driver.

'How would you say he is?' she asked.

'Astonishing. Complete recovery, I'd say.'

The other asked, 'How do you think he is emotionally?'

Ellen, from lack of comprehension, echoed, 'Emotionally?'

'Does he – does he get moody?'

'Yes, but – well, he was always a bit that way.'

Out of loyalty, she did not pursue: instead she asked, 'How much should I tell him – about, you know, about the time he was unconscious?'

'Tell him as much as he can take,' they concluded.

'He doesn't seem to like being told of things that happened while he was –' she halted.

'Tell him slowly. Spoon-feed it to him. You know how to spoon-feed by now, I should think.' A smile. 'No overloading. As I said. And be circumspect. I mean, like they used to do with the shell-shocked men, the soldiers. Remind rather than tell. Do you know what I mean?'

'Shell-shocked?' repeated Ellen. 'Yes. Yes.'

All smiled.

Up to then she had deflected Thomas's questions, promising answers when he had recovered further. That evening of the doctors, she began working carefully backwards. Of the actual shooting she spoke least, and finally told him in one terse, quiet burst.

'You called to take me and Helena home from the nursing-home. It was a lovely May morning last year. You put the hood down on the car. Coming down Canty Hill, the accident happened. A man out shooting hit you on the side of the head. The car crashed and there we were. I was up and about within a week, Helena not a

17

scratch. But poor you. The pellets put pressure on your brain.'

He stared. And stared.

She pressed on, looking him straight in the face, as she had done with her parents while lying in childhood. 'Dan Quinn. The poor fellow died the following Christmas. The family all left and went off to to England.'

Neither glossed, nor glossed over, she told him no more, and never would. He never asked.

Day in, day out, he took her hand as she raised him from his bed, led him like Lazarus into the light. At night she lay with her cheek to his face and whispered, 'Welcome back, my dear, dear man. Welcome back.'

As she sat across from him, she splurged in her excitement.

'They all wanted to see you, didn't they? Did you see the crowd in the church, Thomas?'

Everybody perceived the appalling difference in him. They had waited weeks for this: they had prowled past the house for a glimpse. And would have climbed the trees by the windows had they not feared being seen. Now, how their eyes feasted. That night, by the lamplight in their kitchens, speaking with little puffs of wonder, they mimicked his gaunt walk into church – stiffened necks, their heads held rigid. His shoes with steel heel-tips used to ring firmly on the stone floor. Now, he clinked like a broken bell – one, two, three, pause: one, two, three.

They said afterwards, 'Wasn't it in a way like the opposite of a funeral? D'you know what I mean?' All through the Mass, they scrutinized him. They took in his unprecedented hesitancy, his uncertainty, the half-vague expression on his face. Was this ever the same proud and aloof martinet, their great gunman-hero of the Troubles, who held himself as if banded with steel hoops?

They watched her as keenly: nobody had seen her for weeks. At his elbow they saw her display the pages of the Missal to him, and guide him through the prayers with a finger. She steered him upwards when he should stand: she sat him down again.

At the end of Mass nobody moved until they did – not even the slackest worshippers, who usually ran like hares before the *Last Gospel*. All stayed to watch.

The inner door had a glass panel: a frosty Crown of Thorns.

Here, the couple stopped. As she stepped forward to negotiate the complicated door-handle, he stood waiting, not looking any-where. A man helped, cap fisted to his breast – with a nod and a whispered 'Hallo, Missus'. Like damaged royalty, the pair stepped through the doorway, into the sunshine of the open church porch, and Thomas Kane blinked his long white face in the glare.

The congregation bulged out after them, but in the yard most people held back, content to walk far around him and stare. Chil-dren, agog, jostled for a better view. Senior men and women of the parish began to approach, and they spoke awkwardly to him, the men sweating in the August warmth.

Their thoughts showed. Should they shake his hand – or was it still lifeless? How could you welcome a person back when – when, well, he had been here all the time?

Eyeing the press of bodies, Ellen threw an invisible cordon around her confused husband. She clasped his arm with demon-strative responsibility: she glanced up at his face from time to time. Some of them said afterwards that she kept looking at him as if checking for something.

'Thomas. C'mon.' Ellen flicked a handkerchief from her sleeve and unfolded it. She reached up and dabbed a gem of sweat from his temple, where some blue flecks remained on the skin, and would never quite fade.

He looked over their heads, his eyes distant to the other hilltop, and took a deep breath, about to speak. Now they all pressed forward – but no. No word. They stepped back, disappointed: they had hoped he would wonder aloud who fired the shots. Among the few tall slabs *in memoriam* of dead canons and *monsignori* lying beneath the parade of beeches on this hilltop, the knot of people stood gazing at their local myth. Kindly they backed away from him, in the front yard of a country church whose walls today are painted a bright heliotrope. The tall man at their centre had returned from the dead, and his wife had brought him back, her plump lips in her worried face.

After eating, Thomas and Ellen sat by the bay-window. Dandelions gleamed like yellow stars in the long grass under the two apple-trees. At three o'clock, Canon Williams, coat open and flying, stalked through the gate. He flicked again his dark ageing eyes to

Ellen's breasts as she arranged chairs outside the front door.

'I've new glasses, haven't I,' he said into Thomas's face, 'and I can't with them see as far as the end of my nose. I declare to God the collections got smaller since you weren't here, getting money out of this crowd is like getting blood out of a turnip.'

He sat. 'I'll pour myself out if 'tis all the same to everyone' – and he tipped the bottle of stout towards a glass, both vessels held at an angle to make a wide 'A' in his hairy hands.

He poured. 'I was thinking and I seeing you at Mass this morning that you used to be a wonderful figure of a man;' sipped the cream froth on the black ale: 'A wonderful figure of a man.'

Canon Jeremiah Anthony Williams took another sip. 'We stormed Heaven for you, so we did, didn't we, Ma'am, we had every child from here to Timbuctoo in some clatter of a novena or another. We had so.' Yet he had refused to lend Ellen a walking-stick for Thomas's early upright days.

The Canon gazed ahead. 'I never liked Dan Quinn, I never did at all.' He shook his head. 'Nor did you, Missus, did you?'

Ellen, sharp as a tack, moved on him, asking in a hard voice, 'Canon, would you like something to eat?'

Soon, Helena, cheeks red and fresh from sleep, twinkled in and out through the door. Her pretty, plaid skirt flared like a tutu.

She said, 'Hallo there,' to the Canon, and showed him her skirt: he ignored her. His collar rose dignified to his chin, scoring a red weal above the Adam's apple. He snorted catarrh inwards, burbled, sipped stout again, then fell into one of his leaden reveries.

A village woman called Mamie arrived, and brought a gift to stave off her unwelcomeness – a finch in a small painted cage. Thomas rose from his chair, turned the cage this way and that.

Mamie preened at his admiration of the little bird, and ran her hands through her thin hair again, half-laughing. Thomas Kane flicked his fingernails on the tin of the cage.

The Canon said in a burst, 'Miners take songbirds down the mines to tell them of danger. If the bird dies, they know there's a dangerous gas around.'

'Good job there's no mines in this part of the country, so,' laughed Mamie.

Helena played 'hide-y' with Mamie, who winked at the child, and Helena stumbled off in a giggle.

'Fire-damp,' uttered the Canon. 'Yes, yes. That is what the mine gas is called.'

Thomas reached a long finger towards the caged finch who hopped back in dismay.

'Fire-damp. And. Talking of fire,' asked the Canon, 'is any of ye going to Dromcollogher for that memorial, that's next Sunday they're unveiling it.'

Thomas looked at him, puzzled.

The Canon comprehended. 'Last September. 'Twas while you were out cold. In your ould coma. The picture-house, and fifty they say now, or is it forty, I don't know. Dead, so to speak. There must be a lot you don't know, so.'

Thomas Kane glared at him, put the finch's cage on the window-sill, walked indoors and closed the front door. A moment later Ellen opened it, emerged and said, 'Essie made a sponge-cake. I think the Master's a bit tired.'

'Does he even know about Lindbergh?' asked the Canon.

The Canon munched. 'We should tell him everything he missed. Sure he probably knows nothing. Isn't that a queer one all the same, a teacher that knows nothing?'

'I think,' said Ellen primly, 'he will be all right. I'm making sure he knows all he needs to know.'

'Death is always looking for customers in new nations,' said the Canon, a man shaped by irrelevance.

Long after, when the visitors had gone, Thomas reappeared on the stairs.

'Oh, you must be exhausted,' said Ellen.

He walked through the hallway into the kitchen and sat down in his own wide low armchair. Helena came barrelling through with a gurgle and began to climb on her father's knee. He plucked her firmly from his thigh and planked her untenderly on the floor. She tried another climb. He detached her again, and this time he skelped her hard; his hand bit into the thigh beneath the fluffed-out plaid skirt and its pretty lace edge. Helena squealed, gasped and wept in fright: for moments the child could not catch her breath. A blue and red weal bloomed on her skin.

Ellen did not voice her shock. She led Helena away, distracting her with the finch in the cage: 'Look, Helena – birdie, birdie!'

He dozed in the armchair. Sunday night filled in, always a time of stillness. The house quietened and they went to bed.

'Thomas,' she said, 'I have news for you.'

She turned to see his face. A waning moon and the night light of late summer kept the room semi-bright. 'You know me, I'm as regular as clockwork.'

His eyes flicked open.

'Dear man, if it's a boy we'll call him after you, no arguments.' He said nothing.

'If it's a girl, we'll call her – "Grace". What else could we call a child so conceived?'

He still said nothing, and closed his eyes fervently: impossible to tell whether in joy, or in dread.

They had days filled with gold in that first year of their marriage. Like all newly-weds of the time, they knew no familiarity with the bodies of others, and not much with their own. Once they discovered, though, how beloved is the skin of the beloved, they never stopped touching each other when alone. He – who could have believed it? – deferred to her, asked her an opinion on every matter.

They had the codes of twins, or sweet conspirators, and the same dependence each upon the other. She could not get close enough to him: at night, when she crowded him in his chair, or got her arms around him in bed, she would try, it seemed, to climb inside his actual skin.

Her kisses landed everywhere. Only his ears were taboo: any touch there irritated him. Otherwise she kissed every fibre of his face and head and neck, his closed eyes, the corners of his mouth, the hollow above the bridge of his nose where his black eyebrows met – kisses, kisses, kisses, and the little 'pok' of her lip-sound that went with them.

No man could have been more different then from the taciturn and forbidding face he showed to the world. Night after night, and on dreamy gold dawns or frosty mornings, he talked to her in their deep bed. Murmurs. Whispers. Questions. Stories. Except during those difficult times, when he had to accommodate her piety while pregnant.

Now, she did the talking. She told him of Helena's first steps, of the child's first word – 'Dada! Dada!' Of the Teaching Union meetings she organized in the house so that his colleagues could pretend to include him. Of the children reciting their poems over his supine body so that his brain might hear, however faraway, the sounds of words that he loved. The food she placed on his tongue: rhubarb with ginger; coconut chocolate; the dust of grated orange peel. Of how she held fresh flowers and wet earth beneath his nose; of how she touched his face with silk or tweed, or new grass: 'There was only one sense I knew was not working, your dear eyes. So I tried all the other four. Sort of like the Last Rites, Thomas, only in reverse. You know how the priest anoints the Five Senses. I suppose that's what I was thinking of.' She counted in a remembering tone: 'Hearing. Smell. Taste. Touch. Yes.'

The night she conceived, in those nervous, gasping weeks after his awakening, she knelt beside and above him, and raised the nightdress to her waist. She pointed, tracing a finger along her abdomen.

'See. This line appeared on my stomach after Helena was born. They told me after the birth that it's known as "the life-line".'

In the gloom, she peered at his eyes, allowed her tongue a moment's rest on her lower lip. He beckoned and she lowered her face: he drew his forehead and eyes across her breasts. As she climbed across him, she bent and kissed his mouth. A small bruise like a mauve stain lurked for days afterwards on the edge of Ellen's lips, where he had kissed her too hard.

2

Dennis Emmett Sykes was born in St David's, south Wales, on 1 September 1914. Twenty-nine days later, his father died in mud and shrapnel, at Vitry-sur-Beche. Dennis's mother, with her tiny baby, had, initially, considerable difficulty: war pensions had not yet been properly put in place. Bernadette Murphy knew nobody in St David's: she came from Wexford, and a year earlier had met Patrick Sykes, while both on day excursions to Liverpool. As she had abandoned her Catholicism in order to marry the squat and pleasant Welshman, she had no good way of making friends by the usual local means of church, chapel or meeting-house. Her husband had few in family. A brother, estranged from him, lived in Swansea. Their dead mother descended from Irish labourers who had crossed to Wales for work on the railways.

However, Bernadette Sykes, *née* Murphy, from a family of ten children and swingeing poverty, had two assets. She was unusually pretty, with classy looks that made her seem like someone from a higher, wealthier stratum; and she had a combination of numerate intelligence and emotionless cunning. Her bereavement never fazed her. She had known within months that the marriage would eventually prove difficult: her bridegroom never had her speed of thought.

The day after the news came from France, she sat at her kitchen table in St David's to plan her survival. Assessing all her possibilities, she figured that her marriage connections were useless – other than the house. Paddy Sykes had been an engineering foreman's mate at one of the medium-size collieries in south Wales. The company had just introduced a policy of housing some employees, but were not quite ready when Paddy Sykes had asked for permission to marry. They almost did not offer him the St David's cottage, sixteen miles from the colliery. Bernadette, though, having seen it, took it immediately – for its prettiness, and for the distinguished general air of the place: near the old monastery, within sight of the sea inlet.

When her husband seemed doubtful, she cajoled: 'We only have to be here until we get a place nearer your work.'

Thus she ended up with a house so attractive, even if small, that one of the mine-owner's wives complained what a pretty summer house it would have made. Later, the photographs of the house helped confirm the status and identity Bernadette was about to invent.

What an advantage that sixteen-mile distance from the mine proved. In mourning, she would have been expected to fraternize with her late husband's workmates and their wives. Once the dismal small service ended in the Methodist chapel near the colliery, she, baby Dennis in arms, accepted the condolences in the hallway – and the envelope from the General Manager's office. She returned to St David's that night, and very few of them ever saw her again.

Her first act, once that 'recovering' month of October had passed, took her to the village post office shop, where she purchased a notebook and borrowed a copy of the electoral register. At the kitchen table, she listed all the names in the St David's area, and along the coast, a resort and retirement area for wealthy folk, and all their addresses. With the mine condolence money, she bought a pram, and mobilized. Then on fine afternoons, walking miles, she systematically assessed the wider locality, noting down especially the large houses where, according to the register, the address showed a single resident.

One afternoon, she left the baby with a neighbour.

'The doctor. Trouble with the milk': she indicated her bosom (although she had long since stopped breast-feeding).

'Grief, I suppose,' murmured the neighbour.

An hour later, Bernadette knocked on the door of one of the larger houses in Pembrokeshire, which, according to the register, had as its owner an E. G. Hilton.

Bernadette said, 'I'm simply looking for work.'

The woman at the door, pleasant and rosy-aproned, asked, 'Can you typewrite?'

Bernadette shook her head.

The woman said, 'Pity, he'd take on someone who could. He has a lot of letters, see. Financial matters and that.'

After checking local newspapers, Bernadette went by train to Cardiff the following week. Typewriters, she discovered, cost a lot – more than she brought with her. And – 'to learn you must go to school,' they said. 'But there are correspondence courses.' She read their catalogue, at lunch, in a pub.

The watchful barman said, 'I think you're in the wrong place.'

'I'm only having a sandwich.'

'Girls work here. Working girls.'

She looked at him. 'I'm a working girl.' A full understanding arose. 'Or I would be if I got the chance.'

'You don't look it.'

'What's wrong with my looks?'

'Oh, no, I mean – you look too good for – work.' The barman leaned against the pillar by her chair.

'That's my stunt,' she replied. 'I don't look it.'

'Are you working this afternoon?' In the huge, three-quarters-empty pub, nobody could overhear.

'Depends.'

'On what?'

'How much?'

She turned three grimy tricks in a room nearby: three pounds. Bernadette bought a Royal typewriter. They arranged for her to have it delivered free when the van next went near St David's: scheduled for the following Thursday.

She went home, gave the neighbour some chocolates as a 'thank-you' gift, and took Dennis in her arms. For several weeks she checked her body for infection, and never prostituted herself again.

Tongue sticking out of the corner of her mouth: lamp drawn closer the better to read: baby asleep: for eight months the young widow Bernadette Sykes lived the life of a hermitess. Her neighbours understood that delayed shock sometimes produces grief and withdrawal.

The *Typewriting and Shorthand Correspondence Course* arrived with a handbook called *The Perfect Secretary*, and the package taught its purchasers how to get up up to 'London Speeds',

120 words per minute shorthand and 60 wpm typing. She returned to the Hilton household.

The same woman opened the door.

Bernadette said, 'I can typewrite now.'

The woman said, 'But he's dead.'

'When?'

'Nearly four months ago.'

Bernadette shook her head in disappointment, her auburn curls, specially ragged last night, flying out.

'Thanks, anyway.'

The woman scented something and as Bernadette turned the white ceramic gate-knob, called down the ivied path, 'But his widow's here.'

'Widow?' She turned.

'They were estranged, see, but never divorced. She might need help.'

At this moment, Bernadette pulled her greatest stroke. Waiting in the hallway, she noticed the family photographs, read the captions. The women all had boys' names (Protestants, of course, as Bernadette from Ireland recognized): 'Billie Hilton'; 'Charlie Gage'; 'Gussie Hilton'; 'Nicky Hilton'.

'Go in now,' said Mrs Rosy-Apron.

The woman at the desk, elbows in mounds of paper, had a small, fierce, well-bred face.

'What's your name?'

'My name,' said Bernadette Sykes, formerly Murphy, 'is Bryan Cooper.'

The woman registered and said to her, 'Can you clear all this? Intelligently?'

To which 'Bryan Cooper' replied, 'Without question'. She never said, 'Madam', or 'Mrs Hilton', or 'Ma'am'. And thus did Dennis Sykes's mother's survival begin.

Mrs Asia Hilton, who did not wish any part of her late husband's complex administration, left St David's a week later. In her absence, when 'Bryan Cooper' came across a piece of paper she did not understand, she simply wrote to the originator – broker, lawyer, bank, Government Stock Issue department – asking for help. At the end of one year, Bernadette had settled the entire affairs of the late E. G. Hilton and sent his will for probate. She worked five days a week, nine to five, for an excellent, agreed salary. Amid myriad and complex finances, she never stole.

Mrs Hilton did not even once have to return from her house in Northumberland, having been persuaded of the remarkable effectiveness of this young woman with a 'past' too painful to discuss – perhaps an outcast from a somewhat good family somewhere in Ireland, who cares?

The next move looked after itself. Asia Hilton recommended 'Bryan Cooper' to her young cousin Dorothy Bayer, who had just come through 'a foul divorce'. Dorothy came to Pembrokeshire for a rest, exhausted after proving that her twenty-five-year-old husband, his senses hammered numb by a shell in Ypres, was not fit to administer the funds. All the other Bayer-Hilton men died on the Somme and on Vimy.

'But I must be able to keep my house in St David's,' said 'Bryan Cooper', who had by now bought it from the mining company. (She attributed the 'unexpected capital' to 'a small legacy from Ireland', rather than a year's utter frugality plus Asia Hilton's generous wages and bonus.)

'Of course, of course,' said Dorothy Bayer, looking at the photograph of the house and saying, 'How pretty.'

'And you know, Mrs Bayer, that I have a small child?'

'I do,' said Dorothy Bayer. 'You can live in one of the two lodges. Ensure that they're warm. Northumberland gets cold.'

Bernadette Sykes leased the house in St David's to a couple from London – husband recovering from war wounds – and got herself to Alnwick.

Dorothy Bayer read magazines the way other women of her day ate chocolates – in bed, with greed, and little thought to digestion. 'Bryan Cooper' gathered each finished magazine and devoured it likewise – but with a view to learning. In one, she read a short story, which described how a young man, bastard son of a cookhousekeeper, became the toy and plaything of the house's rich young women, and went on to marry wealth.

As her son Dennis neared the age of three, sweet child, his mother taught him little rhymes and songs to which he danced. One afternoon, when the time was right, he entranced Dorothy

Bayer. She had no children, did not want children, but at twenty-five, whatever her riches and liberties, still had a biological clock.

So, Miss Bayer clapped her hands when Dennis Sykes, in his sailor suit in the summer of 1917, sang 'It's a Long Way to Tipperary' – Dorothy led the local war effort. Even more enchantingly, the child recited 'The Green Eye of the Yellow God':

He was known as Mad Carew by the subs at Katmandu
He was hotter than they ever cared to tell;
But for all his reckless pranks he was worshipped in the ranks,
And the Colonel's daughter smiled on him as well.

As Bernadette planned, Baby Dennis Sykes was taken up by Dorothy Bayer. She rode him on horseback in front of her: she drove him around the estate and into the village in the new car, standing him up in the passenger seat. He had to sing and recite for all her friends everywhere they went: he became her doll, lips by Botticelli. All the while his mother, watching, watching, chose his clothes for prettiness and dressed his hair in angel curls. She taught him new songs and poems, and hoped desperately that his looks would be hers, and not Sykes's from Port Talbot.

Above all, she manipulated young Mrs Bayer into taking Dennis to her heart and house. Dorothy kept him always around, the only child in the place. When her friends came to call, they brushed his curls. He spent hours in Dorothy's bedroom as they all tried on clothes, and they chatted and chittered and chattered. They bathed him, tried their new body oils on him first, even perfumed him, a plump and dimpled little rent-boy. Once, with shrieks, they taught him how to rouge their nipples and little Dennis pranked on, encouraged by their squeals. When the girls were not there, Dorothy, alone, prattled to him as mindlessly as if he were a spaniel, and he thus witnessed every aspect of her boudoir.

In Dorothy Bayer's bedroom – 'Dots' as she insisted he call her – he saw everything, including Dorothy's irritation at the fact that it took ages to depilate her hairy thighs.

'Dennis, do come over here and talk to me. I'm bored.'

So he grew, pampered by his mother's rich employers. Occasionally he played with another child, a steward's daughter who lived in the town of Alnwick, but usually he spent hours every

29

day with Dorothy and friends. If not, he curled on his mother's office floor, a brown-eyed, golden-haired cherub, reading the advertisements in *Woman's Weekly*.

Membership of a ten-child family had early produced in Bernadette Sykes, *née* Murphy, a desperation for privacy. She turned that passion into 'Bryan Cooper's' discretion and reticence.

To explain away Dennis's surname to the Bayers and friends she murmured, 'A big mistake. But a boy should have his father's name' – and she would go no further.

Her Irish accent modified until it became 'charming': and with her efficiency such a legend, employment never failed her. The Bayers passed 'Bryan' around among their friends. Rich enough to take no interest in her, they never enquired into her life, sent nobody to St David's to check on this odd woman's background: enough that she saved them such headaches. She became a kind of county-society administrative secretary, who, huge advantage, had no men friends, and no lovers.

'Once bitten three hundred times shy,' she claimed, making them laugh – and feel safe. And added, 'I have my son to rear,' enabling them to enjoy a tinge of vicarious conscientiousness.

Her triumph lay in sinking herself so totally in her work that they did not notice her, and rarely had occasion to talk about her. If they did, they compounded her fiction that 'Bryan Cooper', genteel Irish, had eloped with some rake who then got himself killed on a bridge he was building in South America. Or something like that.

Thereby, she freed them so that she could use them discreetly. In the early years with them, working beneath their sight-lines, she created a life of comfort while maintaining an outward show of modesty. As her son grew, she exploited them in another way.

Dennis had inherited – and increased upon – his mother's intelligence. In the village school he shot so far ahead of his classroom peers that his teacher, Miss Campbell, felt liberated by him, could give him extra books, tuitions. In all the earliest little school tests, he scored full marks. Systematically, although it seemed random, his mother also kept him at home from school – 'illness'. The ploy worked: Miss Campbell came up to the house with books and homework. On those visits, her occasional accidental conversations with young Mrs Bayer clicked, and now, Dennis's mother could set out to fulfil another of the Bayer circle's fantasies – the cliché of the servant's brilliant son, which Bernadette understood from her magazine fiction.

One day, she mentioned to Dorothy a modest and small preparatory school near Manchester. Nothing too flashy: Bernadette knew where to draw the line. She did not want them pulling out of his financial assistance when they understood that a servant's child was going to 'too good' a school.

'They're strong in mathematics. His father wanted him to go there –' Pain flitted across her face briefly.

At the age of nine, sweetly uniformed and fully funded by the Bayer-Hiltons, Dennis went to boarding-school.

On his first Christmas holiday, Dennis came home by train and bus. After tea with his mother, he ran up to the house to see Dots.

'In the bedroom, as usual,' they told him in the kitchen, and in he charged: it was about six o'clock in the evening. She stood there, stark naked, drying herself with a towel. But where was the wonderful warm greeting for him, the hugs and kisses, the admiration?

'Haven't you grown?' she said coolly. Then out of the bathroom strolled another woman whom she introduced casually.

'This is Bobbie. Bobbie, this is Dennis, he's the secretary's son, he's at school. Where are you at school, I've forgotten the name of the place?'

Bobbie, a genuine redhead, shook hands with Dennis, and said, 'The secretary's son? I didn't know Bryan had children?'

Dots said to Dennis, 'Bobbie and I love each other. Aren't you thrilled?' The women touched noses gently.

Suddenly embarrassed, Dennis left the room and heard Dots call, 'Oh, you're not jealous, are you?'

Thereafter, he never again sought Dorothy in her bedroom, even though he had enough shrewdness to remain exceptionally affectionate whenever they met. Besides which, Dorothy had discovered travel, and rarely stayed long at Alnwick.

=

31

At boarding-school, Dennis Sykes studied intensively. He could draw well, had excellent mathematical capacities, fast brain, plus high verbal skills. Debating, stage-managing the school play, the library – he took on all the activities of boys too small for, or not good at, games. Although he never joined in any of the school fads – collars turned up, hair parted in the middle – he monitored all relationships with bonhomie. He knew everyone amiably, no one well.

Commerce occurred early. By whatever means, he seemed to persuade as much food as he wanted from the (female, naturally) kitchen staff, and by selling or giving it to chosen boys he purchased acceptance.

At the same time, in his paradoxical way, he developed a distancing air: in due course he came to recognize that this aloofness empowered him, because people mistrusted it. Some of this separateness got put down to study, a swot. In all his examinations he finished in the top three of the class, mostly at number one or two. Alongside, he read voraciously: novels, life stories, newspapers, the *Reader's Digest*.

In his last two years, he took off academically like a comet, uninterruptedly top of the school, always likely to win his university scholarship. Of this achievement, he remained openly proud all his life, and never forgot that August day, a week before his eighteenth birthday. When the letter arrived, he wandered in a dreamy glow all over the Bayer estate.

Late that afternoon he found himself in Dorothy Bayer's deserted bedroom. He stood in front of the cheval glass, where Dorothy habitually stood, on the spot where the carpet had been worn through to the boards by her feet. She had long gone to Ischia for the summer.

Dennis examined himself. With her ivory hairbrushes and combs he fussed with his hair, as those rich girls had done. He peered at his brown irises and long lashes; he picked up the perfumes and smelt them. Slowly, he took off his clothes, squatted, examined his genitals, turned, tried to inspect his anus. Next, strutting back and forth, prissing and preening like the mannequin they once made of him, he sang one of those little old lisping songs to the mirror:

Hallo Patsy Fagan, you hear the girls all cry,
Hallo Patsy Fagan, you're the apple of my eye;
You're a decent boy from Ireland, that no one can deny;
You're a harum-scarum, devil-may-care-'em –

Dennis stopped, turned from the mirror, looked the length of the
room and walked to the adjoining bathroom. There, he opened
every cupboard, examined every jar, every tin, every phial, bottle,
packet and pill. Next, he went to the rows of wardrobes and rails
in the dressing-room, pulled out with minimum disturbance, and
sniffed, every garment. Finally, he invaded every drawer and
inspected every item of clothing, looked at the labels, the stitching
– smelling, smelling everything. As the shadows gathered, he sat
on the edge of Dorothy's bed, burst into tears and did not dress
or leave the room for another hour. All his life, when alone and
in distress, he sat forever with a finger on a wrist, taking his pulse
as if ascertaining that he still lived.

Dennis spent that summer reading, and cycling through the
countryside. He used the abundant pocket money from his mother
to watch women. Always women: in cafés he observed them having
tea, or working as waitresses. In shops, he made meaningless
inquiries just to gauge how they reacted to him. As they stood
on street corners chatting, or walked ahead of him, he watched,
following a little, or walking by.

3

Helena obeyed, white-faced: she clasped each hemisphere of onion, like headphones, to her ears. Ellen bandaged them firmly into place with a long torn strip of old sheet. First she bound it widely under the child's chin, and eventually tied it on the top of the little girl's head in a big merry bow.

Ellen leaned back, hands folded like a renaissance madonna on the pregnant curve of her large stomach.

'Now, Helena,' she comforted. 'All we have to do is wait.'

From the doorway, Grace, motionless with fascination, watched her older sister. Neither said a word. Helena's blue eyes shone fearful, her legs not reaching the floor from the chair.

Hard footsteps on the yard: the little girls started. He loomed.

'They're just watching,' Ellen said pre-emptively. 'Helena's poor earache. We're just fixing it.'

Helena screamed, and her hands panicked towards her left ear.

'Ooh, that was quick, that was *quick*,' gasped Ellen, and rushed to take off the bandage. Helena's screams rose. She began to roll her head from side to side, getting out of control. Thomas looked on.

Ellen grabbed the child's head and began to undo the bandage.

'Helena, Helena! Easy – easy, love. Okay. Okay. Shhhhh. Shh. It's all right.'

Grace's eyes widened at her sister's sufferings.

'Easy now, eeeee-asy now.' Ellen soothed and soothed.

Thomas pleated his lips in approval of the old cure. After a moment he walked by, into the depths of the house somewhere.

The child was moving beyond reach of comfort. Ellen unlooped the bandage rapidly and took away the left hemisphere of onion: she peered at it, and Helena sagged and gasped in sudden relief.

'See! See!' Ellen held the flat, fleshy side out, a conjuror showing the audience the missing card, 'See! It worked!'

One russet earwig, tail waving like a man fallen into a barrel, had embedded itself head first in the onion.

'No more earache, Helena. See? And the other ear. Is it all right?'

The child nodded dumbly, and Ellen removed and inspected the other onion half.

'Now, the washing of the ears, there's a little bit of blood. Grace love, get me that clean towel will you.'

Grace moved to the table to pick up the earwig-containing piece of onion.

'No, Gracey, no,' Ellen commanded not unhumorously. 'Sweetheart, I bet Helena would like some bread with sugar on it.'

Ellen towelled the child's head and face, and hugged Helena: 'You're as brave as anything.'

Once her husband had made that first Sunday morning appearance, Ellen Kane regenerated quickly. The village knew she was making apple jelly again, because she sent for a windfall in late September. Betrothed girls once more began to visit for advice. Women bearing new recipes, other pregnant mothers – the parish streamed afresh to her door. She wondered at their frequency. Did they come because what she called 'normal business' had been resumed, or because they hoped to glimpse, even meet, Thomas? She knew they had called him 'the Living Dead', a morbid curio of the countryside.

But they took home no reports of him. He avoided all her visitors. Some observed distant sightings – but after that first ghostly Mass, nobody saw him regularly and normally for a full year: longer than most people expected. In time, he had resumed his Principalship of Deanstown School. By the early 1930s, he had returned to his stature as a main force in local matters, tall, grey-faced and austere, with a young wife and a growing family.

Nothing much ever changed in Deanstown, and the pace of the village allowed the Kanes to find their own tempo again. No hurry. His recovery, wrote Ellen in her ledger, could be 'like a flower opening, or a tree growing'.

As for her, whom they watched like a queen – she *seemed* back to her own, old self. A question for everyone; advice, food and old

35

clothes to the desperate poor; on fine Sunday afternoons, she still met the Protestant Miss Harpers on the road for talk of flowers. When she trained the choir, she still beleaguered the unfortunate harmonium.

Yet – there was a fresh cautiousness, a watchfulness. Difficult, they said, to put a finger on it. If you hadn't known her well before 'the incident', you would never see this change in her. It fell across her demeanour like a faint shadow: they said she was always watching in case something went wrong.

From now on, the parish scrutinized her even more than they observed each other. If that were possible. These people survived by eyeing their neighbours. The underground currents of hatred and bile that drench those who know each other too well had flowed among them for generations. Few had gone untouched by violence. Most struggled for a living. Some had lately received a few envied fields from the Land Commission in the breaking-up of the gentry estates. In their passion for secrecy, all tried to know each other's business, and competitive envy kept them alive.

Ellen could have painted Deanstown as one great, long, humpy dragon, with each scale a neighbour's face. To any outsider, the people of the village and the parish constituted a single, and often troublesome beast, that had to be fed, and kept calm. When it prowled out each day, the dragon could be fought, as her husband did. He stabbed the lance of his tongue into its ignorance; he thumped his fists into its face. Or Deanstown could be appeased, spoken to friendlily but with great caution, given offerings – as Ellen chose to do.

From the moment she married Thomas Kane, she understood that the village was a vital part of her life, as clearly defined as any relationship she had ever known. She set out to win the villagers over – insofar as they ever could have welcomed someone so new. Her care for their children in her classroom impressed them: 'The young ones even – they don't even want to come home from the school these days.'

Then, as they watched her in difficulties, their natural doubt of an incomer halved: 'Oh, the way she looked after that man and he stretched.'

As Thomas recovered, Ellen's intelligence was released, and she could advance her place in the community with greater clarity: 'Oh, yeh, she's back to us again.'

Just like their lives, pregnancy followed pregnancy, and she began to balance adroitly the difference between privacy and shared experience. To show the way, she took Helena for the first government-ordered inoculations – but said nothing of the child's panic. She lent sheets and candlesticks for wakes, baked for funeral breakfasts. A rumour of typhoid had her visiting the cottages, explaining the leaflets, helping to boil the water: she never divulged Thomas's distaste in such things, for such people.

And, unlike him, she welcomed their favours returned. When Grace got croup, Ellen tried every cure they offered: poteen rubbed into the baby's chest; a teaspoon of whiskey every four hours; camphor balls boiled permanently near the child's cot.

Tacitly, by testing her boundaries, most of Deanstown learned her one golden rule. Ellen Kane never discussed her husband's temperament no matter what they observed, nor his health no matter what they rumoured. They granted her this licence ungrudgingly: they turned away their own chagrin at such secrecy by praising her, by hailing her 'innocence', her 'modesty', her 'devoutness'.

Within half an hour Helena grew frisky again, cotton-wool in each ear, bread-and-butter-and-sugar in her hand. Ellen bound Grace's hair in green ribbons. At eleven o'clock, the Kanes left the house and climbed the wall across the road into the Demesne. All around them, too distant yet to identify, other people walked in the same direction, their talk borne on the autumn air. Thomas Kane soon strode off in front.

In the second field, Miriam Hogan called out and ran up.

'Locusts. Wait until you see, we shall all turn into locusts today. Or vultures.' Miriam made talons of her two hands. 'Have you ever been to one of these fiascos? We will be fighting over spools of thread. Will there be a thousand people here, will there, will there? That's what I want to know?' said Miriam. Morning dew darkened the light leather of her boots.

The village never liked Miriam Hogan. She never behaved in a way they could address; she made smart, cutting remarks. Of which she boasted to Ellen: *How to Deal with Their Curiosity*: 'Smile blandly and ask about their drunken brother/father/husband – or better still mother/sister.' *How to Avert the Most Personal Questions*: 'Say to her – Was that the Vermin Man/the Health Inspector/the Debt Collector/the Cruelty Man I saw knocking at your door the other day?'

To fight back, the dragon's salacious tongue stained Miriam, and its breath blackened her feckless, drinking husband. They quoted her, mockingly: 'Maybe Jack met somebody' – meaning he could be found in his cups anywhere in the county, brought home at night on a cart by a farmhand.

Up the fields ahead of them, the auction banners, MOLUMBY & STAKELUM, hung out over the leaded windows of the Castle stableyard.

For years, Jack Hogan entreated.

'Miriam, it is perfectly ordinary for people to want to have children.'

She used a variety of obstructions.

Argument: 'If it is born deformed? Or mental?'

Silence: 'Ah, come on, Miriam, come on, talk to me.'

Distress: 'The smell. I hate the smell. The smell, Jack, of what comes out of your thing.'

As he jumped to defend himself and all male biology, or to say how could she know when they had never, not even once in eight years, done what married people do – she shouted like a pouting child.

'I do know the smell, I do know, I do! When you're drunk sometimes, you leak it onto the back of my nightdress when I'm asleep, and it smells like stale wet newspaper and I hate it.'

At least, thanked Jack, she no longer scratched, no more of that dreadful, scabbed tearing of her lovely, sable skin.

'No, Mrs Gardiner,' he told her mother, 'she's all right. Miriam's good, she's a grand girl and wife. She's all right.'

Miriam said, 'Jack has a dispensary all the morning over in Outrath and he'll come on after. Unless he meets someone. Very smart, the auctioneer, to hold it on a Saturday. Where's Thomas?'

Ellen pointed to Thomas, ahead by half a field, Helena and Grace in his wake by several yards.

'How is he these days?' asked Miriam. 'I can hardly walk myself, I'm bleeding like a pig this morning, I knew yesterday and d'you know what, I'm sick of it, three weeks, five weeks, four weeks, six weeks, I defy all calendars.'

Ellen said, 'That's the thing about having babies. All that stops for a while. Miriam, what have you your eye on today? That's what I want to know' – a teasing mimicry of Miriam's catch-phrase. They fell into step beside each other, one woman tall and barren, one strikingly fecund.

'They say he shouts a lot at school these days,' said Miriam, eyeing the distant, straight-backed Thomas. 'Yes, a lot,' said Miriam. 'No patience, they say. A sideboard, maybe?'

Ellen wore her hair up today.

'Jack had a boy in the dispensary the other day with his hand hurt after Thomas's "discipline" in school. Did you know that?' Miriam looked down at Ellen, whose face had reddened beyond pregnancy's blush.

She called out to her girls. 'Gracey, stay with Helena now, won't you?' Fixing her hair she said, 'Oh, Miriam, we're looking for a table, a good dining-room table. Of course there's nothing wrong with the one we have, but Thomas says, that if we're going to have such a big family we have to have a table that we can pull out. And add those extending leaves to.'

Miriam pressed. 'But blisters? As big as coins? On a young fellow's hand? Not fair. No. I mean the lad is only ten years of age.'

Ellen hastened. 'Oh, look Miriam, there's Cyril Stephenson's aunt, they're taking over the Glebe, Captain Wallace's old house, they arrived yesterday, they say she's a scream.'

'Munch and Viva,' said Miriam cryptically.

'Munch and Viva?' asked Ellen puzzled.

'Ulverton. Her children. If you'd call them that. They're ancient items too.'

'Munch and Viva Ulverton?' Ellen laughed. 'Munch and Viva? Is that what they're called? Funny names.'

An auctioneer's lackey shook a powerful handbell, and it ba-ranged off the Castle walls. Ellen and Miriam quickened their steps.

Miriam, still forcing the issue, asked Ellen, 'Is there anything anyone can say to him – about toning down his "discipline", as he calls it, in school? I mean – men are saying there'll be trouble. There will.'

Ellen, when uncomfortable with a topic, had a way of holding herself stiff and unreachable; for a moment or two neither questioner nor topic existed. When she chose to emerge from this storage, all hope of resurrecting the subject died.

She murmured thoughtfully, 'A sideboard? A sideboard, Miriam, you're bidding for? Children!' she called. 'Stay where I can see you.'

Miriam re-directed her frustration to the *Notice of Sale*, her voice climbing.

'The cheek of it! Saturday-the-12th-of-September-1932- Monster - Auction - at - Deanstown - Castle - Sale - of - Furniture - and - Effects-by-Order-of –' and she yelled. 'Jesus! *Admission a shilling.* Don't say we have to pay in? For the love of God!'

She hooted at the man with his blue, numbered tickets, 'I'm not paying, I'm buying!' – and waltzed herself and Ellen past the assistant. He and his sagging jaw cared less. Hours ago he discovered that his writ would not run: nobody paid.

In the old grass courtyard, Ellen caught up with her two little girls and straightened their coats and their ribbons. Up the slopes from the Lake, by the Concubine Tower, the last distant stream of people pushed forward in a thick insect trail.

'Make sure! Make sure! Make sure!'

The Auctioneer stood by the entrance, as outrageous as some bald, cabaret ringmaster.

'Make sure you have your money in your fist! Come on now, girls, today's the day you *don't* keep your hand on your ha'penny.'

Miriam said to Ellen, 'I think that's supposed to be quite a rude thing to say.'

Ellen laughed back, 'You'd know, Miriam, I wouldn't.'

'Miss Goody-goody,' said Miriam.

With motley chairs from within the auction stock, Molumby & Stakelum had turned the old Servants' Hall into a saleroom.

'There y'are girls, we'll be auctioning what you're sitting on today. Priceless, I'd say, only priceless.' The Auctioneer ignored Thomas's withering look. 'Ah yes, we'll be selling what you're sitting on.'

Miriam laughed: Ellen blushed. Thomas, by the wall, waiting to choose a suitable chair, continued to stare at him, unwilling to lose in this contest of dignity, and the Auctioneer said, 'You'd better sit down now, sir, or we might sell yourself into the bargain, there's all kinds of queer things in this catalogue today.'

He walked away, winking to a pal, and Thomas looked hard but unavailingly at the man's disrespectful back.

In this small community, the people's ears seemed unusually large and cupped – genetically formed for the catching of other people's business. They leaned forward for this Sale as they never did in church.

'Well, I declare to God, look at the lot of you,' said the Auctioneer. People laughed.

'Is Dinny Kavanagh here?' he asked. A man rose at the back.

'Dinny, the wife says you're not to go home without buying a commode,' and the Auctioneer, pleased at the joke with an old acquaintance, rubbed his hands.

A sparrow flew from one rafter to another. Two expensive women, strangers, came forward to the front-row seats they had claimed earlier with their folded coats.

'Dealers,' whispered Miriam to Ellen. 'Buzzards. They'd bid the coat off your back. None of us'll get anything half-good here today.'

Deanstown looked around and marvelled. Their servant ancestors had cleaned this furniture: ball-and-claw mahogany, leather ottomans, salon chairs with gilt legs and saffron brocade. By the Auctioneer's podium, rows of huge paintings leaned against each other, some almost three-quarter way up the high bare wall. Gossip believed the best pictures had been taken away to London and Paris, and even a few to Dublin. For any of those left today, not even the Canon had a wall large enough. Grass grew through the stone floors.

Most people had come out of curiosity, or at best for practical items – pots and pans, any bit of bedding which had never been affected with damp, bric-a-brac. One man, known at all such

41

auctions, had come to buy brushes – shoe brushes, clothes brushes, sweeping brushes. All who knew him enjoyed the fact that he had a small brush of a moustache beneath his nose.

The sale began. Grace alerted Helena urgently. The Auctioneer's assistant held up a doll: the patter opened.

'Right lads, there's not another doll in the parish like this one, whatever you might think of your missus.'

Everybody laughed, some cheered.

'Which of you is she going home with?' Hair-oil glistened on his forehead.

'God, that's a *Jumeau*,' whispered Miriam to Ellen.

'Is that good?'

'What'll we christen her? I'll tell you what. We'll call her Lucky, she's my luckpenny for the day. Now who's going to start the bidding on Lucky?'

Grace tugged Helena's hand desperately and pointed to their father. He had shown interest.

'I'll give you a tanner,' shouted a voice at the back.

'You will in your fillet.' The Auctioneer caught Thomas's eye, saw the fingers, and took the bid.

'Five shillings, now there we are. Five shillings starts me for Lucky the Doll. Who's going to go in against that, any advance on five shillings, any advance?'

A hand said six shillings and Grace hunched her little shoulders in excitement as Thomas went to seven.

The Auctioneer called, 'Come on now, warm me up, warm me up. Any advance on seven shillings, she's a doll in a million, buy Lucky and be lucky. Eight, I have eight, come on who'll make it ten bob, come on a half sovereign as it used to be when men were men and geese went barefoot. Am I hearing ten bob, am I? Ten bob, who's ten bob, ah, we have ten bob, thank you madam. Ten bob here sir, will you rise me, who'll rise me? Hold her up there, Eddie –'

The lackey held the doll like a lantern.

'Not as high as that Eddie, there's decent people here,' said the Auctioneer. 'Eleven shillings, I have eleven.'

Thomas dropped out of the bidding at fourteen shillings: the doll went for three pounds: Helena, wistful, and Grace, irritated, subsided.

=

Canon Williams, standing stretched up against the wall, bought a walking-stick topped with a dog's head.

'If he has any more walking-sticks,' whispered Ellen to Miriam, 'he'll soon never need to use his legs again.'

Two pairs of candelabra went for more than they should have done: rivalrous wives. A long man draped S-shaped like a hook around the back of his chair and looking at everything sideways, bought a riding-crop, he who had never owned even a pony.

'He'll use it on the bicycle,' someone heckled.

The Auctioneer targeted Ellen and Miriam when he saw them laughing. To buy off his banter, Miriam bid, and again and again and again, for a delicate parasol with black-and-cream-and-red *chinoiserie*.

'But six quid!' whistled Ellen.

Item by item the Castle's history came tumbling down, down, to the minor fripperies. The long-closed household had not functioned since 1914. At the onset of the Great War, black marketeers filched the lead from the roofs and sold it to munitions dealers. When bad weather came, good-spirited neighbours broke in and removed the best of everything to the security of the stableyard wing. The land agent later said that some items vanished in the neighbourliness.

A woman, beaming like a moon, paid two shillings for a half-bottle of lavender water and pressed it to her nose: 'The smelling salts of history,' she said grandly.

One little oval tin of sun cream showed a palm tree and bore the word 'Cannes'. The purchaser said this was the French word for 'tin' and passed it from woman to woman. Her sister worked for gentry in Buckinghamshire: 'That's what France smells like, I remember my sister describing that smell exactly. Her mistress goes to France every summer of her life, and she comes home smelling like that.' They goggled as she put the tip of her little finger into the cracked pink cream and applied it as daintily as a society filly to her goitred neck.

Lots 200–380, Domestic Utensils, brought the auction to its feet. Nurse Cooper from the nursing-home, her profession rendering her unembarrassed, bought all the chamberpots and two commodes.

'I'd say we'll have a dirty week-end,' released the Auctioneer.

Ellen bought a wide copper preserving pan.

'This winter's jam?' remarked Miriam.

Thomas Kane, alone as ever, viewed everything. Occasionally he took out a wad of old letters and wrote a tiny note on the empty back of an envelope. Those near him stared from time to time: five years on from his recovery, he was still a curiosity. If not too absorbed, he returned their inquisitive glances with a glare. His dress sense had returned, blues and greys of soft cloth; and his fingernails again the cleanest ever – as they said. The face and head never moved, only his chilly eyes.

Most of the remarkable furniture went to dealers, including two small cabinets that Miriam said were worth a mint: 'Olbrich. Austrian.'

The two expensive women sitting in the front row bought them. Several men, standing by the wall, one behind the other, leaned forward or back to make comment. None outbid another. When a significant piece of furniture, or a maker's name materialized, acknowledgement or recognition passed among them.

In turn, the Auctioneer played to them whenever he gave a brief auction pedigree.

'Now, the comrade [he pronounced it "cumm-a-raid"] of this very piece was sold up the country the month before last for record guineas.'

Thomas fastened on these dealers, and watched them closely. As each bid, he frowned at their smiles and collusions. They took no notice of this tight-mouthed man. Thus they never saw the moment of sadness in his eyes as *An Irish Versailles*, a painting of the Castle in the eighteenth century, entered the bidding at a hundred guineas, a price Thomas could not approach.

One of the smooth men bid and won. Brief contest, a mere finger-flick, his hand as close to his chest as a card sharp. At the Auctioneer's knock, one of the women turned back and raised the eyebrow she used for smiling with. The buyer inclined his head towards her.

=

44

By four o'clock, the Sale reached the farm items. Ellen, Miriam and most people prepared to leave. None of the heavy agricultural equipment could work again without grave attention. Men bought ancient harrows, rakes, ploughs and hay-turning machines for spare parts or for scrap.

Outside, Thomas saw the dealers laughing arm-in-arm, picking their steps in the mud from the castle down towards the Lake. As he walked briskly past them, one said, 'Excuse me, what's the quickest way of getting back to the main road?'

He stopped and faced them. About to speak, he changed his mind, shook his head in disdain and anger at them, turned and walked away. From the green crest of the ornamental lawns, Ellen stood and watched Thomas. He walked down the Bell Walk, towards the kitchen-garden wall, his shoulders stiff with disapproval.

Miriam ruffled Helena's hair and said to Ellen, 'Helena has your lips and Grace has your eyes. A fair division of the spoils.'

'Daddy walked away very quick,' said Helena, 'he's gone down the long way.'

'Very quickly,' corrected Ellen.

'Well, I'll see you so, Ellen, I think I'm going to go for a long walk, Jack won't be home until cockcrow if he wasn't here so far. You didn't spy him anywhere, I suppose?'

'No,' said Ellen.

'He must have met somebody.'

Miriam waved a resigned hand, and flapped away.

Ellen Kane herded her two children, and gave them the preserving pan to carry between them. She began her walk home down by the lime trees, towards the main road. If she timed it right, she would come tangentially to Thomas's shoulder. From the brow of the hill by the sunken fence, she could now see him again: he strode down these sloping beautiful fields between the beech hedges.

Helena and Grace, sure of the route, ran ahead and Ellen, hands deep in her coat pockets, contemplated their skipping. When they reached the place where their path joined their father's route – he was now out of sight once more behind the hazel woods – they raced each other back to Ellen. Grace banged on the preserving pan like a drum.

45

Soon, all three climbed the wall together in front of their house. Ellen looked back into the fields, saw Thomas coming and waved. He did not return the gesture; perhaps he could not have seen her.

Ever since his recovery seemed final and assured, she had tried many stratagems to raise difficult matters. Throughout the past five years, she worked out moments in which she could be alone with him, where he could neither leave their room, nor evade conversation. Yet, if she blurted, as she had twice, 'Why won't you talk about yourself?' he shunned her for three grim days.

At odd, strange daytime moments, he thawed. The smell of October woodsmoke did it once, and summer's new potatoes, like little white babies, his own crop brought to table. She made a raspberry cake one Sunday – Leah and Herbert had taken the children on an outing to the Grey Valley. Thomas, never lifting his eyes, reached across the table and held her hand.

In bed, though, he had never changed. The first roughness after his recovery waned once his urgency calmed down: he became as tender as before. This bred Ellen's dilemma: how to adjust her spirit and her family to a man infinitely sweet when inside her body, bitter as acid in his discipline towards their children? After a day of cutting slaps across their legs, shattering them with hurt, or corrections spoken abusively – and to two children aged five and three – he still buried his face in Ellen's shoulder that night.

Not a soul could she tell, not even Leah. Thomas's passionate requirement of utter confidentiality had also become her creed. Nor could she have claimed uniqueness: just another local woman married to a man of uncontrolled temper.

As they entered their gateway, Ellen heard the loud call.

She turned in delight. 'Oh, Leah, but where were you? Where were you? I never saw you? And what in the name of God did you buy?'

Leah Winer, and her husband Herbert, walked to meet her: their two shy girls came too.

Ellen exclaimed again: 'Did you come on the bus? And what time are you going back? Are you getting a lift? Isn't it great I have a fresh chocolate cake baked?'

46

They stood aside from their greetings to let a crowded car rattle by on the narrow dusty road.

'Come in, come in, Thomas will be here any minute.'

Rhona Ulverton looked out of the Lagonda window and said, 'This place is like Bombay.'

'We're just as poor ourselves, Mamma,' said her daughter beside her in the back.

'This country is finished,' said Rhona. 'Bloody finished.'

'*We're* finished,' said Viva.

'This dreary place!' exhaled Rhona.

'We'll just pretend not to be finished,' said her son, in front beside his uncle Henry.

Viva Ulverton shook her head and smacked her wet violet lips. She drew a finger along the back of her brother's neck.

'A chicken. That – is – what – you – look – like.' She tapped his neck in time to her words. 'Munch – a chicken, you look like a chicken.' Viva tugged a knitted hat so hard down her forehead that it left a red circulation mark an inch below her hairline.

As they drove past Ellen Kane, Rhona turned. 'Jesus, she's pretty. Who's she? Now – she. Is. Pretty.'

'That's twice you said it,' observed Viva.

'Once would be too much where you're concerned,' interrupted Munch.

Rhona asked, 'Henry, who's that flower?'

'Mother, can't you ever call me "Munchin"? My full name. All I ask. You gave it to me. "Munch" sounds like an instruction.' Today, little or no saliva lapped his mouth; today he had done his best to clean himself.

'Or a description. No, an instruction, that's funnier,' said Viva. When Munch was like this they pressed normality upon him.

'She,' said Henry Wallace, 'is a Mrs Kane: she's the wife of that fellow, d'you remember the ex-Sinn Feiner who was in a coma for ages.'

Sometimes Viva went too far, or forgot. 'And you've been wetting the front of your trousers again, it's actually turning yellow, actually yellow.' Viva leaned forward and peered over his shoulder. 'Munch, you should never wear light grey trousers, your pee is a horrid yellow.'

47

Rhona looked back again. 'Well, she's too pretty for this place.'

'City girl,' said Henry Wallace, Rhona's brother, 'Janesborough. Litter of children by now. Husband's a sour pill.'

'Mother, you might as well have called me "Do". Or "Fetch". "Munch". It's a terrible name.'

Rhona sighed. 'We have had this conversation, my dear boy, a thousand times in forty years.'

He protested, 'I wouldn't mind but I like the full name. "Munchin". "Saint Munchin".'

'A saint?' shrieked Viva. 'You want to be called after a bloody Irish saint?'

Rhona said, 'A sour pill? Henry, can a man married to a woman like that afford to be a sour pill?'

'Of course he can, Mother,' said Viva, 'this is Ireland. Married people can do what they like to each other. *If* they're Roman Catholics.'

Rhona, still reflecting, concluded, 'If we had a half-decent civilization, a pearl like that woman would not be buried out here.'

'Mamma, that is ridiculous, what about those beautiful Indian women?'

'Exactly.'

Herbert Winer said, 'No, no, the kitchen table, don't disturb the parlour. And only a cup out of our hands, Ellen, we have to go back.'

'Now come on, what did you buy?' asked Ellen.

Leah, not usually hesitant or reticent, shook her bangles, a sign of embarrassment. 'Well –' she began. 'We didn't buy –'

Herbert took off his spectacles, peered into them from a distance, replaced them and said justifyingly, 'I find those auctions confusing.'

Leah, who had clearly been expecting a different type of remark from Herbert, gathered courage and speed. 'Although we could have bought all round us because did you hear? Our good news?'

Ellen alerted.

Herbert said, 'Now, now. Don't burden people.'

'Good news a burden?' Leah queried.

'It often is. Ellen, where did you say Thomas was?'

'He'll be here any second, he should be here now. Grace, go and see can you see Daddy.'

Leah's words flew out. 'We came into money. A lot.'

'Wha-at?! Oh!' Ellen turned to her friend. 'Oh, Leah!'

Herbert winced. 'Leah, why don't you listen to me? People get upset by money.'

Grace bounced back into the kitchen. 'No, Mamma. Daddy's not.'

'Not what little chickie?' smiled Leah.

'Cluck-cluck,' mimicked Grace.

'But Herbert, that's wonderful news,' said Ellen.

Herbert sighed: Leah shrugged.

Up the long, gravelled avenue, the car listed a little to starboard. It stopped at the door. In the empty hallway, Viva asked, 'Is Cyril bringing his little Roman Catholic to meet us?'

'Ask him,' Munch Ulverton said from the window, and sang out like a ship's watch, 'he's ten yards away and bearing down fast.'

Cyril Stephenson said, 'Hallo, Uncle Henry, hallo, you must be Aunt Rhona, thanks for your letter, no, she's away.'

'Are you lovelorn then?' asked Viva. 'Do you miss her? I'm Viva, this is Munch.'

Rhona Ulverton said, with her gift of instant intimacy to a nephew she had not seen since he was two, 'Oh, Cyril, it isn't any of my business, but couldn't you think again? I'd rather you married a Nonconformist nearly, than a Roman Catholic. Christ, this house is cold. Are we sleeping in your house until the furniture comes? Have we enough furniture by the way, have you any spare? We need another bed?'

'The auction,' said Henry Wallace thoughtfully, a very long man. 'You should have bought.'

'With what?' asked Viva. 'Beads? Wampum?'

Cyril said, 'We still have the old beds.'

'Didn't people die in them? Oh-ho, no-oh, thanks, I'm not sleeping in them,' said Munch. 'Ghosts, ghosts.'

'Munch,' said Rhona, 'go for a walk, dear. Jesus! Look at this floor!'

The planking beneath Rhona Ulverton's feet needed attention, but she held herself as if already reigning over the household. Face-powder that she spread on her liver-spotted hands had flaked again, and dotted her black blouse-cuffs. Her nephew, Cyril, who blushed quickly, and who never wore anything but a check sports jacket – his wife-to-be once asked if he wore it in bed – looked out of the window at the rusting tractor derelict in the fields. It had never functioned. The factory blamed Cyril, said he tried to drag too heavy a load, refused to observe the guarantee: Cyril's life ran like that.

On account of the large windbreak to the west of the house, twilight came early to this room. Rhona paced.

'Cyril, this is an announcement. Now that we are back – I'm refusing to be bound by the the whole politics of everything. We chose to return.'

Viva barked, 'Mamma, you are so manipulative! You'll get us into trouble!'

'Cyril,' Rhona pleaded, 'I didn't want to do what so many others did. I didn't want to go to Scotland. Or Belfast. Or whatever. If we went over to Devon or somewhere, Somerset, say – we'd still be Irish. Paddies. Yes, we'd be Paddies, we'd be the very same as the Catholics. That's no choice.'

Viva said vehemently, 'But Mamma, for Christ's sake. We have *no money.*'

'So, Cyril,' Rhona continued, 'be warned, I expect to be active in this locality. By which I mean political. We're surrounded by ignorant people. These bloody peasant gunmen, they can't run this country. I'm jiggered if I'm going to let all that we have evaporate. Christ!'

'Mamma! The guns are silent now.'

Behind Rhona's back, Henry Wallace caught Cyril's attention and shook his head slowly and reassuringly.

'God Save the King,' stated Munch to nobody.

'They're not silent. This country isn't fit to rule itself. Did you see that thing the other day where one of the members of parliament brought a pair of six-guns into the debating chamber with him?'

'Mamma! That wasn't yesterday, that was nine bloody years ago,' Viva phutted.

=

50

Thomas did not reappear and Herbert played with Helena, who read for him her new book, and Grace who explained to him every article of her doll's clothing.

Inevitably Leah said, 'I need your mirror, dear,' and followed Ellen upstairs.

They whispered dramatically: Leah told all: an ancient uncle, fifteen thousand pounds and a small-ish commercial property in Cork with an income of eight hundred pounds a year.

'And you know what he's like. He's been flinching ever since. Saying we'll be obliged to pay in some other way. That we'll fall ill, or one of the girls won't do well at school.'

'Poor Herbert,' murmured Ellen.

'And we argue about it.'

'But,' queried Ellen, 'you two never argue?'

'We do now. He won't buy anything and I want things.'

'Awwwh!' sympathized Ellen.

'Anyway,' said Leah with finality. 'And you, dear?' She patted Ellen's pregnant bump. 'You look in a bloom.'

Ellen smiled. 'It is still tiring, I'm amazed at how tired I get.'

'And Thomas? Is he – ? I mean, how is he?'

'Oh, fine. Oh, Leah, you may even be able to move to a new house.'

'By the way.' Leah fished into her handbag. 'Yours.'

'What's this?'

'Two hundred and sixty pounds. All told.'

Ellen pushed the envelope away. 'No, they weren't loans, I can't take that.'

'Yes, you can. Or I'll give it to the girls and then where will you be?'

'Oh, Leah, I was only helping you out.'

'Fifteen or sixteen times, some helping out, huh.'

Ellen turned over the envelope but never opened it. 'It was a pleasure to me. But Leah, is Herbert, is he going to be all right about the money?'

'Who knows? I don't. Maybe he doesn't. Who knows?'

Rhona looked through the door at the rhododendrons, the monkey puzzles and Cyril's red roof.

'I don't think I realized until today that these two houses were

51

so close to each other. Just as well. I can't walk much any more. Viva, my stick, would you.'

Rhona leaned on Cyril's arm. She stopped by the huge mirror.

'What do you see, Cyril? The family nose, for one thing. You have it too.' Rhona pointed her stick into the mirror at Cyril's nose. 'You look much nicer in the mirror. Isn't that an odd thing?'

Rhona and Cyril walked past the the dead plants and their stippled-brass pots in the vacant old house.

Outside, Cyril Stephenson said sheepishly, 'You'll like my fiancée, Auntie Rhona, she's very likeable.'

'She's a Roman Catholic,' sang Viva behind him, smelling the inside of the knitted hat, her shingled hair curling into her eye.

'Quiet, Viva. And Viva, I am sure your cousin Cyril doesn't want to know about you and your own little Catholic in Ranpore, does he?'

Viva reddened: Munch stilled.

'He slugged her and he left her,' Rhona said to Cyril. 'Black eyes he gave her. I used to see them from my bedroom, and Viva, well, Cyril, you know the phrase "bent over backwards for him".' To Viva – 'Didn't you, darling?' Rhona laughed.

As they walked under the trees, across the 'U' where the main avenue bifurcated to the separate houses, Viva lagged behind, pretending to fix her hat.

Rhona, who truly needed neither a walking stick nor an arm to lean on, continued, 'Now come on, Cyril, continue. You're set on nuptials. Is that what you're saying?'

Cyril nodded dumbly.

'Well,' Rhona arched her neck. 'If you are going to marry, I'd better accept it. We shall have to celebrate. When can we cele-brate? When can we *meet* her? A glass of madeira one afternoon, maybe?'

Cyril mumbled an unclear something.

'I hate weddings,' said Rhona. 'I hate them.'

Munch said, 'I don't think we'll be going to this one, Mother?' 'Of course we will. Of course we will.'

Munch insisted. 'Oh, no, we won't, and do you know why? There won't be a wedding in public, the girl will be excommuni-cated, that's why.'

'Not a good year to marry a Roman Catholic, Cyril,' said Rhona, 'this Eucharistic Congress thing, cardinals from kingdom come. The whole Irish'll be in a fever.'

'Nineteen-Thirty-Two – the Year of Fervour. That's what the papers say,' declared Munch. 'A fever of fervour.'

'I didn't say I was marrying this year, Aunt Rhona.'

Herbert said, 'I missed Thomas. Do you think he knew we were there?'

'Ellen said he was fine. And she looked fine.'

'Even if I'd seen him at the auction,' said Herbert, peering through the window of the bus.

'Of course, you know Ellen, she will never say anything.'

'He's a man who knows what to do about things,' said Herbert with approval.

Leah glanced at him, but did not challenge. Herbert continued.

'I often feel for him. All that time out of his life. He must think we all know things he doesn't, things that he missed.'

'He has a good wife.' The late sun through the bus windows caught Leah's great frizz of red hair.

'I mean. His face when I asked him, d'you remember, what he thought about Lindbergh? Why does that haunt me?'

'Things haunt you, Herbert. That's why.'

The Ulvertons dined on corned beef and cabbage with Cyril Stephenson that night.

'Small helpings again,' scoffed Viva, 'nothing new in this house.'

'I hated that auction,' said Rhona before she went to bed. 'More of the old order gone.' She walked like an ageing heron, but when alone and unseen, moved more spryly: she was only fifty-eight and wished to appear more venerable.

'Mamma,' said Viva, 'Deanstown Castle never belonged to our side, it was owned by French Catholics.'

'Yes, but French Catholics aren't like Irish Catholics, they have a bit of style about them, they're not bloody slaves and prudes.'

Miriam stood in the hallway, wincing.

'But you are, you definitely are, and you said you wouldn't get drunk again. You said.'

'Ah, Miriam. Who was there anyway?' he coaxed. 'Look, smell.'
He hawed on her.

'Yu-htsss!' She recoiled, twisting her mouth away.

'Seriously, Miriam.'

She sat on the stairs. 'I asked her. I asked Ellen – d'you know? About the boy's hand that was swollen?'

'Did you make your tea itself, Miriam?'

Miriam shivered in the dim hall, drew her feet up from the brown tiles. 'And she said nothing. As usual.'

Jack clicked his teeth, scratched the palm of one hand. 'Whuh-huh. Did your man come with the new ointment, d'you know?'

'Although – she looked great. Great. She won't say a word against him, though.'

Jack said, 'Miriam, I'll tell you one thing, I'm never again putting that new petrol in the car, it gave the engine the hoose, like a calf or something.'

Miriam shook her head. 'And he was there, too, moving around as if he walked inside a glass case. He put up a bid for a doll. The girls are getting to be lovely little things. That's what he's like, like a glass case, no, not like the glass itself, like one of those figures in, oh, like, Jesus, I'm too tired to think, those tall domed glass cases you see in museums, you know, old uniforms.'

'Thomas?'

They stood in the bedroom. Every night he washed beneath his arms with a cold face-flannel.

'The boys in school. When you have to discipline them.' He stood at the ewer in pyjama trousers; she walked over and pressed her big pregnant stomach to his back; she laid her head between his bare shoulder-blades.

'If their hands hurt afterwards, you know – when they get an answer wrong, or something. Maybe you don't know your own strength.'

She felt his spine stiffen and she clung. He stood in rigid silence and Ellen Kane knew he could stand there all night, unmoved and umoving.

4

At one point in the 1920s, Bernadette Sykes calculated that Dorothy Bayer's income from all sources amounted to six thousand pounds a day. The Bayer-Hilton old money lay in property and other possessions; new cash arrived daily from investments. Two centuries of marriage alliances in Europe, South America and South Africa, had increased the core fortune. Among recent generations, infertility, war and homosexuality whittled the family down to a few outer cousins. Only the widowed Asia Hilton remained at the heart of the fortunes, and, childless too, Dorothy Bayer.

When Dorothy returned to Alnwick from Tunisia in September 1932, Ramsay MacDonald's tax laws had begun to reap. Dorothy may have oozed languor, but she lived by shrewdness: despite some unusual chemical indulgences learned in north Africa, she retained a clear view of her wealth.

'We have to make some decisions, Bryan Cooper,' she said. 'Tax paid is wealth lost.'

Without (as usual) showing too much knowledge, 'Bryan' pointed out that Trusts had advantages; Dorothy concurred and began to liquidate several income-generating assets.

'Yes, I'll form Trusts for all the people I love;' 'Gerry' – Geraldine, who, many years since, had replaced 'Bobbie' (and others in between) – became the first beneficiary.

'But,' sighed Dorothy, 'what about my Dennis? What will he do?'

Years earlier, Dennis's mother learned the value of timely silence – and after such a long moment Dorothy decided.

'Oh, well, let's give Dennis a Trust too,' she said. 'But not a very large one. A man must earn his own living, we don't want him turning into a little tart, do we?'

By now, Bernadette had secretly rearranged her own future.

In the years of administering the properties and estates, she discovered that insurance companies and other financial institutions paid commission on new business. Gradually, she carefully restructured all the appropriate policies – and thus guaranteed herself a life of security.

In personal terms, her accent, demeanour, appearance and presence had also reached levels of consistency. Firm within herself, she never unlocked the greed and breeding that she once feared would let her down. Dennis was at university, financed by his scholarship and, soon, by this new Trust of Dorothy's: the estates were running smoothly: at forty-two, she had space to re-think. Her new solitude, and her financial safety, told her that she had achieved her goals: time to move on. This mood ripened one day in Newcastle-upon-Tyne.

Over and over she had congratulated herself on never having let a man through her defences: her secrets remained intact. Of late, however, she seemed to notice that not a few had begun to observe her with interest. One, the accountant for the solicitors with whom she most often dealt, asked her to lunch. Bernadette accepted, and discovered two facts that alarmed her.

He said to her, 'I hope you don't mind this remark. But your careful twin-set doesn't altogether conceal something exciting about you.'

Although she answered, 'Mr Cathcart, long ago I lost my heart and never got it back,' his overture registered a great deal lower than her head and shook her composure. Awake that night, she concluded that if her body now seemed ready to betray her, then her guard was dropping, meaning her long task was over.

More worryingly, the accountant, malicious at being rejected, had remarked as they parted, 'I love the way you've taken the Bayers.'

'*Taken?*' she queried.

He winked, and waved good-bye.

Some months later, the first instalment of Dennis's Trust Fund arrived at Alnwick. Bernadette opened the envelope, verified the cheque, and sent it with the letter she had already written.

Dear Dennis,

This is the first payment from a Trust that will give you an income for the rest of your life. I have therefore seen to it that you will always have at least some financial means. The money will increase because interest rates will go up.

As I have also benefited from Miss Bayer's money, I am now going to give up working for these people whose sort I have always hated. But I had to do it for you, to get you a start in life.

I will go back to St David's, only for a few days, and then I will do some travelling, as I have always wanted to. It is my turn to have a decent existence, and maybe I will meet someone suitable. When I find somewhere in which I think I will settle, I will get in touch with you.

But I have set you on course. With the brains you inherited from me, you have guaranteed yourself free education with your scholarship and bursaries. Miss Bayer says you can use the lodge for holidays for as long as you are at University.

Until we meet again,

best wishes for your studies.

Yours,

Mother.

Dennis ran to the Dean's office in such distress that they let him use the precious telephone.

Dorothy herself answered.

'No, my Dennis, she's gone. Went yesterday. Didn't you know? Oh, yes, she told me a month ago, I thought you knew. No, she didn't go to St David's after all. In fact she's left the keys of St David's here for you.' Dorothy paused, then said, 'Hallo, hallo, are you there, Dennis? Dennis, darling, are you all right? Do come here for the week-end if you're feeling peaky. Although I shall be in Edinburgh, I fear.'

Like a mad fiend he walked through that day of dismay. It rained when night fell; anguished and breathless, he stood under a shop arcade; the rain stopped and he walked on. In a doorway on Lantern Street, he found a prostitute, and for a ten-shilling note, she plucked deftly and agitated rhythmically until he ejaculated into her hand.

He rested against the brick, making meaningless conversation to her in the archway. A raindrop inside his collar chilled his neck. For a further ten shillings she lifted her skirt and let him look, and he tooth-combed his fingernails softly and edgily through the lank hair at her crotch. In their third transaction, she hauled at him softly once more, the coldness of her hand an exciting detail. When semen whitened her black skirt, Dennis drifted away and hailed a taxi to the University.

At the mirror in his room he scanned every lobe, aperture and follicle of his head and face. He inspected his underwear and genitals, sniffed his hands, then washed them with fierceness and sadness. High on a cocktail of triumph and self-repugnance, he climbed into bed and fell deep asleep.

Several dreadful weeks followed. In the early, early mornings Dennis sat up against his pillows and, finger to his pulse, stared at the thin line of red which brought the dawn to Manchester. Once, he went to the doctor and complained of breathlessness, but never gave away any possible emotional causes. Over and over, he patted his face as tenderly as if he were his own child. He ate nothing, drank goblets of tea; he washed his hands again and again and again. Then, like some god gone wrong, on the seventh day he rested from his distress.

To recover, he began to formulate what would become his story and his attitude. His peers already knew little about him, this gregarious but never forthcoming, slightly pretty swot. So he felt free to replicate – if unwittingly – his mother's example. In other words, he reinvented his own life.

To begin with, he returned to Lantern Street. One of the other tarts identified the whore he described – 'Betty'. Later that night, Betty duly reappeared. Thereafter Dennis saw her once or twice a week, and on Betty he tried out his new identity – to test credulity, to gauge reaction. He always chose the same type of meeting: a door, alley or archway; no intercourse, vaginal or oral; one-sided verbal exchanges – he had no wish to learn of Betty's life, or full name, even when she offered. After each ejaculation, he told her yet another tale from his great new fiction, and she listened – with attention, so it seemed.

She did not respond in depth, was not required to – but he was pleased to retain one comment she made: 'Any man with as much spunk as comes out of you is going to be rich.'

When he had sufficiently invented the fiction of where he had come from, he next wished to decide where he was going. To do this, he needed to map-make. Clinically, he charted the pattern of his visits to Lantern Street. Any reverse in study, some slight, some hurt or depression in his general life, a feeling of unease – all such contentions sent him to her. The need turned into a scream on two occasions. A loving letter from Dorothy Bayer, with a cheque for Christmas, gave Betty more cash than usual – and a complaint about an aching wrist. She also observed a development: Dennis had never uttered a swear-word in her presence up to then: when he did, Betty said, 'That's more of a man!'

His harshest demands came after a chance meeting with the aggressive Alison Kettley, the Alnwick steward's daughter. Dennis bought the girl coffee, he had to; she asked. At the marble-topped table, amid the spilt sugar of the Saturday afternoon crowds, Alison pried into his student life, fingered his scarf, asked about his adventures – she 'would bet' he had girls in love with him.

To his dismay, she began to talk about his mother.

'She must have loved your father hugely, to have carried a broken heart all those years?' Bernadette's fictions endured.

Dennis nodded.

'Such a looker, too. Did you know that? Did you know that she was, I mean, she is, such a pretty woman? Boys often don't know that about their mothers. She must be so proud of you, is she? If you were a few years older she'd have you marrying Miss Bayer. We used all think that's what she was up to, getting you a rich wife out of that family. I bet now that she's left Alnwick, your Mum comes to see you really often does she? And all that money she was left by your father? You'll inherit that, Dennis. Where's she living?'

Talk, talk, talk – but he practised his warm-eyed look. Later, Dennis manoeuvred her through the streets with such svelte force that they had reached the railway station before she knew where they were headed. Alison gasped that she had forgotten two chores, but Dennis's smile so rewarded her that she entered the train thrilled and philosophical. As he waved from the platform, he congratulated himself on having kept her from meeting other students.

That night, Betty of Lantern Street said, 'Go easy, go easy, you'll hurt yourself. Oi! Oi! Stop, you're pinching my arm, stoppit.' Two streets away, two hours later, Dennis bought Carla, black, strong and impatient at his delay, for which she charged him extra.

When Dennis moved to Birmingham for postgraduate work, he began the long and safe journey into the myth of his past. To make the legend consistent, he gave it very few major component parts. That way he could never forget, never make an error.

To the widowed mother in Glasgow, he added a wealthily married sister called Dorothy in Witwatersrand. By now, his father had been a sportsman, an engineer and a gambler, cast out by a good family. One grandfather, a clergyman, had married money. Dennis just missed his University blue owing to injury. As an undergraduate, he had been almost engaged to an unnamed blue-blood – but, probably for class reasons, the girl left him for another; he remained heartbroken. The legend rolled on.

His academic brilliance needed no invention. Although never visibly boastful, it somehow happened that all who met him knew of his distinctions within minutes.

Only once did he return to Alnwick, having checked that Dorothy was abroad. Others had just come to live in the lodge; he told the cabbie to drive by. Dennis never entered the house proper, simply collected the keys to St David's, where he walked and walked the lovely coast. As before, his treks always ended up in towns; he haunted the summer cafés and teashops of Tenby.

On that riviera south coast of Wales, how the girls and the women jawed! Dennis watched and overheard everywhere. Always with enough money in his pocket to afford a room in a hotel – never, never a bed-and-breakfast – he eavesdropped, while pretending to read his serious-looking books. Clothes. Men. Relatives. Men. Children. Family. Mothers. Money. Relationships.

He heard. Yet, he avoided contact.

'Not yet ready,' he told himself. 'Wait, Dennis, wait.'

To grant himself a more withdrawn air, he even bought a pair of horn-rimmed spectacles with clear lenses.

'For a play,' he told the optician. 'I'm up at Cambridge, *Bitter Sweet* – you know, the Noël Coward. Yes, you're absolutely right, it *is* lovely. Marvellous fun.'

Girls did approach him: why not? Very good-looking: obviously well-to-do: blazer and knife-pressed flannels, and clean, so clean: he smiled them away. Not yet, Dennis, not yet.

Next year, he discovered that people had come to live in the St David's house. His mother had sold it by remote control. All her goods, packed by a neighbour, had been sent to a furniture store in Bristol. Where, they told him, they had sent it to a shipping office, who took it to a boat bound for the south of the world. Dennis walked from the shipping office to the water's edge and sat for an hour, completely still.

'Bryan Cooper' vanished – with many thousand legitimate pounds. When she first left Alnwick, she did not go far: her cunning told her no need: she rented an excellent apartment in Torquay just as the summer season ended. Two trips to London fitted her out in the amber and grey colours of that autumn's fashions, plus a black coat and three black dresses. She called herself 'Madeleine Ring', a widow. Twice a week she dined alone in the Imperial Hotel, choosing the absolute best of the menu, and being shrewd with the half-bottle wine-list. By the third week, with the discreet collusion of the pompous, gossipy maitre d'hotel, she had sized up a divorced man from South America – who proposed.

Bernadette never had one ounce of mothering in her; she felt only duty. Whether she missed Dennis, how can we ever tell? When Patrick Sykes made her pregnant, a logical consequence of all marriage, she accepted the burden of a baby's dependence by looking ahead to his earliest possible maturity, and with it her own freedom.

Had Dennis been unintelligent she would have shipped him off somewhere, a children's home, a working farm, into service. If she had not pulled off her various coups with the Hilton-Bayer set, if she had failed to get out of south Wales, she would have sent her son down the mines at the age of fourteen like all the other boys in and around St David's. In recent years, when she ever contemplated his possible life ahead, with the typical prospect of a daughter-in-law and grandchildren, she shuddered again.

Accordingly, her cool decision to vanish had nothing to do with his feelings – only hers. Her care of him had also been a manipulation of him – towards money, preference, and above all unto her own eventual liberty. Once that had been put in place, and once he had proven his intellectual ability to build his own life, she felt no more ties.

Her coolness of spirit and her simple greed had kept her life on straight lines, led her to play a long game. Through the Asia Hilton experience in Pembrokeshire, she first carved out an understanding of herself that connected to money and possessions. At Alnwick, she found how powerfully she could manage the rich, and their ways and means. Her greatest vulnerability – a fear of others' poor opinion of her – came under control after she discovered the advantages of false identity.

It never occurred to Dennis to register his mother as a missing person. Such a course of action simply did not fit her. It took a long time, though, before he could stop himself in public staring at every remotely similar woman. In the years following her disappearance, Dennis believed he saw Bernadette twice: once from a train window at King's Cross, once in Paris, on the Boulevard Haussmann. On both occasions he was wrong. He never knew what became of her, and when they came to clear out his effects, no trace of her, nor of any family existed anywhere, no 'departed mother in Glasgow', of whom he told such dotty and loving anecdotes, no 'wealthily-married sister in Witwatersrand'. Nothing.

All the big engineering corporations kept in close touch with university faculties. Dennis was offered one, two, three, four jobs during his postgraduate studies. He opted for a surveying firm in Liverpool. Was it because his father had met his mother there? We do not know. Some wish to give himself a family past? He never said.

It was in Liverpool that he established his permanent general pattern. Get in. Settle down. Good digs, first, then a flat. On his own. Always. At work, get well-liked and admired for performance. Pleasant to everybody, 'especially secretaries and clerks, because

62

they talk, they have to, their work is so boring.' Outside, check the population at large. Inside, check the society of the workplace. In both, assess the means of creating 'friends'. Next, measure those circles against each other. Figure out where to circulate for good commercial practice – plus: in what milieu to move with social safety? And, finally – where to live the secret life?

Public. Private. Secret. Three lives. 'Public' meant 'warm'. 'Private' meant 'genial, if gently aloof'. 'Secret' – he prowled. That is how Dennis Sykes lived the three lives. Committed in work. Shy but loyal with such companions as he made, always office-derived in those early days. In secret, he learned soon the charms of devastation.

His first 'field experiment' resulted in a most satisfying piece of emotional savagery. Two Liverpool foundries had merged; the parent company closed one plant and wished to enlarge the other. Dennis's employers liaised with the Council in discussions to widen roads, to increase the capacity of a railway bridge. He did the first surveying, and reported an extraneous difficulty. One house would suffer. Increased loads, noise and dust would spoil the enjoyment of its long, lovely garden.

'I think we should confront it,' he said in his quiet way. 'Meet them. Go and see their faces.'

He rapped the lion's-head doorknocker. 'Them' was an American woman alone; husband worked weekdays in London. She and Dennis sat facing each other, armchair to sofa, drinking coffee.

'No, I will take the decision,' the American woman told Dennis. 'I have to. He's away Monday to Friday.'

'That can't be easy?' He pursed a sympathetic lip.

'You said it!'

She, a stranger in Liverpool, had made no friends yet. Dennis sensed her irritableness, primed her: 'Does – does your husband, does he, ah'm – *have* to work in London?' – and then listened.

She spoke, he reckoned later, five minutes non-stop: then came the embarrassment, then the gratitude. Dennis listened. Dennis listened on.

Audrey Gee said, 'You know, I've never had a chance to say it all before, I've never said it. Not even to him. I mean not fully. I'm sorry to pressure your ear like that.'

'No, no. Shush.' He waved a hand.

63

When he returned to the office he said he felt certain they might 'crack this nut', but it would take a few weeks.

He wrote – his fine handwriting on the firm's letterhead.

Dear Mrs Gee,
Thank you for the coffee. If you need further advice, please get in touch. I will keep you informed as to progress.
Yours faithfully,

Dennis prepared himself for Audrey as a priest for a rite. He remembered some creamy languorous girl, drawing on new stockings, and recounting an *amour* to Dorothy.

'Then, he put his hand –' How she stood, and posed, both for the cheval-glass and Dorothy.

'Just here.' Leaning like a fashion model, one hand on one bare hip, she asked the rhetorical question.

'Now, why is that so – oooh!?'

The girls laughed deliciously.

Second and third visits to Audrey began to yield a gentle familiarity over the drawings unrolled on the dining-room table. Dennis picked up clues, and on his fourth visit brought the week-end *Sketch* which had a special photo supplement on Wimbledon.

'Oh boy! What a memory you have!' Two weeks ago, Audrey told Dennis that her sister back home had played a schools championship against Helen Wills Moody.

She stood in the hallway glancing at the newspaper. Dennis closed the front door behind him. Audrey had a mirror on the closet door at the end of the hall. She stopped momentarily to fix her hair. Before she could walk on, Dennis, right behind her, stood and put one hand on her hip.

Quietly he said, 'Don't move. Just – just – don't move.'

He spoke very softly.

They stood there. One hand only, on one hip. Then she turned and, slightly taller than him, put her head down on his shoulder.

All afternoon he stayed tenderly near. Sitting beside her, he lodged a hand on the edge of her lap. When she stood, he rose and touched her hair, lifted it a little, let it fall. As she gazed into the long garden, he stood behind her, his shoulder just touching hers. In the hallway again, before he said good-bye, he put his fingers in her mouth.

Next morning she had a note pushed through the door: it only read, 'Thank you. *Thank* you.' No signature.

Four days later, he came by. Each afternoon she had taken care to dress with edge, just in case, just in case . . .

Dennis stepped inside, stood with his back to the closed front door. He covered her face with his hand and spread his palm like butter all across her features.

They halted on the stairs twice, scrabbling, kissing, falling to their knees on the landing. He calculated every move, every breath. She kissed with her eyes closed, he with his eyes open, as he would forever.

Standing above her as she lay on the bed, he hesitated.

'What?'

He lowered his eyes. 'I believe – I believe I may need instruction.'

'Oh, Jesus! Oh dear, sweet Dennis.'

The widening of the bridge went ahead.

'I must say,' said Dennis's office admiringly, 'I don't know how you did it. If it were my house, I'd never agree.'

Audrey overruled all her absent husband's objections because she had a secret. She knew she would not have to live in the house much longer. Dennis had struck – but only when he knew for certain that he was being moved to London.

'Darling Audrey.' Every Monday over the four months, he had found her frantic after her wifely week-end. A Wednesday, consequently, more leisurely in mood, seemed suitable for the *coup de grâce*.

'You know there's going to be a war.'

She said, 'I can think of nothing else. Can't you avoid it?'

He had checked and re-checked the shipping timetables.

'When I was a boy,' he said wistfully, 'there was a postcard my father had sent from Santiago. That is where his first office was. It had a blue sign. On a terracotta wall.'

She lifted a breast, and with it touched his face and eyes.

'Audrey, would you – if I asked . . . ?'

'Come with you?'

'She had green eyes, my first girlfriend,' he reminisced fondly
forty years later. 'And sort of off-black hair. She was, she was –
great *fun*.'

Audrey embraced his head. 'Where? When? I'll be there.'

He made the elaborate arrangements. She left a note for her
husband. Half an hour before Stanley Gee was due to arrive from
London for the week-end, Audrey departed for the docks, panting
like a bride.

Afternoon after afternoon, evening after evening, 'Your tongue,'
she said, over and over, 'your tongue. Oh, Jesus, Dennis, honey.
Oh, Jesus Chriii-iiiii-issst!'

'No,' he said each time he lifted his sweating curly head, 'I'm
the one who knows where the honey is.'

Lying back he asked, 'What did you daydream about? About
men, I mean? Before I came into your life? Did you used to think
about men – and that?'

He licked the back of her ear, moistened the edge of her hair.

'Yeah, but I never thought –' and that habit he had of never
letting her finish what she was saying, of stopping her words by
laying his cheek to her lips. Four and a half months of immersion.

On the days before he arrived at the house, Audrey would hug
herself and say out loud, 'How I love him! How I love him! I
wonder if I'm good enough for him?'

Each day she had a new greeting for him. 'Who do you look
like today, Dennis? Let me see, I think you look like –'

After they had seen *Bringing up Baby*, Audrey changed her
mind and said, 'No, honey, I was wrong, George Raft has too sharp
a face, you're like Cary Grant. Yes, you're Cary Grant.'

Not once did he say, 'There's no need to apologize.'

Not once did he say, 'You're too self-effacing.'

Not once did he say, 'Yes, of course, you *are* good enough for
me. Don't be silly.'

Every little service, every cup of tea, every sandwich she
brought to the bed – he accepted them like a firm little sultan.
Yet, each afternoon before he arrived she still asked herself out
loud, 'I hope I'll be good enough for him today. How can anyone
love someone so much?'

Audrey looked in the mirror and hoped for a big moon at sea, so that they could lean on the rail and gaze at the stars and the ocean.

She embarked as Dennis instructed, on a dockside full of exotic cranes, with barges in the river. In the cabin she drew from her new suitcase a new slip, a new négligé. He had done all the planning; she had done all the booking.

They had before them a nine-week voyage, an 'advance honeymoon, and think, honey – no war, I won't have to fear you'll get killed overseas.'

'Qualms?'

'Nope. Oh, no! Because I guess, I guess – I'm leaving an all-right marriage for a thrilling one.'

He had warned that he would not come below until under way, had smiled in that crinkle that made her body fizz: 'I'm bringing you a gift.'

As the boat cleared the harbour, a train passed overhead, en route through Crewe to London. In the first-class compartments sat Dennis Sykes, wearing a suit of chalk-striped navy-blue, with a white, foaming pocket-handkerchief. He shook out his *Times* and settled to read. Out to his right, the lights of a ship slipped away and Dennis blew a mental kiss to all who sailed in her, and to all in Santiago.

In his pocket he carried a letter, from his old to his new office, which began, 'You are getting, if I may say so, a bit of a treasure this time. DS is a remarkably clever and able chap – and terribly popular.'

Dennis Sykes had a habit of rubbing the edges of his fingernails against each other. He had no self-abusive gestures, such as picking at skin, and he virtually raged if he cut a finger or bruised or scratched himself. Dorothy Bayer took a photograph of him once – a three-year-old boy with long curls and the lips of a decadent angel. He wears a button-through little tunic with an over-elaborate white collar, and he has cocked his head archly – a cherubic show-off. Over twenty years later, in the London office-group photograph, the lips have merely grown to manhood, and dark wavy hair hides the forehead; the eyes mistrust the camera.

=

Public. Private. Secret. After Liverpool, Dennis added very few geographical moves to his *curriculum vitae*. Between 1938 and 1949, he worked for the same company, a fact of which he was proud: he believed it demonstrated stability in him. He meant to grow into a sharp and ambitious executive, ready for each significant moment that came along. Every movement in his career took him upward. Alongside, he built his private income astutely by spending carefully; setting out to earn as much from investment as from employment, he more or less succeeded.

The way in which he approached work typified the life-method he had worked out. A seeming lightness of touch, with quips and accommodating-ness, concealed a ferocity of commitment. He worked harder, longer, swifter than any colleague his age. No extra work fazed him; no new complication irritated. With unnoticed control, he used his superior capacity to become a rescue service for overworked colleagues: 'If you're busy, I'll finish that.'

While doing so, he watched how the company functioned. Preferment, he observed, came to those who got nearest the senior managers. Dennis chose the Deputy Managing Director and made him the recipient of all his design and client problems; by doing so he gave the man an opportunity to develop a protégé. They discussed, experimented, exchanged ideas; they drank together – Dennis never touched alcohol, but encouraged the other man to relax. Together they kept up with the literature of their profession, and discreetly considered personnel difficulties in the firm.

The senior man trained him. *At meetings never contribute until asked. Service the primary requirement. Innovative but solid drawing-board and site work. Elegantly presented and conducted. Put the client first, then the project. Listen. Listen.*

Within a year, by dint of drawing and listening, and by means of ideas, courtesy and evident responsibility, 'DS' had made himself into as perfect a young managing engineer as the firm could have wanted, or ever had. Promotion jumped him two grades, unheard-of for a man in his twenties.

Method. Perception. Control. It had begun to work – especially control. Therefore – private life next. He had long perceived that he needed extensive social experience. All in good time. The time is now. At Dorothy Bayer's he had taken in the rudiments by osmosis. But now – how to move easily in company; how to become liked by women; yet how to avoid involvement. At the same time, he wanted to know every wild and absorbing carnal trick. Could he get both?

The conundrum absorbed him. Although conducted entirely in secret, the affair with Audrey, with its element of sexual instruction, had boosted his self-confidence in dealing with women. Intimacy. Sweat. Tight curls of hair like little serpents. Such a drug. And to think it could lead to power. To stay always in command, though, he needed ever more experience.

One path to follow: enjoyment without commitment. He wanted this combination for two reasons. Popularity with important wives and daughters would enhance his office reputation. Plus – he needed 'bodies' for his secret life. All things bright, Dennis, he told himself, everything on course. Young, evidently comfortably off, clothes-style already admired, and he had never known women liked men's hair so much.

'I wear rags of silk in it every night,' he teased the women in the office, 'silk from China. In little rolls, red and yellow.'

He began by swimming in the nearest pool. Maturer, but still young, women colleagues, of senior responsibilities, took to him. He accepted one in every four of their invitations – to a party, or a supper, or a lunch. Dennis listened and smiled, listened and smiled.

He primed their instincts, filled them with images of Dennis the caring son: 'My mother – anyone know how to ease the pains of rheumatism? Her knee –' and he would tap his leg. And Dennis the emotionally interested. He would look pensive and they would ask why: 'Oh, a friend of mine,' Dennis would sigh. 'His marriage is going wrong. I have to go round and see them tonight – but I never know what to say – in these situations.'

Soon, these slightly older women colleagues told him everything. Past loves, passions, unrequitements – he heard amazing things: of abortions in backstreets, of ruinous obsessions; incest. Upon which the confessor would say, 'It's like talking to a girlfriend talking to you, Dennis.'

Dennis would smile but make no move.

Which led them to ask among themselves, 'Is he a bit – pink? You know – no girlfriend in evidence?'

He heard – and kissed one of them. Once. On her doorstep late at night, without coming in 'for coffee'. Then he apologized, and when she told all the others of the kiss in all its splendour, they concluded, 'No – definitely not pink.'

After that one tongue-and-lips kiss, he increased his attractiveness by holding them all warmly at bay. By which means, he also kept his doorstep unfouled.

Without knowing it, the women leaked him information: who was being moved off which contract; what manager was now favouring whom among Dennis's contemporaries; who was having problems with what client. He even knew the content of his own Annual Report before his Annual Interview. With such intelligence at his command, Dennis moved like a panther into all corners of favour.

All also told him about sex, even though they called it love. He learned how they dreamed, how they hoped. Knowing they included him in their wishes, he played gently along. At the point when he had four girls in the same office hovering and crazed, each never telling another of their love for him, he received his second promotion. Unusually high he rose – therefore, time to escape gracefully into darker suits and stiffer collars, to move up the company hills, in among the management wives. He heated up the ailing-mother-in-Scotland story – 'wasting disease, you should see the medical bills.'

Or – 'She desperately wants me to marry, but do you know what she said? So that she would have a daughter-in-law who could nurse her.'

They loved him even more. As they smiled in disappointment, they understood why he could not yet wed.

While the public and private lives were being set up and managed, the secret life raged on beneath. When he 'played', as he called it, Dennis followed an undulating pattern. First came a period of extraordinary promiscuity, typically lasting a period of some weeks, for which he always paid in cash. After, for some months, he would, as he put it to himself, 'lie fallow'. Then, out again, and into the fresh carnal burst he hurled all the pent-up insults and reverses since the last period.

He did not like it. Even if the self-disgust had a power source within it, even if the sheer release made him walk tall with the force of its secrecy, he wished for more control over it. He knew control must be available; he knew he could tame these outbursts and convert them – to another pattern of behaviour. They could be different, methodical, useful. Sexual activity could have a purpose, like an energy harnessed. He could use seduction for professional advancement, and it could still satisfy that curious, unexplained but utterly driven sense of revenge. But – so difficult to learn. Whom could he tell – or on whom could he practise without having to say why? Then one Saturday morning in 1940, he found his tutor.

On the corner of Lisson Grove stood a mansion block of flats needing repair. Attractive prices, therefore, and if you had money for renovations, you got rapid access to a high standard of London living. Furthermore, if your repairs seemed comprehensive and exciting, people in the block talked about you, speculated, invited you for drinks. These buildings had their own social micro-climate.

Dennis Sykes stood inside the open door of his new apartment. The decorator swiped different colours in wide soft swathes across the walls as a test. A bony woman walked by.

'I like that russet terracotta,' she said. 'Are you one of the boys?' Then she said, 'Forget it, you're not,' when she saw Dennis's puzzled face. 'Thank God, darling.'

Her name was Binnie Maxwell. 'I'm on the floor above. 34B, same as my bust.' The decorator laughed and arched an eyebrow at Dennis.

Binnie glared. 'When Michelangelo here is gone, why don't you come and have some coffee?'

She had a leather sofa.

'Dennis? And how old are you, Dennis?'

'Twenty-six.'

'If Herr Hitler really starts chucking the ordure – Dennzy, you'll be cannon fodder.'

'No. We've talked about it. The company says I'm to be Reserved Occupations.'

'Another cigarette, please?'

'What do you do for a living, Binnie?' He lit it for her, and the sofa-leather creaked.

'Reserved Occupation, too, darling, but whisper it please, I'm also a lady. I'm a *fille de joie*.'

Binnie, mid-thirties looking fifty, racked with coughs and mascara, formed the core of a like-minded and like-bodied bunch. Obliquely well-bred, most were the daughters of financially-stressed divorcées whom the titled and rich had cast aside for younger flesh.

'*Les Louches*', Binnie called them, and they lived on their wits. Some had unsteady inheritances, or allowances. Several had addictions. All needed money, usually in desperation. They got it in tough ways: tarting on a closed and abusing circuit; servicing elderly wealth; hitting the resorts after wives had gone home.

Binnie had a frail side, too. For all her wild living she longed for some kind of protection, some kind of undemanding stability that would yet not deny her the raciness of it all – 'I have to box on the ropes too often, darling.'

She and Dennis clanged together like a pair of magnets. Binnie, smelling Dennis's rapaciousness, offered the deal. He, a near neighbour, would frequently be so nice to come home to: she, a woman of the world, had a lot of knowledge to impart.

They shook hands: she kissed him with her thin, carmine lips, then broke away to the high bar stool by the peeling kitchen counter.

'Phase One: the practicals,' and she wheezed with saloon laughter.

On their first full afternoon together she told him, 'Of course we start with an advantage, darling.'

'What's that?'

'For a little chap, you're hung like a Zulu. Not at all dinky in that bureau.'

Soon, she made other expressions of agreeable surprise, and he made her laugh like a whisky drain. The tuition began.

'Darling, look in our eyes all the time. Lead us gently but firmly and always, always push us down to a soft landing place.'

'Darling, here. Put your tongue just inside our lips, and run it around. Lick the inside of our lower lip. Lick it like your tongue was a little busy snake. Aaaahhh!'

'Darling, the most wonderful stunt of them all, Say to her, "I was dreaming about you last night." And then quick as a flash, say, "No, tell you later. A lot later." Nothing more flattering, darling, than being told by a man that you've been on his mind while the bugger's been *asleep*, for Christ's sake.'

Binnie sighed, 'Now – slip him back out, darling, and lie back. Thaaa-at's it. A little rest, shall we? A little nicotine relief for Binns and Denns? And then we begin all over again.'

She taught him how to use his fingernails lightly up and down her spine, how to run his tongue from ankle to thigh – 'Always, always on the inside, darling. On the outside you might as well be tongueing the table-leg. No-no-no-no-no-no, darling, that is not *at all* what Binnie means by ball-and-claw.'

For several consecutive week-ends, they spent afternoons and early evenings in bed, with Binnie hailing Dennis's fortitude, and correcting his ploys: 'Think of it as training the animal, darling, think of me as an animal-trainer.'

In return, Dennis, glad of the sweats and aches, bought her cigarettes, drink, and food. Early at night, before the hard people came out to play, he took her to meals in the solid, well-fed restaurants where she would never ever see the folk from what she called 'the bright side' of her life. Afterwards they went back to Binnie's where they clanked and tussled some more.

Yet, even if he stayed until three in the morning, Dennis never slept overnight, always closed the door of 34B behind him and like a jaded musketeer slipped quietly down the dark green stairwell, his empty scrotum aching.

In Phase Two, Binnie taught him about targets.

'Watch wives, darling. Watch the corners of their mouths. In fact, watch the corners of all women's mouths. Mine don't droop, darling, do they? Say what you like about me, call me a fast and lanky jade if you will, but the corners of my mouth do not *droop*! And I am proud of that!'

She dragged on the cigarette with horse's lungs.

'Watch this. You go to a party. You find a woman, a wife. She's – heavy-ish. But not too heavy. Or bony – not as bony as me, nobody is. But too bony for her own good, and evidently wed to a wealthy animal. He will have sleek fur. So will she – but the gloss will be a little dull. Bit artificial, paid-for rather than natural. Listen to her for half an hour, keep refilling her glass. Don't, for

73

Christ's sake, *talk* to her. Listen. *Listen* to her. You know about listening. Next afternoon, you'll be round there for tea and buns and handkerchief-pandkerchief. Binnie knows, darling. How does she know? Because while you're round there, Binnie's actually hogtieing the article's animal? That's why the corners of the wife's mouth are drooping, darling, poor wet hen that she is. But – for Christ's sake darling, tell them you're married. Otherwise, they'll be round here with their pointy teeth – going after you like pike in a fucking trout stream. Another of your ciggos, please, darling.'

Binnie paced towards the long window and looked down at the traffic; shadows of the afternoon darkened her high, thin, nude haunches.

She turned, thin long breasts a-swing.

'Why am I telling you this?' He lit it for her; the lighter flame gilded her face. 'Yes, they are tears in my eyes, you little shit – no! Don't ask! No! Shut up! None of your fucking business.' Binnie tightened her act again and slipped back into character.

'And another thing, darling, if you're into social bullfighting, you can have the most wonderful anarchy, the greatest fun stirring it between husband and wife. In a way a woman in the same position never can. Heed Binnie, darling, and you'll be the social equivalent of one of those guided rockets Herr Hitler is supposed to be building. Yes, ye-es, go to it Dennzy.'

She turned and, cigarette askew in her lips, began to hammer the bed fiercely with her fists.

'And be delicate when reporting back. Binns is not made of fucking tin after all. Am I?! Am I?!'

Dennis launched himself: Phase Two: The Social Life – Intimacy without Commitment. With ease, he built a separate existence away from the office and, above all, away from clients. New circuits: he purchased a car, joined a motor club; he bought clubs and played golf. New women: alphabetically, and in code, he kept count in his notebook: Clarrie, Diana, Elizabeth, Faith, Hazel, Iris, Joan, Lorna – one a fortnight. Or so.

All feared losing their comfortable homes: all knew disappointed marriages. Most had for years gone along with the ordinary pretence of marriage in exchange for the patterns of house, car, clothes, by which they now felt comforted.

Dennis brought relief. At least they could tell him what hurt at home.

Marjorie remarked, 'I've never had the courage to tell him how his hogging the newspaper at breakfast annoys me.'

Nicola said, 'And he didn't even know that to give somebody a gift of gloves is a bad omen, it means breaking a friendship. Not that we were best friends, we've been just – well – married, I suppose. I'd love my husband to be my best friend.'

Olive complained, 'And I go to the most careful lengths, I choose the writing-paper carefully, I've always been extra-careful about the way our address is printed on it, about the lettering, and then suddenly I find that half of it is missing, and that he hasn't even said how nice it is.'

Petra said, 'I'm married to a man I don't love.'

Dennis clucked and shook his sympathetic head.

He soon understood that he had guessed the paradox right: sex and business could mix if kept apart. 'The Binnie System', as he called it, brought him a dividend even beyond the sex-without-emotion, a career bonus by way of by-product. While warming briefly these sad-faced, hurt and cautiously angry women in Kensington, Burgess Hill, Wimbledon and Harrow, while 'apologizing' to them for his 'marriage', they also told him all their husbands' business strategies. As he studied their bodies, Dennis also learned of their friends and associates. Each night in his flat, he wrote down all the names they had mentioned: husbands, companies and connections. As well as storing for future reference, the information enabled him to appear knowledgeable of industry and finance, to drop names as delicately as a Chinese diplomat.

Rarely did he see Queenie, Roberta, Sheila, Thomasina twice. How sweetly and wistfully they parted, she still in a robe, secretive and kissy behind the closed front door. But Dennis reassured them on the telephone two days later – that it was a once-only time for him too, and now, oh, how guilt would haunt him! He felt 'funny' seeing his 'wife' that evening, he explained ruefully.

Dennis had only three breaks in this routine, when three times he contracted Non-Specific Urethritis from Binnie. Red-edged and oozing, he showed Binnie.

'Me, darling, I fear,' she said. 'I'm a carrier. Apologies all round.

But my friend Edmund will look after little Dennis's every need. He has a clinic for these things. He's a hickory-dickory-dock. So to speak. A dick doc.'

5

As her family increased, Ellen Kane found that she stood in the hurtful middle between her children and her husband. The cold and jagged outer ire he showed in the earliest days of his recovery never abated; it often intensified. Those cyclical undulations of mood, common to many men of his age and time and experience, began in him at a higher level up the roller-coaster. His household angers were more vicious; in his calms, bitterness lurked a bare inch below the lid. And yet, and yet – once the bedroom door closed behind them, he had such tenderness for her: lips pressed to her hair, hand held in both of his.

It took her several years to regulate the confusion caused by this split in him. She watched him closely, looking for perhaps one clue, a key that would release him. What, for instance, could she make of his sudden disappearance sometimes, after he had been particularly harsh to a child? Once or twice she found him sitting on the chair in their bedroom, his head erect, eyes closed, like a man keeping pain at bay.

In front of the children, she had to brave him with tact, diffuse his powerful, general force. Never smile, she learned, when a crisis of what he called 'discipline' blew up as suddenly as a bomb. Be grave, she discovered: take his side somewhat, to appease him: but never quite join in his harshness.

Afterwards, she had the next difficulty – of how to calm an afflicted child while not betraying her husband's authority. She hugged; she kissed; she praised the weeping daughter or son for other things, and for hours afterwards never failed to smile with warmth when they caught her eye. If she prayed after such incidents, it did not mean that all her old piety had returned, but that she meant to give example to the children. With all these warmths and diligences, Ellen believed that by and large she had reduced or explained to the family their own bewilderment. Some of her loving worked: the children did not grow resentfully, nor – on the face of things – uncontrollably distressed.

Helena seemed to have the greatest difficulties, to such a degree that from above, her mother, and from beneath Grace – and even the younger ones – often rushed to buoy her up. Ellen spent particular time in developing Helena's reading habit. By the time she was ten, the child, as pretty as porcelain, could immerse herself in a book. When she had finished the latest Laura Ingalls Wilder, sent by cousins in America, or a new Eleanor Farjeon from the school library boxes, Helena could sit and dream, untouchable. By these means she occasionally escaped any gale of violent 'correction' that suddenly swept across the kitchen from where her father sat. She never raised her voice, and in following her mother's lead of creating family exchange, she taught Grace and the younger ones impossibly long passages from vivid poems.

> Then saw they how there hove a dusky barge,
> Dark as a funeral scarf from stem to stern,
> Beneath them; and descending they were ware
> That all the decks were dense with stately forms,
> Black-stoled, black-hooded, like a dream – by these
> Three Queens with crowns of gold – and from them rose
> A cry that shiver'd to the tingling stars

– and the young ones would shiver in delight and repeat the words, with Helena nodding as if keeping time to music. Her mother encouraged and encouraged – and fed her warm milk to try and cure Helena's recurring diarrhoea.

One April Saturday night in 1937, Ellen conceived again. A few days after Grace's ninth birthday, a red-faced man appeared at the gate, embarrassed not exerted, and asked for help.

'What kind of help?' asked Ellen: it was late morning.

'Urgent help, Ma'am. The car's broke.'

Ellen no-nonsensed him. 'It's "broken" not "broke" – and since when did a broken car become urgent?'

The man replied, 'Since John McCormack got into it, Ma'am.'

Ellen dropped her hands into the dough. 'Jesus, Mary and Joseph!'

'That's the form, Ma'am.'

She clarified. 'You mean to say that John McCormack is out there in the car? On the road?'

'I do, Ma'am, that's the form. His wife is along with him there, and the son.'

Ellen, flustered at first, began to organize.

'Bring him in, bring them in, we'll at least give them a cup of tea. My husband knows about cars.' The man went.

'Helena!' Ellen called, and sent her to fetch Thomas from the garden.

'Grace!' – who was sent to find other children, so that faces could be wiped.

Essie lumbered in and was sent for a clean apron and a clean tablecloth. Thomas appeared.

'Wash your hands,' Ellen urged, 'John McCormack is coming through the door at any minute, his car broke down.'

'What?'

'Go. ON!'

Thomas hared upstairs, Ellen ran after him, and they changed like lightning, in time to see from their window the small party step through the gate. Lily McCormack wore a small velvet hat and pearls and, on the gravel, walked carefully in suede shoes.

Thomas, peering, said to Ellen, 'He's bigger than I thought,' and they raced downstairs again to stand at the door as a couple, just in time to shake hands and introduce themselves.

The embarrassed driver spoke to Thomas, who sent him to Hand's pub, where a mechanic from Dublin, in charge of the steamroller on the New Road, had been staying. Ellen led their visitors to the parlour.

Thomas spoke first. 'I was saying to my wife – you're bigger than I thought.'

McCormack smiled; 'A big noise comes out of a big drum.'

Scuffles in the gravel outside: the children wrestled to peer in at the window.

General talk began – of the difficulties with cars, new roads, weather. Tea appeared: John McCormack began to praise the scones.

'Well, you're lucky,' said Ellen, 'I put them into the oven just as your man came through the gate.'

Lily said, 'I wish I could bake like that' – to which her husband replied, 'Just as well, or I'd be even bigger.'

It became a Kane household joke for years: 'Mama – can we have some of John McCormack's scones?'

All the time, Thomas had not stopped smiling or half-smiling – in a rictus of shyness; or in genuine pleasure at having one of the world's great singers in his parlour; perhaps from a feeling that he knew he had the capacity to belong in such company. He commanded the room, steering the conversation from one adult to another and if necessary extending the courtesy of an explanation to the McCormack boy, who sat as meekly as all boys in their best clothes. Thomas had a habit of looking at the back of his outstretched hand when making a point, and of then turning the hand palm upwards, flat, to conclude the statement. He sat upright, forward on the edge of his chair, courteous, forthright and confident.

So, it was Thomas who accepted when John McCormack turned to Ellen and, tapping the dark piano said, 'Mrs Kane, since you're after giving us the fruits of your talents with your lovely baking, I hope you'll let me repay the compliment.'

Thomas beamed. 'You're going to sing for us? Well, well, that's just tremendous.'

'Have you any music of your own here, Mrs Kane?' McCormack asked. 'Because we have some in the car.'

Ellen said, 'I have, but surely you know them by heart?' and she smiled.

'Of course I do, but I want you to accompany me.'

'Oh,' was the only little sound she could make, 'Oh.'

Thomas helped. '"Panis Angelicus", maybe?'

'Yes, yes, we have that.' Ellen foraged within the piano stool.

Thomas rose, went quickly to the window and pulled back the lace curtains, alarming the lurking children – startling them even more by the fact that he was smiling at them.

'No,' he said, 'no, stay where you are,' and he lifted the window open. Then he whispered to Helena, 'Get Essie to come out here and listen.'

Inside the room, Ellen had at last arrayed the sheet music. McCormack, in his dark suit and yellow tie, bulky as a grizzly bear, stood on her right as formally as if on a concert platform. She settled, and with all the composure she had absorbed from

Sister Agatha at Teacher Training, played the opening bars. Then, when she nodded gently, McCormack began.

Panis Angelicus.
Fit panis hominum.

The great voice, with the power of gold, they said, could be heard, they said, at the weir four miles away, they said. And, listening, Thomas Kane sat with fingers splayed across his own lips in astonished pleasure. The children outside the window stood still. Essie, out of sight, froze her big body at this molten sound that seemed to hang in the air above the house and the garden. A man on the road with a pony stood like a statue of stone.

Ellen played the piano calmly, and now played on, in simple accompaniment to every note that was sung. Thomas Kane took his fingers away from his thin mouth, and he joined his hands in his lap as if in prayer. Lily McCormack, who had heard it all before, still sat transfixed. The last note lasted as long as a long kiss.

When it was over, McCormack bowed to his blushing accompanist: 'Mrs Kane, I can assure you, if ever you need a job as my pianist –'

The mundane man who drove the car arrived in time to say that the engine had been fixed and was now making a grand noise once again.

All evening, Thomas murmured in wonder, 'John McCormack? John McCormack in our house?' Twice he told Ellen the story of McCormack meeting Caruso.

'And he says to him, "And how is the world's greatest tenor today?" And do you know what Caruso said? He said, "And since when did McCormack become a baritone?" Well, well. John McCormack? Singing in this house!' He laughed. 'We should be putting up a plaque.'

As they lay in bed, he stroked Ellen's shoulders over and over, down to her hips and back to her shoulders again, then stroked her spine with hands as soft as kindness.

'The excitement of it!' he said over and over. 'The honour. You played the piano for John McCormack. My wife!'

81

'You must tell the children how you feel,' she said.

'No. Oh, no! This is for you and me,' he replied in the darkness.

This, however, is how the Kane household heaved with pain and confusion. The following afternoon, even though still agog with stardust, Thomas addressed Helena ominously.

'But what was the name of the hymn he sang?' A Sunday visit had been paid to a distant farm.

Suddenly, all the others in the car fell silent. He asked again.

'I don't – remember, Daddy.' Helena's breath caught.

'What are you, a little fool? With your mouth hanging open? I'll ask you once more. What was – the name – of the hymn – Mr McCormack sang?'

Helena's lips contracted: she squeezed her fingers, and said tentatively, 'Was it "O Salutaris" – Daddy?'

'I'll give you "O Salutaris" when I get you home. You'll have your legs bared for me when we get out of this car tonight, Miss. Now – I'll ask you again? What was it?'

Helena shook her head wordlessly.

Thomas said to the windscreen, 'Are we rearing a complete fool? A clown? What are we wasting food on? Why are we feeding her?' He hissed on his teeth.

Grace nudged her mother's shoulder from behind, but Ellen did not intervene. Helena's face had turned completely white and not another word was spoken.

In the kitchen, the others sat at the table silent. Soon, Helena walked through them blindly. Her long white stockings were down: red marks faded from the backs of her legs. Even the small ones were silent as they heard her climbing the stairs.

Grace whispered fiercely, 'Mama, Mama, you should have stopped him doing it, he's always doing it, you should have stopped him.' No answer.

The Kanes once more ate a silent evening meal. Thomas did not appear in the kitchen for some time. When Ellen searched, she saw the light of his old carbide lamp in the garage: not a sound came forth: she peered through the crack and saw him merely sitting on an old chair.

Upstairs later, Ellen went to see Helena, who lay quietly in bed.

'Dear girl, aren't you undressing at all?' Helena had climbed under the blankets fully clothed, coat included. Ellen took her hand, and Helena tightened her grip so hard that Ellen had to ease it. She stroked her daughter's blonde hair over and over.

'Here. I've been keeping this for you.' She handed Helena *The Story of the Amulet* by E. Nesbit. 'This was my very own copy.'

Helena took it and put it under her pillow.

'Aren't you going to read it, love?'

'No, it'll only tell me what I'm missing in this house.'

Ellen stroked and stroked, saying, 'Shhh, now, shhhh, love, shhh. The hymn, by the way, was "Panis Angelicus". *Panis. Angelicus.* Will you remember that?'

'He told me while he was slapping my legs. He told me three times. Six words. Six slaps. *Panis. Angelicus.*' At last she began to weep. Ellen gathered her and sat with her in the dark until the girl fell asleep.

To change her own mood, Ellen went downstairs and washed socks, even though Essie tried to stop her. Then, finally, preparing for bed, she eyed Thomas.

'I never asked you, Thomas. Did you sleep well last night?'

He half-smiled. 'Last night? Like a log.'

'I bet,' she said, and chuckled to get his attention, 'I bet that there will be news soon from that department –' and waited until he turned.

'You can't tell that quickly, can you?' He reached forward and loosened her hair from the fixings at the back.

'What will we call it? I know I'm right. I've known with each of them.' She put her head on his chest. He grabbed her hand and held it.

'If it's a boy we'll call him – "McCormack",' he smiled.

She eased his hand away. 'Oooh, Thomas,' and rubbed her fingers. 'Don't you know your own strength?'

'Did I bruise you?' He looked down solicitously. Ellen shook her fingers loosely.

'You have such huge hands.'

He hugged her again. They lay.

'Thomas?'

'Nn-mm?'

'I know you are so anxious that the children use their intelligence, and that they know things. No!' she said panickily, 'Don't stiffen your body.'

He raised his head. 'Are you about to criticize me? I hope not.'

'Oh, Thomas! That dead voice you use, it's like steel.'

He rose quickly, put a cardigan over his pyjama jacket and clumped his way downstairs. Ellen still lay awake when he came to bed two hours later.

In the decade since Thomas's full recovery, the children's pattern had been established. At three o'clock, they had a meal after school; an hour's play afterwards, and then, until tea at half-past six, lessons with Thomas at which Ellen hovered.

'They must be ready for secondary school when the time comes,' he said frequently.

Age difference brought no concessions. Helena, aged eleven, was asked the same addition and subtraction as Grace aged nine, and down the line to all except the very youngest. Then came the learning by rote, in the manner of the period's education. Like Evensong, the Kane children could be heard at home, long after classes had ended, chanting tables and spellings. Thus they grew up sharing a high, if curiously uniform, standard of intelligence. Grace, alone, went beyond the mere recite-to-memorize, and showed the least fear of using her imagination. By and large, however, she, too, had to conform to the 'learn-it-off-by-heart' dogma drummed in by her father, and supported, apparently, by her mother.

No visitors were comfortably received in the house during the evenings of the school week. Afterwards, Thomas, and only Thomas, read the papers in front of the family; Ellen did the crossword when the children had gone to bed at night. As an extension of the education, Thomas read out news items he considered appropriate to their lives. In March, they all gasped at the fire in Texas which killed five hundred schoolchildren. In May, the *Hindenburg* exploded, and Thomas gave them the history of airships. From mid-June to the General Election in early July, he taught them the political process.

Grace asked, 'Who are you going to vote for, Daddy, is it Mr de Valera?'

Thomas looked hard at Ellen across the table. 'Tell her.'

Ellen said, 'Gracey, it is very bad manners to ask anyone whom they vote for.'

Occasionally the outside world arrived with the postman. In September, Father Peter Nolan in Wolverhampton, a friend of the Morris family – of Ellen's mother, in particular – sent Ellen one of the new English threepenny pieces. It sat propped up in a glass for all to admire, high above the tallest child's reach.

Apart from such bright bolts, outside matters came in so rarely and then under such control that anything worldly seemed magical. A film came to the school, dental care instruction: animated molars fought off black, pitchforked invaders called 'Bacteria'. In another ten minutes of flickering black-and-white, gap-toothed exotic children smiled up at Irish priests and nuns on Foreign Missions. For whose upkeep the girls delivered magazines such as *The Far East*, and travelled the parish to collect the subscriptions from the parishioners.

On one such journey, both girls saw a cow about to be serviced by a bull. The farmer had a rope around the bull's neck; the big wrinkled beast slipped and slid on the stone-flagged yard and the farmer winked at the girls, saying the bull needed 'a dose of coaxyorum'. When they relayed their puzzled story at home, Helena and Grace had never seen their mother so angry; she forbade them to go near that farm again.

Next day, Ellen reconsidered her rage, using different justifications. She suggested to Thomas that, with Helena now eleven, perhaps it was time the two older girls began to meet more people.

'Why?'

'They need social development, too.'

'Why?'

She played one of her few good cards. 'Thomas, love, we can't have them looking backward. Helena'll be going to the convent in September. She'll have to get a chance of being accustomed to people outside the house.'

He looked up from the parlour table where he had been writing.

'They're never to talk about life in this house. Do they understand that? All those people would love to know our business.'

'Oh, they know that, Thomas, they're good girls. And anyway,' she added, 'I suppose they can't say anything if they have nothing to say.'

He looked at her sharply but made no comment.

'I'll start them cautiously,' she concluded. 'I'll watch carefully which houses they visit. They can run errands for me.'

In this way, Helena and Grace met Mrs Ulverton. Ellen sent them on a visit to an old brother-and-sister farm, where Rhona also called.

'Oh, by the way.' Rhona had an unconscious rhymer lying within her who sprang to life now and then. 'I brought you a bird, though Munch says I'm absurd.'

As Helena and Grace watched, amazed, this exotic, strangely-spoken woman, whom their mother knew, began to undo her blouse. Beneath lay a peach satin slip and some white, enormous arrangements. In the no man's land beneath her bosom and above her waist rested a large parcel wrapped in newspaper.

Feeling it, Rhona remarked, 'And it's still warm. You see, newspaper is so good to us all. If you want to keep cream cool wrap the jug in newspaper. If you want to keep a goose hot, ditto. That means the same, ditto means "the same", child,' she explained to Helena. Rhona had just killed a neighbour's gosling, but did not know whether such a young bird could be cooked.

'Here, help me,' and Helena, standing up, took the gosling from above Rhona's waist with all the ceremonial care of a doctor handing over a new-born baby.

'I use my greaseproof paper more than once, there's a good tip for you, child, the greasier it gets the more it insulates, and after all, it's all only food. Now, child, what is your name, pretty things you two, whose love-children are you?'

'Helena Kane, Ma'am.'

'And yours?'

'Grace Kane, Ma'am.'

'Ooh, good manners. Helena of Troy, and Grace and Favour, and how old are you both? Or should I say each?'

'I am eleven since last month.'

'I'm nine since April.'

'And so precise. Pretty children. That's *my* daughter – over there in mauve.' She indicated Viva, who waggled long fingers at them.

'Now,' Rhona sat and addressed the large cold farmhouse kitchen. 'I want to hear all your views on this bloody excommunication. Is there anything we can do about it, I mean can we stop it? It is barbaric.' Neighbours shuffled.

At which moment, the woman of the house, thick spectacles gleaming in the lamplight, ushered the girls out of the house and sent them home with eggs for their mother.

Unfortunately for Ellen's new scheme to widen the girls' horizons, Thomas met them at the door.

'What new words did you learn?'

Grace, still as excited at Mrs Ulverton as if she had seen a parrot, blurted, 'We heard "bloody excommunication". And we heard "barbaric". That's all, we knew all the other words. Oh, and we were asked whose "love-children" we were?'

'Fetch your mother,' said Thomas.

He asked the girls to repeat the words to Ellen. She contrived to have the girls expand the context.

'I won't have it,' exploded Thomas. 'That woman will fill their heads with Protestant ideas.'

Ellen traded again, and won. 'As long as they know we're right,' she said. 'The wrong views of others will only reinforce their faith.'

Then she lost, by not thinking ahead.

'In that case,' said grim Thomas, 'they had better all come to the excommunication.'

'Oh, Thomas!' She bit her lip.

'Yes?' he asked unbrookingly.

'It – it used to be a very harshly worded business.'

'All the better. Remember – "the fear and love of God", the fear is important too.'

'Even the little ones.'

'Oh, yes, oh, yes. No question. They'll remember it all their lives.'

Ceremonies cemented the church's power. To practical effect. The children's First Holy Communion every year boosted retail trade: new dresses and veils, new suits and shoes. Confirmation every three years brought a state visit from the Archbishop, with local catering. Occasionally the Church received a golden opportunity to demonstrate its darker authority.

Archbishop Edward Ahern, and his Administrator, Monsignor Tom Kelly, sat like cassocked impresarios.

'The bigger the church the wider the message your Grace?'

'Yes, Thomas.'

'Therefore, Mooreville. And – early in the Mass, middle or late, your Grace? Canon Law leaves it open.'

Edward Ahern said, 'The latter, I think.'

Monsignor Kelly, who was a pedant, replied, 'By that, your Grace, do you mean the last-named of the three? "The latter" can only be one of two, it is a construction very like "the alternative". Do you see what I mean?'

'Yes, Thomas. I mean, as late as possible. After the last Gospel, even.'

'Yes, your Grace, yes.' He approved. 'Yes. Yes. But they won't be away until nearly one o'clock? And after half-eleven Mass, isn't that a bit long?'

'No longer than on Easter Sunday, Thomas. Or a Confirmation,' replied Edward Ahern.

Powerful psychology: the Monsignor beckoned an altar-boy to remove all flowers. Edward Ahern watched from a throne to one side. The small Monsignor began to excommunicate Joan Merrigan whom Cyril Stephenson had at last married.

'A child of this Archdiocese has placed herself outside the fold.'

The candles on the altar had been doused; the crucifix draped.

'Her name is Josephine Brigid Merrigan, known as Joan Merrigan. She abandoned Mother Church for selfish reasons, namely to marry a non-Catholic.'

All sacred vessels had been ostentatiously removed from the altar.

'Thereby she allied herself to a man who can never see the face of God. And now Mother Church, after many efforts to have the child reconciled, will abandon her, and reject her.'

The clappers on the sanctuary handbell were bound in black crepe cloth.

'She will be consigned to the exterior darkness. On her deathbed she will not receive the consolation of the Blessed Sacraments, nor the valedictory comfort of Extreme Unction.'

No sunlight activated the colours on the stained-glass windows.

'She will not pray with her family, nor will there be a place of welcome for her children within these walls, they will not exist in the sight of God. As she has chosen to put herself distant from God, so He now chooses to forget her.'

The little Administrator paused, wiped his brow. Congregants in the front pews looked only at their hands or at the floor. The altar-boys in their scarlet and white sat still.

'If she calls for God He will not hear her. Though she writhe with agony on her deathbed, or in all the days of her life, He will not ease her pain. Though she kneel and plead with Him, He will not heed her. For her there will be no Communion of Saints. For her there will be no glimpse of the sight of God. That is what the word of Holy Mother Church, the term "Excommunication" means. The word of God.'

Not for years had so many people packed this church. Nobody coughed. Archbishop Edward Ahern held his crozier at a powerful slant.

'Let me repeat her name: Josephine Brigid Merrigan, known as Joan. She is no longer a member of this Church or Catholic community. She is shunned by God, by His Blessed Mother, by Saint Joseph and all the Saints. Her prayers no longer have efficacy; they no longer go up to Heaven. A murderer, provided he show contrition and do penance, will have a greater chance of passing through the gate of Heaven than Joan Merrigan will henceforth.'

A tear rolled down Ellen's face; Helena caught her breath; Grace looked across at her father on the outside of the pew.

'And it is His wish that her former community, embracing her family, her parents, brothers, sisters, nieces and nephews. And her new neighbours in that part of the archdiocese to which she has now removed herself. It is God's wish that they become aware that she has been decreed by God unfit for our society. That is also what "Excommunication" means.'

Grace and Helena shifted. The younger Kanes snuggled under Ellen's sleeve. Thomas sat upright, his eyes never leaving the face of the Administrator, his head a gleam of austerity.

89

'Josephine Brigid Merrigan, known as Joan, is hereby excommunicated. And to you my dear brethren, gathered here this morning in the love of God, I say this. Even though it is not technically a sin, if you find yourself consorting with an excommunicated person, it would be as well to seek your confessor's advice. As the proverb has it, you cannot touch tar and not be blackened. Let us kneel and pray for her poor, unfortunate soul.'

In the Kane car, mother and children spoke not at all.

Thomas said, 'Well. There you are. She would not listen to anyone. She thought she was right. She would not take heed. And that is what happens to people who do not take heed. Are you listening?' He addressed his remarks over his shoulder to the children in the back of the car. Nobody replied.

'I said. Are you listening?'

Grace ventured. 'Yes, Daddy. We are.'

'And what did I say?'

'You said, "That is what happens to people who do not take heed."'

'Good girl. And what is it that happens to people who do not take heed? They get excommunicated. What happens?'

Grace replied, 'They get excommunicated.'

'Are you the only one back there with a tongue in your head, Miss?'

Helena, alerted, murmured, 'No, Daddy.'

At two o'clock, the Winers came, Leah still gesturing in argument with Herbert on the unfairness of his never learning to drive.

'And I, Ellen, I! I. Look. My hands! I have to drive all the time. I have to turn the starting-handle.'

She subsided with the mood she found.

'The children have had a shock,' whispered Ellen to Leah. 'We had this excommunication today. It was very grisly and upsetting.'

'But why did you take them?'

Ellen evaded.

Leah took the hint and declared, 'An outing.' She called. 'Girls. Girls. Best feet forward, we're going for a drive.'

The Grey Valley represented some kind of collective memory for the locality, a wild place, of strangeness and ancestry. At its deepest

90

it had sheer sides of limestone, haunted in summer by strangers on bicycles with sketch-pads, or small hammers and satchels. They captured the gentians and whins in their purples and yellows; they hacked serene fossils from the ripples of shale that shelved like an ebbed beach down to the gorse.

Shaped like an upturned, three-quarters-open fist, the valley cradled thirty or so houses. Those dwellings from which children had done well in America had been able to continue thatching their roofs. Others yielded to cheaper measures – mainly corrugated, galvanized iron. All maintained their colour codes of ages past: russet-washed walls, or *belle-époque* red, or whitewash, or deep green, or mauve, or bluewash.

Leah, Ellen and the girls climbed from the car and stretched. Grace ran ahead, then turned back and said, 'Oh, Mama, why didn't I bring my paints. Look!'

Helena, a book omnipresent under her arm, trotted after Grace into the wooded interior, and the two women strolled the path behind them.

No invader, not even Cromwell, had violated the Grey Valley, and Deanstown people rarely told outsiders that it existed. Those bicycling summer strangers, in their khaki shorts or billowing flowered dresses, had read of it botanically or geologically, in specialist publications. The Natural History Museum in Dublin still displayed the great honey-coloured ammonite found there in 1907. An English botanist claimed that the Grey Valley had a micro-climate.

'The thing is. If you look at Herbert. We never used to differ.' Leah clenched her fists. 'But he has changed, Ellen: he's changed.'

'My father always says that men aren't generally well-known at all, that they're very different inside themselves.'

Houses in the valley contained priceless handmade furniture that had been built-in over two to three hundred years. Kitchen dressers still had chickens in the open-drawered compartment beneath, straw peeping out between the slats. One wall-bed, which folded out by night, had been made in 1598, and the maker's adze-marks still ridged through the generations of pink lead paint.

'And did you ever think,' asked Leah rhetorically, 'that you would hear me say what I'm going to say now? I'm going to say that we'd have been happier while we were still poor.'

'Of course,' said Ellen, 'men want to earn, don't they, they want to earn the things they have.'

In the deep, foggy wood, Helena and Grace called to each other. Grace chanted, 'Bliss-bliss-bliss-bliss. Bliss-bliss-bliss-bliss.'

Helena chased Grace, then hid, then frightened her from behind and they chased again. Then Helena dropped her book, reached up and began to swing from a bare old elm branch.

On the valley's floor, beneath the greenery, rock formations had created areas like ice floes. Leaves piled in a bronze mulch. As the girls ran on, the women walked the dark pathways to the interior, and eventually lapsed into silence, savouring the peace of this foggy oasis.

6

In his three chosen lives, Dennis Sykes matured quickly. The partnership had huge and essential contracts from the War Office and assigned him, as promised, to Reserved Occupations: he designed airfields and hangars; he engineered the secret bunkers to which the politicians would retreat if Hitler got across the Channel. On his private circuit, his value increased as husbands vanished into the maw of the burgeoning war. Indeed, on one significant day, he was the only man under fifty when Royal Wimbledon hosted Moor Park in their annual fourball.

And for the secret life, Binnie remained a sufficient receptacle. He had met her just before his twenty-sixth birthday, and, infections excepted, their heavings had continued apace. As she had asked, he kept his suburban pathfinding hidden from her, unless he wished to taunt her. His barbs always took comparative form: he would look at her body thoughtfully and say, 'I sometimes wonder . . .'

'What, Dennis?'

'Nothing.'

'C'mon.'

'Nothing.'

'Come ON!'

'Well – whether I like the more, the more, well, the fuller bodies I meet?'

'You are such a little shit!' – but it drew tears.

Prostitutes rarely figured again: he had adjusted his revenges and found how to satisfy them in his London and Home Counties 'social' life. Then, in mid-September 1942, Dennis began to discover the pleasures of broader horizons. The war swung between the RAF bombing Dusseldorf and Bremen, and Hitler laying siege to

Stalingrad. With pride the firm appointed DS to their most secret project.

'Possible necessary relocation of ultra secure building,' said his mentor, now the Managing Director. 'Deep under Stirlingshire or Ayrshire, perhaps the eastern Borders. Should the Americans fail Europe, Herr Hitler's jackboots could grow seven-league status. Scotland's farther away.'

Binnie fidgeted. 'Well, darling, mission accomplished around these parts, eh? The chaps say, according to your reports, that you're "A man's man", and the gels say, "He really likes women". Talk about having it both ways, but not fully. Dennzy, dear, don't ever go sweet, will you? Never go pink?'

'No fear,' said Dennis, 'no fear.'

'Are you sure? You're for ladies, darling, not for men.'

'Sure.'

'Sure as eggs is *ova*, darling? Speaking of which.'

Binnie had three abortions during her intensive two years with Dennis. Each time he wrote what she called 'a respectable cheque'.

Before they left the restaurant, Binnie said, 'Top of the tree, now, little Dennis, darling.'

He asked what she meant.

'Well it's one thing, darling, to pierce the hearts of all these creatures in the Home Counties. But Scots ladies are different, purer. And the Scottish gentlemen, they watch their wives as closely as they watch their money. They see them as their chattels, Dennzy, darling. So – big challenges for a little boy.'

Binnie bag-of-bones, with her smoker's cough, rinsed out by abortions, alchohol her dominant body fluid, outlived Dennis. A rasping, pink-flannelette, Bette Davis lookalike, she slumps today in one of those Home Counties homes called The Cedars or The Pines. When Dennis's obituary appeared in *The Times*, she held it up to a friend.

'I used to know him. Unhappy little fella. Never pretended it, though.'

After six months' research in Edinburgh, with secret briefings back in London, Dennis, under orders, moved into the countryside. In the Cheviot Hills, at Mervinslaw near Hawick, he found Iain and Mona Nicolson. They had no children and a calm household. The Agriculture and Fisheries Department, Dennis's 'cover', preferred its 'operatives' to stay with 'approved' local people. Given the powerful nature of his work, the hosts had to know what secrecy meant, or ideally have 'official' experience.

Ten years earlier, Iain Nicolson had come home from 'Government security' in Africa. While he supervised the finances on the Mervinslaw estate, he met and married Mona, a secretarial factotum for the Countess of Mervinslaw. Her mistress was a lady-inwaiting to the King and Queen when in Scotland: Balmoral for the summer holiday, functions at Holyrood House. These required that Mona stayed once a year in Edinburgh; otherwise, she and Iain had not spent a night apart in their clockwork and rigorous marriage. They were fifty and thirty-eight when they met Dennis Sykes, who, within weeks, had begun to divide the couple as never before.

Husband and wife both liked him; to each other they spoke of him enthusiastically. Iain Nicolson's resentful nature eased because Dennis was the same small height; Iain had also found a male talking companion for his 'six-o'clock dram'. Mona saw in Dennis, rare object, a man interested in clothes and furniture, in flowers, even, and society gossip. And he knew so many people, discussed names she had only read in magazines.

On his third week (Dennis never rushed things, no need) in their large, stone, dormer-windowed house, Dennis said to Mona (out of Iain's earshot), 'If you don't think it impertinent of me, that colour suits you.'

Mona looked down at her blouse, plucked it out a little to inspect. 'H'm? Some people say green's unlucky.'

'Works with your hair,' he said, 'that tinge there,' as he pointed vaguely to the brushed wings of grey.

Mona, after that pause in which the hesitator is lost, said, 'Iain never notices things.'

Dennis practised his look of surprise. 'Not even – you?'

Mona might have blushed, but took it in her stride. 'Maybe if we lived in the city?' she said. 'Iain's not a city man.'

'Full many a flower is born to blush unseen,' murmured Dennis.

He then allowed Mona to see him stare at her breasts. Next day, she dressed less austerely.

Dennis had learned well. He initiated with Mona conversations which dwelt on the senses. When he brought up the subject of touch, he said, 'Let me see your hands.'

Mona showed, and Dennis was careful to look, not touch.

He murmured, 'I have a doctor friend who believes that the hands [Dennis held out his own] can cure anything.' (He had no such friend, and apart from Binnie's Edmund, did not even know a doctor, had not met one since breathlessness at university.)

Whenever he thanked Mona – for food, or a fresh towel – he spoke quietly, so that the softness of his voice obliged her to draw a little closer. When alone with her in the house, indeed when addressing her, he looked first at Mona's mouth, and then straight into her eyes.

Above all, he made her laugh: 'I heard that Lady Milly Haig has a wooden leg and that she has her maid polish it with furniture wax.'

Mona changed a little, confusing Iain. She had her hair altered and Iain did not like the new hairstyle; he licked disapprovingly upwards at his moustache.

Dennis said brightly next evening, 'I met a man today, don't know his name, he was *very* complimentary about your wife when he heard where I was staying.'

Iain Nicolson blinked. 'Oh aye?'

That night, he snapped at Mona – in front of Dennis.

Next morning, Iain long since gone to work, Dennis said, 'None of my business, but is Iain, is he a bit, well –?'

She said, 'Moody? Yes, snappy. Wee men are a bit like that, aren't they?'

'Me too?' he asked with a grin. She shook her head; he saw that she did not find the subject amusing.

'Like Napoleon?' wondered Dennis. In the kitchen he sniffed the wind near her. 'What's that perfume? What's it called?'

For the following week, he paid Mona no attention, allowed himself to be utterly absorbed in his work, smiled vaguely at meals, deep in papers. In due course, he apologized for his preoccupations.

Mona came to breakfast one morning in – for her – a completely unprecedented white sweater.

96

Iain looked at the sweater, at her. 'Can you work in that?' She did not answer. Dennis's eyes licked the sweater – then he turned to Iain earnestly for 'advice' on the size of a local laird he was about to meet.

Iain drank twice as much as usual that evening, called Mona 'foolish' in a discussion about the war, and went brusquely to bed. Dennis raised a sympathetic eyebrow.

Within two more days, Dennis was touching Mona's elbow as he poured her evening drink, before 'sharing' some of his work questions with Iain. Two weeks afterwards, Dennis stayed in bed untypically late. Shortly after he heard Iain leave for work, Mona rapped gently at Dennis's door; 'Would you like a cup of tea?'

He made room for her to sit on the bed, and they talked. A week later, Iain went to Stirling for the day, leaving in the very early morning. Dennis again received tea.

On the day Dennis left Mervinslaw three weeks later, Iain took his leave of him and wished him well. At the front door an hour later, Dennis said to Mona, 'Do you, ah, do you ever – have occasion to be in – I mean, what I'm asking is, do you know Glasgow?'

She looked away and said, 'Ah'm, I have a friend there, whom I haven't seen for a while –'

Dennis asked, while also looking into the distance, 'What's – what's the best, I mean, the best way of, you know – of, well, getting in touch with you? Do you still answer the Countess's phone?'

'In the mornings, yes.'

He took both her hands, and with tenderness kissed her twice, just each side of her mouth. 'I will, as you know, be writing a note, but, I mean – to both of you.'

She nodded in understanding; he released her hands and walked to his car.

He telephoned: Mona failed to find Dennis at the rendezvous he gave. This was not surprising. On that promised evening, he had gone back to Mervinslaw, where, over a drink, he asked Iain Nicolson whether he could have seen Mona in Glasgow, no, he must be mistaken? Dennis had had his own studio photograph taken, and in the next breath he presented a copy to Iain, who put it on the sideboard with warmth.

Dennis contacted Mona at the Glasgow rendezvous, apologized most tenderly, blamed 'matters hush-hush', laid another false trail, kept her from home a second consecutive night, never met her. She came back flustered, and with badly-delivered excuses. Small Iain became a suspicious man, especially when Mona received a postcard from Glasgow with just a '!' on the back. It took the Nicolsons some time to repair their marriage.

7

The parish held pagan oddities. For generations, the Shea family owned a healing stone that never dried, dripped eternal moisture. Over in Corrbridge, a yellow light swooped across the sky when a Clinton died anywhere in the world. Bede Regan had a potion to cure ringworm in animals and children; he got it from his friend, Chief Burning Cloud, in Wyoming where they had worked on the railways. Look at that Carney woman. One fight with Peter Gleeson, and Peter Gleeson lost his whole herd of calves. Those animals died like flies the day after the Carney woman was seen running through them at dawn scattering ashes.

Oddly, this spirit of otherness, of superstition, preserved the two Stephenson mansions. In the years after the Civil War, many such great houses fell in flames all over the country. Pub talk, and old rebel songs, aroused clandestine arsonists who, on their way home at night, reduced much of the Ascendancy to embers.

Not in Deanstown. A respect, born of eerie wariness, prevailed towards that family up there on the ridge. In the Wallaces and the Stephensons something strange had always run. The hallway of the dower house (now Rhona Ulverton's) was once filled with long, striped masks, and drums, and spears with tufts. Someone had seen an angry little human head on a mantelpiece. There was a leg-bone lying in a glass case.

Even that farmland felt queer: two fairy forts; an old cemetery; and how come they had more mushrooms in their bottom field than the rest of the parish? Walk through the Ulvertons' woods to this day and you will see trees with two different growths sprouting like Siamese twins from the same bole. Nobody had sufficient lore of flora to understand that Rhona's ancestor, the great amateur botanist Captain Wallace, had merely grafted and budded in fits of spring fever. An oak still bloomed there last year with camellia-like flowers; and a lilac with the red tight buds of japonica.

Consequently, such a rite as excommunication fitted them. 'Look at that Mrs Ulverton,' clucked the village. 'Was she related to them other Protestants, the Maudes,' they wondered, 'where the devil stuck every deathbed to the wall?'

See her hooked-ish nose, the purple lipstick, her scarab ring? That devil's-head walking-stick contained poison in the prongs of the horns.

Rhona, unwittingly, contributed to this view of the family's bent towards quasi-sorcery.

'I can fly,' she told homegoing schoolchildren. They believed her. 'But I am not in the mood this minute, I'm not wearing the right-coloured clothes. Watch out, though, when I'm wearing vermilion.' She pulled a string of yellow chiffon from her open mouth, made a coin disappear completely and then found it in her shoe, blew cigarette smoke from her ears.

'In India,' she told them, 'I grew up watching the fakirs. Did you notice how I pronounced the word?' Only one grinned.

'Smart boy wanted, eh?' said Rhona to him sideways.

She resumed. 'Those fakirs – they knew how to climb a rope and disappear. Stop here tomorrow,' she instructed, 'and I'll show you.'

As they walked along the road towards her next day, she waved a pull-out set of six dangly postcards. Between the first and the final picture, the fakir climbed the rope and vanished.

'I can do that,' she said, pointing to the rope-trick, 'my nickname at school in India used to be "Magic", I was known as "Magic Wallace". But I need jodhpurs to climb a rope. Otherwise everybody would be, wouldn't they, looking up under my skirt and seeing my knickers.'

The children dissolved into giggles.

When Mrs Ulverton became friendly with Mrs Kane, Deanstown whistled in surprise. Until Mrs Hand recalled that well – didn't Mrs Kane always after all sprinkle the crops with Easter water on John's Eve, cause being she found egg-shells in the potato ridges one year, someone trying to steal the crop? And she had, after all, taken her comatose husband to a healer with stone amulets in north Cork. The stones failed. But a cure is like fork-lightning, they said – you never know if it will hit.

The excommunication predisposed Ellen towards the Ulvertons and Stephensons. In this, justice, kindness, humanity, diluted her usual religious loyalties. Her feelings intensified after a conversation which produced a surprise from Thomas.

On their return from the Grey Valley that evening, the girls scattered. Herbert and Leah, with Thomas sitting by, listened carefully to Ellen's account of the morning's terrible rite. Ellen quoted: 'It is God's wish that they become aware that she has been decreed by God as unfit for our society. That is also what "Excommunication" means.'

Herbert, considerably shocked, summarized. 'To be an outcast. Terrible.'

Thomas looked at him carefully.

'Think of it,' said Herbert slowly, fixing his skull-cap yet again. 'Think, Thomas. If you could not face that village tomorrow in case you loved someone. That girl might love that man she married. What does it matter so long as he's a decent human being? I mean to say, I mean to say. Look at what's happening to us. I mean to say, under Adolf Hitler.'

'Why give such a man his full name?' whispered Leah.

Thomas respected, and may even have feared, Herbert's calm wisdom.

Ellen asked, 'Should we do something?'

Herbert replied, 'Such an ordeal. Do you know them?'

Ellen shook her head. 'They don't mix at all. You know. Protestants. But – they're not from here, they're from India.'

'Ordeal?' echoed Thomas. 'That's an interesting way of looking at it.'

In bed, Ellen murmured, 'What could we do? About the Stephensons, I mean.'

Thomas surprised her. 'Well,' he said slowly, 'that elderly woman, Mrs Ulverton. Talk to her.'

Ellen swivelled her head. 'But – but I thought you didn't like her?'

'Herbert knows what he's talking about.'

'He does, doesn't he?' admired Ellen. 'He's not a bit vague.'

=

Ellen, characteristically, spoke up.

'Strange that we've never met. But we never see you or your family out anywhere?'

'No.' Rhona wore an old black riding-coat, and a long ivory skirt.

The women connected immediately. A week after that conversation with Herbert, Leah and Thomas, Ellen set out for the Ulverton house, heavily noticeable in her 'John McCormack' pregnancy.

In a shower of rain, she stood under a tree. Suddenly, like a figure from a dream, Munch Ulverton loped across the fields. He bowed while striding, and carried on past her. Ellen next heard the woman's voice calling 'Munch! Munchin!' and on the brow of the hill Rhona appeared, trying to shake life into a crazy umbrella. She came down the hill more spryly than Ellen would have imagined. Near the tree she stopped, and looked askance.

'My son.' She indicated the fleeing figure. 'He will catch cold. He's used to a hotter climate. I can't chase him, I'm sixty-three.'

'Step in here and shelter,' said Ellen, making way. 'You'll catch cold yourself.'

Rhona lowered the umbrella and walked so directly to Ellen, and with such hard intent, that for a split second Ellen feared the tall woman would strike her. Instead Rhona held out her hand in greeting.

'So – your manners are as sweet as your looks. That is the first word of kindness anyone has spoken to us in the last three months.'

'No?' said Ellen in disbelief, and then corrected herself, 'Oh, of course, the excommunication.'

Rhona looked down at her. 'The forbidden word? You dare use it?'

'It was all – unfair,' said Ellen. 'Uncharitable.'

'But aren't you Queen Catholic around here?' said Rhona.

'I'm not.' Ellen blushed. 'I only pretend to be, but you mustn't ever tell anybody. I have to be like that for the children's sake. I found the excommunication – I found it so unkind. Unkind. And indecent.'

'You're very open.'

'I amn't always.'

'Only my grandmother ever said "amn't". If you're going to be open with your secrets – well, you can completely trust me.'

'I guessed that,' said Ellen.

'Here's my secret. Or one of them. We have no money,' said Rhona, 'and we're often hungry, and now we have no credit. Since the "excomm." as we call it. That's why we never met, that's why we never see anyone. We have no means of returning hospitality. I used to entertain all the time in India. D'you imagine how I feel now? Here? Penniless? I was reared for entertaining, for being a hostess – it was what I was. Now I can't even sit by myself at my own table.'

'Why can't you?' The shower passed by. Lemon sunlight broke through.

'I've had nothing to eat for three days.'

Ellen said, 'What?! My God in Heaven!'

'I mean it. Last week too we didn't eat for three days.'

'Can't your daughter get a job? Or you?'

'No one hires Protestants like us. You know that. You look embarrassed, you shouldn't be. Everyone has secrets, even you have.'

Ellen took the big decision: she spoke her besetting concern. 'I know. I can't get my husband to be calmer.' Then she bit her lip, stuck it out as a preliminary to tears.

'It's all right, oh, it's all right.' Rhona laid a hand on the younger woman's arm. 'What am I to call you? I'm not going to call you Mrs Kane, are you Eleanor?'

'Ellen.'

'Perhaps your husband is a lonely man? Does anything work?'

Ellen swallowed the tears and replied, 'And I want to bring my children up, I mean, I want to rear them well. I want them innocent for as long as I can, I want them merry. And nice to people. Yes, innocent.'

'My grandmother,' said Rhona, 'believed that love and affection were better than a warm bath.'

'Now, today for example, my husband, he's in better humour because he got a gift in the post of something he's never had before, a box of cigars.'

'Oh! Oh!' Rhona exclaimed. 'Bless you, bless you! Oh!' She halted in recollection. 'Of course today is the eleventh of the eleventh, I knew something would go right when the numbers lined up.'

Ellen asked with a half-laugh, 'What is it, I mean, what's the –?'

'Will you meet me here next week?' asked Rhona, moving away.
'I will.'

'Same place, same time?'

'Yes.' Ellen still looked puzzled.

'Cigars! Cigars! Have you magic powers, or what?'

Ellen laughed. 'Lord, if only I had. Cigars, though?'

Rhona stalked off, still speaking. 'By the way – that brown coat doesn't suit you. And the next time we meet don't give the impression you're trying to please me, you don't have to, I like you.'

Ellen said, 'Now I don't know where to look.'

Rhona, from a few feet away, the grass wet at her feet, spun around and said, 'Do you really want something to think about?'

Ellen cocked her head to one side like a puzzled bird.

'Think about my son,' said Rhona, 'my dear beloved son, Munch. I think he's mad. I mean – insane. If he is, I shall be so hurt.'

Their five and a half years in Deanstown had brought the Ulvertons no influence. Nothing had happened in their lives. So much for Rhona's brave political words. Her greatest fear – that they would dwindle into friendlessness – had been coming true. The excommunication hastened it.

Lack of money controlled everything. Henry Wallace, tighter than wire, helped not at all. Instead, he and his wife hovered five miles away, watching, poised to buy any remaining heirloom: the famous silver humidor, say, or the Meissen tea-service. So far, Rhona defied her brother and avaricious sister-in-law, with some desperate scraping. A small batch of Tate & Lyle shares came via Trinidad, a remote great-aunt's bequest. Residual colonial pension payments on her long-dead husband arrived out of the blue as a result of a clerical error made in London.

Once or twice, in hunger, her stomach plunged almost down to danger point, to inanition. She awoke one morning dizzy, her hands not gripping. Natural foods were out of season; mushrooms and fruits long over. All credit in Mooreville had vanished; the shopkeepers there, ultimate insult, had even stopped asking for repayment once they knew of the intended excommunication.

Somehow, some desperate how, Rhona conjured food. She found a box of apples in hay; she stole a winter hoard of nuts from a tree. 'Bugger the squirrels,' she told Viva, 'our need is greater.'

Late that week, a straying heifer fell in an adjoining ditch and died; the farmer could not be bothered to recover it; Rhona bartered with the butcher – he could have a quarter of the beast in return for his work. Did she lure or chase the animal to its death? Nobody could prove anything – yet, on neighbouring farms they strengthened their fences.

As to cigars – she rushed up the terraced lawn calling to Viva.

'Dress! Pack! Quick!' That evening, Rhona sold her mother's Georgian hairbrushes to Henry and his wife. On pawn principles – to be redeemed or not, and she fought off their protests. By way of revenge, Munch was billeted on Henry for three days.

Rhona and Viva took the train from Goolds Cross. En route, she explained to Viva.

'Your grandfather had a remarkable taste in cigars. He had a box at Hound's. I had forgotten.'

Mr Lusk at Hound's fetched a ledger. The record had been maintained intact. When David Wallace died in 1910, Hound's had held exactly a hundred and eleven pounds' worth of cigars in his box.

'Good omen,' said Viva, who also liked these things. 'One, one, one – again.'

Mr Lusk had the jelly eyes of the inquisitive. He spread the papers on the glorious wood of the counter.

'Now, the position is this now. When the late Mr Wallace died without having given us instructions as to what should become of his cigars, we waited a decent interval and we sold them now. A decent interval. Are ye married yeerselves, girls?'

'You sold them?' boomed Rhona.

'If we kept them, Ma'am, they'd have gone like all humanity, dust to dust now. But hold on, hold on.' Mr Lusk had the patience of men in old purveying trades. 'We didn't know the first thing about what to do. We wrote to the widow, and we even sent a letter around by hand – d'you see?'

Mr Lusk pointed to brown-ink entries made in the ledger. 'But, out of grief or what now, we'll never know, the poor woman never replied.'

Rhona knew why: alcoholic haze.

'So the money sat here now, so it did, accumulating at the rate

105

of somewhere between a fluctuating three-quarters to one and a quarter per-cent-per-annum.'

'Where is the cigar money now and whose is it?' asked Rhona.

Mr Lusk beamed; a good-natured man, Mr Lusk, with a cyst on his forehead.

'Oh, 'tis here, Ma'am, and now – 'tisn't ours so 'tisn't. 'Twill be in the Ledger. We do it every half-year.' He hauled again at the huge marbled book and hummed a 'yah-de-dah-de-dah-de-dah' under his breath. 'We do always round up or down to the nearest pound. To this very day. And now you'd be surprised how it comes out even in the long run. We'd be half a guinea up on one year and the next year we'd be half a guinea down, now we do always say 'tis the same half-guinea.'

Rhona, tiring, said, 'I daresay it is. But – is there money? Now?'

'If you're the heir. The heiress, I suppose, although these days you can't be too careful.' He stubbed a big finger and read, 'Wallace, David Warrington Jasper, San Giovanni, Sandycove: accumulated to end of financial year, 1937, that is to say, April 4th; six hundred and eighty-six pounds.'

And from Mr Lusk, as to be expected, 'And you'll notice now – no shillings nor no pence.'

'The money doesn't work,' said Viva, 'at between three-quarters and one-and-a-quarter per cent interest, even if you compound it. On a hundred and eleven pounds it wouldn't be that much.' Today her hair looked like a schoolmarm's.

'Ah, Miss.' Another thing about Mr Lusk: he had letters after his name in finger-wagging. 'The cigars now – they were worth a hundred and eleven pounds the way the original gentleman, the original Mr Wallace, paid for them. But the year he died wasn't there some sort of a row in the international trade markets and you couldn't get Cuban cigars for all the tea in China, that's a joke we have here, Ma'am,' he explained to Rhona. 'And now a gentleman in the Vice-Regal Lodge, he said he'd pay what we asked that we thought fair, and he paid four hundred and forty pounds for the whole box. A good investment. So the interest is on that, not the hundred and eleven. D'you get me, like?'

'We get you. Like.' Rhona proved her identity, an ancient

passport, in her maiden name. Mr Lusk said, 'We'll draw up a cheque, Ma'am, and we'll send it round to the hotel. I s'pose you're in the Hibernian.'

On the street, Rhona said, 'I'm exhausted.'

Simultaneously, each said tenderly to the other, 'Don't cry.'

They clasped hands. 'The worst thing has been not being able to tell anyone,' said Viva.

'No, the worst thing has been not being able to feed my two dear children,' said Rhona. 'Now, I need to buy some powder, have you enough scent, dear Viva?'

Deep in some kind of gratitude, they stood quietly, self-effacingly, on the street for a moment, the two tallest women in Dublin that day.

Rhona came home to Deanstown, and clawed back the Georgian hairbrushes from her brother Henry: 'Never you mind where I got the money!'

She kept her appointment with Ellen. For an afternoon hour the women strolled back and forth in the same patch of field, near the same tree. Behind them, the dower house with its colonial portico smiled through the woods. Rhona told her cigar story; Ellen exclaimed. Then Rhona stooped to listen. Out in the open fields, with no apparent context, the two women absorbed each other. One, tall and aristocratic, and vividly dressed, carried a silver-topped cane; the other, small, bulged almost outlandishly in her pregnancy.

'How is your husband? Is he – well?'

Ellen said, 'The main problem is – I'm no more than a kind of a go-between.'

'Explain, my dear.'

None of the children asked Thomas directly for anything they needed. Few of them spoke openly or straight to him: none easily.

Cash for schoolbooks: 'Mama, tell Daddy I need –'

Pocket-money for an outing: 'Mama, the school is going to Dublin for the Spring Show, and we've to bring five shillings for the bus and the whole day –'

'Aha,' said Rhona. 'It's like the king who will listen to one courtier only – and only in private.'

'That's a good way of putting it,' agreed Ellen, 'but they all assume that the court chancellor, that's me, will get all their favours granted.'

'I don't like men when they won't be friendly,' said Rhona. 'Dear girl – you need a *modus vivendi*, you do.'

'A way of living?' Ellen the teacher could not stop herself translating. 'Do I?'

'You need a means of surviving your poor husband's lack of rationale. May I think? Look! I knew that goose was laying!' In the grass she found a small cache of big eggs and stowed them in her skirt pockets.

Ellen said, 'I am taking a terrible risk. He hates anyone talking about him, in any way whatsoever.'

Rhona pointed to herself dramatically. 'I have been called a marble mausoleum. My secrets die with me.'

'I live,' said Ellen, 'in the fear that something awful is about to happen.'

'Anxiety. My husband suffered from it. How many children have you? I've lost count, I mean how many beyond those two lovely girls?'

'Before you go,' said Ellen. She led Rhona to the hedgerow, where a napkin-wrapped parcel lay among the nettles like Moses in his basket. 'Three others, and this one invoiced': Ellen patted her stomach.

'What's this?' asked Rhona.

'I'm a lovely baker they tell me,' said Ellen, without immodesty. 'These two are my best. There's a meat pie and a gooseberry tart.'

'I will eat them with pleasure. Thank you.'

They had parted when Rhona called out, 'Don't forget one thing. You have a rare natural gift – of affection. It'll carry you through anything.'

Inventively, the two women found many means of seeing each other. Thomas was appeased by references to the excommunication: 'I suppose it's a good thing to show people we're not all savages.'

To Ellen the relationship became vital, because it repeated a pattern: it re-ran the Mrs Greege experience. In the doldrums of those awful early days and weeks after Thomas's shooting, the house plummeted into near-squalor. Hidden behind her locked gate, nobody witnessed Ellen's weeks of unwashed hair, the same clothes day after day, a baby infrequently bathed and changed.

Then, Herbert Winer visited intuitively. The tender provocativeness of his enquiries first led Ellen to recognize the frailty of her situation. He directed her to find resources within herself, rather than within piety.

Herbert spoke gently but at length. Herbert pointed out her isolation. Herbert urged her to seek help from a senior woman. Herbert ruled her mother out; May Morris's need for attention would have diverted the concentration from where it was needed.

Ellen wrote in her housekeeping ledger after Herbert's visit, 'I have the following choices as to what to do with my life and this predicament.' After deep thought, after contemplation that was at first plaintive and then energetic, she recognized that only one woman she knew in this place of strangers had the inner fire to help her.

When Ellen first came to Deanstown she lodged with Mrs Greege, who tried to regard her as a kitchenmaid, and insisted she scrub the floor; then she unapologetically opened all Ellen's letters and parcels. An unlikely saviouress this woman may have been; harsh and cutting the words she addressed to Ellen; antagonistic their joint history. But – she came when asked. Ellen now believed that Mrs Greege's intervention saved Thomas Kane's life, the bathing, the powerful nursing, the instinct. Likewise, now, Rhona Ulverton – only infinitely kinder, and in need herself. This time, Ellen had chosen an emotional rather than a practical ally.

For the 'John McCormack' baby, a boy, Rhona came to the nursing-home, with a small posy of the earliest possible snowdrops.

'I regret they're not celandines. They're supposed to grant a new baby the gift of keen sight.' She smiled. 'And I brought no dance music with me, we should all dance when a baby is born.'

Ellen asked in a discreet *sotto voce*, 'Did Essie, did she come to see you?'

Rhona nodded. 'Delicious, too. You were right, you are a great baker.' Rhona leaned forward. 'Ellen my dear, will you help me with something?'

'Of course, of course.'

'How can I keep my son out of the asylum?'

'Oh, the poor boy! Is he violent?'

109

'Oh, you *are* a good girl. Most people are afraid to ask. No, he's violent like a lamb is, or a mouse. But he is so difficult. People in the village. They want him put away. He frightens the animals. Apparently.'

'I'll think hard,' said Ellen. 'Of course I will.'

A month later, her own depression began. Through the glass partition between the classrooms, she saw her husband humiliate his own son in front of the entire room. As the boy stumbled over an answer and blushed, Thomas called him out, made him hold forth his hand and gave him four slaps of the ash stick. Ellen, hardly knowing what she did, dismissed her classes and left the school an hour early. Thomas watched, never intervened.

Later, at home, he asked, 'Did your clock go wrong or something?'

'No.'

'Did you know you let the children go home an hour early?'

'Yes.'

'Why?'

'No why.'

In her heavy tweed coat Ellen left the house and walked.

The black moods continued for two and a half months. Her depression worried them all, and scared Thomas. She had never been silent at mealtimes; now she could not even respond to a ripe story about a neighbour, or a report of some strange event in the farms. In brief respites, Ellen knew enough to wait, that a remedy would appear the way birds returned in the spring.

Rhona saw her that first week, said a knowing 'Aha!' and simply walked by her side, in silence.

During the next week, 'No, do not try and cheer up,' insisted Rhona. 'I won't have it. No, never mind about Munch. When you're ready. When you're ready. Not before.'

Finally, weeks later, Ellen told Rhona what triggered it.

'The child was humiliated. Humiliated.'

'You made an error,' Rhona observed. 'Of judgement. You should have said to him immediately, "Please don't do that to our son again." You should have said it up into his face.'

'Oh, you don't know my husband!'

110

'Try it!' said Rhona. But Ellen never raised the subject with Thomas.

Throughout 1938, Rhona's moral support gradually reduced Ellen's anguish at Thomas's parental harshness. Nor did she feel as fearfully isolated by his paranoid fear of neighbours' inquisitiveness. The knife's edge of his humours, along which she had so long teetered, had become a slightly softer, broader place to walk.

Rhona employed contrast in their discussions.

'I mean, your husband, he's not like Hitler, Ellen, is he?'

'No, Rhona, oh no.'

'So – in your own words, what is it you loathe?'

Ellen explained how she hated Thomas's failure to apply the same intelligence to his feelings as he did to his working life.

Rhona said, 'Easy. He is a man of parts. Some parts have spikes. Some have hurts. Some have warmth. Blunt the spikes. Put balm on the hurt – if you can find it. Heat yourself on the warmth.'

'Easier said than done,' said Ellen indignantly.

'When we have no choice,' said Rhona, 'we have to use our energy to put up with our lot. Not be passive, not lie and moan. Say, "Well, that's tough, he's like that." But don't let him get away with it.'

In return for such support and sympathy, Ellen virtually fed the Ulvertons. Essie belted to and fro with full and empty bowls and jars and great pans. Tact became paramount. For Rhona's latest conjuring trick – learning how to poach salmon at night – Ellen provided the accompanying vegetables. Or, saying, 'The children hate the taste,' she would share home-made butter from Thomas's sister-in-law in Bishopswood. Or ask for an opinion on a new soda-bread recipe, or potato cakes.

In September 1939, war broke out. Munch Ulverton lay in the roadside ditches and fired imaginary artillery at passing strangers.

'Poor Munch,' Rhona said to Ellen, 'and I love him so. My heart is broken. I loved his father, and I had so hoped that when Munch grew up I would have new conversations with an adult male. I love Viva too, but I can never bring myself to tell her so. I'm often horrible to her.'

'I'll tell her,' said Ellen.

111

'Would you? Please?' asked Rhona.

'Of course, I will.'

To Rhona's delight, Munch would do anything for Ellen. She called him from the ditches, wiped his briar-torn face as if he were Christ and she Veronica. To Rhona's greater delight, Ellen gave Viva tea one Sunday, and said, 'There is no shame in having mental illness in the family.'

'Lunacy, we call it lunacy,' said Viva, who picked skin from her hands all the time.

'Call it what you like,' said Ellen smartly, 'there's still no shame in it.'

'Mamma is useless.'

'Oh, no she's not,' said Ellen. 'And I've never met a mother who likes her daughter so much.'

Viva turned a bright red, but did not look displeased and for the first time managed enough tenderness to walk Munch home from the stream where he said there were U-boats in the water-cress.

By 1940, the Kane household's emotional structure was forever fixed. As Rhona summarized it, the home ran in three concentric circles of relationship. The outer circle comprised all the children, in their groups and cliques, revolving around each other. They posted watchmen for their father's irruption into their wary ring. The next, inner circle contained Ellen's relationship with the children – bouncy, loving, teasing, warm, strict. Finally, in the innermost circle, Ellen conducted her secret marriage to Thomas.

Years earlier, she gave up hope of ever seeing again in daylight the man who used to round the corner of the house, or walk in from the garden, with a smile. In bed, however, he still seemed to find his old love for her. Like a swimmer coming up from the deeps with a treasure in his hand, he would approach her with gentleness, then lie exhausted on her shore. Downstairs next morning, something would annoy him, and the knives of their lives would again be unsheathed.

Even if he never discussed his harshness to the children, he knew Ellen loathed it. He had ways in which he tried to circumvent, or apologize for, his cold, bullying attitudes. In May 1941, he discovered a source of liquorice ropes, her favourites; he brought home a dozen on the day of a library meeting. He bought lemons, too, if ever in stock either at Mooreville or Janesborough. If a war report seemed particularly important, or bizarre, he scissored the piece from the newspaper and folded it carefully to keep for her: they talked for an hour about Pearl Harbor.

About the house and school, though, his unrelentingness did not thaw, and no matter how she told herself that she could see a red heart beneath the pack ice, she never knew what mood each day would produce. On his bad days, the awful times of his supine silence long ago had a kind of echoing innocence.

All the circumstances of the society ensured that she could not leave him: no divorce, no separation, no laws of marriage other than union. Therefore she compensated, as did all women of that time and similar circumstance, by investing in her children. Apart from never shielding them from Thomas's excesses – certainly never sufficiently for Grace's demands – she found riches with them. She mothered them abundantly, never sentimentally. Although she would not discuss their father, she never otherwise played them false, and she behaved in general as an amused and amusing, loving parent. Just once, on a grievous occasion, she fought him on their behalf, but without their knowledge.

On Christmas Day 1941, Helena gave Thomas a green tie, and Grace gave Thomas a spotted handkerchief; both girls had saved birthday money; they had hand-painted the wrapping paper and woven the string from coloured raffia. He opened the packages carefully.

To Helena he said, 'I'd never wear a green tie, did you ever see me wearing a green tie?' – and handed it back to her. Grace watched apprehensively, as he then opened the wrapping around the blue handkerchief. He unfolded it, inspected it – and walked away.

This happened in the hallway; Grace and Helena looked at each other with horror. Typically, Helena's tears began.

Grace tightened her mouth: 'I'm going to talk to Mama about this.'

'About what?' asked Ellen, coming downstairs, baby in arms.

'About Daddy,' said Grace, in a voice just below a scream. 'Do you know what he's after doing. He's after throwing Helena's Christmas present to him back in her face.'

Ellen dealt with it too slowly, did not shush Grace in time.

'In our faces. He threw them back. He's a Bastard!'

'GRACE!' Ellen, hampered by the baby, moved forward, but too late.

Grace opened the kitchen door, and shouted, 'That's what you are, a bastard, a bastard, a bastard, a bloody bastard, a bastard.' She hurled the balled wrapping paper at him, and in her new dress ran from the house.

Thomas rose calmly, took his hat from the hallstand, put on his scarf, chose his second-best coat, collected his walking-stick and set off.

In the fields, Grace sometimes glanced over her shoulder. Thomas, in no hurry, strode three hundred yards behind her, swishing at the grass, a man out for a walk. She ran and ran. Both eventually disappeared from view, over the slopes.

Almost two hours later, the white dot of Grace reappeared in the distance. He had caught her just before she made it to the safety of the Grey Valley, and Thomas now walked directly behind her, policing. Every few yards he reached out and stung her legs with the tip of his stick, or flicked it sarcastically to her buttocks through the thin white party dress. From her bedroom Ellen watched alone.

When they neared the house, the children heard Grace's squeals. Ellen stood at the hall door, the kitchen closed behind her. Grace rushed to her, but Ellen fended her off and said, 'Go upstairs, Grace, and begin to wash.'

Ellen quickly steered Thomas into the empty parlour and closed the door. Nobody heard what transpired between them. Helena applied mercurochrome to the series of stinging cuts on the backs of Grace's legs.

Behind the parlour door, Ellen swallowed hard and said quietly, 'I felt every blow you gave Grace. Don't move, Thomas, don't move,' as he made to leave the room. 'Sit still. Say nothing, nothing. Just think on what I said.'

'You did brilliantly well,' said Rhona. 'And you say he blushed? Yes, yes! Embarrassment is a wonderful weapon. How was he afterwards?'

'Odd,' said Ellen; 'he was very affectionate.'

Until the schools opened on the seventh of January, all those Kane children remained quieter than usual in a house into which a stronger chill had drifted.

They said that Miriam Hogan had a miscarriage in March 1942, but few women in Deanstown believed it.

'Must be another immaculate conception,' they cackled.

Over four to five months Miriam did appear to change shape, and she moved from customary peakiness to apparent bloom. Nobody asked about her 'condition'. Aged twenty when Jack married her, and now even wealthier since Mrs Gardiner died, Miriam was forty in 1942, a year older than Ellen.

Rhona Ulverton saw through the 'pregnancy', and caused the 'miscarriage'. Too alike, the two women never became friendly. The Ulvertons, uncomfortable in their poverty, hated the way Miriam dropped in. Ellen Kane had become accustomed over the years to Miriam's disconcerting way of appearing: in a doorway, over a wall, popping up from behind a hedge. Thomas, in a rare moment of light-heartedness, said, 'She'd have made a marvellous guerrilla.'

On St Patrick's Day, as Miriam walked along the Stephensons' and Ulvertons' shared avenue, Rhona appeared in a heavy coat and a man's hat. Miriam, again true to form, wore no coat, only what appeared to be a light summer dress, making her bulge unmistakable.

'Oh – oh, my dear girl,' said Rhona and she claimed later she said it artlessly, with no malice aforethought. 'I was going to say come up to the house and I'll lend you a coat on this bitter day, but with all that padding around your stomach you won't need it.'

Miriam fled. Someone saw her climbing into the doctor's little green car, 'thin as a rake as usual'. She did not return for two months.

Rhona said defensively to Ellen, 'She's a silly little bitch anyway.'

In April, Helena began to menstruate. Grace followed immediately: two years apart in age, two weeks in maturity. Thereafter, as some euphemism would forever be required, they would call it 'the aeroplane'.

On the last Saturday morning of the month, the house was filled with a harsh and huge noise. Ellen later paraphrased when telling the story, 'You know, like in the Bible, "And there came a noise as of a mighty rushing wind," only it wasn't the Holy Ghost.'

All rushed to doors and windows, excited and shouting. Low over the roof of the house, against the sunlight, the wide black shadow dipped and waggled. It rose again, struggled up above the trees and limped through the air towards the Castle.

Thomas gathered a notebook and pencil. All followed him. Up ahead, through the old gate, they could see the tip of the tailplane, a black and grey upward fin.

At the top of the slope a figure appeared in the gateway, his hands to his face. Thomas turned to his own oncoming family and shouted, 'Stop! Wait here!' But the stranger held both hands in the air like a supplicant facing a gunman. His face streamed with blood. As they watched, the young man took off his flying helmet, laid it on the ground, then spread his arms wide and dropped – a kneeling cruciform.

Thomas called to Ellen, 'A German! A German plane.'

All drew level with the kneeling airman.

Ellen said, 'He's cut. Is he badly hurt, do you think?' She stepped forward a pace. Her bosom rose with the exertion of the rapid walk. 'Are you hurt?'

The man looked at her and said, with a nervous smile, *'Ich spreche kein Englisch.'*

'I beg your pardon?' asked Ellen, her smile for strangers in place.

'Ich spreche kein Englisch. Ich bin Deutscher.'

Said Thomas, 'Maybe he doesn't understand you. Try something else.'

Ellen raised her voice to more or less a shout and asked him, pointing to his wound. 'Is that cut deep?'

'Blood. Red.' The German boy looked confused – then with his sleeve began to wipe his own bowed forehead.

'Awhhh, goodness me,' said Ellen. She stepped over and shook the aviator's hand, then helped him to his feet. He staggered.

Thomas looked on, did not offer to help.

'Girls!' commanded Ellen. Helena and Grace walked over, and Ellen handed Helena her handkerchief. 'Wipe his face. Over there.'

116

Helena, so tall for her age, only had to reach up a little. Gently, gently she dabbed the cut on the German's forehead. Grace, responding to another instruction from her mother, began to undo the leather cuff buttons where blood also appeared. The boy made himself completely available to them, and stood still. Thomas began to write in his notebook – the day and date, the time, the description of the young flying officer, the number of persons present.

With a shout – 'Master Kane, are all you safe?' – men arrived; one brandished a four-pronged fork in hand; all had been working in the fields.

Thomas spoke. 'It seems to be a German war aeroplane that has got into difficulties, and the pilot seems to have hurt himself, I'm just taking a record of the details for the authorities.'

Four-pronged-Fork strode forward and began to threaten the airman's face.

'Have you bombs with you, have you?'

The boy recoiled and Ellen, placing herself between the flier and the farmer, turned and snapped.

'What do you think you're doing?'

'Ma'am, but he's a German!'

'Do you not know your politics? This country is innocent in this war. Ireland is *neutral*!'

They took the young pilot home, down through the fields. The farmers, under Thomas's direction, stayed to 'guard the aeroplane'. Michael Ryan went to fetch a rope so that they could tie it to the old gate 'in case your man escaped and took off again.'

At the house, they sat him at the kitchen table. With slow, unthreatening movements, they eased off his flying jacket and the heavy vest-shirt underneath, until he sat naked to the waist.

Ellen sent for Doctor Hogan: 'In case there are any broken bones or that.'

Grace took up a vantage point at the table, and watched as Helena sponged the boy's blond forehead. Ellen checked his shoulders, back and chest for bruises. Essie stood by, refilling the basin where blood ran like a thin red oil, drifting in the water. Grace placed a dreamy hand under her own watching chin.

Thomas arrived with the Sergeant, who peered at the stranger

117

through the bay-window, then entered the kitchen cautiously. The boy stood, clicked his heels and saluted: *'Heil Hitler!'* – to which the Sergeant said, 'Hallo yourself.' The boy sat again, and Ellen began to help him dress. The inevitable news arrived that Doctor Hogan could not be found: 'We'd never want to have the plague come,' said Ellen.

'The military'll be here shortly, Ma'am,' said the Sergeant. 'We sent a wire to Southern Command in Clonmel, that's what Procedures says we're to do in the event.'

'There'll be no Procedures until he gets something to eat,' she replied. She and Essie fed the boy, now dressed in a shirt of Thomas's. Bacon and eggs, sausages and black pudding, tea and soda bread with her own apple jelly: all watched him eat. When he had finished, he stood, bowed and burst into tears.

The Sergeant turned to Thomas and said, 'He's not what you'd call much of a soldier. Hitler'll never beat Churchill at this rate of going. If all he has in his army is crybabies.'

'Sergeant!' rapped Ellen, and he subsided with an embarrassed shrug.

They bade the airman good-bye when the lorry arrived. Sixteen soldiers disembarked with guns; they lined the gravel from gate to house. Some, such excitement, crouched under the evergreens. The young man first bowed very formally and deeply to Ellen.

She shook his hand and said loudly at him, 'Now, I hope you're going to be all RIGHT! And that you get back eventually to your mother and your family in GERMANY! These people won't harm you, we're very friendly in THIS COUNTRY!'

He clicked his heels again, bent over her hand, but did not kiss it. Then he shook hands with Thomas, who had to put aside his notebook and pencil in a hurry. The flier saluted the Sergeant, and when he came to Helena, took her hand and kissed it carefully, and said, *'Danke. Danke.'*

Then he twisted a button from its metal clip on his jacket and handed it to her, clicked his heels and bowed.

'What did it mean, what he said? "Donk", or "dunk", what was it?' hissed Grace to Helena in bed that night. 'I think it meant "beautiful". I think it's the German for "beautiful". It is, it is, I bet you. He said you were beautiful.'

=

118

Next morning, even through the rain, Grace at the window could see the tail fin and part of the fuselage peeping over the distant side of the castle wall.

'Helena, if the rain stops, we'll go up and look all over it. Because the soldiers are coming with a tractor the next few days to take it, the Sergeant told Daddy. Oh, Helena, what's up, why're you crying. Oh, lookit, you're all bloody, you cut your bottom or something!'

Helena said, 'Get Mama, quick, but don't tell anyone.'

Grace returned minutes later. 'I whispered. She looked real hard at me and said she'll be up in a minute.'

Ellen arrived.

'What is it?' Ellen had a small parcel under her arm.

'I don't know. I think I'm sick. Look.' She pulled back the bedclothes. 'Will it wash out?'

At secondary school in Mooreville convent, the Kane girls were known not to mix well. Each time they mentioned any other girl's name at home, Thomas made a disparaging remark about the family. Thus, the Kane daughters made no friends, and on the cycling journey to and fro, sought only each other's company. Consequently, they were denied the usual, colloquial channel of puberty information.

Ellen unwrapped the parcel. 'I've been expecting this.'

'I have a pain.'

'Where?' asked Grace.

'Will Daddy be angry?' queried Helena.

'No, love, he won't know.'

'But he will be cross,' she insisted. 'He'll see the sheets?'

'I'll hide them,' said Grace.

'Shush,' said Ellen, 'and Gracey, you'd better listen too.'

Ellen spread open the contents of the parcel and covering the bloodstained sheets for the moment, sat on the edge of the bed. She began.

'Now. God gave women the blessed right to have children and to bring them up in His image and likeness. It is a great honour.' Ellen had been rehearsing this since the day Helena was born. 'This is how it happens. In foreign countries, because of the heat – or the cold – they all have to marry very much younger than we do. So they marry when they have a lot of energy. At sixteen or so.'

119

Grace chimed in, 'That's you, Hellie, that's you.'

'Quiet, Gracey,' said Ellen. 'Now. In order to have babies, women have to carry around food in their tummies. A little of what you eat every day is stored up in a tiny room inside you and that's called your womb.'

Grace, tossing her long hair, said, 'And blessed is the fruit of thy womb, Jesus.'

'Exactly. Now. Because you couldn't go on storing up food for-ever God cleans it out every month. Every twenty-eight days – and it comes out as blood.'

'Out of everyone?' asked Grace. Helena said nothing; she stared at her mother's face and listened.

'Everyone.'

'Even Essie?' asked Grace, and Ellen, with secret knowledge of Essie ('I'm flooded again, Ma'am'), smiled.

'Indeed even Essie.'

'And Mrs Doctor Hogan?'

'And Mrs Doctor Hogan.'

'Forever and ever?' pressed Grace who had never heard any-thing so interesting.

'No, Gracey. First it stops when you're having a baby. And the second time it stops and forever is when God knows a lady is too old to have babies any more that it wouldn't be good for her or the baby. At about fifty or so, although John the Baptist's mother, Saint Elizabeth, she was over sixty when he was born but that was a special message from God. So what this means, Helena,' and Ellen smiled at her oldest child, 'is that God has now told you, He's sent you a special message, that you're going to be able to have babies when you marry.'

'But,' asked Grace, 'how does getting married affect it? Can she have babies or can't she?'

'She can and she can't,' said Ellen, funking it. 'God doesn't *mean* her to have babies until she's married.'

'But how does it work? If she knows now she could have a baby, then she could have one, couldn't she?'

'Only if she's married, Grace.'

When Ellen dropped the 'y' from her usual affectionate 'Gracey', her second daughter knew to steer clear.

Ellen said, 'Pay attention the two of you. There are rules about

120

this. First of all, you're never, ever to tell anyone, especially not a boy or a man. It is none of their business. You can tell each other, or you can tell me, or if you're not feeling well in school, you can tell a teacher. Preferably not one of the nuns. One of the lay teachers. Because sometimes, like you have now, Helena, you get a pain with it.'

Grace butted in, 'Funny message from God, so.'

'God's ways aren't our ways, amn't I always telling you that? Now, when it comes, this monthly message from God –'

Grace butted in again. 'Is that what we're to call it?'

'No. You're to call it something that will hide it. Your Auntie Rina calls it her cousin, she says, "My cousin is after getting off the bus." Or Leah says, "Her nuisance of a relative." I only say, "My friend has arrived," because it's a message from God, therefore it must be my friend.'

'I know,' said Grace bouncing on the bed. 'We'll call it the aeroplane,' and in spite of herself Ellen laughed. Helena joined in.

'This little belt goes around your waist, love,' said Ellen to Helena, 'and these loops, look. And these are like little face-towels, or flannels. I got you the very best towelling.'

Two weeks later, Grace cycled home from school, for once not racing Helena. As she freewheeled into the back yard and Ellen greeted her, Grace sang, 'God's been in touch. I'll need one of your parcels.'

Her mother laughed.

Where Helena had stayed in bed for a day and a half, Grace pranced – and organized a picnic for both girls next morning to the Grey Valley. Ellen encouraged such excursions, protected the girls' privacy, their right to such times. The Grey Valley was their counterpoise to the Castle, where their father roamed incessantly. He never came to the valley, was disliked there. The girls, consequently, looked forward to their rambles with leaping hearts, and always returned refreshed, peaceful, animated. Grace said the valley had warmth even when everywhere else was cold.

By half-past ten on sunny Saturday mornings, their chores finished, the girls climbed on their bicycles, sandwiches packed; they purchased lemonade in Silverbridge en route. In the valley, they climbed the stone sides, scrabbling and halting and looking. They discovered beetles, and the trails of foxes, the sett of a badger which they treated as reverently as a shrine. Hidden in clearings among the deep grasses and heavy-hung groves, they lay and turned their faces to the sun.

Helena liked the high white cliffs of limestone at the far end. Grace loved the nestled houses, and ran her hands over the large settles that sat outside fixed to walls, where people sat in the evening and chatted, the men smoking, the women darning.

Occasionally, Ellen joined her daughters, and the three enjoyed days of which they talked again and again. Helena found a pointed stone – Ellen said that it must be a flint arrowhead. And she sat peacefully beside Grace for two hours and more, and watched her draw. On rare afternoons, she even lowered the shoulders of her own blouse and lay with the girls to catch the sun on her shoulders. Helena gathered the alpine gentians and the moss and the powerful little orchids that botanists said grew nowhere else in the country: Grace drew them in pencil, then coloured them at home.

Always when leaving, they stood on the eastern rim and looked back, watching the chimney smoke climb the evening sky, waiting until, at the far end, a light or two appeared in the windows. As dusk fell, the valley disappeared into a velvet pocket.

In these pursuits, and in other small, careful ways, the Kane girls grew, in a centrifuge of innocence, in a naïvety controlled and imposed by their mother. No boyfriends: Ellen's prayers for purity had the force of Thomas's insistence on discipline. They moved up the grades of secondary school unsullied. In their late teens, Ellen, still in control of their lives, dressed them staidly, in shoes and socks, coats and suits: a lace collar seemed risqué.

Their father joined in this eternal purification. He excised from newspapers and magazines any articles with even the faintest carnal tinge. Once, from the *Reader's Digest*, Thomas cut 'How to Have Fun in Bed' by Cornelia Otis Skinner, but forgot to erase the title from the Contents page. Grace showed it to Helena on a week-end home from college, and they puzzled upon everything from pillow-fights to breakfast.

Ellen, taking a cue from Thomas, removed all magazine advertisements showing underwear or foundation garments. She sacked a dressmaker for describing too graphically with her hands how

'Empire Line' meant a fall of cloth from directly beneath the bust.

Grace, more than Helena, sensed the naturally erotic denied them by their parental conservatism. When she challenged once or twice – she had heard of a shop in Cork where you could buy a black under-bodice – all Ellen had to say was, 'Ask yourself what Our Lady would do. Could you see her wearing foundation garments the colour of sin?'

Grace muttered, 'They didn't wear those kind of clothes in Galilee, it was too hot, and anyway she's always wearing white or blue. And black would show through that.'

Ellen would have no argument.

Academically, the children set a local record – no other family in the history of the parish had ever received second- and third-level education. Helena gained first-class honours as a Domestic Economy teacher; Grace came first in Teacher Training in Janesborough, Ellen's old college.

As the girls became women, containment of their father proved a little more possible. In one good example, Ellen persuaded him to light the candles at Helena's twenty-first birthday party.

'I never had birthday parties,' snapped Thomas.

'I did,' retorted Ellen, but with a smile: one of Rhona's ploys. She further manipulated him into good grace by inviting people in front of whom he could not misbehave – her own parents, plus Leah and Herbert, and a selection of neighbours she knew he found impressive. Not the Ulvertons: Ellen always kept Rhona for herself.

People who left the party together spoke of the two oldest Kane children: 'Beauties – and as tied as twins.'

Helena had Thomas's build, tall and rangy, and her aunt Rina's blonde hair. Grace looked so like her mother, small, voluptuous, that she teased people with photographs of Ellen taken nearly thirty years ago.

8

Dennis Sykes returned to London in late 1945, and received official plaudits at a secret dinner for three hundred people, whom Churchill praised as 'the unseen'. On his thirty-first birthday, the firm made DS a partner, and he throve in the myriad post-Blitz rebuilding contracts. Binnie and he struck up again, though never as powerfully – more friendly than raw. She had had, as she said, 'a good war'. An elderly American munitions industrialist found her warm streak, and rewarded it with money that did not run out for several years.

In London, Dennis found a new breed – the officer widows. At one stage, he ran seven concurrent relationships. By 1948, even his voracious palate had tired, and in his longest 'fallow period' – almost twelve months – he never even 'hunted'.

In 1949 Dennis landed in Dublin, Managing Partner of the firm's new Overseas Division. With recruitment among local engineers and graduates, he set up a forceful office.

This prowling urban animal noticed an outstanding fact: when you got close, everybody in Dublin seemed so *rural*. Finding them easy to approach, he began to ask people at work, or the barber, the waiter: 'Where are you from?'

Very few said, 'Dublin.'

All had either come direct from the country, or descended from people who had. He soon heard the joke, 'A Dubliner is somebody who doesn't go home for the holidays.'

From the evening newspapers, Dennis noticed that it all stratified consciously. County Associations sponsored weekly dances: the Mayo Men's Association, the Kerry Men's, the Galway Men's. Dressed to the nines, he went to one of these dances one night, the Monaghan Men's Association in the National Ballroom. The night failed him. They seemed so raw and ill-paid, and he had overdressed. Nor could he understand what they were saying in their thick, involved country accents; and they danced like brown bears.

At breakfast next morning, he told his landlady where he had been, and how different he found it.

'They're all very innocent,' she said, eyeing him carefully. 'Very innocent,' she repeated. 'This is a very innocent country.'

A land of virgins: his appetite roared into heat. Dennis Sykes cased the city, like a robber seeking plunder. He checked restaurants carefully: impressive but not flashy. Three of the cinemas had dining-rooms, the Carlton, the Metropole and the Capitol, white tablecloths, white linen napkins; the waitresses wore white starched caps. Girls whose banter, he observed, contained no sexual knowingness: he could ask them the most double-meaning questions, and receive innocent replies. Women never dined alone: only with aunts, or husbands, or in families. Therefore, he drank soft drinks in lounge bars, where he got two jousts. Both ended in disaster.

'You dirty thing,' said one.

'I'd only let a husband do that,' said the other.

Research, Dennis, research. He drank on – and listened.

'Mothers and priests. That's how Irishwomen grow up. Mothers and priests. They know nothing about men.'

'Nationwide?'

'A nation once again,' said a bank clerk. 'Virginity is a national institution. I had a girl once and she used to arrange, if we were going to the pictures or that, that we'd meet on the steps of the church. And go in to say a prayer for purity.' The bank clerk laughed. 'I think she had a contract to supply purity to the south of Ireland.'

Such a challenge.

Dennis laughed. 'The mothers I can understand,' he asked. 'But the priests?'

'Hah, you never heard a fire-and-brimstone merchant. That's another great national resource, fire and brimstone. Listen. There was a scheme on here not long ago. Now, you know they wear pins in their lapels to show if they don't drink. Pioneer pins, they're called, it has the Sacred Heart on it. They have a pin too that you wear if you speak Irish, you'll see it, a little silver ring. Or if you're

125

an expert, a native speaker, a gold one. And a while ago, someone came up with the idea of a chastity pin. They did,' he insisted to Dennis's incredulous face. 'Oh, aye. A genius called Father Goode. "The Goode with the Bad" they call him; he's always giving out to women about their morals.'

Dennis realized that 'morals' meant what he had in mind.

He heard Father Goode late one Sunday morning.

'Don't tell me you might be interested in taking instruction?' asked the landlady in delight.

Dennis smiled noncommittally.

Father Goode, astride the pulpit like a horseman of the Apocalypse, attacked courtship. One by one he listed its evils:

Touching: – 'It will lead,' he cried, 'to inflammation.' Dennis did not quite know what he meant.

Kissing: – 'Two mouths sliming together like slugs, God alone knows what they were eating or drinking beforehand.'

Immodesty: – 'Women wearing tight clothes, they stick out in them, my dear brethren.' Delivered with, Dennis observed, a flair for alliteration: 'Lewd. Libidinous. Licentious.' Whether the predominantly female congregation understood the language, it listened tensely.

Dennis made notes when he came home. A catechism, purchased at the church door (and left lying around in his room sufficiently 'hidden' for the landlady to find), showed him that the Catholic Ten Commandments differed slightly in sequence from the ones he had learned at Sunday school in Alnwick. Next evening, a large, playful smile on his face, Dennis wrote his own Ten Commandments.

Thereafter he took his time, bought a small sweet house in Heytesbury Street, moved in the renovators. When his appetite temporarily outgrew masturbation, he visited Binnie in London.

Renewed after Binnie's body, and invigorated by her comments – 'A land of opportunity, Dennzy darling' – he returned and dived back into his researches.

He saw her eventually. Age – forty-one or so: height – 5' 3"; large-faced, quiet-eyed, buxom – in the Oriental Café, South Great Georges Street, early on a Saturday afternoon, among the coffee things, the spoons, the napkins, the saucers. He followed her that afternoon – on the 16 bus to a pretty little house in Terenure: no other residents. Then, he tracked her for weeks.

To the laundry in Camden Street where she worked.

To Mass on Sunday, where she sang in the Pro-Cathedral choir.

To the cinema, almost every Sunday night, one in three with a girlfriend.

She walked in Bushy Park. Alone. No man in evidence. A lot of time spent alone, he noted. For tracking purposes, Dennis had an assortment of hats, caps and coats.

Two week-ends away in three months: from the quays she took the bus marked 'Roscommon'.

Above all, she sat with her shopping bags in the Oriental Café for an hour from two o'clock every Saturday afternoon of her life: a beaker of coffee, a large currant scone with butter and a soft slam of raspberry jam, the *Evening Mail*, and then the eager first pages of a library novel.

Where to strike? How?

Dead easy in the event: he knew her table, sat at the next one. She arrived, struggled with a tray: he helped, then, after her pleasant thanks, lapsed into his book, the title held so that she could see it: *Dubliners* by James Joyce, what else?

Next week, when she smiled and said, 'Hallo again', he allowed his face to recall her.

'Ah. Yes. Hallo.'

'You're a slow reader,' she smiled.

Again, a moment to recollect; then a compliment, 'Oh, how observant of you.' Then a dash of homely naïvety. He looked at the book jacket and said, 'Relish, really. I'm reluctant to finish it.'

'Oh, isn't it lovely,' said she, 'when a book does that to you?'

'Yes. Yes.' Dennis pleasantly returned to his reading.

Week Three, he helped with her tray again.

'You're housetrained,' she said. 'You're not Irish?'

He smiled with his brown eyes. 'How did you know?'

Rose laughed. 'A woman could be hiking coalbags and an Irishman wouldn't help her.'

'I'm half-Irish,' he said. 'Irish mother.'

Said she merrily, 'I knew there was something good about you. And the other half?'

127

'Father? Oh, dead, a long time ago, killed in the First World War.'

Next week he didn't show. Tactics.

The following week, she said, 'Oh, there you are.'

'Hallo. Nice to see you again,' said he.

'Were you away?' said she.

'Yes. My mother's very elderly. Well – I mean, she's been hanging on by a thread for years. I go to see her as often as I can.'

'Where is she?'

'Scotland. Just outside Glasgow, place called Helensburgh.'

'That's a nice name of a place,' said she, drawing her crumbs to the centre of her plate.

'Yes, the man who built the town named it after his wife.'

She lit her cigarette, then thought of offering him the packet; he waved a refusal with the second and third fingers.

'You're not married yourself?'

'No.' He shook his wavy head.

She laughed her little silver laugh. 'Man your age, should be ashamed of yourself, you're like the Irish fellas.' Not quite a coarse voice, a little deep, but there had been some local attempt at refinement.

He smiled his famous rueful smile. 'Yes, you're right.' She was perfect meat, perfect, just the right degree of forwardness. 'But. Well.'

'Now, no excuses.' She genuinely had no guile.

'No, no excuses.'

First: I am the Lord thy God. She must be rendered completely devoted.

Her name was Rose Glacken. Today, not her usual shopping clothes: Rose wore a bottle-green twin-set, plus those nice beads Nuala gave her a few Christmases ago. And a good skirt, that small herringbone pattern, a Gor-Ray, she bought it in Kelletts. Nylons were a bit more plentiful now thanks to somebody out in Loughlinstown who had imported a huge amount from America. Her brown court shoes, newly soled and heeled: she collected them the day before yesterday from that little cobbler in Harold's Cross: a bit of a detour getting on and off buses, but worth it.

They talked of other things. Of the war: yes, Dublin had had bombs, more of an accident really. Over on the North Strand. No, he was in what they called a Reserved Occupation, lucky, yet he felt bad about it.

Of his house. 'Heytesbury Street.'

'Oh, very nice,' said Rose.

Rose asked him, 'But what do you do with your time? I mean when you're not working? You read, what else do you do?'

'I think,' he said. 'I think.'

'It has to be said,' agreed her friend, Eily, 'a man who thinks in this day and age is a rare article.'

Thereafter, Dennis Sykes systematically ruined Rose Glacken and her ordered life. As surely and intuitively as if divining for water, he found her lethal streak of duty. All the women he had enslaved and then walked away from, had that pressure point in common – responsibility: conscientiousness, some passivity. Better if they were tarnished with a little greed: his evident financial well-to-do-ness hurried them if they proved slow.

Second: Thou shalt not take the name of the Lord Thy God in Vain. As a tactic, all previous boyfriends must call from me expressions of the vilest jealousy.

'And if I can ask you the same question,' he said the following Saturday. 'Why aren't you married?'

She smiled: 'Past history' – and he allowed her to see his brow darken just a smidgen.

'I had a friend who broke off his engagement,' Dennis said later, 'because his fiancée couldn't stop talking about her past boy-friends.'

Binnie taught, 'Always discuss relationships. They are meat and drink to women, little Dennis. Viandes et Vin.'

'Oh, I can well understand that,' said Rose. 'I have a friend who's as jealous as anything of her fellow's girl that he had before her. In my case, there was only a couple of times we went out. It came to nothing, he wasn't going to get the farm until he was pushing sixty, 'cause his father was as healthy as a fish, he's still alive, and his mother wasn't going to let another woman in.'

'Was he good-looking?' asked Dennis quietly.

'He had curly hair,' Rose said. Dennis smoothed his own locks.

One more week should do it, Dennis believed. Correct.

Seven days later, she said to him, 'If you're not doing anything Sunday, a few friends of mine are dropping in.'

Against Dennis's rules. In his secret life, he would not be 'vetted' by friends. Absolutely not.

'Oh, no! Oh, no! I can't.' He sucked a piece of regret. 'How very civil of you. But I have to go and see this ancient creature out in, I think it's called Palmerstown, an old friend of my mother. And I don't know what time I'll get back.'

A lie, a complete lie: he was golfing: 'But will you ask me again?'

'Oh, I will, of course?' Rose fell down, down. 'What about the following Sunday?'

'Yes, please. Thank you. You'd better give me the address now.'

He wrote down the address carefully in his beautiful leather notebook, checked it meticulously with her and said, 'I'll be there.'

Last sip of Grand Oriental coffee. Quick tentative question: 'Do you ever hear from that old boyfriend now?'

Hasty reassurance. 'Not for years.'

Third: Remember that thou keep holy the Sabbath day. In a pious society, women are likeliest to be most bored and therefore most susceptible on Sundays.

He stepped like a dancer up her little Terenure pathway, with its diagonal red and yellow tiles. A fire in the grate; and the table set for tea for two in the neat parlour; Rose looked both rounded and suitably pointed – she'd bought a new bra the previous afternoon in Arnotts. Today Rose was wearing a pink Kayser slip and matching knickers: that stiff roll-on still pinched, one of the suspenders dragged to the side.

Rose Glacken, like so many women of her age, took love where she found it: nieces, nephews, ageing relatives, firm friends. She would, say, have willingly nursed aged parents; would have sacrificed all aspects of her life to take, say, her sister and her sister's husband through lifelong illness, had such occurred. No effort of nurture could be too great. To pass the long time, Rose, stable, rarely took a drink, unlike Nuala. Nor did she yet rely on prayer, although she had long ago begun the spinster's pattern of repeated socializing with the same friends. Of such fine heart, she told

herself that she could love a man, a good man, truly love him –
even in the way he wanted to be loved.

Sundays, though, were tough days, down days. Passable in summer: walks, cycles to the mountains, bus trips to the shore. Dreadful in winter, although Rose luckily had the element of a real, coal
fire in her grate; Nuala could only afford electric or gas heaters,
those narrow blue flickering bars of thin comfort.

Oh, to have a man to talk to on a Sunday: that came straight from
daydreams. A well-mannered man, too. Who brought an armful of
the Sunday papers in case she had not seen them. Who wiped his
feet on the mat. Who admired the colour scheme immediately.
Immediately.

Who – and he not even a Catholic – was able to discuss Father
Goode's sermons. And once Dennis uncovered that Rose went to
hear Father Goode frequently, he knew, if any doubt lingered,
that he had found marvellous quarry.

'He's very powerful, isn't he? I mean, he's a very powerful
speaker.'

Rose, in her parlour, agreed.

'When has he been at his most powerful?' asked Dennis.

'I heard him one Easter,' she said, 'the Easter before last, and
he tore into women about the way we dress in front of men going
to dances and that we can expect men to want to – to want to not
respect us.'

'Is he very specific when he's like that?'

Rose said, 'Yes, and he's a fright to go to Confession to, he
asks very direct questions.' Dennis allowed her to fall silent and
muse.

'Darling, don't give me that guff about the heat of the fire,'
hooted Binnie.

Because Rose's nipples had risen under her new blouse as she
recalled Father Goode and his prurience.

*Fourth: Honour thy father and thy mother. Never choose a woman
with a family who can interfere.*

'Are there many in your family, Rose?'

When he discovered the sad answer, Dennis made his first
move.

'I'm terrified of *my* mother dying,' he said, then stepped from

131

his chair by her fire and kissed her tenderly on the top of the head. Nonchalant. Confident. Brotherly. But in doing so he put his hand for a second on her neck, and then sat down, and for the rest of the evening behaved like a gentleman, and a little aloof.

Yes, good: both parents dead; the proceeds from their farm in Roscommon helped buy the house in Terenure. Pristine and aromatic with floor polish and, in season, flowers: it simply waited for a husband. Inside sat Rose at her loom. Did she have moral guardians? A lone sister eighty miles away in Roscommon, married to a man thirty years older, and both a little unwell, with no children, therefore, no troublesome visitors for weekends.

'Happy birthday, dear Rose!' – a Cusson's Gift Set of soap, talcum powder and lavender water: mauve box, mauve ribbon.

After the reams of bashful gratitude, Rose said, 'I'll tell you one thing, you'd never get an Irishman walking into a shop and buying that for a girl. Or if he did he'd get his sister to do it.'

'I buy all my mother's clothes,' said Dennis, 'and in fact when I'm buying her a present it's always clothes I buy her. But of course I've known her taste a long time.'

Rose made tea. Dennis stoked up the fire and they sat in their opposite easychairs.

'Come over here,' and he indicated where she should kneel down. She squatted by his knees, her back to him, and they both watched the fire in silence.

'It's your birthday, Rose.'

He placed a hand on the back of her neck, then bent down, turned her face up to him and kissed her – softly and not long – several times, then ran his hands through her hair. She caught the hand, held it, then let it free again and it roamed and roamed through her hair, and they kissed and kissed. Very soft kisses, never prolonged, no tongues.

As he left, he said to her, 'You'll have to buy a sofa for this room,' and grinned.

Red-faced from the fire in the grate and the kisses on her face, she touched his moustache.

'What's Father Goode going to say to me?' she asked.

'I'll wait for you outside the church,' he joked.

=

Binnie always said, 'Women are addicted to kissing. If men only understood that they'd conquer the world.'

'I thought we did already?' asked Dennis.

'Darling, there are only two things around which the world revolves. That –' she made a 'gimme-cash' gesture with her fingers, 'and this –' she pumped a strong forearm. 'Moola and muff, darling. Pence, darling, and puss. But – kiss. Kiss. Kiss us. Just, kiss, us.'

After every meeting now, he kissed Rose. Especially on Sundays, after, perhaps, a walk, or even an uxorious silence digesting the Sunday papers he had brought. He kissed her and kissed her. And left her lips waiting for kisses like fields waiting for rain.

'When I wake up of a Monday morning –'

He corrected with smile: 'Ah – *on* a Monday morning.'

'Of or on, my lips are full of your kisses.'

Rose in love.

Fifth: thou shalt not kill. Of course not. Nevertheless, use just a little agreeable violence. And call it Passion.

He declared Heytesbury Street finished in May: it had been completed and furnished long before that. The cork popped.

'Never? Not until now? Well, well. I hope you like the taste. Do you know how champagne was invented, though? Oh, *you'll* love this, Rose. Wine fermented too long in a monastery in France and when the monks came to pour it they found it full of bubbles, and then when they tasted it they said, "Look, we are drinking the stars."'

He raised his glass. She tasted and swooshed, 'Oh, it's gone up my nose.'

He laughed kindly.

They walked indoors from his little garden, and he cooked her lunch. She marvelled at his skill, his kitchen command. That evening, by his fire, as they both knelt on the floor, he removed her blouse and her bra. Just what he hoped for, exactly the right amount of hanging weight he loved! And he thanked her for the privilege, and still he kissed her and kissed her and kissed her. He stilled her flinchings by his gasps of admiration and his devotion, then assisted her in her modesty by hugging her so tight he could not see her. Never once touching her nipples, he circled them and then helped her to dress, apologizing.

'Passion. I got carried away.'

'We're only human,' she helped.

Within a month she was helping him undo the blouse buttons, and he was making jokes.

> There was once a young couple of taste,
> Who were beautiful down to the waist.
> So they limited love
> To the regions above
> And thus remained perfectly chaste.

A verse of Binnie's, who never said anything a mere once.

'Oh, Dennis you know everything,' Rose praised.

Sunday after Sunday, they knelt by his fireside or hers, naked to the waist, adoring.

Heavier kisses, wild pawing at Rose's hair, drawing it through his fingers over and over. He sucked her breasts as if to milk them.

Lying back with a subsiding gasp, he said, in the dreamy version of his voice, 'The Milky Way was formed because Heracles drank too fiercely from his mother's breast, and as she tore it away to stop the god-baby hurting her, her milk squirted out across the sky. That's the Milky Way.'

Rose thought Dennis a genius.

Impossible nowadays to imagine the depth of innocence in those country girls. Rose Glacken, and younger by a generation, the Kane daughters, and all their friends, older and younger – all the women growing up in country parishes had minimal carnal information. A few *double entendres* shouted in banter as they cycled through a village; or a chance viewing of animals' copulations. If unfortunate, they had been pawed, or worse, by relatives or neighbours. Pregnancies without the girl knowing the reason for her swellings were not unusual. Families lived in terror of the stigma of illegitimacy – it caused havoc to land inheritance rights. Ignorance was deemed the best defence.

Dennis Sykes seduced Rose Glacken by two means: one, by assuring her she was now old enough to enjoy all the fruits of life, and after all what was Confession for? She didn't always have to go to Father Goode – she should find someone sympathetic to the idea of Love? And, two, by the use of his Sixth Commandment.

Sixth: Thou Shalt Not Commit Adultery. Tell them there's never been anyone else. If they're single, always tell them it's your first time.

'But – how do you know,' asked Rose, 'how to kiss?'

'Same way as you do. You're a wonderful kisser.'

'I'm not.'

Dennis said, 'You mean I do it all on my own? No, Rose. Wonderful. Maybe it's just the natural force of loving inside you. And of course we both read a lot.'

Rose nodded, happy to agree.

He smiled shyly. 'Do you feel like a child, Rose? I do.'

By now he customarily put his tongue in her mouth. He took it out and asked, 'Makes a nonsense of sin, doesn't it? As if God would keep a girl like you out of Heaven on account of me?'

Rose replied, 'I found a priest in Clarendon Street who's real nice.'

'"Really nice",' corrected Dennis.

'Yes, he's very nice.'

'Besides which,' said Dennis. 'We're like children playing.'

Seventh: thou shalt not steal. Her intimacy must be appropriated openly; I must know everything about her, especially the three 'Ms' – her mates, her money, her monthlies.

Friends – three very close: Nuala, oft-quoted by Rose; Eily, clever and bookish, and Mary Pat, a keen dancer; all of the same age, and (could be tricky, so watch it) all *desperately* interested in romance.

'You must meet them.'

'When we're ready.' Good touch, the 'we': hint of promise.

He asked, 'What are their boyfriends like?'

'They don't have any. That's why I tell them so little about us. You know. People get jealous.'

Not the full truth from Rose; her friends were expressing some alarm, and she knew it, at her long evenings with Dennis the Mystery Man. But she had begun to relax more and more, and at his encouragment, did a lot of the kissing. Of late she did not

135

always wear her roll-on, or her stockings, when he called. Once, she even had to throw the key down when he arrived early and caught her in the bath. Ever the gentleman, he sat and read while she assembled.

'Here.' He thrust at her one Saturday afternoon an enormous bunch of flowers.

'God! Dennis! This is like *Social & Personal*.'

'An investment came through rather well. I can't wait to tell Mother.' All untrue. Well, technically Dennis had a point. 'Bryan Cooper' had invested so shrewdly that Dorothy Bayer's Trust took a sudden lurch upwards: one squad of dividends came from a company contracted in the rebuilding of Dresden.

'Don't forget. If you ever need help,' said Dennis.

Rose said, 'I have a thousand I could let loose.' On money, the great point of peasant confidentiality, Rose told Dennis everything.

'Give me three weeks with it.' Dennis smiled his cat's smile.

He returned with the money doubled.

She gasped and offered: 'I've another three thousand.'

Did she lick her lips? It seemed so.

Dennis shook his head. 'It doesn't always work. I'll tell you when the next good time comes.' And she reminded him almost every fortnight.

Yes. Worth five hundred of his own money, Dennis reckoned.

One week-end, picking up the acid on her breath, he asked, 'Are you all right, Rose?'

She blushed.

He put an arm around her. 'I watch you very closely,' he said. 'I keep an eye to see you're all right.'

'Some months are worse than others,' said Rose. 'And I mean, I'm not as bad as Eily. She has to go to bed for two days.'

Dennis clucked sympathetically. A thoughtful half-hour later, he announced, 'We'll go out for our tea,' and on the doorstep that night kissed her chastely, did not come in.

Unexpectedly, he dropped by next night. She was ironing. He looked.

She remarked, but unblushingly, 'Stop looking at my undies.'

He smiled.

=

136

Eighth: Thou shalt not bear false witness. Wrong! Thou shalt always bear false witness.

All going according to plan.

Including his success at keeping her from ever meeting his colleagues; 'We have a very difficult project; we are so – so touchy with each other, that we all agreed to avoid each other socially for the moment.'

Including his success at avoiding her friends: 'Put it this way, Rose. Before long, there may be a very, shall we say, a very appropriate occasion to meet them, I mean – an excellent reason for a party. And we'll get your sister and brother-in-law to come for the night. Besides which – I'd rather spend the precious time with you.'

Once or twice, when Rose pressed harder for social exercise, he frowned. She hated to see Dennis frown. When displeasure appeared, she let him 'play' longer next time, and for his next visit baked a cake. Once, when she asked how much he earned, he told her. She took it like a lady – but with glittering eyes when telling Eily. To whom she explained the burden of the aged mother in Helensburgh.

He also used his displeasure to invade her, and to make rules. A little after a 'mood', he would say a little edgily, 'How is Father Clarendon Street these days?'

'Great, he never asks too many questions. Not like Father Goode.' Rose mimicked. '"Did he touch under your clothes, my child? Where did he touch you?" Nuala used to say we should all agree to answer, "In Palmerston Park, Father."'

'Speaking of which, Rose,' Dennis replied, and reaching a hand up, snapped the elastic in her knickers. 'Let in some air one of these days, it's a hot summer.'

Week by week he undermined her modesty.

Some evenings, out of the frustration of waiting for the ripe time, Dennis on his way home handed some of his folded banknotes to the whores with their big lips and their shiny skirts on the banks of the Grand Canal.

Ninth: Thou shalt not covet thy neighbour's wife. If she ever shows the slightest interest in another man, drop her until she comes crawling back.

137

He arrived late one Saturday afternoon to the Oriental Café
and saw Rose in animated conversation. Dennis allowed her to
see him leave in a hurry. Within an hour she rang the bell at
Heytesbury Street. Surlily, he opened the door; he turned his
back and walked ahead of her, into the house; he stood looking
into the empty fireplace. A light breeze blew through the open
french doors.

'What's up?' she asked, behind him.

'Who was he?'

'Oh, Dennis! Is that it? The man in the Oriental? That's Billy
Nicholl, they own the laundry, I've known him since he was
sixteen. It was his father made me manageress.'

'You never said.' His jaws bit into the words. For an hour he
froze, an hour of mood, an hour of her cajoling, an hour after which
she wept at last. Then she allowed her to thaw him. By six o'clock,
the late sun heating the carpet, she lay naked. Dennis's tongue
started the long-postponed work: Rose had her first orgasm in
association with his displeasure at her.

Thereafter, Confession and Absolution came into their own:
Rose never hung back again. If she had become addicted to his
kisses, she began to die for his tongue. Rose asked for more dates:
she got them. One Saturday, in the strange heat of an Indian
Summer September, he kept her up all night, taking her to the
edge of her own control and back again.

'Fair's fair,' he then said, unbuttoning.

'Statues look different, don't they,' whispered Rose.

*Tenth: Though shalt not covet thy neighbour's goods. Thou Shalt
Physically and Rampagingly Possess Them, Lock, Stock and, yea,
even unto Barrel!*

At work they noticed the change in Rose. Nancy Hanley a
presser; Nancy who had eight children despite her husband's working the Liverpool boat – 'I wish to God he'd a-been doing Africa'
– noticed it first.

'Some fella's polishing Rose's shilling,' she said to Maureen
Phelan, both women blueing the shirts, perhaps even Dennis's.

'Well, whoever he is, there's a tune in her fiddle right enough,'
replied Maureen. 'I hope she'll be all right but.'

Rose had always been so fair to them; good about time off for

138

sick children, strong in her compliments when she spot-checked the work going out; bonus at Christmas; holiday money.

'The thing to watch for,' said Nancy, 'is if she stops going to Mass.'

'No,' contradicted Maureen, older. 'Them country girls always goes to Mass. The thing to watch for is if she stops going up to the altar rails at Communion.'

Which Rose did. He had blasted his sermon into her.

'The inside of you,' gasped Dennis in wonder – and was that a tear in his eye? 'The inside of you is like silk, Rose.'

For the next three and a half months, Rose learned Dennis's rhythms and preferences, fourteen weeks which took her from shyness, to abandon, to a private sense of shame about which she could do nothing. At the end of which time he had her reactions as trained as a pet monkey's.

Hallowe'en, 1951. Rose rang Dennis's doorbell. No answer.

Feeling certain his mother had been taken ill, perhaps died, Rose returned to Terenure and baked his favourite dark fruit cake. A week later, certain that his mother's funeral had just about happened by now, she put a note through the letter-box. The week after that she did the forbidden, the unthinkable: she rang his office.

A voice said, 'Who's calling?'

'Oh. A friend of his.'

Impressive transfer to another voice, who asked, 'Who's calling him, please?'

'I'm a friend of his.'

Impersonally, the voice said, 'No, Mr Sykes isn't in today.'

She thought of asking the police; she even scanned the newspapers; essentially, she fought off her instincts.

Saturday morning, five days later, she said, 'Who are you?' to the woman who answered the Heytesbury Street doorbell.

'Ackland. We've just moved in.'

'But – I thought Mr Sykes lived here.'

'He did. But he's left Dublin. Oh, do you know where there's a good laundry around here?' asked the fresh-faced woman, whose husband worked at the British Embassy.

=

139

When Rose went into Holles Street Maternity Hospital after the first complication, she wore Eily's mother's wedding ring and she was able to give her own address, Mrs R. Glacken, 15 Mayhill Terrace, Terenure.

'Wasn't that lucky,' said Eily, 'having an address of your own like that?'

She miscarried; by chance it happened in a check-up visit to the maternity hospital, and ended as a wide, soft red squelch in a bathroom, with much sympathy from the nurses.

'And you there? Actually in the hospital at the time?' said Eily in wonder. 'God, Rose, you're always lucky.'

Rose sat in her quiet little sitting-room for two months, and then went gently back to work.

'Hanging's too good for a shagger like that,' said Nancy Hanley to Maureen Phelan, because eventually in Dublin everything gets out.

'He's a fool to himself,' said Maureen; 'he'll never meet a nicer girl.'

In Dublin next spring, Rose Glacken accepted finally that Dennis was not coming back, and she invited Eily around for 'a bonfire'. They sat by the fire in Rose's parlour, and Eily watched in amazement as Rose put letter after card after photograph after letter, on the coals. She read one especial letter lastly, but not aloud, before she consigned it.

Darling Rose,
You asked me last night what it was I felt that you give me. I tried saying the sun, moon and stars, but you wouldn't have it, and then I promised you that I would go away and think about it. Now I know.

You give me myself. I was nothing until you came along, a small figure in the landscape, over-devoted to his mother, solitary, accustomed only to sitting quietly in my lodgings, reading or thinking.

Before you I had only had desultory relationships with girls and never for very long. And now there is even the chance

140

that we might march onwards side by side. What more can a man ask – to have a girl such as you?

My love always, forever,
Dennis.

She folded it, and put it back in the green, deckle-edged envelope, and said to Eily, 'It was the day after that letter, that was the day he went.'

Eily said, her glasses winking in the firelight, 'Well, he's going now, isn't he? Watch him burn, the bastard.' She pointed to the flame-licked letter. 'He'll burn hereafter, too.'

'No,' said Rose, 'that's where you're wrong. That's what I learned. His likes get away with it all the time. What we have to do is not let them make us get sick.'

'Will we kneel down and say a Rosary?' said Eily helpfully.

9

Electricity came late to Deanstown. Rural Electrification had been planned for several years, but the mountains supervened. In addition, farmers and smallholders refused to allow cables across their fields. Cattle would die from rubbing off the pylons. Storms would bring down wires, burn grass.

Lurid folklore added extra hazards. Firesides heard what exactly happens to a human body when electrocuted – what shade of blue it turns; how far out of their sockets bulge the eyeballs; when the fingernails crack open; why the penis ('the lad himself') springs erect.

Many, on visits to cities, had met electricity and disliked it. Bill Clements, who married late and then to a woman of only forty acres, took her on honeymoon to Janesborough, all of thirty miles away. ('Exotic,' commented Ellen.) The new Mrs Clements returned telling how Bill 'sat up in bed, and he blew and blew at the light, and it wouldn't go out, and he had to call the girl downstairs up.' Other stories told of people going blind in the new glare.

They might have been a tribe fearing some bizarre, silver force that would sear their innards, confound their reason. Wasn't electricity used to try and make mad people less dangerous? Didn't it change the patterns of the inside of the head? The old gunmen said, 'Any power that's hard to control is a dangerous thing.'

It might alter Life beyond their future. To many, electricity meant lightning sheets, cracking against the high summer skies, or the blue zig-zags, whose rainy voltage split rocks. Everyone knew of someone cleft from poll of skull to sole of boot while sheltering under a tree. Everybody had heard of lightning running like a mad chrome ghost along the galvanized iron roof of some barn, tearing at the rivets with its wizard's talons.

Electricity belonged with miracles when safe, with death when untrammelled. Electricity danced along water. Electricity struck the metal eyelets of boots; it tore harness-pieces from horses' foreheads; it flew like a bright fast metal comet along the ground, hitting horseshoes, turning riders and carts upside down.

'Think,' they said. What might it do on the loose inside a house with, as John Shea pointed out, 'every man woman and child in the parish sleeping in an iron-framed bed?' In the middle of the night would their mattresses and palliasses be upturned and would they find themselves pitched rafter-high? Think of the speed of electricity – upon you, like violence or gunfire, before you knew it had seen you. There were men they heard of – in the next county – who watched it turn corners seeking the metal food it desperately needed. With a loud blue-red-turquoise-flash, it rendered that metal to powder.

Electricity was the gelignite of the gods. Small wonder that entire countries in Africa and Scandinavia and the Far East would have nothing to do with it.

So the stories ran. So the regressed part of Deanstown viewed this new force, that threatened to hurtle across their land and shake the mountains when it danced.

After college and their first teaching posts, Ellen made one stipulation to Helena and Grace – to come home every second Sunday by one o'clock for a family meal. They could bring some washing with them for Essie to do, and they had to make a small financial contribution 'to the education of the younger ones'.

She always made an exception of the New Year's first Sunday, given how much they had been at home for the festive season. Thus, neither girl heard the exciting news of the Rural Electrification Scheme until halfway through January.

Ellen showed them the Notice. 'The boys say the very first thing they want is toast with scrambled eggs on the new cooker.'

Helena asked, 'Are we definitely getting it?'

'We have to,' said Grace. 'This place is like the dark ages.'

'Oh, Miss, oh, Puss,' mocked her mother sweetly, 'is it awful for you altogether?'

'At least,' said Grace, 'we'll be able to see our faces in the mirror for a change.'

'And would that be such a good idea?' asked Ellen. All laughed.

'Is everyone applying?' asked Helena.

143

Ellen laughed again and said, 'Your father is on the committee collecting the names and listing geographical difficulties. You know – getting the poles across fields and that. And you'd be amazed at some of the objections. There's an old woman up in Banter and she says "Yerra, it'll never catch on." And there's another old fellow over in Cairncrow says he doesn't want that "oul' lightnin' sparkin' and fizzin' at him outa the wall"' – Ellen did one of her mimicries.

She had grown up with electricity, and her immediate comment had to do with how dirty the house would prove when all its corners were lit up.

The Application Forms came to Thomas at the school, great boxes of them, and the senior schoolchildren distributed them on allotted days off, one form to every household. Some returned, requesting more forms. For instance, the Canavans in Horganstown asked for three – one for the brother, and one for each of the sisters. The siblings in that house had not spoken to each other since the parents died twenty years ago.

In the village, notices appeared. 'Evening Meetings will be held at Deanstown National School on Monday, Tuesday and Wednesday, the 14th, 15th and 16th of January, 1952. Admission Free. Questions Welcomed.'

Fog came down on the Monday night, and swirled like an old friend through the high and mysterious trees. By the lights of his oil-lamps and his stoked school fire, Thomas Kane introduced men in spectacles who carried blueprints and survey maps. The people sat crowded, cramped and smiling among the desks of their childhood. Feet shuffled; neighbours muttered and buzzed.

The first man, courteous and warm, stood before them as strange in his strong blue suit as the school inspectors used to seem. 'National Supply' was explained. They learned the history of Poulaphouca reservoir supplying Dublin, and of the Ardnacrusha scheme which harnessed the Shannon. In the film that whirred against the white, thick wall, a double-decker bus drove through one of the great turbine pipes. New, holy words floated through the flickering room – 'Head Race', 'Tail Race', 'magneto'.

When the film ended, the man and his colleague unpacked a number of flat cartons. They heaved and wrestled the heavy contents across two conjoined trestle tables at the top of the room. Thomas moved a lamp closer, and the men stood back to unveil their trump – a map of the village and district in relief.

Look: there flowed the river, made of a silver ribbon. Ridges of wrinkled, earth-brown plasticine made the mountains. Tiny balsa-wood boxes, painted bright, created the farms and the village – 'There's the master's house, there's the Canon's,' they whispered. The green metal trees came from doll's farms.

One by one, the gentlemen plotted little pylons into slots. By the light of the school lamp, their minute tines squared like shoulders as they marched through the undulating map, toys on a child's counterpane. From these pylons, the tiny, tiny serried rows of poles, made of creosoted half-matchsticks, radiated off to right and left. On 'cables' of metal thread, thin as gossamer, the 'power' floated to the eaves of the little houses. The junior gentleman moved Thomas's lamp away; the senior man clicked a hidden switch cabled to the film-projector battery beneath the table, and a street light illuminated a building with the minutest of lettering over the door: M. J. HAND: LICENSED TO SELL WINES & SPIRITS. Gasps.

Then, one by one, the little houses on the relief map, both in the village and along the outlying roads, lit up, until eventually, as a *tour de force*, a hidden 'moon', on a rigid wire so thin it could hardly be detected, glowed last of all with the words *Deanstown & District*.

The electricity gentlemen called for questions. Viva Ulverton had eaten apples throughout the meeting. She peeled each one elaborately in a spiral, taking as many risks as she could, but never breaking the skin. Eventually, she had a continuous narrow whorl of apple peel which she wound around her finger and then ate. She champed the cores like a hyena and asked, 'How much will it cost?'

They offered her national figures, provincial averages.

She shook her head, asked again. 'How much will it cost?'

They smiled at her, with the county breakdown, the typical household: Viva said, 'No. How much will it cost *me*?'

Nobody gave her an answer she liked. She rose and left, throwing her huge shawl over her shoulder.

=

That first Electricity evening did much to counter the old super-stitions. Deanstown welcomed conjurors. Since the German war-plane, nothing so diverting had come by, and that was ten years past. The travelling shows never played the school any more, not since Thomas threw them out. Canon Williams had grown quiet in his ancient old age, and he made no more lightning visits: how he used to throw houses into frenzies of respectability! Nor did he lambast them from the altar.

True, they joined in impersonal successes, from outside the parish. The county team had won three All-Irelands in a row: 1949, 1950, 1951. Word had it that Vincent O'Brien owned a horse that might win the Grand National. At last, though, they had something of their own to talk about.

Just as well. The war rationing – which should never have reached this far into a neutral country, should it? – would end soon, and no longer provide conversation. Those Ulvertons proved useless as a spectacle, now that the mad son was in and out of 'the Hospital' (as everyone called the asylum). Through her father's friends in Janesborough, Ellen had found a place for Munch in the quieter wing, and he came home when doctors observed he had entered a 'good phase'. From time to time in there, he met Cyril's excommunicated wife, who often disappeared 'for a rest'.

Mrs Greege died. Ellen laid her out, with the best linen and her own good candlesticks. Her sons approached Thomas for financial advice. In two biscuit tins and a suitcase under her bed they discovered twenty-four thousand pounds in banknotes. More poignantly, they found intact the wedding gift Thomas had returned to her in May 1925 in revenge for her disrespect of Ellen. To post it, he had cruelly reversed the same wrapping paper in which Mrs Greege had sent it. The boys handed it to him, thinking their mother had somehow mislain it.

The Home Economics of Rural Electrification: How to Light a House for a Penny a Week; How to Cook for a Farm Family for a Week for Half-a-Crown. Everyone who had attended the first meeting, plus fifty per cent more, came to the second. Could the school fit them all?

A woman with a pleasant face and a small enamel badge bearing

146

a lightning flash, held up a grill-pan; then some baking tins; then many brochures of electric cookers. She explained.

'And from now on, ladies, dirt is gone from your cooking forever – and as for your men. Well, I have bad news for them. A week's supply of hot water is only going to cost fourpence.' All laughed.

'Look, ladies,' she said, with Ellen near the front nodding in the agreement of a woman who had seen it all before. 'These are pictures of the way a cake of bread will rise in an electric oven. Now I know some of you get great results already, and that's because you're great bakers. But when you have an electric oven, even your husbands will be doing the baking' – at which, of course, they laughed and laughed.

The woman turned on an oil-fuelled generator. On the table sat a small electric cooker. She greased a pan, she cracked eggs.

'Watch the speed,' she said, 'it does an omelette with.'

Not everyone knew what an omelette was, but they watched. She impressed them with her wristy one-handed cracking of eggs on the rim of the bowl. Onion and butter smells filled the room.

'See – no flames, but all the heat you want. And it is *concentrated* heat.'

This placid conjuror, her buttocks square beneath her large skirt, heeled the pan back and forth on the round, metal cooker-plate. Little rivers of egg ran fugitive from side to side, seeking the heat at the edge of the pan that would cook them too. One last circular glide of her wooden spoon around the rim and – 'There y'are ladies!': the omelette lay folded in surrender on a plate.

With a fork she offered morsels. A wag suggested, 'Taste it yourself first, Ma'am,' and she, who came from similar stock, said, 'You'll get none.'

She played her heckler. All through the morsels that she visited up and down the benches and children's desks, she told him, 'You're getting none.' Finally, with a flourish, she pounced upon the wisecracker with the last fluent piece.

'Come on – open your mouth, we'll see will this shut you up,' to the delight of all.

He blushed and took it. As she walked away, she asked, her back turned to him, 'Well, did you like it?'

'Not bad, not bad,' he said with a merry grudge.

'Well,' she said, facing him, 'you're going to be a busy fella – for

147

I put number Nine [a well-known cattle purgative] in that bit you ate.' Her victory was complete.

From a box beneath the table she drew, with the care of a jeweller showing samples, cakes she had prepared in advance.

'See the height of that sponge,' and they admired the little domed mountain sprinkled with powdered sugar.

'Slice into this,' she said with the fruitcake. 'Now ladies! Doesn't that beat all the arguments you hear that electricity makes our fruitcakes sink. It does no such of a thing.'

The sleight-of-hand escalated. 'If you have someone special coming home from England, what about a Battenberg cake?' They ooh-ed and aah-ed at its marzipan beauty. Tapping the desk in rhythm with her words, she said, 'You can't. Go wrong. When you control. Your own heat.'

Finally she drew forth the staple diet of the countryside, a cake of risen soda bread. She did not cut it, she broke it, and it came away in her hand. They peered, tapped, prodded and sniffed.

'How long?' she asked them. She could have sold the Elixir of Life from a Medicine Show in Tombstone. 'How long did that take?'

Nobody answered.

'I'll ask you a question you all know the answer to? How long would that take in your own bastable oven on top of the fire with *spris* [the ember piled on the iron lid of the pot] – you all know that?'

The room said, 'An hour and a half to two hours.'

'In this – thirty-five minutes! And at the same time you're cooking the dinner here on top. And you've no smoke, and you've no ashes to clear out, you've no mess, or bother, or old filth.'

As the evening disbanded, women asked Ellen, 'What about makes of cooker, Ma'am?'

'Well, the make I'm getting is the big Belling,' she declared. 'It has a good big oven, it'll take a fifteen-pound turkey or a sixteen-pound goose, and it has a drawer underneath for keeping the plates hot, and it has a grill. And there's three plates on top, one is rectangular, and then there's a big round plate and then a small round one.'

'What about for the cleaning, Ma'am?'

'I think we'll buy the Electrolux. Because the long tube and the different-shaped nozzles means you can get into corners, and God, girls, we're going to need it. When that light switches on, 'tis then we'll see the dirt.'

One woman, who once gave Ellen an excellent recipe for lemon tartlets, and who, a naturally embarrassed woman, shifted her shoulders up and down when speaking, said, 'We have the Sacred Heart lamp ordered already and that's the only thing.'

'Oh, so have we,' said Ellen, 'there's a great run on them.'

True: the most common item they would order in the preparation for electricity was the little lamp to shine in front of a picture of the Sacred Heart of Jesus. A red glass dome encased a three-dimensional blue cross that flickered and glowed permanently. In front of this the families would now kneel when saying their rosary. At present, they had small fat oil-lamps, with red glass globes and wide, blue-striped wicks.

'Think of it, girls, no more paraffin oil, no more smells, isn't it great?'

Ellen rubbed her hands, enjoying her self-given role of leading the women into general acceptance. The myths of electricity had been made by the men.

'Ma'am, tell me now.' John Relihan's wife from Kiltynan turned every utterance she made into a matter of importance. 'Do you yourself, like, do you think 'tis safe?'

'Oh, of course I do,' chirruped Ellen. 'I grew up with it, it is a Godsend, that's the only word I can think of for it, a Godsend. God sent it to us.'

When Ellen got home (Thomas always stayed to lock the school and leave it tidy for the morning), Helena, surprise, waited. She had been visiting nearby.

'And don't you look nice?' said her mother.

'Mama, did you hear?' Helena blushed in excitement. 'Did you hear what they're paying the new cookery demonstrators? Nearly twice teachers.'

'Do you know what, we must have been thinking of each other? I was just saying to myself coming up the road, because we had a cookery demonstration tonight – wouldn't that be a lovely job for Helena?'

'I'm going to apply. Will Daddy be cross if I do?'

'Apply anyway,' said Ellen, and winked.

The third meeting, called for Wednesday night, was, as the expected bombshell meeting, the most crowded of all.

Two senior men, of gravity and authority – 'They look more like surgeons,' Mrs Hand said – waited in a car until all the foggy stragglers seemed to have at last entered the school. The men shook hands with Thomas, and he introduced them to the audience: Mr Michael Quinlan and Mr Andy MacCarthy. A third man, unannounced and unintroduced, came in late, nodded to the two officials, and took up a place in the shadows, standing by.

Mr Quinlan, smiling, hesitant, opened the meeting's topic – 'Where Deanstown and District is Going to Get its Electricity From.' He outlined their geography.

'Ireland is a saucer-shaped country, with high mountains all around its edges and a lot of liquid in the middle, all the lakes.'

Most of the people in the room had heard almost identical words from Thomas Kane, and they all smiled with memories of school-days. So far so good. The official next addressed the particular difficulties of their large area.

'Deanstown is not necessarily the obvious choice for a focus of all our planning, but it is the most centrally located problem we have,' he said, 'and therefore it acquires a new importance.'

They nodded quietly.

'Especially as it is going to be a place in which we have to exert the sort of new skill the whole world is interested in. What we do here will have an influence on projects in Africa, in India, in South America. Deanstown will lead the way.'

For weeks, he and his colleagues, smarting from previous bad experience, had been working on a form of words. In the car on the way from Dublin, Mr MacCarthy and their passenger had 'heard' Mr Quinlan's words, like an an actor rehearsing lines.

'Here in Deanstown, we cannot get you the kind of supply much of the country has.'

How quickly he had elided into the communal spirit, how swiftly he had become one of them.

'So much derives from the Shannon and similar sources, as with the great scheme at Ardnacrusha. But here, the mountains are

150

in the way.' He paused. 'Now I know that faith can move mountains –' he allowed them their chuckle – 'but we are only humble engineers.'

Was he a Corkman? He might have been; there was a trace of Cork in that accent, but he'd probably been in Dublin a long time.

'We've looked at this problem in every way. We've even flown over the entire area in an aeroplane, and you'll be glad to know that most of your roofs are in very good repair.' A smile again. 'And we have considered every way of getting the electricity in here, and we have rejected all but one, because ladies and gentlemen – Deanstown and District is a special case.' Buzz-buzz – and again he permitted it.

'So, instead of bringing you electricity from the Lee scheme in Cork, or from Ardnacrusha, we are going to *build*. We're going to construct. A special. Local. Scheme. You will have your very own electricity, and it will be generated and provided locally.'

Each listener turned to his or neighbour.

Mr Quinlan pressed on. 'Now. You'll know from the talks you've had here during the week, that electricity is generated, for Ireland's purposes anyway, by two methods. By the turf- or peat-burning stations in Clonsast and the Midlands. Or by harnessing the water, like the Shannon at Ardnacrusha. And as you know, there is another way of harnessing water. At Ardnacrusha we took the widest part of the Shannon, where we had the biggest supply of water and we redirected it into channels at such speed that it was able to turn the huge turbines. In other words, we have to give water strength and force – if it hasn't enough already. There is another way of doing that, and for that' – he held up the big photograph they had already seen on Monday night – 'we're going to use here a smaller version of what happened at Poulaphouca. We're going to build a dam. A hydro-electric dam.'

'The Ulverton one,' everyone said afterwards, 'she started it.'

Some hazelnuts Viva ate tonight, which she had previously cracked, and whose kernels she dipped into salt from a twist of paper.

'Oi?' cried Viva, and Mr Quinlan turned. 'Don't any of you know what happened at Poulaphouca?' She pronounced it 'Poolapooka' and Thomas, from his high desk, corrected her: 'Powel-ah-Fooka.'

'Powel-a-whatever-you're-having-yourself,' Viva replied in the

151

lamplight; and her cheek to Master Kane sent an approving hum around the room. 'When they built that dam,' she said, 'two thousand people lost their homes.'

'No. That's not quite correct,' said Mr Quinlan urbanely.

'Right,' said Viva, who had the full, and suddenly tense, attention of the room. 'Give us the correct version.'

'Some displacement of domicile is inevitable in projects of such magnitude,' said Mr Quinlan.

'What's that in English?' someone said.

'In Poulaphouca, because Dublin is such a huge supply zone, we had to take a lot of land into consideration.'

'I notice,' Viva said, 'you're very careful not to tell us where you're building this dam here.'

Mr Quinlan said, 'I was coming to that.'

'I bet you were. Could you hurry up?'

Whatever his experience, his status, his general demeanour and presence, nothing in Mr Quinlan's upbringing had prepared him for Viva Ulverton. Viva, when swimming naked in the river where others had gathered on summer afternoons, did not even deign to cover her breasts when towelling. Nor was there any point in Canon, Curate or Minister having a word with her: Viva had let it be known after the excommunication that if she saw a clergyman on their land she would shoot, and claim bounty.

Mr Quinlan turned to the blackboard and took down the large and glamorous photograph of Poulaphouca Dam, then gestured to Mr MacCarthy, who with his smooth and pleasant smile took over.

'Ladies and gentlemen, good evening, my name as you heard is Andy MacCarthy.'

Viva crunched her last few hazelnuts. 'Get to the point.'

'I am, I am.'

'You're taking your time about it,' she said.

He rubbed his hands and began. 'The thing about a dam is that it must be sited in a place where you can get a lot of depth. So that the water gathered there is deep enough to put very considerable pressure on the dam wall. And the strength of the water pressure that comes through the dam – that is permitted to get through the dam – comes from releasing some of that force. Like a big hard tap. Or a hose nozzle. Have you all here seen a hose or a tap?'

'How could they?' said Viva. 'There's no running water around here.'

Andy MacCarthy smiled and said, 'Nevertheless I hope you get the idea.'

'They do,' said Viva. 'We're not fools here, and if you're not going to tell them, I am.'

Mr MacCarthy produced a series of charts: many had illustrations of taps releasing water.

'This is the force you need,' he pointed to the first tap, a dim, dull trickle, 'to light a bulb of twenty-five watts.'

'You can always tell a man,' said Viva, 'who's afraid of coming to the point if he knows he's going to cut his finger on that point.'

Mr MacCarthy smiled bravely. 'And this,' he said, 'is the sort of force you need if you're going to light a hundred-watt bulb. You'd need two of them for this room, for instance,' he said helpfully.

Viva addressed the packed room. 'You none of you know what he's up to, do you?' she asked caustically. Her Anglo-Irish accent and forbidding bearing quelled any likely hecklers.

Mr MacCarthy's next chart showed a much healthier tap, in brighter flow. With an amateur attempt at drama he reached for a last chart.

'And this,' he said, 'is the kind of water-power you need to bring the electricity to Deanstown.'

Waves beat on a blue shore: a seagull wheeled, caught forever in Mr MacCarthy's big coloured picture. 'You need oceans of power,' he said. 'Oceans of it.'

Viva snorted. 'You're afraid to say, aren't you?' – and she stood. 'Who's here tonight from the Grey Valley?' she asked.

Several hands rose. Viva fluttered her fingers like a fan-dancer.

'Your houses are going to be filled to the eaves with water soon,' she sang. 'Because that's where the dam's going to be. They're going to empty the Grey Valley of people and they're going to fill it with water.' She waved her skirt in a frou-frou and sat down again.

Andy MacCarthy turned to her. 'How did you know that?'

Viva smiled at him, a big, gay smile.

Mr Quinlan came forward, smiling like a nervous deacon.

'If I may reinforce what Andy, what Mr MacCarthy, said? You are pioneers in a technological development that will be copied all over the world.'

He raised a hand to quell the buzz.

'We also have a huge financial consideration. If we don't bring in this hydro-electric scheme, you will never get electricity, nor will a very large section of the county.'

Viva said, 'Around here, they don't care about anyone else.'

Mr MacCarthy re-entered the conversation, and glid smoothly over her.

'We chose the Grey Valley,' he said, 'because it is geographically ideal, and because there are no large farms. There's quite a bit of scrubland in it, you have to admit.'

He began to explain the valley's aptitude for the dam project.

'It is the only natural high-sided valley anywhere within reach, capable of containing enough water to house a hydro-electric dam. Not only that, you have the River Carry and the River Lene.' He pointed to his map.

'They're close enough to the mouth of the valley to be easily diverted, and powerful enough to fill the valley. You see – we have to ensure that the water levels never drop.'

They expected opposition: they had planned for it. In their meetings and conferences in Dublin, they had dealt entirely in anticipation. In the end, it all fused into one substance: money. Thus, Mr MacCarthy and Mr Quinlan decided in advance when to play their ace. The budget allowed for it; they would play it only when people seemed extra-restive. Mr MacCarthy nodded to Mr Quinlan: the moment had come.

'And of course,' said Mr Quinlan, 'we didn't get around to talking about *compensation* yet.'

Compensation. Instantly the room quietened. They understood compensation as salmon understand a waterfall. In effect, money for nothing. Mr Quinlan became the good parent.

'Compensation will be paid for every person, for every man woman and child in the Grey Valley. Compensation that will not only be adequate. Compensation that will be generous. This project has international funds behind it. Because several countries are interested in how a project of this compact size will be able to generate such huge power. This dam is something special.'

He knew he had them, and he warmed.

'Now – normally compensation for the kind of disruption the Grey Valley residents will have to go through would take two forms. They would either be rehoused in something comparable elsewhere, usually better. Or they would be given the cash to do so. On this occasion we will be doing a bit of both. In fact –' when he smiled, his nose changed shape '– in fact, a lot of both.' He never, ever, throughout the entire project uttered the phrase, 'People will have to leave their homes.'

The room was his. No question. He knew it; Mr Quinlan knew it. Finally, with authority that increased at every word, Mr Mac-Carthy said, 'I want to introduce to you – and he will speak to you at another meeting next week – the man who is in charge of the project. He is a very distinguished engineer, even though he doesn't look old enough to be long out of short trousers. And you will be seeing a lot of him. He will be living here.' He beckoned to the man in the shadows.

'Ladies and gentlemen, this man will be with you for the next year so get used to looking at him. As you'll hear in due course he is an Englishman, but he has a bit of good in him, his mother is Irish. His name is Mr Dennis Sykes. He's the man who will build the Deanstown dam.'

Dennis came forward and they looked carefully at him as he smiled. The light in the room dimmed a little as, simultaneously, the oil in both lamps, always filled at the beginning of the evening by Thomas, burned below the halfway mark. Then both wicks recovered, and went on to draw on their second half of fuel supply. The room brightened again.

Mr Quinlan said, 'Well, that's all, now, ladies and gentlemen. Oh, there is one more thing. Mr Kane here, whom you all know and respect.' He indicated Thomas, a sentry in the flickering shadows by the fireguard.

'He will be your representative to us. He will be the man who will take all your complaints to us, and I think you must agree that your interests could not be in better hands. So when we get this project going, Mr Kane will be keeping an eye on everything on your behalf. He'll note down your queries about poles going across fields, about wiring houses, about where your meters will be put. And so on and so forth.'

=

Dennis's brown eyes roamed the dim schoolroom, with its Mercator's Projection Map of the World, with its partition. Through the many panes of glass, from waist height to the ceiling, Thomas Kane with his unblinking eyes and his raven hair in those days, and his forceful physical presence and his strong demeanour, wooed Ellen Morris when she first stepped off the bus to teach in his country school.

'Well,' said Ellen. 'What did you make of all that?'
    'I knew all along,' said Thomas.
    Ellen whirled. 'And you never said.'
    'They asked me not to.'
    Ellen faced him. 'Thomas, the girls are going to be very upset.'
    Thomas looked surprised. 'Why?'
    'Well, the place is special to them. Extra special. Since they were small.'

Thomas Kane never told anyone that he had no welcome in the Grey Valley. He had accused the place of failing to harbour a wounded colleague during the War of Independence. It had also and ever been his contention that the children from the Grey Valley were among the most stupid he had ever taught.
    'Interbred,' he said. 'They're pig-stupid. And unsteady.' As with all things he disliked, but to which within all manner of reason he could not object, he had always ignored coldly the girls' Grey Valley expeditions.
    Now, he made a face with his mouth.
    'Oh, well,' he said, putting sugar in his tea and picking up the newspaper. 'Can't be helped. I've seen all the maps. It's the only place they can put the dam.' He shook the newspaper. 'You can't hold up progress.'

10

Next week, all the Grey Valley people arrived for what had become known as 'the Compensation Meeting'. Even the oldest tribespeople rumbled out, some of whom had been too infirm, they claimed, to go to Mass. The women wore grey or black fringed shawls, the men had huge boots. They sat around the schoolroom walls, on benches, in respectful and shy silence. Since the news reached them, the word 'compensation' had echoed off the high limestone cliffs above their houses in the valley, had whispered through the dense thickets. In conversation, many had already spent the compensation money before they got it – or even knew how much it would amount to; and they looked forward to new houses, with no damp, with sound windows.

Mr Quinlan was back: he welcomed them all. On the blackboard easel behind him stood a large and glowing 'Artist's Impression' of the valley. He told them the picture would be raffled in a free draw when the dam was built. Miriam Hogan and Jack stood at the back of the room in their tall expensive clothes; Jack sent his hand over and over his sandy hair.

Mr Quinlan said, 'Now those of you who were here last week will remember that I introduced you to the man in charge of all this excitement. Still there's nothing lost by introducing a good man twice. Here's our Chief Engineer, Mr Dennis Sykes.'

Dennis began. As he spoke, the room stared. Predictably, the men did not like the look of him – too well-dressed, too sure of himself, little bantam-cock. The women took in the gleaming cuffs, the razor-pressed trousers, the white stiff collar on the blue-striped shirt; the brown eyes, the abundant, unoiled hair, the smile. Viva Ulverton stood to her full height (she claimed her stoop came from bending down to hear what people were saying to her). Miriam Hogan crossed her legs without knowing she did. Ellen, equally

157

involuntarily, closed her coat across her bosom despite the fact that she sat near enough to the fire.

'Ladies and gentlemen.' Dennis used his hands when he talked, not quite like a Frenchman, but not with a countryman's reticence either. 'What is different about this project is the size. If this works – and I mean to see that it works – we will have built a system where in a third of the usual volume we will generate three times the amount of electricity. It is nothing short of revolutionary. This will be one of the smallest dams ever built and a great deal more powerful than many which are much, much larger. Where we have an advantage here –' he turned to the artist's impression – 'is this: there is an unusual sudden depth. At this end.' He pointed.

The painting on the easel showed the Grey Valley as a rocky deep cavity, whose floor was a cushion of bushy greenery. Commissioned and directed by Dennis, the artist had conveyed nothing of the valley's privacy. This air of secrecy began outside, where woods almost camouflaged the only entrance. Unless a stranger understood where to view the valley from – and only habitués, like Helena and Grace Kane, knew the exact spot on the ridge – he would never guess how many houses had been hidden among the groves and stands of thick woods and copses. A clue could be had in the late afternoons, when the light shifted around, highlighting the rising plumes of chimney smoke. Deliberately, the artist had now portrayed the valley as it had been before dwellings were built in it.

'Up here,' Dennis pointed to the last rising canyon at the sealed end, 'as you know, the two rivers flow from opposite directions. Here. And here. The River Carry and the River Lene. They're fairly wide, but – and this is most important – at this, their nearest point to each other, and to the Valley, they're very deep. And they're fast. They pelt down the side of Knockmore, which you don't need reminding is the second highest mountain in Ireland. It's only when they flow separately away through the country that they become placid, and turn into ordinary meadow-rivers. Now as you know, these rivers are rarely empty. Our plan is to divert them and bring them together for a stretch – here. Then lead them through here – by blasting a channel in this end –' He waved the pointer Thomas used for singing lessons.

Dennis created a dramatic pause, then said in urgent, controlled excitement, 'Now here's the beauty of it all.' He clenched an upturned fist like an orator. 'After they have made our electricity, the rivers will again join their own beds where they now flow. And in fact – listen to this, ladies and gentlemen. No grazing land anywhere will lose water. That stretch, where we take the rivers away from their original courses, is all scrub and moorland.' The room sighed in wonder.

'So – the water will pour down here and fill to this height.' Dennis removed the artist's impression and replaced it with another. This second picture had obliterated all physical aspects of the valley interior – the bushes, the foliage – and presented the place as a huge, ovoid skeletal bowl surrounded by high cliffs. 'It will in fact fill to here.' He pointed to a blue line near the top of the valley. 'How simple! Water comes in one end. It creates a deep and powerful enough lake – which is contained by the wall of the dam, and some of it is allowed, in a controlled fashion, to pour through the turbines.'

'Jesus God,' said Miriam Hogan later, 'did you hear the way he said "rather"?'

'In due course,' Dennis purred on, 'in fact if the valley growth patterns are anything to go by, in no time at all, we will have a *rather* beautiful, new tree-fringed amenity – here, on the edge of these meadows. The only thing will be – anyone going swimming will have to remember it will be about half a mile deep.'

He produced a third and final artist's impression called, in glorious lettering, THE DEANSTOWN & DISTRICT HYDRO-ELECTRIC DAM: OPENED 1 FEBRUARY 1953.

Dennis interpreted the gasps of the room as he pleased, and said, in a confirmatory tone, 'St Brigid's Day, an ancient feast-day. Yes, we will build it that fast. Little over a year from commissioning to completion. It will be a world record.'

The artist had painted a smooth and brilliant curved dam, like a picture from a futuristic comic. Through the dam, the water pumped like streams of foam; tiny men in white coats stood on important platforms looking up at the dam wall in awe. Of the Grey Valley no more could be seen.

'And just a word about that timescale,' said Dennis. 'In the end it will all happen very quickly, and it will be very exciting. I hope you'll all be there.'

159

Mr Quinlan eased forward. 'Now. Who's going to ask the first question?'

Nobody, least of all Dennis Sykes, foresaw how he would lose control of that meeting. The first twenty minutes or so raised no difficulty. How will the compensation be decided: will it have to do with the size of the smallholding, or the square footage of the house being vacated? Had any relocations been talked about yet? Where were they looking at? Would those new county-council houses being built in Mooreville be part of it? Will there truly be cash as well as rehousing? How much? Would local men get jobs on the scheme?

Mr Quinlan's nose curved more and more, as his smiles suggested that they could hardly believe their luck. No opposition. No attacks.

How far would the power reach beyond Deanstown, would it supply the North Riding? There was a rumour that if it did, Deanstown would get its electricity cheaper.

Miriam Hogan, still focusing on Dennis, returned from her reverie when the pensive old woman sitting just in front of where Miriam stood, turned round and said urgently, 'Give me a hand up.'

Her name was Mollie Stokes. Helena and Grace knew her well. She smoked a pipe, still spoke much Irish and often asked the girls to read to her, saying her eyes were fading. They had never been fooled. Anyone who could crochet in that half-light would have no difficulty with print or handwriting. Last year, Grace told Helena she would one day find a way of teaching Mollie to read 'without Mollie knowing what was happening'.

Helena laughed at Grace's idealism. 'You won't catch her. She can hear the grass growing.'

Mollie Stokes gathered her shawl and held up a hand like a child at school asking a question: 'Sir?'

'Yes-ss,' said Dennis, crisp and benign.

Miriam Hogan gushed afterwards, 'What I want to know is, where did he get such good manners?'

Mollie Stokes said, 'Sir, I listened to all you said, and I looked to your pictures.'

People whispered her identity to each other: Ellen wondered

whether she was the woman the girls had talked about so affectionately. Mollie began a calm account of her day.

Morning sun in her eyes, winter and summer. Woodcocks. Pheasants. Apples, and even cherries red as a child's cheek. She was born in her bed, as was her mother and grandmother, and the whole line of Stokeses back to before the curse of Cromwell. Ninety next Whit, she wanted to die in that bed, be shrouded and waked in it.

Mollie Stokes had reached her understandings of life in and through the Grey Valley. It explained to her thunder, and colour, and solitude, and the taste of food that she grew herself. She got from the valley her sense of Time, of health, of calm; it had taught her growth, and the seasons of the year, and logic. Death threatened with less fear; life's burdens could be anticipated because, as she said to little brown-eyed Dennis Sykes, 'That valley is my system, Sir.'

She, and the others who lived there, had ancestry and descent, had means and nature, had sequence and recurrence. If spiritual advantage comes to those who have unbroken blood continuity in one place, if they have accumulations of simple understanding by which they can live fulfilled lives, the people of the Grey Valley had more than most. Without having the means to articulate it, they none the less understood, as did Mollie Stokes, what they would now lose. Compensation might appeal and even appease, but their spirits would none the less be charred by the loss of their old place.

Dennis Sykes, accustomed to women, recognized immediately the force of Mollie Stokes. He stepped back a little, let Mr Quinlan take charge – who gestured it back to Dennis. For a moment or two, any forthcoming response seemed to bobble between the two men, wordless ping-pong. Dennis finally accepted the challenge and spoke with good grace and thoughtfulness to the standing old woman.

'I know exactly what you mean. I recognize what you are saying, that you know already what you are going to lose. And I think you are also saying that there are no values in money that can compensate for what you must leave behind you.'

Mollie Stokes nodded: she looked like the old woman with the samovar in a Russian play. Dennis drew a deep breath.

161

'And,' he said, 'I'm very sorry. Very. Sorry.'

'Is there nothing to be done?' she asked, then stood immobile and unblinking.

Dennis repeated, 'I really am. Very – sorry.'

He turned again to Mr Quinlan, who raised helpless shoulders. Nobody said anything for some eternal seconds. Someone's foot scraped on the wooden floor.

Mollie Stokes broke the silence. 'In that case, Sir,' she said, 'I may as well do my mourning now.'

Only Thomas anticipated what she meant. He was probably the one person in the room who could have stopped her. But he had heard her long ago, and, perhaps overwhelmed by the memory of her force, and by the emotions her voice would call up, he failed to move. Mollie Stokes opened her mouth and began to keen.

Victorian and Edwardian travellers through Ireland described the keening women. The term came from *caoine*, the old word for 'lament'. In her *A Lady's Tour of the South-West and West of Ireland*, Mrs Florence Handscombe wrote, 'Three women arrived with the coffin on its farm-cart. They were dressed in poor black, their hair blown by the sea wind, and their eyes blackened around the edges as if with sticks of charcoal. From the moment the funeral entered the overgrown cemetery, they began to "keen". To "keen" is to make a wild, high noise. It disturbs the hearer with its intensity, and its griefstricken shrill cadences rend the heart.'

Vita Sackville-West compared the keening women of the west of Ireland 'to the worst that German legend can yield, or Furies and Harpies can render. For many months afterwards, I woke at night, harsh voices in my ears, their tragic blackened eye-sockets staring at me from diverse points in the dark room.'

General Arthur Crabbe believed that 'not even the Indian dervishes at their most fearful can reproduce the wild effects of these simple but terrifying creatures.'

Mollie Stokes had serviced many funerals, keening in a voice that the opera stage would have acclaimed for its range. On the long notes she remained without vibrato. The short notes built to peal after peal of bereavement and misery. All who heard it chilled at the sound: Dennis Sykes smiled at first in embarrassment, then turned a little white and looked away.

162

Miriam Hogan looked at Jack who shrugged his eyebrows. Nobody left the schoolroom.

At funerals, when keening for their own beloved, such women usually lapsed into a kind of desperate sobbing, punctuated by sudden high returns to the keening, as if somehow their voices were still tearing through the fabric of their normal behaviour. More composed relatives then led them away, and – perhaps even more harrowing in some ways – the sound floated back to the graveside, even from a long distance.

Miriam Hogan reached out a long, thin red-freckled arm and coaxed Mollie Stokes from the room. Those people bunched inside the door made way. Mr Quinlan, Dennis Sykes and their sentry Thomas Kane, watched the small old woman protected by the tall younger one, hesitate in the school door and then walk out into the night.

Lost to eyesight, but not to earshot; her high-pitched sobbing, which borrowed notes from seagulls and eagles, lasted several minutes more.

Finally Mr Quinlan broke the silence in a voice he dare not raise.

'Ladies and gentlemen, I think that's all. Mr Sykes will be coming to live nearby. Mr Kane will channel all enquiries. Thank you. Thank you.'

He withdrew, a shattered glass. The people dispersed.

Dennis Sykes reintroduced himself to Thomas Kane.

'Mr Kane, that was, I suppose I may use the word "extraordinary". I certainly can't think of another word.'

Thomas nodded. 'Yes. It's a very old tradition, it's called "keening", it was an old mourning custom.'

He told Dennis some of the history. The smaller man listened, nodding as if in fascination.

Next, Thomas called across Ellen, and said to Dennis Sykes, 'Oh, this is my wife.'

Dennis Sykes took Ellen Kane's hand. Dennis had a dry hand, yet Ellen recoiled. He fell short of wrapping his grasp round the full breadth of her smaller hand: instead, his fingers invaded her palm, and loitered. Too long. Her hand tried to improve the encounter by shoving forward, into the handshake a little, but

163

his grip, though light, had no intention of changing. Twice she registered – the fingers: the duration. A part of her brain thought that this man shook hands like a thief – even though she had never shaken hands with a thief.

With people moving around the room, and shadows heaving across the light, the schoolroom lamps denied Dennis an adequate view of Ellen's face. He craned quickly, still could not measure. She seemed to him quite an item – not as countrified as the other women; unusual; almost Italianate; full-mouthed.

'How do you do, Mr Sykes?' Not a local voice: no burr; a clear tone. He allowed the handshake to come to an end, then put his hands like royalty behind his back.

'I'm bound to say I'm having an interesting time,' he replied. She half-smiled.

He continued, 'My friends have wondered whether I will find it slow here in the countryside. But you have your moments it seems.'

'You're very welcome,' said Ellen, bowing her head a little in her manners – but why did the words stick in her throat, she wondered; why could she not say them as easily and fluently as she had always done?

Thomas and Mr Quinlan conferred a little longer, then Mr Quinlan fetched Dennis.

To whom Thomas murmured, 'Mr Sykes, this isn't the time or the place to make arrangements, but sure we'll see you again.'

And all left. To face unpredictedly intense complications.

Helena and Grace, in an exchange of letters, agreed to meet in Mooreville, prior to catching the bus out home for the week-end. Grace had heard, and now told wide-eyed Helena, of Mollie Stokes's keening.

'Hellie, they're going to drown our valley, it's going to disappear.'

'I know. I know.'

'Hellie, our lovely place! Our valley! They're going to make it a lake!'

'I know.'

'All our foxes! And the badgers! And the wild apples! God, it's awful. Awful!'

'Awful,' agreed Helena.

164

'I've never been so hurt about anything,' said Grace. 'And you know about Daddy?'

'About him helping them? Yes, Mama wrote. She said in the letter, here it is, that he couldn't do much else. Apparently all teachers, all over the country, have been doing the same in all the electrification schemes. The school is where it is more or less organized through.'

'Yes,' said Grace, twisting her mouth, 'but you know him. Look at the relish he'll be doing it with.'

'Easy, Grace, easy.' Helena had many of her mother's intonations.

'No, Hellie, I won't go easy. This is only part of it. Look. Last week-end, I went and stayed at Ruth Clohessy's house, I told Mama and Daddy I was doing a week-end course in case they called to see me, I didn't tell them I was staying with anyone, you know what he's like about us mixing with people at all. And Hellie, I think I know now why he never wanted us going into other people's houses.'

Helena, leaning away, looked troubled.

'He doesn't want us to see that other fathers are nice to their children. Ruth's father talks to her, he says "hallo" to her when he comes in. God, he even ruffled her hair when he walked past her chair. He teased her, I mean, nicely. And he's the same to all the other children.'

Helena stirred her tea, and sighed. 'Yes, I've noticed the same, but I didn't want to say anything.'

'Well, I've noticed it for ages and ages, for years now, but I didn't want to say anything either,' emphasized Grace. 'And you know what Mama will only say, she'll say he's had a hard life or something. But Hellie, I'm sick of it.'

'Oh, Gracey, don't cause trouble.'

'Well, you tell me this,' said Grace. 'Why were we always ill? Why were you always getting diarrhoea? Until you left home? It's because we were all the time frightened, that's why. Look. Since I started teaching, the one thing I know is we're not allowed to frighten children in school. Or say hurtful things. Look at our father. Look what he always did. And still does to the younger ones.'

'Don't, Gracey, don't.'

=

165

Helena spoke in vain. Conflict began from the moment the girls entered the house.

Thomas said to Helena, 'Where in the name of God did you get that blouse? Was the circus in town or something?'

Slowly, over the past two years, the girls had been allowed by Ellen to buy their own clothes: Grace had argued and argued for their independence.

Helena winced – but Grace blew. She blew so high and so hard that Ellen, for the first time ever, scattered the other children out of the kitchen. They listened, anyway, at doors and windows. Thomas and Grace faced each other down in a shoot-out.

'What did you say to my sister?' snapped Grace. 'Apologize! Go on, apologize! No Hellie, I won't shut up, he has to say he's sorry.'

Thomas stepped towards her. 'Mind your mouth, Miss, you are forgetting yourself.'

'I suppose you're going to hit me. If you do, I will tell everyone in this parish. Go on. Hit.'

Ellen did not need to intervene: Thomas, amazingly, stepped back.

'Is this what all your "independence" is doing for you? Fine teacher you'll make,' he sneered. 'If this is what you think constitutes respect.'

'You're the one with no respect,' spat Grace. 'Look at the way you have just completely disrespected Helena.'

'I said – watch your tongue, Missy.'

Men would have stepped back from Thomas when they saw him like that. Not Grace.

'Go on. Bully me. Like you bullied every single one of us all our lives so far.' She had his eyes, and they blazed.

Thomas Kane had made himself legendary by knowing how to move through hedgerows and dark fields by night with a gun in each hand. He had stalked patrols of soldiers, taken out their rear-guard silently and escaped through the trees; he had blown apart army posts from the inside. All these heroisms, between 1916 and 1920, when, inexplicably, he walked away from the violence in the middle of it all, had made him a hero. Otherwise, the other hard men of the parish, whose children he 'disciplined' at school, would have faced him long ago. Yet Thomas Kane had curiously weak antennae for general life. His wife picked up the slack, dealt it to him, guided him along the ropes of each day. After the keening incident, she had anticipated an outburst from Grace, even if not of this strength. Sure enough, Grace switched the issue.

'Look at you! You won't even lift a finger to help that old woman Mrs Stokes.'

'Grace, that isn't true, your father has a great sympathy with Mrs Stokes.' Ellen, when agitated, spoke with her hands pressed to her jaws.

'When will we see it? When she's in the County Home with all her possessions rotting at the bottom of this dam?' asked Grace.

'Gracey,' said Helena, 'Gracey. Easy.'

'You don't know what you're talking about,' said Thomas, but his rigidity now slapped no curb on his fiery daughter.

'This is what I'm talking about,' said Grace, and she held out her fingers to make point after point exactly like her father always did, but perhaps the mimicry was unconscious or inherited.

'I'm talking about the destruction of an old place of great value. I'm talking about the removal of our history from in front of our eyes. I'm talking about the disappearance of something we will never have again, those rare plants, the rocks with their fossils. I'm talking about buying people off so that engineers can have their way. How do you know that this is the only scheme that will work? We've only their word for it. I'm talking about the way they're going to appeal to people's greed, by giving them cash. And you, you of all people who have always complained that people are too conscious of money, you're going along with it, you're even working for them.'

Faced with her force, Thomas gave up his righteous position by deciding to answer her last point. 'I am working for the Government. It is my duty.'

'Duty! Duty! You made duty your god! Look at you! You haven't one friend in the world. Name one man you talk to. And I know why you've never had a friend. It's because you're afraid someone else could ever make you change your mind.'

Ellen shouted, 'Grace!'

All stopped. Helena caught Grace's arm. Thomas turned and walked away.

'Grace, you've gone too far.' Ellen did not know where to look.

Grace spoke with the brusqueness of finality. 'Mama, I haven't. And you know it.'

Grace took Helena's arm and said, 'Come on, Hellie, I'm going for a walk. Are you coming?'

Thomas went to bed at eight o'clock, and appeared to be asleep by the time Ellen joined him, an hour later. The girls had not returned.

Next morning, nobody spoke. While the family in general went by car, Helena and Grace walked to Mass together. When all returned, Thomas received his breakfast alone in the parlour. The other children sat quietly, except the youngest, Hugh, who asked, 'Why is everybody saying nothing?'

Grace smiled and said, 'We're trying to teach you the virtue of silence.'

Mid-morning, Helena and Grace left the house together, with a basket containing food. Ellen did not ask where they were going.

Thus ended the first altercation in the Kane family which challenged the autocracy of the parental knowledge. Nobody had ever before dared. Complete control over the children's opinions had held sway. Every item of information, or thought, or learning that they brought to the house had been altered parentally in some way. Mainly by their father: he put their world through his filter; he changed, challenged and reordered, until all things they ever knew or considered had been rinsed through his mind.

Ellen had continued to serve his utter writ, living separate lives, wife and mother: that according to her lights, seemed best, in the fitness of things. She had never contemplated that it had, eventually, to crack: too extreme. Now his wife did not know how Thomas Kane would react to this revolution under his roof.

At six o'clock that evening he gave his response, when he opened the parlour door and summoned Ellen.

'She.' He paused. '*She* – is not to come into this house again. Nor will I speak to her – until I have a letter from her setting out her apology in the form I have drafted here.'

He handed Ellen a sealed envelope. As she spoke, he held up a hand. 'No. I've said it.'

He closed the parlour door in her face. Ellen stood in the hall, looking at the envelope.

Helena and Grace returned.

'We went to the Grey Valley,' said Grace matter-of-factly. 'We saw Mrs Stokes.'

'Grace. Helena, love, you'd better hear this too. Grace, your father says he wants an apology from you. He has written out a letter to help you.' She handed it to Grace, who, leaning on the handlebars of her bicycle, took the envelope and, without opening it, tore it in half, then dropped it to the gravel.

'Oh, Grace!' said Ellen, in dismay, not anger. 'He says you can't come in unless you apologize.'

Helena picked up the torn letter and held it out to Grace.

She shook it away. 'Simple. Then I won't come in. Hellie, get me my travel bag, will you, and I'll go.'

'Grace! Grace!' said Ellen.

Helena went indoors and packed Grace's bag, while mother and daughter stood beside each other. Ellen talked; she wheedled, she attacked, she cajoled, she wept. Grace did not move. Helena came out, handed Grace her bag; the girl fixed it to the carrier clip at the back of her bicycle and rode away, saying, 'I'll drop you a note, Hellie, 'bye, Mother.'

Helena said to Ellen, 'This is awful.'

Late that night, Helena read Thomas's draft apology.

Dear Daddy,
I am heartily sorry for having offended you, and for having shown you such disrespect. I undertake and give you my word that I will never do so again, and that I will support all your actions on the Grey Valley.
Your obedient daughter,
Grace Kane.

Nor was it lost on Helena that the Act of Perfect Contrition, which they had been taught by Ellen to say every night of their lives in case God called during their sleep for their immortal souls, began with the words, 'Oh my God, I am heartily sorry for having offended Thee.'

=

169

Next evening, as Thomas and Ellen took a late walk, she remarked as if thinking aloud, 'I have to say – that was very moving what Mrs Stokes did in the school. I haven't been able to get it out of my head.'

Thomas cleared his throat. 'She keened like that at my father's funeral.'

Ellen looked up at him in amazement. 'You never told me.'

'She did.' He stopped himself speaking, as he always did when anything of feeling came near the surface.

'People get attached to land, don't they?' asked Ellen later. 'I mean, if it is only a haggard garden?'

'They do,' said Thomas, still thinking, 'they do.'

Ellen tried to clinch it, moved too soon.

'I suppose you feel a sympathy for her so?' she asked in a tone of hope.

He withdrew at a typical speed. 'No, I have a job to do.' And as he so often did, he vacillated, leaving her unsatisfied either way, 'But I understand her distress.'

'So –' she chose carefully. 'So – if a few people take Mollie Stokes's side, what way, I mean, in what manner do you think they should be spoken to?'

'Depends on who they are.'

Local debate had begun. As no compensation figures had yet been struck, hostile mutterings had started, initiated mainly by those outside the valley who did not qualify for cash or rehousing. Five other families in the valley had come out and said they would not leave, that the waters could close over their heads.

Ellen said, 'Well, the Griffins, the Careys, the Ryan Jacks, the Hallorans and the Healys. As well as Mrs Stokes.'

He followed her list. 'The Griffins are scroungers. The Careys no better. The Ryan Jacks don't belong there anyway, they're incomers, they only went there at the turn of the century. The Hallorans will smell money like a cat smells fish and they'll go where that is. The Healys aren't worth talking about.'

Ellen waited, then said, 'And old Mrs Stokes?'

'She'll be dead by then.'

'But if she's not.' Ellen stopped.

'H'm.' Thomas stood and thought.

170

11

One remark of Grace's cut into her father – her observation regarding his lack of close friends. It attacked his view of himself as a man who had command over his world. He knew from old days the value of comradeship, knew how a friend warned of a possible bullet in the head, or mopped a wound with a handkerchief or scarf. Although capable of relaxing with people in exalted positions, he had no confidants.

Now he began, not necessarily aware, to change this – difficult in a system where he required himself to remain above the people, in order to retain his authority over them. Not that a good confidant proved easy to come by.

Jack Hogan: too drunk too often, with a talkative wife.

The Canon: would use a confidence as a weapon in an argument, and now too old.

Herbert Winer: the husband of Ellen's friend, and anyway had to have everything explained to him twice.

On the day during which he most reflected upon Grace's remark, a confidant appeared, to whom Thomas would open his heart. Completely. The appointment had been made the previous week. Dennis Sykes asked Thomas in a letter if he and his wife would care to come to the Royal Hotel in Mooreville for a drink.

Ellen did not go, said she had arranged to talk to a girl – coincidentally from the Grey Valley – getting married the following week. Thomas arrived in the hotel on the dot of five o'clock. Dennis looked at his watch.

'Punctuality. The mark of the gentleman,' he said. 'How do you do, Mr Kane, how nice to meet you again,' and held out his hand. 'Mrs Kane not with you?'

Thomas explained. Dennis ushered him to the far end of the bar: 'I've asked the barman to keep this little corner free so that we can talk in private.'

'How are you getting on in general?' asked Thomas.

'Settling in, settling in. I have a house now, and I am getting a telephone, believe it or not.'

'A telephone? Yes, I suppose you would need one,' said Thomas.

'I'm being driven everywhere at the moment,' said Dennis, 'and – ah, yes, now you'd know. I have to buy a car, or at least the company is getting me one. What's a good make of car?'

Dennis Sykes had made careful enquiries. They told him Thomas Kane saw himself as an important person, liked to be viewed as a figure of authority. Kane, they said, acted as if in charge of everything, had no idea that many people hated him.

'A cold man,' they said, 'very big in himself.'

'A bad bastard,' said others in Dublin; 'he's vicious and he thinks he's above everyone. But – he's a man you have to keep in with, he knows people. Since the old days.'

Even if these remarks ran along a scale from half-mockery to sneering, Dennis sensed that people feared the teacher. Therefore – woo him.

Dennis believed in his own luck – provided he assisted it. On the very day he had chosen as the date on which to leave Rose, the Government approached with the Deanstown project. An afternoon of discussions persuaded him. At a party two nights later, he met the people who would rent his house: everything up and running within three days.

'Amazing, Binnie, wasn't it?'

'No, little Dennis, there are only two kinds of people in the world, those who make their own luck and those who have none. In other words, darling – you and me.'

'Only drawback, Binnie, I'm going to be soon sick of these peasants.'

'Have you left her with one, Dennis? The Dublin lass? Bun in the proverbial?'

He reflected: they were sitting in the small bar at the Mayflower Hotel off Park Lane.

'Don't know. Still – not my problem.'

'Dennis darling, somewhere inside me – but I can't find the place – I hate you.'

'Come on, Binnie, I'm your star pupil!'

172

'But Dennis, darling, I'm a woman. Sister-feelings.'

He shifted. 'Oh, yeah? Well. She was nice. All right. But you know. Time to move on. God, she was boring, though. Bo. Ring. Still, I weaned her off religion, I did that for her.'

'And,' asked Binnie, 'you think that's a favour?'

Thomas Kane replied, 'I think the Wolseley is a lovely car.'

Dennis replied, 'Then a Wolseley it will be' – but Dennis had ordered a Wolseley long before Thomas Kane mentioned it.

'Yes,' he reflected. 'All that nice leather. And wood.'

'Exactly,' said Thomas Kane, his hat carefully on the seat beside him.

'I can't tell you how excited I am about this great project,' said Dennis. 'This is my big opportunity. And I have to say I'm quite nervous. Now – a man like you, you must have had some challenges in your life. Tell me something – if you don't mind my asking you, if I'm not imposing on you.'

Thomas said to Ellen that night, 'He's an extraordinarily sincere individual.'

'No,' he said to Dennis, 'you're not imposing on me, not at all.'

'How do you overcome fear? I mean – I wake up at night sweating with fear in case I get this project wrong. In case the day we press the button to let the water into the dam catchment, nothing will happen.'

Thomas smiled – the smile he used for the Archbishop, the smile he used for John and Lily McCormack.

'Yes, yes,' he said thoughtfully, rubbing his chin. 'Are you a religious man at all?'

Thomas said to Ellen, 'And do you know something else, something really surprising? He's taking Instruction, he was attending a priest in Dublin. Father Goode in Merchant's Quay.'

'Oh, isn't that ideal,' said Ellen with a dry edge, but said little else.

'Oh, by the bye,' said Dennis to Thomas (a phrase Thomas soon began to use), 'I hadn't realized about Cardinal Newman's great connection with Dublin?'

'Oh, yes, oh, yes. Very much,' said Thomas. Who then returned to the subject. 'The thing about fear.'

Dennis leaned forward flatteringly to hang on every word.

173

'The thing about fear is. Fear is one of two things. Fear of that which you don't yet know anything about. Or that which you know from experience, and therefore you know you have good reason to fear.'

Dennis sat back and looked thoughtfully into the middle distance. He paraphrased Thomas's words.

'Mmmm. "That which you don't yet know anything about. Or that which you know from experience is worth being afraid of." Is that what you're saying? Gosh, that's an intelligent remark.'

Said Thomas to Ellen, 'He's very stimulating to talk to. He grasps things immediately.'

Dennis continued, 'So what you're saying is. I have to ask myself. Which am I afraid of? Something I already know. Say – if I had done something like this hydroelectric scheme, and it didn't work. Which isn't the case. Therefore what I must be afraid of is – that this project won't work?'

He stood to order another drink, absolutely refusing Thomas's intervention and protest.

'And they say,' said Thomas to Ellen, 'that the English aren't hospitable. I could hardly buy the man a round of drinks.'

From the bar, Dennis called to Thomas, 'Now I notice you like your water in a separate glass. Like the Americans.' He returned and mused and quoted. 'Mmmm. "Two kinds of fear." I can see now what Mr Quinlan meant.'

'Mr Quinlan? You mean the man with you?'

'Yes,' said Dennis. 'He's one of the head men. He said one of the reasons Deanstown was chosen, it wasn't entirely a geographical decision. Although it has turned out that way. One of the reasons was that the support on the ground – meaning you – would be as intelligent and sensitive to all our needs, he said, as we'd find in Ireland. I hadn't realized you were so well known.'

'Ah!' Thomas jerked his head in a modest demurral.

Mr Quinlan had said no such thing. He had remarked that an old gunman he knew told him Kane was once known as an 'icy savage'.

'Have you lived here long?' asked Dennis. 'It's quite a lovely place. Did all that sense of – of –' Nobody struggled for a word more impressively than Dennis Sykes. 'Civilization. Did all that

174

civilization – did it come from that gorgeous-looking Castle? I'm looking forward to exploring it.'

He had also heard of Thomas's love of the Castle.

'It looks so like some of the châteaux I've stayed in in France,' said Dennis, who had never been to France.

'He's a much-travelled man, too,' said Thomas to Ellen.

'Jesus, Binnie, don't joke, this really is the back of beyond. I mean this is so remote the birds can't get there!'

'You'll be able to go native, darling, you can shag all those thoroughbred cattle.'

'There are no such creatures as thoroughbred cattle, Binnie.'

'Oh yes, there are, Angelica's new man-friend's got them.'

'Binnie, I have no indoor plumbing in my house, for God's sake.'

'What no bidets, no douches for the ladies? Dennis darling, what *will* you do?'

'Did you know that Dean Swift stayed there?' Thomas eagerly sought new listeners to the history of the Castle.

Dennis swivelled. 'Don't tell me he wrote my favourite book there?'

'And he seems very well-read,' said Thomas to Ellen. 'I mean he quoted from *Gulliver's Travels*, and not from the part we all know, not from Lilliput, but from Brobdingnag.'

'Goodness,' said Ellen, washing under her arms.

'No,' said Thomas to Dennis. 'He had that written before he came here.'

Dennis allowed his crest to fall.

'What a pity the place seems to be falling in ruins,' he said.

'Ach!' said Thomas. 'Don't talk to me. I fought and fought to save that place. I think it should be preserved, I mean it has a great history.'

'So important,' said Dennis, 'so important, a sense of history.' He insisted on Thomas joining him for supper – 'unless your wife might be discommoded?'

'And such a great vocabulary,' said Thomas, watching Ellen pull the nightdress over her head. 'Lovely to hear someone speaking good English. "Discommoded". "By the bye".'

=

175

'And you should see this guy they all defer to, Binnie, this head-master. He's like – he's like a hillbilly in a suit, no, he's posher than that. He's like, he's like – a bad sheriff in a Roy Rogers film. He has these eyes as blue as the worst kind of glacier, he's twice my height –'

'Well darling, in all conscience – *would* that be difficult?'

'Shut up, Binnie. He wears these homburg hats, he's really frightening. Ask him a question and he takes up to five, ten seconds before beginning to reply and he – he –'

Dennis stopped.

'He keeps putting his hands together like this.' Dennis made a gesture of prayer-folding. 'But he does it as if he has to control them otherwise the hands might of their own accord reach out and strangle you.' He twinkled at Binnie. 'Wife's a peach, though. Absolutely right for me. Little partridge. Face like a renaissance madonna.'

'So you're going to divide and rule, darling D?'

'Don't know, Binns, don't know. Doubt if she's ever had a production number.'

Binnie punched him. 'Christ, you're a vulgar little punk.'

Ellen, seeking the advantage of Thomas's mellow mood, straight-ened a pillow and murmured, 'I had a note from Grace. I think she might be home for an hour or two tomorrow night.'

'No.' Clear as a handclap.

'She's only passing –'

'No.'

'Thomas, she's –'

'No.'

'But –'

'Look. I spent the evening with a civilized and decent young man who understands the function of respect. She is not coming into this house until she writes that letter of apology.'

The conversation ended. Thomas slept and, as always after some whiskey, snored. Ellen heard the mantel clock in the parlour strike three before she began to doze.

Munch had come home for Easter, much spryer again, as he always seemed after one of his 'holidays' in the 'hospital'. He lurked in the woods when Dennis Sykes arrived; then, like an Indian brave, long-legged Munch raced the new Wolseley as it glid through the shrubs that lined the avenue. A last dash via the walled garden and thence to the kitchen where Viva sat glueing a mug handle and – 'He's here at last,' gasped Munch.

'Who? The dandy Jim?' Viva rushed to the window. 'He is, by Jove, he is. Mother! Quick, up the stairs. Fast.'

Rhona left the hall and lurked at the top of the landing.

Dennis tugged the bell-pull, and stood admiring the view through the windbreak straight across to the Castle.

'Mother,' Viva called dulcetly, 'a gentleman to see you,' and bowed to Dennis.

Rhona then made her entrance, descending the staircase like a dowager in an opera.

'Good afternoon.'

'Mrs Ulverton, I believe?' asked Dennis.

'Credulous of you – but entirely accurate. And you? Do you have a card?'

'No. My name is –'

'I know who you are, I'll tell Mother,' said Viva. 'This is the dam builder.'

'Viva!'

'Mother,' said Viva patiently, 'the man who is building the dam, not the damn builder.'

'Hooh!' trilled Rhona. Every moment of this had been rehearsed – with Munch playing Dennis.

'Mr Sykes,' said Viva. 'Isn't it?'

'You must be having the Dickens of a time,' said Munch from near the bamboo.

'Oh, forgive him.' Rhona smiled.

Said Dennis, 'Charming house.' He gazed around.

'Yes but do you get the joke?' insisted Munch. 'Sykes, Dickens. *Oliver Twist*.'

Dennis smiled.

'Not very flattering, is it?' said Rhona.

'No, that's all right, Ma'am,' said Dennis.

'No, I mean your name, Bill Sykes. Do come in here. We use the morning-room in the afternoons, that's the way we are. *Bill Sykes*. Shall I call you "Bill"?'

177

'My name's Dennis, Ma'am. Call me Dennis.'

'No. Sit down. You're too late for tea, I'm afraid, and too early for drinks.'

Viva sat across the table and, chin on her hands and elbows on the table, looked steadily at Dennis.

'I just called,' he said, 'because I'm making it my business to meet everyone affected by the electricity's arrival.'

'Thoughtful.'

Viva said abruptly, 'I know something about you.'

'Oh?' said Dennis, turning pleasantly.

'You are – a little fucker.'

Dennis shook his head as if to clear it. 'I beg your pardon.'

'By which I mean, you're pint-sized and you fuck women.'

'What my daughter means in her inelegant way, she's known too many military men' – one smile in Rhona's repertoire fluttered like a lace handkerchief – 'is that she believes you are a seducer, Mr Sykes.'

Dennis's mouth fell open.

'You do, don't you. Yes, you do fuck, admit it?' Viva pressed with glee.

'Don't worry, Mr Sykes, don't worry, in this house we like men who like women. It's all right. "As you were, troops." Were I younger, I'd take you myself. Please don't answer because you're likely to come out with some asinine compliment and I couldn't bear it.'

'I bet you never did it in a haybarn,' said Viva, 'because you'd have thistle spines up your B-o-t-Tom. Everyone thinks haybarns are great, but that's what happens.'

'Yes, Viva, we needed the depth and width of your experience, thank you,' said Rhona. 'Now Mr Seducer Sykes, I suppose you have persuaded everyone to take your electricity?'

'Apparently not,' smiled Dennis a little recovered, but edgy.

'Ohhhh? And why not?'

'Superstition in some cases. Fear in others.'

'Who says?' asked Rhona.

'Mr Kane has been canvassing.'

'He hasn't called here,' said Rhona, 'and we haven't decided.'

Dennis reached in his briefcase. 'Well, he has spoken to me

about you, and that is in part why I am here. I have some forms here that will help.'

'*Forms* that will *help*? A contradiction in terms,' said Rhona.

'Mr Kane's idea,' said Dennis, his energy returning. 'You see, we have schemes whereby people can join, but if there's financial hardship, they can abate the payments –'

He got no further. Rhona rapped the table. 'What did you say?' She stood. Dennis looked up in alarm. Viva came and stood behind him, as tall as her mother.

'Out! Go, seducer. Leave!' Rhona glared.

He said helplessly, 'What have I said?'

'Little fucker in more ways than one,' said Viva.

Rhona snapped, 'My grandfather was at Sind. My great-grandfather co-owned the yard that built Cook's ship. Abate!'

Rhona swept from the room. Viva followed. Dennis sat alone, then rose, gathered his forms and found the front door. As he closed it behind him, he saw Munch behind the bamboo in the hall inside, waving, making a hand like a child saying, 'Bye, bye.' Rhona and Viva watched from the landing.

Dennis drove his Wolseley slowly down the drive. Inside him, in the woods, Munch ran fleet as a deer through the short-cut in the trees and, to Dennis's amazement, stood at the head of the avenue and waved good-bye again.

'Twins? No, no twins. Why do you ask?' said Thomas Kane when he and Dennis met the following night. 'A daughter and a son, that's all. No twins.'

'Well,' said Dennis, 'that is most confusing. You see, the son was standing in the hall when I left, and then a man looking exactly like him was at the gateway at the far end of the avenue when I drove out.'

Thomas smiled. 'Oh, that avenue loops quite a lot, so he simply raced through the wood in a short-cut.'

At Dennis's aggrieved look, Thomas remarked, 'Those people, they're quite – quite strange.'

As if to make up for the failed performance at the Ulvertons – and Dennis had rarely had a failed performance – he turned it on for Thomas Kane. They had met, by arrangement, at the school.

179

Dennis showed Thomas the Wolseley, let him drive it on a short spin.

'I approve. I approve,' said the teacher solemnly.

On their return, Dennis unloaded neat rolls of paper in drums. He uncoiled the first one on Thomas's high desk.

'Since you're so involved in this – it seemed only right to get your advice on one or two of the plans.'

Thomas, stiff with importance, took out his spectacle case.

'Now, this is what?' He looked at the drawings.

'This is the actual point of force, this is a cross-section.'

In one chamber of Dennis Sykes dwelt an uncontrived man, who planned, drew and executed engineering projects, who tested weight, mass, flow and energy, who led teams of other men excitedly and excitingly. From this, his only spontaneity, he made a reputation that would raise him up and up. He could not resist the challenge of imposing Man's will upon landscape, of making machinery subdue Nature. Now, still in the early reaches of his career, he pored over drawings with a country schoolteacher as enthusiastically as if he had been a student examining the works of Leonardo da Vinci. It proved to the good of his scheming that this, less calculated side of him assisted his campaign to capture utterly the support of Thomas Kane.

Before he arrived, however, he had invented a 'problem' on which he could consult the white-haired authoritarian. He wanted to flatter the man further – into thinking he had a contribution to make in matters completely beyond him.

'The difficulty,' said Dennis thoughtfully, 'is whether the fall of ground here, where the two diverted rivers will eventually meet, whether the fall of ground – at this point – will be enough to get the water through at a pace that will fill the dammed valley fast enough to meet our deadline. Because if you look here –' he produced another section. 'This is based on a geological survey of that far end.'

Thomas scrutinized.

'Now – we know we're going to blast this end,' continued Dennis, 'but there is a theory that we can only blast so far without damaging the underneath, core material. We can blast a channel, certainly, and it will be wide enough to accommodate the flow of water, but it might still be too high.'

Thomas's stern face always seemed grimmer behind the spectacle rims. He asked, 'In other words, because you can't blast as deep as you want – the water might have to climb a hill? If that's not putting it too simply?'

'Mmmm, quick grasp you have,' murmured Dennis, but did not labour it.

Thomas asked, 'And you're certain you can't blast down that far?'

'Not yet. We think so. There's one more survey. You may have seen the men, taking up cores.'

'Aha, is that what they were doing?' said Thomas.

'You must come on to the site more often,' said Dennis. 'Local knowledge is hard to come by. Of this calibre.' He almost lost the last words.

Thomas said suddenly, 'Have you thought about pumping?'

'Pumping?' Dennis lifted his head from the drawings. He looked at Thomas sideways. 'Pumping?'

Thomas showed him. 'A pumping station – just there, on that ridge. Would that be too expensive?'

'Show me?' Dennis animated.

'You know that at Shannon they pumped the water to create force. Into the Head Race,' said Thomas. 'The river is too placid otherwise.'

'Oh, my goodness, so they did,' said Dennis. 'So they did.'

The entire discussion was a set-up and a fallacy. At the far end of the Grey Valley, the limestone had proven soft enough to permit blasting safely down to any level they wished. Core sampling, a routine procedure, would go on until they ascertained that no serious flaws lay beneath the rock. This routine took place in all such projects to check for geological faults. Undiscovered underground channels could suck the two new rivers away, if the rock were blasted right through. A pumping station, therefore, had always seemed essential – but to control, rather than assist, the waters.

Yet Dennis Sykes allowed Thomas Kane to gain the impression that he had made an important contribution – to a project that had long passed this stage of planning, even before Sykes joined the team.

'Pumping,' said Dennis. 'Pumping?' He straightened and

sounded wistful. 'You should have been an engineer, Mr Kane. My late father was an engineer. And a very brilliant one, by all accounts.'

The school door clanged, and Ellen asked through the shadows, 'Thomas, is that you?'

'Come in.'

'Working without a lamp. You'll go blind, love.'

She started when she saw Dennis Sykes, who stood respectfully. Thomas introduced them again, and, more pleased than she had seen him for ages, said, 'We've just been looking over the plans for the construction, very complicated.'

'Your husband has been making some very valuable contributions,' said Dennis.

'Oh, I hope you are not straining your eyesight,' said Ellen to Thomas.

'I'm just going to take this man and give him a drink,' he replied.

'I'll run over and tell Mrs Hand,' said Ellen, moving away.

'No need, no need,' said Thomas. 'She'll know when she sees us.'

A postural stalemate began between the three people. Thomas stood and thought; she fiddled with the lapels of her coat; Dennis, hands behind his back, waited for Ellen to say something, judging the distance between him and her very carefully. He did not move his feet; he leaned a little in her direction. From Dennis, Ellen caught a faint aroma of soap, unusual on a man in Deanstown.

She opened her coat to tug down the hem of her woollen jumper, patted it into place on her hips, closed the coat again, and settled it with both hands down the front of her body: she might have been buttoning armour.

'Yes,' said Dennis eventually, 'there isn't enough light left, is there?'

'What time do you think you'll be home, Thomas?' said Ellen.

Nor did she take any notice of his saying there was no need to tell Mrs Hand. Thomas Kane did not drink in either the public bar or the saloon of any pub in this part of the world. Mrs Hand and everyone knew that. Therefore, just before he and Dennis Sykes arrived, the parlour was cleared on Ellen's instruction, and the fire stoked.

=

Like eighteenth-century gentlemen, they sat facing each other.

'Everywhere I go,' said Dennis, 'people know who you are. That couldn't happen in England.'

'Really? Is that the case?'

Dennis nodded. 'People say you were a great – hero.' He halted respectfully over the word.

'Ah!' Thomas looked into the fire. He had taken off his coat.

'I know I'm the opposite side, so to speak,' Dennis began, 'but in England we know nothing of what happened here, it was never taught to us in school.'

'What?!' said Thomas, incredulity ablaze.

'Nope. Never.' Dennis shook his head.

'But – but that's extraordinary.'

'Not a word. All we know is that twenty-six counties of Ireland became independent in 1922.'

'And the other six still shackled.' Thomas shook his head.

Dennis asked, 'If I may, the thing I'd like to ask is – what was it like for a young man like you, obviously with great potential, what was it like suddenly to take up a gun and become a guerrilla?'

From that moment, Thomas Kane finally decided to make Dennis Sykes his close friend. He began, 'I'd have to tell you the full story. I'd have to go back a little before that, my own family background, and that sort of thing.'

'Please do. Please do.' The younger man spread his hands in kind invitation. Such were the gifts that made Dennis Sykes a successful chooser and leader. He had the capacity to make a figure like Thomas Kane trust him and, in Mrs Hand's parlour, Dennis heard a view of the man's life never before spoken, unknown to Ellen or the Kane children.

Thomas began. 'I was the oldest child of a family of eleven children, and I believe my mother had three other infant losses. My father's father lived with us, and both he and my own father were men of great intelligence. But that was no good. There was no system whereby we could rise much above menial livings. My grandfather was a quiet and lovely man, said little. He had the worst of things happen to him – he was predeceased by one of his own children. Which was my father.'

Thomas paused, sipped. 'I was eleven and very tall for my age. And one day my father sent for me from the fields where he was working. We were cottiers, a big family, small cottage, usual story. My father worked as an agricultural labourer. When I got there, it was a pleasant spring day, much sunshine and the big cloud formations we get around here. My poor father was standing under a tree, all alone. He was leaning against the bark, against the trunk, his head back. Like this.' Thomas in his chair indicated with his own high head.

'He saw me coming and he smiled and beckoned me. I, for some reason, began to run. Now, my father was the nicest man who ever lived. He had a smile in his eyes for everybody. He talked to me all the time, since I was – since I can recall. Going for water to the pump, he'd take my hand. If he found an unusual shape of vegetable he'd give it to me first. He'd watch the birds nesting, so's he could show me.'

Thomas stopped to reflect.

'Jesus! Talk about maudlin,' said Dennis to Binnie. 'He told me this long rambling sob-story about his miserable family. I had to sit there and listen like a confessor.'

'Father Dennis,' she coughed, 'that would get you the girlies' secrets. Father Dennis Sykes.'

Thomas continued. 'Suddenly I found I was having to support my father's weight. He said to me, "I have to go home." And we began to walk. I don't know how I knew, but I knew it was serious.'

The drama became so inherent in Thomas's voice that Dennis leaned forward without ploy.

'We walked home, and he said to me as he sat by the fire – my mother had gone to the village, the younger children were playing around somewhere – he said to me, "Find your grandfather." He liked his father the way I liked mine.'

Suddenly Thomas broke off and looked at Dennis, 'Isn't this a bit insensitive of me? I mean, knowing that, well, your own poor father – ?'

Dennis waved a hand. 'No, I've always wanted to know about other people's fathers.'

He nodded, and Thomas carried on. 'So. My grandfather came in. He looked at my father and said to him, "Where are you complaining?" and my father said, "Here," pointing to his cheek and throat. To cut a long story short, I went for the doctor, who said he couldn't come. He told me to bring my father to him. We put him on a neighbour's cart and when we got to the doctor's surgery, we had to wait while the landlord's dog was having a splint put on its hind leg because the landlord's wife, "the Lady", as she was known, would not go to a vet, only Dr Williams would do.'

Thomas Kane paused, passed a hand over his eyes.

'Dr Williams looked at my father, said very abruptly "What's wrong with you?" My father said, "Pains, doctor," and began to show him. "I suppose you drink too much," said the doctor. "No, I don't," said my father. To cut a long story short, he said after a while, "You have cancer, it will be busiest in your jaw, you will live about four months." That's all he said.'

The teacher grew agitated. 'I helped my father out to the cart where my grandfather waited. There was no bed in the hospital, my father never even got a nurse. The doctor came to see him only once more. And I used to see that doctor driving in the gates of the house to the landlord and his wife, oh, once a fortnight. While my father rotted in front of my eyes. I never got over it. It made me silent. My children find me silent. That I know. My neighbours find me silent. And I *am* – well – silent.'

In an attitude of attentive sympathy, Dennis Sykes listened. Nobody came to the door: enough drink, as was the custom for Thomas Kane and his guests, had been provided to obviate the need for any disturbance: he had seen to that years ago, knowing the size and eavesdropping range of Mrs Hand's ears.

Thomas Kane said nothing for a long time. Then he spoke again.

'And it is that experience that more than anything else helped to make me the way I am. I should have been a – a professor. A mathematician –'

'Well, yes, I can see that –' chimed Dennis enthusiastically.

'Or, a lawyer. Not buried in this place, not teaching the three Rs to this, this –' Thomas struggled for a word. 'This hole-in-the-wall.'

12

In the ordinary scheme of things, Dennis would have used Thomas Kane as his local touchstone, as his local protection, his eyes, ears and advantage: Dennis worked that way.

That following week-end he said, 'Binnie – you can only call me heroic. I mean, I listened. I actually listened. With some attention, I may say. To his boring, boring, droning story.'

'Little Dennis, darling, I've been thinking about you. You're all ulterior and no interior.'

'No, Binnie. I need the fellow. I have to stomach him.'

What Dennis did not yet know was the degree to which he would suddenly, urgently require Kane. He had not necessarily chosen the most effective local representative: Dennis, being an outsider, should have selected someone closer to the people, some-one who heard things – not a man from whom the locals shied away. And there would be things to hear – as Dennis only discovered on his return from his seasick-making 'relief' week-end in London.

He drove back to Deanstown in foul weather, on the bad roads. Early on Monday morning he visited the site, to find that the men had stopped work on the main infrastructural artery: 'Aah, too wet, Sir, sure you couldn't get a duck to work in weather like this.' From under the trees they gazed happily to the dark-grey skies and leaned on their shovels.

Sensibly, he realized he would have to raise their wages: fortu-nately, the international funds were about to flow. He telephoned Dublin – but heard something else.

Dennis spoke to Dublin three times a day: from the Post Office in Mooreville: his own telephone had not yet been 'rushed in'.

'I don't quite get what you're saying. You'll have to interpret the signs for me,' called Dennis down the crackling line. 'Serious or not?'

'Not unserious,' said Mr Quinlan.

'Is there a balance that can be tipped?' yelled Dennis.

Mr Quinlan, who somehow seemed not to have to shout, replied, 'Well, as you know, I'm not an alarmist.'

Cried Dennis, 'What will they do?'

'There will be a letter in tomorrow's papers, apparently,' said Mr Quinlan. 'We'll confer again. Once you've seen it.'

'Do you know what the letter says?' called Dennis, mindful of listeners outside the call-booth.

'I can give you a whiff of gist.'

Dennis listened, and sucked a vicious 'Dtthh.'

'Can you get those telephone people moving?' called the irritated Dennis.

'Strategy: to commandeer irrevocably TK's support.' Dennis looked sideways at the quick note he wrote. 'Does TK know?' he scribbled – does he know that his own blasted daughter Grace Kane had left her teaching position to organize a Grey Valley Campaign?

'A fast mover too,' said Mr Quinlan in his whiff of gist.

He told Dennis's ear that so far she had enrolled the help of a historian from University College, Dublin, two from University College, Cork (one of whom had been born in the Grey Valley), a couple of scientists from Trinity College, and the Deputy Director of the Natural History Museum.

'Yes, I'd say they're what you'd call medium important,' considered crackling Mr Quinlan; he pronounced it 'meejum'.

Grace guessed she needed a year. 'NN-mmm,' she nodded. 'A year's leave of absence. It will take a year. Or so. N-m.' She smiled like an attacker.

'What are you going to live on?'

Grace said, 'Um.'

'Your father's not going to help, surely?'

'Dlok,' clicked Grace with her tongue. 'Probably not,' she said.

'I can see your passion for it, though, and I'm a great believer in letting passion have a run for its money. Let me think. We'll talk tomorrow.'

Next lunch-time, Grace went to see her headmistress again.

'Well?' she pounced.

The Principal never ate the crusts on her sandwiches; she piled

187

them like little planks all over the place. 'If you're fighting for these people – I'm assuming they want you to fight for them?'

'Oh, they do, they do,' said Grace.

'Grace, are you extending the truth?'

'No! Look –' Grace began to justify.

Miss MacNamara put up two restraining yet submitting hands.

'All right, Grace, all right, all right. I can tell that the hordes of Hy-Brasil wouldn't stop you. Goodness, you're like your mother.' Grace grinned.

'Practicalities?' asked the Principal. 'The food in your mouth, the roof over your head?'

'Oh!' Grace animated. 'I hadn't thought of that.' And she solved it swiftly. 'I could stay with that woman I was telling you about, Mrs Stokes, she has no one.'

'And she wouldn't be too hard on you in terms of what she'd charge you?'

Grace said, 'Oh, no. She'd now be very glad of the company.'

The Principal, tearing off a soft perforation of bread, said, 'I can't, you know of course, give you full pay for a year off. Matter of fact, I can't give you any pay for a year off. The Department wouldn't have it.'

Grace waited. Miss Mac's chewing would stop one day. It did.

'But if you'll agree, I'll mix things a little. And this is what I'll do. If you continue to take the adult classes four times a week. And you can do two on one night, if that suits, I'll be able to manage to put you on three-quarters pay.'

Grace clapped her hands.

'Ah. Ah. Provided. Provided.'

Grace had already complied in her own mind with whatever the Principal would demand.

'Provided – when all this is over, you guarantee to teach here for at least two years. And. And. In that two years, you do the adult classes free until you make up the three-quarters pay I'm giving you. It may even be up to three years, I haven't worked it out.'

Grace said, 'Oh, ye-ssss, Miss MacNamara, I will, I will. I promise.'

The Principal said, 'Well – I know you will.'

Grace left the room – and was called back.

'Grace, do you know where you're going to get the money for this campaign of yours.'

'Money?' said Grace.

'Yes, posters and train fares – you'll have to go to meetings. You'll have to see people. They'll have to come and see you. All of that.'

'Oh.' Grace stopped.

'It's okay, it's okay. There is a fund in this school,' said Miss MacNamara, 'not very large, but never called on and entirely at my discretion. You know the photograph in the hall?'

'John Francis Clancy?' asked Grace.

'He left money for what he called "Civic Projects". He left it for the education of the children who wanted to find out how their country worked. Very loose rules, really. It's a bursary. I administer it.'

Grace ooh-ed.

Miss MacNamara said, 'I'll start you off with fifty pounds.'

'That's a fortune, Miss Mac.'

'You have to keep an account of every penny, receipts, everything.'

'I'm not going to have enough thanks in me,' said Grace.

Said the Principal. 'If you're seriously doing drawings of your precious Valley, I'd love a drawing of one of those fiddle-fronted dressers.'

'Oh, I'll do you a water-colour!' cried Grace.

'One last question. Your parents. What do they think?'

Grace said without a blush, 'Oh, you know what they're like.'

The letter had beneath it, 'We would welcome correspondence on this subject. Ed.'

Dear Sir,

We the undersigned wish to draw attention to a scheme being undertaken by the National Electricity Board, who propose to drown the renowned Grey Valley of Deanstown for the purpose of building a hydro-electric dam. The Grey Valley is an area of outstanding natural beauty, with major fossil resources, unusual botanical life and a considerable depth of

189

natural, built-in homecraft. It contains, for example, the last fiddle-fronted dressers and settles handmade onsite in this country: some of them are over three hundred years old and have been in constant use since before Cromwell.

Many of the residents do not wish to leave their ancestral homes, and their lives have become very distressed since the unilateral announcement – with minimum consultation – of this project. No alternative possibility seems to have been considered.

The undersigned seek the support of the nation in the preservation of The Grey Valley and we would ask all interested parties to convene outside Hand's public house in Deanstown on Sunday, 19 April for a march to the Grey Valley. At a rally, several of the undersigned and other dignitaries will speak. Funds to support this campaign will be gratefully welcomed.
signed:
Grace Kane, Campaign Co-Ordinator.
co-signed:
Thos. Considine, dept Botany, University College, Dublin.
Edward Cassells, dept Geology, Trinity College, Dublin.
Michael Edwards, Natural History Museum.
Elizabeth Miller, dept History & Folkore, University
   College, Dublin,
Anthony MacNamee, dept History, University College,
   Cork.
Michael Phelan, Folklore Commission.

Helena waved her arms and said with a feeble face, 'She has been given some leave of absence, Daddy. I don't know how much.'

Thomas shouted, 'What is she trying to do, embarrass us? Make us all look like fools in public?'

Ellen said, 'Let us get some more knowledge. Helena, can you ask Gracey –'

'The girl's name is Grace!' said Thomas. 'What more knowledge do we need? There she is in black-and-white.' He rapped the paper ferociously with the backs of his fingers. 'Where is she now? Where is she? "We the undersigned. Campaign Co-Ordinator." I'll give her Campaign Co-Ordinator.'

He caught Helena's arm: Ellen intervened, persuaded away his grip.

'Thomas, Helena doesn't know. I'll go and find Grace.'

The talk spumed, high as a hot geyser. In Hand's, the newspaper floated along the counter from drinker to drinker, accompanied by words such as 'comeuppance' and 'his high horse'.

Thirty miles away in Janesborough, the Winers read it at breakfast: Herbert always read the letters column first.

'Can there be another Grace Kane?' Leah derisively echoed Herbert's enquiry. 'Of course that's Grace. But I feel for Ellen. Caught in the middle again.'

'You don't understand that man,' said her husband mildly. 'He suffers. He suffers inside.'

'I understand that he makes everyone around him suffer,' snapped Leah.

Everyone who knew the Kanes had an opinion, took a position.

'No, Miriam,' said Jack Hogan. 'No, we won't march in that.'

'You're forgetting, Jack, that I was there. I was the one who got that man to London for his surgical operation. Has he ever as much as said a single word of thanks?'

'Miriam, where did you put the eggs?'

'And as for your trying to say the man may not even know I was in London, be that as it may, Jack, and it will be if life is true to form, it doesn't put a stopper in the fact that he thinks he's above everyone.'

'Ah, Miriam, these eggs are gone bad, look, their yolks are gone black. But sure – what matter?' said Jack with ease.

Last night in bed, for some strange and unspoken reason, Miriam had turned and taken his hand and placed it on her neck and kissed him on the mouth, a kiss fifteen years late but no less welcome for that: 'No less welcome, Miriam.'

Off the Janesborough bus, Grace cycled the last miles from Mooreville to the Grey Valley. By the southern road she went, avoiding Deanstown and her father's eagle eye through the school windows.

As she reached the climb, she learned how fast things moved on big projects. On the high far end, where the rivers would flood in, great lorries moved slowly up on the ridge like saurians. Their

191

engine sounds, revving and slipping, rasped down towards her on the breeze. She turned the last bend to the Valley entrance, and in the other direction saw only the ring fence: no sign of the first excavations for the foundations of the dam wall.

So far, Dennis had initiated these works with a delicate air. He stayed away from the interior. No engine snarled on the Valley floor; only the wind agitated the trees. Although he had prowled the Valley from stem to stern, usually in the white light of dawn, he already knew that limit where molestation would begin. Oh – if he could build the entire thing as cleanly as possible. If he could just slide the dam wall across the mouth, and softly open the channel at the far end. And in the course of it all, let the Grey Valley continue to sit silent.

Problems: problems. He strategized through the nights like a boffin. Would the compensation plus the re-housing remove the objections by the actual residents of the Valley? If so, since they were his biggest threat, one potentially huge problem would evaporate. Before this campaign was mooted, he had figured on buying off the objecting Valley dwellers with a nudge up the compensatory scale, a nudge he would 'sell' to them. After which, the botanists, the historians, the geologists could be invited, openly and with small grants, to pay their last respects. Museum staff could take what they wished from the houses. Acknowledge the people's old furniture: emboss their names on the little museum plaques: all to be done quietly and constantly over a year: everything damped down, with Thomas Kane co-ordinating.

Then – flood the Valley and make the flooding dramatic, make it poetic. Invite the community to stand on the rim of the Valley and watch it filling in. They would drive, he said slickly to Mr Quinlan, from their new houses in the new cars their compensation had bought. He reasoned further that the natural shape of the landscape, the big lips of the valley behind the deep woods, helped him to conceal work-in-progress. He was right.

'Girl, I can't understand it,' said Mollie Stokes to Grace. 'There isn't a sound here, the place is as silent as the grave except for them few lorries at the far end.' She called them 'lurries'.

'Listen, Mrs Stokes, can I stay with you?' said Grace. 'Is that all right?'

192

'The company'll be lovely for me. I'm not right in myself since.'

'Did anyone come to see you?' asked Grace.

'No, girl, only that strange creature and she walking like a heron, you know her, that Protestant woman from over near your house, and her daughter with her.'

Grace took off her scarf, shook her hair. 'Oh – the Ulvertons. What did they say?'

Mrs Stokes said, 'They said I should fight to keep what was mine, that nothing in the world can buy the past.'

'And what did you say?'

'I agreed with them. But sure why wouldn't I?'

'And,' asked Grace, 'nobody from the electricity company?'

'No, girl, not soul nor sinner.'

'And,' asked Grace, 'you say there's no work hardly to be seen going on? At least nothing as much as you'd expect?'

'Child,' replied Mrs Stokes, 'there's nearly nothing.'

Grace said, 'Yippee! Maybe we've stopped them. I knew it, I knew it! I knew we could do it! Well, they didn't have much fight in them! Oh, Mrs Stokes, I think I'll run out and have a good look.'

Mrs Stokes's house stood near the Valley's entrance. Grace took the route she and Helena knew best, cutting up the lower slopes, through the early brush, until she came out on the first slides of shale that led to this part of the rim. On top grew thick hazel, arbutus, some aspens. Here they first saw the vixen and her cubs, even saw the dog-fox bring home a slain baby rabbit.

Thomas had said, 'Tell the farmers about those foxes. Chickens are getting killed.' The girls did not.

Grace stepped slowly down through the heavy groves. Cycling jolted her bladder, and she squatted in the ferns, inspecting carefully for nettles: this always made Helena laugh.

As a small child Grace always believed that the under-earth teemed with people – cities, schools, farms. Not on the same human scale, ten sizes down, she said to Ellen, who never discouraged. To please her mother, Grace added, 'And churches, Mama, and cathedrals. You can see the crowds going into Mass.'

As she crouched now, she saw though a gap in the ferns something which glinted. For a split moment she returned to that pleasing childhood belief. Far below – this was the highest point in the valley – a huge construction site had indeed begun to take form:

some toy huts, several toy trucks, toy men moving. Grace yanked up her knickers, and rushed to the edge of the ferns. From here, you could see for miles; when the light was right you could even catch the weir. Beyond the woods, a tranche of the old commonage had been thickened with works: high wafers of planking; bins; a fence; a tall gate. It seemed, from where Grace stood, as if the people who dwelt beneath the ground had come to the surface at last, and had begun to conduct some concealed and sinister undertaking.

Mrs Stokes asked, 'But tears isn't going to improve all that, girl?'

Grace said, 'But I thought that letter might have stopped them. And that was why you weren't hearing any real work. I thought the lorries we saw were only for show.' She dried her eyes, and held up the letter in the *Irish Independent*.

'Read it to me, my eyes aren't that good the day.'

Grace read.

'A power of names,' said Mrs Stokes. 'A power of names.'

Grace regained her self-control and began to settle in. Mrs Stokes said, 'The room to the west' of the thick-walled house. From a deep woodlined alcove hidden by heavy curtains they pulled down the wall-bed.

'No draught of air in there, girl,' said Mrs Stokes, 'you'll be warmer than at a fire.'

Grace took off her shoes, lay on the bed, looking at the little carved embossed stars on the 'roof' of the bed. The bed-hangings, all handmade, had rich soft embroidery in yellows and blues.

'The county colours,' said Mrs Stokes. 'Blue and gold. And d'you see that patchwork? Four generations of women worked that. 'Tis blankets as well as a quilt.'

She folded it back to show Grace how the work had been built in cosy tiers. Under the dressy cover, each layer could unbutton from the next for seasonal adjustment.

'Your mother now'd love that,' Mrs Stokes said to Grace.

Acrid, pleasing smoke crept in, from the wood on the kitchen fire next door.

Ellen, in affection, reserved Grace's name from Thomas. But she did generate a quiet discussion with Helena. Was there more to this campaign than Grace's usual gift for drama? For example, was there someone 'putting her up to all this'?

Honesty compensated for Helena's timidity. She answered Ellen's myriad questions comfortably. About Grace's art classes; about the books Grace read; about Grace's view of Thomas. All questions came up quietly, not to judge or blame Grace, but to gauge her sincerity, her commitment. Ellen nodded as Helena explained patiently.

'I mean, Mama, don't think I'm getting at anyone, but there were times when the Valley was the only peaceful place on earth.'

Ellen made sympathetic noises and faces. 'I think, Helena love, I'll go and talk to her.'

Even the disliked people of the parish liked Ellen Kane – the Hands, the Burnses, the Brownes, the Cronins, sloppy people, leeches. They said she had 'even hands, she was fair'. Their children experienced no differentiation in the school. Ellen addressed her teaching duties as she did her marriage: richer or poorer, sickness and health. Oh, yes, get on her wrong side and you felt the blisters. If unfair she apologized; compare that, they said, to her husband whose lips had no shape for the word 'sorry'. With that woman you were the same as everyone else, no grudges, until you merited otherwise.

This row between her daughter and her husband disturbed Ellen, jarred the locus of her home. She had explained away or ascribed all other crises variously: blame, for instance, that past 'difficulty' in Thomas's life – followed, when he recovered, by the economic tensions of a big family, exacerbated by the uncertainty of harsh economic and political facts under a bad leader, the headstrong and devious de Valera.

So she spoke to herself, so she reasoned; and through all of this, and through the grim recurring daytime silences of her husband, Ellen Kane ran a good life, and in general outpaced the constrictions upon her. Rhona Ulverton, her confidante, had been such a help; how they talked; how they concluded with, always, a decision taken upon action for the best.

Now, sitting quietly with her housekeeping ledger, she kept doodling mad, interlocking, repeating, question marks.

When Helena came home for the week-end, she sent her with

a pot of soup in the handlebar basket of the bicycle to see Mrs Ulverton.

'Tell her I want to see her. Any word of Grace?' whispered Ellen in the back-kitchen, shooing away Hugh who listened to everything.

'No. I thought you were going over to see her?'

'I'm trying to work a way of doing it without your father knowing.'

Helena whispered, 'Is he still – ?'

'More than ever.' As she heard footsteps, Ellen raised her voice to normal mode, 'And be sure to tell her there's no need to send the saucepan back immediately, we're not in any hurry with it.' But it was one of the boys, whose footsteps sounded so much like Thomas's.

All news of Grace and her activities reached the Kanes as if by homing pigeons.

Always obliquely. Nobody ever said, 'Oh, I hear your daughter is going round putting up posters in all the pubs.'

They said, 'God, Mrs Hand is a fierce woman. She won't put up that poster. Sure, what's wrong with a poster, don't she put up posters for the circus, or for the thistle, ragwort and dock? I s'pose she's afraid of losing all that business from the workmen.'

Another woman remarked to Ellen, 'I think 'tis a shame them workmen going round tearing down them posters, I mean we all have our right to object to something.'

Thomas knew Grace had been in Mooreville, knocking on people's doors; had bought an advertisement in the *Nationalist* for the meeting; had booked seven people into the Royal Hotel; was even expecting two people from London, a reporter and a photographer.

'Does she mean to make a total disgrace of us to the whole world?' fumed Thomas.

In face of this anger, Ellen did not go, but wrote,

> My dearest Gracey,
> I know you're busy – because we hear about you!
> All I'm worried about is your health, that you're getting enough food and rest, and that you aren't making enemies.

196

I know you don't want to come home because of you and
Daddy (who is well, thank God, as are all the others, Hugh
getting as fat as a fool from eating as usual, but he's at that
age). But I would love to meet you if you like.

Remembering you in my prayers always,

Your loving,

Mama.

When Helena reached the top of the Ulvertons' avenue, she
saw Grace's bicycle against the pillars of the colonnade. They met
in the hallway, and each said sweetly, 'Hallo, what are you doing
here?' No touching, no handshakes even: the Kanes rarely made
physical contact of affection.

'Mama sent me with soup.'

Grace laughed, and peered into the saucepan. 'I'll never guess
– chicken and red lentils. Auntie Leah's recipe.'

Helena smiled. 'No, you'd never guess. But c'mon now, what
are you doing here?'

'Enlisting supporters. How's home?'

'Mama's fine. She bought a lovely skirt in Hassett's Sale, sort
of black herringbone pattern. Dad's like a –' Helena stopped.

'A fiend, a demon, a raging devil, a dervish, a bear with a sore
head, a bull in a china shop –' Grace was enumerating on her
fingers when Rhona called.

'Don't stand whispering in the hall like a pair of excited nuns,
come in here!'

She lay on a chaise-longue, in the morning-room, her back to
the light, clad in yellow and burgundy and gold.

'Helena, dear. Here to help your sister, I hope? We have all
kinds of schemes, don't we, dear?' – to Grace. 'India or China tea?'

Both, uncertainly, said they would prefer China tea.

'Milk and sugar?' – and they both nodded: Rhona said, 'One
doesn't have milk and sugar in China tea.'

Helena sat beneath a bamboo plant that had now somehow taken
root within the wall. Grace took the other side of Rhona, and
Munch drifted up and down the room, talking half to himself and
half to his mother. Viva did not appear for several minutes,
and when she did, her face wore a thick creamy covering, some
kind of beauty treatment. She sat without comment.

Rhona hummed various tunes without finishing any bar of them; she also answered Munch's cross-talk. The table wore a wild cloth, red and blue spangles, painted elephants, tasselled, sequinned howdahs; the cups, large and shallow, seemed made of chintzed ivory.

Munch fumbled again and again in his crotch, sometimes with both hands at the front, and each time he did, Rhona gave a loud cough, then clicked her rings in a ching of embarrassment, and beamed at the girls.

Viva, lips immobilized with beauty cream, tapped Grace urgently on the elbow, making her start. When Grace looked up at her, Viva took Grace's hand and laid it on the sugarbowl, then indicated herself by prodding her own bosom. Grace divined Viva's intent and handed her the sugar. Viva took a cube, and, head back, popped it in her open mouth.

Rhona raised a hidden corner of the tablecloth, found a name-tag embroidered on it and held it aloft silently to Helena and Grace. She underlined the name – Rhona Mercury Wallace – with her long fingernail, whose varnish matched the hint of rouge on her cheekbones. Moments later she took her walking-cane, silently compared its elephant-head with the elephants on the tablecloth, and smiled at each girl in turn.

At that moment Munch made a dive for the door and Viva rose so quickly to stop him, that she dragged some of the cloth and spilled a little of all their teas. Munch subsided into an armchair. When Viva returned to the table, Rhona remarked, her eyes dark with concern, 'We have, as you will note, been having our little problems.'

'Mamma!'

'Are they blind, Viva?' and she continued tenderly, 'Viva, darling, you caused this. I told you that you must not tease him, and you must never appear again in front of him undressed. Not ever.'

'He is certifiable, Mamma. Why is he out?' pleaded Viva, trying to speak through the smothers of face-gunk.

'He's a dear boy [Munch was forty-seven]. Now, girls.'

Rhona sat back and drew her walking-cane to her, held the elephant's head between her knees.

'Did you find me diffident today? In certain parts of India tea loses its spiritual efficacy unless taken in some silence. Am I right in thinking you are almost exactly two years apart in age?'

Grace smiled, always the first to speak. 'Nm.'

'And you know about Love? Viva, darling, where are you going?'

'Mother, I've heard you on Love before.'

'You can hear it again. Stay.'

Viva stayed.

'Have men come sniffing yet?' asked Rhona.

The Kane girls looked at each other and smiled. Never kissed nor kissing; never read romances in magazines; the grip of the household had closeted them even from popular songs. When they left home, they were further sheltered. In Helena's Domestic Economy College, socializing with men was forbidden, and in Grace's Teacher Training, the girls took baths in their swimsuits.

Rhona said, 'Stand up each of you. Yes. They will be sniffing like hounds around you two. You, Helena, have the looks a certain sort of man likes, the type who likes a thin girl with a big bust. I, too, was most fortunate. Turn round.'

Helena stood with her back to Rhona.

'I see. And you, my dear,' she said to Grace. 'Turn round too. Yes, I thought so. Lovely creatures. You two will have so many men to choose from. So many. And all must be for love, none of this "good values" stuff, or any of that.'

In the armchair Munch held his hands in the air like wings and began to weep.

'Dear boy! Are you all right?' asked Rhona compassionately; coping with her disconcertment, she turned to the girls again, and tried to shut out the scene across the room.

'I know what I am saying must be heresy, heresy compared to what you have been told at home, at school and at college, but what is life without heresy? And here is another bit of heresy, because now you must go. I think, I really do believe, that no Irishman you will meet will be sophisticated enough to appreciate either of you girls. Viva, do something about that would you? The poor boy's like an animal.'

Munch had sprawled disgracefully wide on the armchair, scratching vigorously.

'So look to the world,' declaimed Rhona, smiling at them, 'look to the wider world for your soulmates and you will be less disappointed, and the wider world will receive a bonus. Those teeth and those beautiful limbs you both have! And your eyes, and your colouring, blue with blond hair, and brown with black hair? Ohhh!'

She held out her hands, one to each. 'So lovely of you to come and see me. I shall be watching for whatever swain you produce, and I will approve or otherwise.'

She released Grace, gripped Helena tighter.

'One last thing, my dear. Are you living in mortal, daily terror of everything – your father, the Roman Catholic Church, the forces of darkness, the Man in the Moon, your own shadow? Ah!'

Grace began an intervention on Helena's behalf: Rhona held up a hand to interrupt.

'Listen to me, Helena, child. You are named after one of the greatest women the world has ever known. Helen of Troy. But not yet Helen of Deanstown are you? You're a sweet girl. And you can be brave. Your mother loves you, loves you both. I know. She tells me. But do you know what's at stake here? Do you know what heroics your sister is performing?'

Helena stood abashed.

Rhona continued. 'If this country is to have any future, people must object. Object.'

Grace said nothing, looked at Helena anxiously – who said nothing either.

'What's the matter with you, Helena? Speak, speak to me.'

'I don't know what to say,' replied Helena.

'Well,' said Rhona kindly, 'you could make a comment. On the validity of what I've just said. Or you could say, "I admire hugely what my sister is doing and it's time I got stuck into it too. And helped her." You now have an Easter holiday, your sister has this rally to organize, and she's trying to do it on her own. Go on, go and live with her in that old woman's house in the Valley, and try to keep some standards in this blasted land. Stop letting your father destroy your life.'

'Helena,' said Grace, hands out, expiating, 'I said nothing.'

'Didn't need to,' said Rhona, 'a clown could see it, Munch could see it – the talk of the bloody place, that man's arrogance. He's worse than a bloody bishop – an RC bishop, I mean. I adore your mother, give her my love. Give her my fondest love.'

=

200

Walking down the avenue, Helena said to Grace, 'Did you understand one word of that?'

'No!' and they laughed and laughed.

'What's a swain?' asked Helena.

'A posh version of pig?' suggested Grace. 'Swine. Swain.'
They laughed again.

Grace said, 'What are you going to do?'

'I think. I think –' Helena grimaced. 'I'll come with you.'

'Wheeeeee!' Grace danced.

So far as Ellen consciously knew, Helena departed that night for
her own habitual accommodation. Yet, as she waved her daughter
good-bye, something troubled Ellen. An untypical furtiveness in
Helena? Why did she suddenly take those heavy knitteds with her,
so bulky in a bicycle's basket? Also, she had said so little about
her meeting with Grace, brought minimal news of Rhona. Helena
usually told everything: so, why did she seem evasive, uneasy?
The queries rolled over and back inside Ellen's brain, over and
back.

On the Wednesday afternoon of that week, Ellen lied to Thomas,
said she was going to call on Mrs Martin Burke. Instead, she cycled
to the Grey Valley. She told herself that she hoped to meet Grace:
she suspected more, but knew not what.

Dennis Sykes, working with two surveyors on top of a crest,
saw her. He stared into his binoculars until she disappeared into
the woods, then anticipated that she would reappear on the upper
line, a mile from the Valley's entrance. The two surveyors had not
seen Ellen Kane – but Dennis, excusing himself, set off in pursuit;
he crashed through the trees, down the incline.

She had her head down, exerting, pushing her bicycle up the steep
slope when he walked through the high ferns, apparently lost in
thought.

'Oh!' Both started: he transmitted extensive surprise and
stopped. 'Hallo!'

'Oh, hallo – Mr Sykes.' They halted, and stood each other off
on the ridge. Dennis pointed down – to the growing construction
plant far below.

'Have you come to have a look? You should have come round

to the site. What do you think? Great, isn't it?' He held his hand out as if promising her all the land she could see.

Ellen gazed, did not speak.

Dennis insisted: 'It is pretty marvellous, isn't it?'

'I'd no idea it was so –'

'Massive. And yet it is a small project.' He turned to her, hoping to dazzle. 'It's Ellen, isn't it?' He nodded. 'At least I think it is, your husband keeps referring to you as "my wife". But I seem to remember it's Ellen. Is this your first time up here?'

'Oh, no, Mr Sykes, we used to come here all the time, I mean, I didn't come that often. The girls did.'

'Ah, yes. The girls. How old are they?'

'Oh, I don't know why I still call them girls, they're young women now. Helena is almost twenty-six and Grace is twenty-four.' Ellen spoke as if to herself, tried not to look too much at him.

'I'm told,' said Dennis Sykes, 'that they're as pretty as their mother.'

Ellen had never heard herself called 'pretty'. Obliquer terminology prevailed in the countryside: 'an eyeful'; or, 'easy on the eye'. More usually, compliments came by comparison: 'I'll say this much for you, Ma'am, you're not a bit like Nellie Cunningham' – who had extensive whiskers, and a goitre the size of a myth.

To Dennis Sykes's compliment, 'I don't know about that,' said Ellen diffidently. Then she warmed. 'But they're nice girls. Well-behaved. And they're well-liked.'

'And I suppose Mother's cycling over to see that they're both settled in well?' Just a pleasant sense of enquiry.

Ellen, fast as lightning, said 'Both? No, Grace is over here, only.'

Dennis put on his quizzical look. 'Oh? Forgive me, Ellen, I've a'hm –'

Ellen's face became a question, which he answered.

'Is your oldest daughter, is she the one with the lovely long hair, blonde? I know the other girl has your colouring?'

Ellen faced him. 'You mean Helena's here?'

'If that's her name. She came two nights ago, no, Saturday. I know it seems like we're spying. But we have to find out everything that's going on.'

'My husband doesn't know Helena's here, I mean –'

'You mean you did not know until this minute? Until I told you? Oh, no! I'm sorry. Sorry.'

Dennis stood beside Ellen. Ellen looked distressed, and he said, 'Look, this is none of my business, and yet it is my business. And I feel I can help in some way –'

No reply: he let a pause grow: he continued, 'I've come to admire your husband hugely, he is a remarkable man – he has told me so much about himself. His experiences and that. His family. He's even going to take me back to where he grew up.'

How often had the children complained that they knew so little about their father's family; how often had they been bitter that they met their father's likeable brothers so rarely. Ellen, who had seen the siblings together before Thomas 'changed', as she described it to herself, wondered whether he avoided his brothers because with them Thomas dropped his guard. She suppressed her sad rancour on the matter, looked at Dennis Sykes quizzically, and said nothing.

'And I really would do anything I can to help.' He gauged her all the time, looked at her forehead, her ears, her neck.

'Now there's this meeting coming up, this big rally, that your daughter Grace is organizing. I should imagine it is a matter of great pain to her father.'

She tried insisting. 'But my husband says very little about himself, Mr Sykes.'

'No. Oh, no. You're wrong, if I may say so. He says it to me. And he does talk all the time about how all of this is upsetting him –'

Ellen looked at him hard and doubtingly.

Dennis remarked, 'You may not know this, but – men, you know. Well – they often tell each other things that they don't tell their wives.'

Seeing his lack of impact, sensing that a retreat might prove strategic, he modified. 'All good men like confidentiality. And great men need more than most.'

Ellen opened her mouth to say something, then closed it again.

'What were you going to say?' he asked quickly.

'Nothing.' She looked at him and changed her mind. 'When are you meeting my husband again?'

'This evening, as it happens,' and then Dennis Sykes trapped her into collusion. 'I won't say a word to him about meeting you like this. Okay? I mean on account of Helena. On account of this – this difficult new development.'

He smiled and held out his hand. Ellen shook it: again the fingers lurking in her palm; again, he held on for too long.

'Very nice meeting you alone, and in such a lovely place,' he said crisply, much too skilled ever to stray into smarm.

Despite herself she blushed.

Dennis remained on the heights, gazing down. First, he watched the swing of her buttocks as she walked to the path. He whipped his binoculars to his eyes as she hiked her thigh to the bicycle saddle on the roadway below. Why did she did not go to Mollie Stokes's house? Anticipate, Dennis, anticipate: reflect upon this new development – he knew that Kane would call it his daughter's 'defection'. What next, Dennis, what next? Can this family be turned upon itself to stop this idiotic protest? Wife doesn't seem susceptible: she must be made so. By whatever means.

Later that night, Dennis enquired, elbow to elbow with his principal road ganger, a man of great ears.

'That, ah'm, Mrs Kane?' The foreman listened and rubbed a lobe.

Dennis wondered aloud, 'Is she – she younger or older? Than she looks, I mean?'

'Ah, older, yeh.' The foreman wore a jacket over dungarees.

'Fresh, so?'

'Ah, yeh. She'd be rising fifty nearly. Else!' He called the woman. 'Else, your man Kane's missus, how long now is she here?'

Else Campion, with one tooth bucked, scratched her apron's strap. 'I know. For Joe had that dog, d'you 'member that good dog, we had, Saffron Stranger, d'you 'member, Liam?'

'An' didn't I make money outa him itself,' said Liam the foreman. 'Saffron Stranger, the very lad,' and turned explanatorily to Dennis. 'He was a coursing dog, like. And light, don't you know, for his size. And in wet going, oh, a pure bullet, wasn't he, Else?'

'He was so.'

Else never grew after the age of ten. On quiet evenings she stood on a crate behind the bar of Keaney's in the village of Silverbridge, conversing over her elbows on the counter; when she stepped down, she vanished and strangers became disconcerted.

'And that'd make her, that Mrs Kane, that'd make her have come here in 'twenty-four, no, I tell a lie, that'd be 'twenty-five, that's right, you can count it yourself sure.' She yelled, 'I'm comin' Jimmy!' She lowered the voice, 'And they said at the time there was twenty-two years between them, I don't know for a fact, like, but the Canon over there, he had the birth certs, sure he'd have to for the wedding. And Kane was over double her age at the time, and if he was forty-four – so she'd be fifty. I'd say forty-nine for my own satisfaction, say.'

Liam gathered a huge ear in a hand and folded it. 'Aw, the fuck, hoh?' He murmured in wonder. 'Forty-fuckin'-nine? The wonders of the world.' The pliable ear comforted his hand.

'Fresh! Fresh!' said an amazed Dennis.

'Grand arse with it,' said Liam, who had divined, if never witnessed, his Chief Engineer's principal leisure. 'An arse you'd take home with you.' He spoke as slowly as a grave and lewd druid. 'Not that anybody'd ever, like. Drop the hand with her. And them dugs on her. She always had them, though, ever before the children.'

Dennis probed. 'Of course, Irish girls . . . ?'

'Ah, no, ah, no.' Liam rushed to defend whatever pliability he had found in the womenfolk he had met. 'Some are great sport. I knew a Roche woman. Where I was working the job-before-last. Two or three mediums of stout and she was the one'd be hauling you into the long grass on the way home. But there's other women and they thinks they pisses holy water.'

'Like, ah'm, Mrs Kane?'

'She keeps her hand on her ha'penny and the other on her beads. Don't she, Else?' he called, but tiny Else Campion had not returned to earshot. 'Oh, listen, sure Kane, he was to retire. And he wouldn't. He's going on an extension, don't you know? Else!?'

Else returned.

'Wadn't Kane for retirement?' Liam asked.

'He wor so, you're right dere.' Else made an 'O' in wonder. 'He wor to retire and he sixty-five, and they gev him an extension 'til sixty-eight, and the Canon said he wor to have another extension 'til seventy-one. That must be nearly up.'

Dennis pulled a mouth. 'He's a very fresh man for his age.'

'He is so,' said Else, 'sure the temper he have, 'tis that do keep him alive.'

Suddenly, Helena stiffened.

'What?' asked Grace, and rushed to the window thinking Helena had seen or heard something. The taller girl shook her head.

'No. Sorry. I mean.' Sometimes, her smile never developed fully. 'No, nobody there. Just, a shiver. A shiver of a feeling.'

Grace let the lace curtain fall from the cottage window.

'Someone walked over your grave?' she asked.

'Yes. Yes.' Helena held both hands to her mouth, a praying gesture.

'Hellie, look at this, I mean – only look!'

Like a builder, Grace ran her hands along the shelving of the deep window-sill and traced it into the shuttering, her water-clear fingernail following the natural grain of the wood. 'Look! I'm on the trail!'

'Trail?'

'Yes! Yes! I'm on the trail of the ghost! The ghost of the carpenter who made this! Look, Hellie! Did you ever see such a kind pair of hands?'

Grace opened out the old shutters, as Mollie Stokes came in.

'Oh, Mrs Stokes, did you ever see such lovely work, and look if you open this here –' she pointed to a weakening section of the frame. 'Nobody else has touched this wood since he made it?'

Mrs Stokes nodded. 'He was famous at it, a man called Michael Banim. Not from here, a Wexford man, but he made for everyone around the place.'

'What year was that?' asked quick Grace.

'Others were that few years earlier, but this house. It'd be what? About the year fifteen-fifteen they say. Or sixteen.'

'What?!'

Even Helena said it, if milder. 'What? As long ago as that?'

Grace calculated. 'Two from six is four. Nine from eleven is two. Subtract fourteen-ninety-two from fifteen-sixteen, that's what I'm doing, Hellie, that'd say that this house was built only twenty-four years after Christopher Columbus discovered America – dear God!'

Mrs Stokes smiled. 'Are you all right here now, girls, the two of you? Are you warm enough?'

Helena nodded, as Grace continued wondering aloud and fondling the wood of the shutters – 'Fifteen-sixteen? Fifteen-sixteen.'

When Mrs Stokes withdrew with her good-night-and-God-bless, Helena turned her back and began to undress, then climbed into the large bed and moved inwards. Grace bounced around the room undressing, and, naked, searched for her nightdress. Briefly, she checked her body profile in the wall-mirror before letting the nightdress fall from her shoulders to her knees. She wiggled her bottom, in delight: 'Fifteen-sixteen. AD!'

Then climbing into the bed, she challenged her sister's angst. 'Hellie, you're sighing again?' she accused. 'Daddy, isn't it?'

'He doesn't know I'm here yet, and he mightn't know until . . .'

'Until when? I'm going to open the window.' Grace jumped out of bed.

'He sees me. Until he sees me at the meeting, the march. I dread Sunday week.'

'Will that breeze blow the candle out, no, it won't,' and Grace turned to check. 'No, don't dread it, 'tis going to be a great day. And if he does, what of it?'

'What will he say to me? What will he say?' Helena drew her lips back in a small worried rictus.

'Let him say what he likes and he won't anyway because we'll all be in public. Sssssttt? D'you hear that?'

Helena rose on an elbow. Grace stood by the window and whispered, 'Probably a badger. Or I wouldn't be surprised if it was a deer.'

No further sound. As Grace returned to the big bed that heaped and plumped like white clouds, Dennis Sykes walked on soft feet away from the cottage window.

13

O ne week later:
    'I brought you this from London.' Dennis Sykes held out
the package. 'I felt you'd like it.'

Thomas Kane opened the wrapping, folded the outer paper,
then opened with careful fingers the inner layer of tissue paper.
The book gazed up gravely: *Moncrieux's History of Guerrilla
Warfare: 57 BC to the Guinea Campaign.*

'It's a translation, of course,' said Dennis. 'I thought you'd be
interested.' He made a drinking motion. 'The same?'

'No, no, man, let me get this.'

'Sit, sit,' soothed Dennis, 'you can buy the next round. Water
in a separate glass?'

Binnie said, 'Thanks muchly, my darling,' ever grateful as she
folded the banknotes.

'Binnie,' said Dennis. 'I am in severe, extremely severe
difficulty.'

'Explain.'

'I need to split the Kanes. Totally. If that girl's protests begin
to succeed, she will at least delay us. And you know what happens
if there's a delay. Everyone rushes to prolong a delay. And then
what happens? Sooner or later someone's going to put the idea of
a public enquiry into that little bitch's head.' He hammered the
pillow. 'Fuck! FUCK!'

Thomas Kane looked at the book's index, fingered the pages, found
one uncut, reached in his pocket for his penknife. Dennis Sykes
placed the drinks on the small table.

'I would have thought –' began Thomas, indicating the book,
and Dennis finished it for him.

'That an Englishman like me would resent you having been at war with us, with my country?'

'You say "at war", I notice,' said Thomas.

'And why not?'

'Well,' said the schoolteacher, fingering the newly-cut page, 'they called us "gangsters" –'

'We,' interrupted Dennis, pointing to his breast, 'we, not "they". We called you "gangsters". And "hoodlums". To say the least.'

'How do you know?' Kane wondered.

'I've been reading my history. I have a friend in London, a university man, a professor, saw him at the week-end. He says Ireland was the most shameful period in English history.'

No: Dennis had spent the week-end with Binnie: she complained of his roughness. He pleaded frustration.

Thomas shook his head, pleased, bemused. 'You're a remarkable man. So – so, understanding. There's no doubt about it. And this book –'

Dennis said expansively, 'Well – you should know the history of your own soldiery,' he said. 'Just because you didn't wear a conventional uniform doesn't mean you weren't a soldier. And by all accounts we could have done with you on our side.'

Binnie soothed. By now he had almost calmed down.

'But they're like the Venetians, the Irish. So do weasel, Dennis. I beg you. Yes. Weasel.'

Dennis fumbled his spaghetti.

'Yes, you're right, Dennis darling. Split them. Split them totally.'

Leah came to stay. She made a good observer at a good moment, loving Ellen, part of her history. Awaiting Ellen and baby Helena's return from the nursing-home, Leah had been there 'that dreadful morning'. For the next weeks, she had seen Ellen upright again, walked by her side as Ellen came back into life, supported her: Thomas seemed without hope, without possibility in an unhygienic hospital.

A quarter-century on, gaudy and warm as ever, she walked from the late bus to the front door. Leah ignored any sombreness of atmosphere she ever found inside the Kanes' house, pretended the children's wariness of Thomas never existed. Always, however, she watched Ellen closely, and never so closely as when Ellen gave little away.

After greetings, and the dispensing of the small confectionery, Leah made Ellen find quiet time. This moonlit evening, they walked. Leah reported 'trouble in Ellen' to Herbert two days later.

Dennis brought more drinks and when Thomas went to the lavatory (a set of galvanized iron partitions in the Hands' back yard), Dennis tipped some more whiskey into Thomas's glass. Mrs Hand brought cheese sandwiches.

Dennis sat again beside Thomas.

'I'm worried about something.'

Thomas looked into his glass and listened.

'I met your wife, did she tell you that?'

'No,' said Thomas, 'she did not.'

'This march on Sunday next. I think she's going to march. And if I lose your support –'

Drink never suited Thomas Kane. It took him through animatedness, into bonhomie, and then into self-righteous, self-pitying anger. Dennis watched and timed.

'On the march? My wife?' Thomas Kane shook his head. 'She will not.' He repeated it. 'She will not.'

'Are you sure?'

'My wife does what I say.'

'But – she's a mother. And your daughters –?'

Dennis left the sentence unfinished.

'Daught*er*.' Thomas emphasized the singular.

'No. Daught*ers*. The – the older girl is on now.'

'Helena?' He frowned.

Dennis nodded sadly. 'Moved into the Grey Valley ten days ago. That's where I met your wife.'

Leah's report fell into two parts – of the walking and talking, with Ellen meeting her problems squarely and, unusually in recent years, discussing them openly; and of the late evening, when Thomas returned, and the anger and division.

210

'Now, tell me about you?' began Ellen, and laughed. 'Do you know, I now think of you as my *wealthy* friend.'

'Oh,' Leah alerted, mistakenly. 'Is everything all right for money?'

'Oh, yes, of course. You know Thomas. The Great Provider Himself. What I really meant was, Herbert must be well used to it by now.'

'He still moans. Says we were better off when we were poorer. But, you won't believe it. I have my own cheque-book.'

Ellen laughed. 'What do I say? Congratulations? I'd be afraid I'd go mad if I had a cheque-book.'

Leah changed the subject – to Ellen. And reported when she went home, 'She has not lost any spirit, Herbert dear, she has gained it. Not that she was standing up to him as such, but she was managing him, not letting him get away. God, he's a problem.'

'He's a fine man,' murmured Herbert. 'He has qualities.'

Ellen Kane had a walk full of energy. Even though she picked her steps carefully, she thrust forward, bosom out. Leah's recurring comment about her beloved friend had to do with inspiration.

'She'll do everything she can in her power for those children. And for him, though in a different way. Do you know what she told me? She told me that she bakes twice when she's baking. She bakes for the children, same as anyone, and then she bakes specially for him. Not that it's any different, it's just that she lets him know.'

As Ellen ended her long résumé of Helena, Grace and their father, Leah looked down at her dark-eyed friend. She saw not Ellen Kane, a country schoolteacher in a small, backward and ignorant village, but a woman who had fought adversity from within herself, who had gone back almost to animal instincts to keep her husband alive.

'So,' concluded Ellen's long tale, 'I have to keep faith with the girls until this thing fizzles out. Because I think it will fizzle out. And I had better be there to help them with their disappointment. At the same time, I have to show him I support his official role.'

She never mentioned Dennis Sykes, who now preyed on her mind like a sin.

=

The women returned, sat at tea in the parlour, all children banished. Except Hugh, who hung around at the door.

'Cake later,' said Ellen firmly. 'Where's Daddy, do you know?'

'He's with the Engineer' – the name now given universally in Deanstown to Dennis Sykes.

'All this time?' asked Ellen. 'Does he know Auntie Leah's here?'

'Will I get him?'

'No-no. No-no,' she hurried. 'Off you go.'

Darkness fell slowly. Late birds, crows from the Castle, returned to their ivy, and one by one fell silent. The two women, figures in a painting, could be seen through the parlour window as the lace curtains billowed apart. Heads inclined towards each other, by the yellow light of the lamp-globe, they talked across the table, and listened. Leah's red lipstick shone: her nose cast a shadow: the red hair stuck out behind her, as ever.

Ellen explained. 'And I know, I know, I should do more. The girls say, well – Grace says – that I should have protected them from Thomas, I mean protected them more. But Leah, I did, though. For instance, every time he cut one of those thin ash sticks he used to punish them with – well, when it got too much for me, I used to go and find the stick and take it away. Secretly in the beginning. And then when I realized he thought it might be one of the children stole it, I did it openly. I never said a word, just removed it. Then he stopped using them.'

Leah nodded, in slow, deep nods.

'But now Grace says to me that he ruined things for everyone.' Ellen's soft voice rose in a hushed inflection of concern.

Leah murmured, 'And what do *you* think?'

'Oh, Leah, he's my husband, and you know me, I do things by thinking what I'm supposed to think.'

Amber tea in Leah's cup: she looked down at it: then she looked up at Ellen. 'Is there something now radically wrong? More than you're saying?'

'Yes. Yes.' Ellen, when cornered, stared hard into the eyes of her cornerer.

'What, dear? What?' Leah opened her palms. 'What's wrong? It isn't money, you said that?'

'No. No. I don't even know. I have a bad feeling. I never told you this, or anybody. But the night before. You know – the night before Thomas's – accident. I couldn't sleep. I was afraid of something, but I couldn't put a name to it. I have that feeling back now, and I have it worse than then.'

Leah asked, 'Is it about Thomas?'

'No,' said Ellen. 'And. Yes, and. It's about the girls, too.' She started. 'Oh, my God!'

Both women simultaneously heard the footsteps strike the gravel, urgent steps, faster than Thomas's usual walk.

'Oh, God. Look –' Leah stood. 'I'll say hallo first.'

She had no such opportunity. He opened the door, did not acknowledge Leah.

'Ellen! Come here please!' Without waiting for an answer Thomas said it again. 'At once, please!'

In the hallway he raged, 'What is the meaning of this, this business with your other daughter? You haven't told me.'

'I was going to,' said Ellen.

'Going to? *Going to?* When? At the end of the century?'

Quietly she said, 'Leah's here.'

'I don't care who's here.' His voice rose. 'What else's going on in this house behind my back and I not knowing?'

'Thomas. Two things. One – Leah's here: I said. And two, you don't normally drink much, so what were you doing? You were with that Sykes fellow, weren't you?'

'He's not a "fellow", and don't call him that, he's a gentleman. What I want to know is – what kind of little bitches are you rearing, that they're doing this to me in public, and you not telling me?'

Ellen said, so that Leah behind the door could hear, 'Under no circumstances call the girls that. Under no circumstances speak to me like that. Ever.'

Leah reported to Herbert, 'And then, dear, she came back into the room and locked the door. He pounded on the door; he then went to the window; she closed the shutters calmly; then the curtains. She sat down facing me and said, "Leah, I'm very sorry. Now – why don't we continue our talk?" Thomas raved on outside and after a while we heard him going to bed. But yet – she slept in the same bed as him that night, and in the morning he was gone before I got up. I didn't see him again.'

Herbert wondered, 'Should I talk to him?'

'Not possible, dear, I'd say.'

Of the two sisters, Helena would not have known – but Grace should have sensed something. Frantic within her own activities, she never looked around to take the temperature of the village.

'Lukewarm,' they said to each other upon enquiry; and 'I don't think there'll be that many.'

'Poor organization,' smiled Dennis Sykes to himself. Only two people felt the thunder of the occasion, Thomas and Grace. Both issued instructions.

'Nobody from this house will even be at a window when that march goes past. Do you hear?' The other children nodded.

'And when the buses come,' said Grace, her hands full of posters and glue and envelopes, 'we'll begin the march as soon as possible.'

Helena made only one observation. 'I think we should have obtained a clearer picture of how many?'

Grace went through the list: 'Each signatory to our letter promised at least twenty people. At least. It will be more. Dr Considine said he'll have thirty. Hellie, look. We've booked five buses. And this is only the beginning. Five busfuls at forty-five people per bus. Two hundred and twenty-five. Plus the locals. We could easily have five hundred people.'

'What's happening about the band?'

'I can't get him to answer my note,' said Grace. 'I even called again and he wasn't there.'

On Thursday morning, Dennis Sykes disappeared. Nobody saw him go; he left no significant message – merely a remark to the second-in-command: 'Urgent. I have to go. Hold the fort.'

He hoped to be back 'sooner rather than later', and at the morning site meeting had praised all progress.

The dam workers talked about him all the time. His nearest equals hailed his acumen, confessed themselves 'staggered' at his scope and grasp. Dennis had located his head drawing office at Rosegreen, eight miles away, in an old Georgian manor full of comfort and eccentricity. There, without any fixed point of his own, he directed the diagrammatic operations, moving from desk to drawing-board to wall-chart like some powerful butterfly, alighting on new ideas, sipping their nectar, and promulgating them to test their stamina.

He had appointed two senior assistants whom he met first and last every day: each brought him full reports of their half of the project. One took responsibility for the 'soft' work – the drawings, the purchasing, the contracts, the payments. The other handled the 'hard' end – men, machinery and operations, the construction drive.

Dennis controlled the impetus. From the beginning, he had pinned his soul to this project like a bright flag. He knew that every engineer in the English-speaking world would know of his success, that he had within his power the setting of an international benchmark. Using hour after hour, day after day, of more solitude than he had ever granted himself, he planned every detail: how he would delegate, where he would aim for breakthrough, and the management of time.

With the smoothness he knew his brain possessed, he fitted all the phases together in his mind so frequently that he could dis-mantle and assemble them like the parts of a gun. He oversaw every detail, down to the nuances of where to hire the greatest number of men – which parishes and even which townlands of which parishes? Hence his wooing of Kane: he recognized the potential of local difficulty, and perceived Kane to have a natural figurehead position.

Budgets, time targets, logistics: no wonder, he smiled from time to time, no wonder his libido had taken a holiday. No wonder, too, that no immature, virgin idealist could be allowed to halt this seething momentum. She had to be stopped: those things had a festering contagiousness. Which is why he left without warning, told nobody where he was going – and threatened Mrs Hand into secrecy by saying he could take away this new, fabulous drinking trade the dam had brought.

Sunday brought great warmth from the sun, the beginning of a premature heatwave. At half-past twelve, dressed in bright colours, Grace and Helena appeared in front of Mrs Hand's public house. Grace wore a straw hat and carried leaflets; Helena appeared nervous. Rhona, Munch and Viva Ulverton arrived.

Viva said in her blurting way, 'How many? How many?'

Grace grinned and said, 'None yet. Two and a half hours to go. Why are we all here so early?'

'Excitement, my dear. And rightly so.' Rhona tapped her stick on the road. 'I hope they're coming from Dublin?'

'And from Janesborough,' said Grace, 'and Cork, and Thurles. And Clare. And Galway.'

'And you're here, I see. Good,' said Rhona to Helena. 'What are you staring at, child?'

She joined Helena's line of sight – Ellen, sturdily walking towards them.

'Don't say,' said Viva, 'don't say she's going to march.'

'Hallo,' said Ellen to all, 'hallo, girls' to her daughters, and after a general exchange, drew them to one side.

She had promised herself to behave normally, not to ask them why they had not answered her letters; she had promised herself not to engage with them in the controversy. Otherwise, she would have to tell them of the fury with which their father had behaved for the past four days – the swearing and door-slamming, the accusations.

'Are the two of you all right? *Will* you be all right? Are there many coming?' Ellen looked solicitously at each girl. 'Dear Gracey! You've been busy, your posters are all over Mooreville, everyone's talking about it.'

'About five hundred we think. About ten buses. Are you marching, Mother?' asked Grace.

Ellen shook her head – 'And you, Helena love, are you all right?'

Helena enquired, 'How's Daddy?'

Ellen nodded in a way that precluded further enquiry, 'He's fine. I just wanted to say hallo to the two of you. Now. Have you – have you everything you need?'

Both nodded.

'Mama, is he cross with us?' asked Helena.

'Sweetheart, this isn't the best time of all for us to talk about this. Daddy has a lot on his mind.'

'Mother, you're still doing it, you're still protecting him!' Grace turned away in disgust.

A bus approached. Behind came another, then another, then another, then two cars, then another bus, then another. Grace cheered. 'But they're so early!'

As the coaches stopped, wheels crushing the grassy verges,

Grace ran towards them. 'You're all very early, but you're all very welcome,' she called, waving a rolled poster. 'Hellie, quick, look how many are here, look!'

With a smile at the Ulvertons, Ellen slipped away from the scene. At her gate, a hundred yards away, she turned, surveyed the gathering, waved to Helena, and disappeared into the folds of the trees in front of the house.

Rhona knew before Grace did, and murmured to Viva, 'Dizz. Ah. Stir.'

'What, Mamma?'

'Disaster. Look.'

Viva stared. A man descended from the first bus, walked to the roadside and began to urinate fatly. Behind him, others lurched out.

'Oh, my Christ!' said Viva. 'They stopped on the way.'

'Many times by the looks of it,' said Rhona: her purple chiffon stole waved in the breeze like Isadora Duncan. 'And those girls don't know what to do.'

'Help them, Mamma,' said Viva. 'Go on.'

'No. I won't. They have to learn.' She nudged Viva. 'Look! *They're* not teachers or students.'

Slowly, all vehicles emptied. Their passengers, men aged from twenty to forty, many unshaven, headed for Mrs Hand's pub. The sun grew hotter. A youth, cheap jacket over his arm, lurched over to Viva and said, 'Where's the fuckin' dam anyway?'

'Where did you come from?' Viva asked.

Grace walked over, baffled. 'Are you here for the rally?' she asked politely.

'Cork. They're from Janesborough, we all met in Mooreville.' He smiled foolishly.

'All of you? You all met in Mooreville?' Viva asked.

'What rally?' He eyed Grace.

Rhona butted in. 'When did you all meet in Mooreville?'

'Yes. Where's the buses we're supposed to be stopping?' He had a bottle in his hand concealed beneath the folded jacket. 'Half-past ten.'

'Half-past ten? Why?'

'Is the fella here?'

'What fella? What d'you mean?' Viva asked.

'Several rounds. He bought me on my own four rounds.'

Rhona asked, 'What kind of "fella"?'

'Friday night. Decent as anything. Couldn't buy a round for him, he bought everything.' The young man licked his mouth. 'Never let it be said the English aren't decent.'

Rhona asked keenly, 'Did he have a lot of black hair and was he small?'

'"A mystery tour", that's what he said, "give's a day of your time and you can have all the drink you can drink." Yeh, a'course he'd black hair. And a fiver each.' The young man walked away.

Rhona turned to Viva. 'No doubt you've guessed.'

'I'm getting there.'

'Master Sykes. A set-up.'

Viva said, 'Little fucker. But there are still the others?'

'Watch, Viva, dear. By the end of it, there will be fighting. Or else you will not see an organized protest here today.'

In all this time, the two cars accompanying the coaches had parked quietly, and their occupants had not emerged. Now they appeared, men in uniform. A senior, braided one asked Viva, 'Are you Miss Kane?'

Villagers came to their doors, but not to take part.

Viva pointed and beckoned. Grace returned. Red of face. Angered and embarrassed. Chagrined.

'I can't work this out.'

'I'm sorry, my dear,' Rhona said to her. 'I fear they're rabble material.'

The Superintendent asked, 'Are you the organizer?'

Grace affirmed.

'May I meet your stewards, please?'

'Stewards?'

He said, 'Over two hundred people, strangers, have come into your village to drink. They're all in that pub by now. You are expecting many more that you have rallied here. Right?'

'To begin at three o'clock,' said Grace.

'How do you propose to keep order? There are several known troublemakers in the village at this moment.'

'Help,' said Grace helplessly to Rhona.

=

218

By sundown, Grace's despair had subsided into, 'But why? Why?'

Rhona walked her up and down the avenue, up and down, a firm hand on Grace's arm.

'My dear girl. Cruel to say, but you've been outwitted. The police simply had no choice. They had to close the village. They had to turn the marchers back.'

'But my people had no drink taken,' protested Grace.

'Worse again, dear.' Rhona paused. 'Do you not recognize what has happened?'

Helena, walking with them, murmured, '*Agents provocateurs?*'

'I fear so.'

Helena and Mrs Stokes went indoors to prepare some food. Grace sat outside and watched the night fall to the Valley floor.

Forever after, Helena chided herself for not having sat with Grace. She wrote over and over again in her notebook, 'Why didn't I stay? By going indoors, I gave Grace the time to think.'

Rightly or wrongly, Helena attributed the beginning of the end, the essence, to that moment. Grace, deep in the depressive aftermath of the march-that-never-was, intensified in her determination.

'I can hear him gloat, that's the worst part. He'll be saying to Mother, "I told her but she wouldn't listen." He'll be saying to the others, "Children of every age should always listen to their parents." Can't you hear him, Hellie . . .'

Next morning, because they had written in advance, and slipped the letters by hand under the old doorways, Grace and Helena set off on their round of the cottages in the Valley. In this search for signatures to their petition, they had anticipated a victory tour, had expected that the rally would have given them stronger cards to play.

'I've two things to say to you, Miss Kane,' said the first woman they called to see. 'Mind your own business for a start. And the second is, 'tis all fine for you with your father and your stuck-up mother. But you never went without money or food or a pair of shoes to your feet, and now I have a fine house coming to me over in Mooreville near my daughter, and you trying to stop me getting it. G'off now, g'wan, and leave uz alone.'

Grace tried to fight. 'But the house and its age, and that furniture you have, the value of these?'

'An' lumbago to go with it, and arteritis, yeh? I'd sooner a good sofa from John O'Dea's shop any day. G'wan, g'off wit' yourself.'

Grace dipped into her next resource of bravery, and walked on. According to her notes, the Connaughtons owned a rare Carbery Settle, a highbacked seat fixed to the kitchen wall. From it unfolded a one-legged table, so that the sitters on either side could turn, face each other and dine.

'Take it away with you girl if you're that fond of it,' said Bernard Connaughton, with his cap to one side. 'Look at this.'

He showed Grace and Helena a letter from the County Manager confirming the offer of 'a bungalow with three bedrooms' in Mooreville, and 'a resettlement compensation of between £750 and £1500.'

Bernard Connaughton cocked an eye at the girls and asked, 'Will you match that? Or your father, 'ill he give me that much for staying?'

Grace said, prim and edgy, 'My father isn't involved in this. We're doing this on our own because we think the Grey Valley should be preserved.'

'Preserved for what, hauh?' The cottier moved off, stranding the girls outside his home.

Of the five houses visited that morning, Eddie Martin alone gave the girls some consolation.

'I was born here, and I never wanted to go outa here but in a box. My heart'll break the night they flood it.'

Grace said, 'They *won't* flood it, Mr Martin, they will not, that's what we're fighting. What I want from you is your signature, and I want a statement from you about the oldness of the furniture you have, and how old your house is.'

He sighed. 'The house is the same age as the rest of them, and there's no furniture here worth the asking.'

Helena enquired, 'Have you a settle-bed or anything like that?'

'I haven't. My daughter over in England furnished the house from top to bottom two years ago and she got rid of all that stuff, we burned a lot of it that winter following.'

Helena asked, 'Have you any pictures of it?'

'No.'

Grace said, 'But look at that thatch? Beautiful.'

He said, 'Well, 'atiz and 'atizn't. There's flax in it and I knew the day they put flax in 'twould be unlucky. Flax never brings luck in thatch.'

Thomas Kane became obsessed with Dennis Sykes. He sought Sykes's approval, his companionship, his praise. Like a man grasping at an urgent opportunity, he careened off at this new, comradely tangent. When the school closed in the heat of mid-July, Kane was to be seen striding in the dam area, observing, measuring, taking notes. He offered comments to Sykes, who accepted them as if they were nuggets of engineering pioneerwork.

Dennis assessed every turn of this relationship in terms of advantage. Notwithstanding his success at obliterating the rally (which Kane never discussed with him – hah! pressure at home), he still feared a call for a public enquiry. Indeed he puzzled as to why none had been mooted. One evening on the crest of the Grey Valley, not far from the point where Sykes had met Ellen, he remarked to Thomas, 'It seems as if you've become part of this family of mine' – and he waved his hand towards the workers, the trucks, the great ants crawling over the site far below them. 'This busy family.'

The massive foundations had now been finished, and the concreting had begun deep beneath the ground. On either lip of the long curved pit stood lines of cement-mixers like tiny watch-towers; each mixer had its own team and they raced each other to fill the pit up to ground-level.

'Yes,' mused Dennis. 'I *have* run them like a family. In a sense they're the only family I know.'

By now he knew the length of Kane's reactions. A planted thought, usually triggered by Dennis in a key word, took time to root: Kane had a proud reputation for pondering. Dennis had observed that the schoolmaster usually renewed such a subject four to five days later.

In their enclave north of Deanstown, the Stephensons and the Ulvertons met frequently. Their two large dwellings had come through a cold winter. Plaster fell away, leaving sores on the pink wash walls of the dower house. Rhona Ulverton repeatedly asked

221

Viva to procure – knit, if necessary – woollen gloves: Rhona had spent many days beneath the heavy blankets and feared her limbs seizing.

A chimney collapsed on the manor one night and terrified Cyril Stephenson's excommunicated wife. Joan had slowly recovered from the worst of her depressions, and she now lay silent in their bed at night, a sullen woman, often tearful. She sighed for hours before sleep reached her, and next morning complained daily of the cold.

Rhona's tentative meetings with Cyril and the wife had produced no financial solution to the problems of heating these houses.

The Stephensons and the Ulvertons none the less loved the place, especially in summer. Old plants grew around the doors. The gardens beamed. Morning glory and japonica flourished like bright bandits in unexpected nooks. Inside, the high ceilings and cornices downstairs remained in an excellent state of repair; the leaks had never penetrated. Feared subsidence had not materialized. Not a flake had fallen from the stuccoed ceilings.

Sunday morning: bumblebees in the blossoms on the high old brick wall. Cyril shrugged; Rhona, wearing a green eyeshade like an antique tennis player, stretched in her deck-chair.

'By when, Aunt Rhona?'

'They seemed unhurried. By September, October I suspect. Viva, no!'

Viva had appeared wearing shorts and a chiffon top through which her tiny breasts and plinking nipples could be seen as clearly as a relief map.

'Heatwave, Mother!'

Rhona rapped her stick on the paving beneath the garden bench. 'No! Look at Cyril's wife! She's sensible' – who, sitting on the grass nearby, wore a green woollen long-sleeved dress.

'Yes, and she's baking. Anyway, she's a Roman Catholic and they don't show their bodies, do you, Joan?'

Cyril's wife never answered.

'Go, Viva and change!' – but Viva escaped, ran down the green slope of the banked lawn, and reached her clearing in the woods.

'And Uncle Henry won't help?' asked Cyril.

The families had become a main topic of electricity speculation. This remained unknown to them – although Cyril's wife, of the people, had suspected. Their enclave, beautiful and sleek when first built, now proved inconveniently sited. This group of houses, above even the glossy woods, had once struck fear into tenants' hearts. The supply engineers, not of Dennis Sykes's team, had finally – after months of dithering – told the houses of the extra work needed. To bring electricity through Wallace's Wood would cost two thousand: they could share it.

'Henry says he has problems finding the money for his own electricity poles.' Rhona sniffed. 'But I doubt it. I believe he's lying.' Rhona worried. 'Cyril dear, I think this is all deliberate. Are you telling me that if a Roman Catholic farm is in a remote place they will have to pay the same as us? And Christ we're not that remote!'

Cyril stood, made his hand into an eyeshade and gazed off at nothing; he looked briefly like some unambitious *conquistador*.

He sat again. 'What are you going to do, Aunt Rhona?'

'I think I'm going to fight – on other grounds – so that if I may make myself enough of a nuisance I can do a deal. I have an idea. God, Cyril, your father and your mother must be turning in their graves! I feel like a non-person in this country.'

Cyril nodded, afraid lest his wife would overhear: but she had fallen asleep in the sun on the grass, and beads of sweat stood on her pale face beside her open mouth.

'Yes,' he said softly, 'the RCs really show us now, don't they. We have no say.'

Behind him to the left, his own house basked. The sun lit the blond stone he could not afford to repair. Down the fields, the yellow, ragged-leaf ragwort rampaged through pastures he could not afford to meadow. He had one horse, and two tweed jackets, and a dark suit that had been his father's. If any of the twenty cows that sustained the house sickened, Cyril could only get a vet of the same religious persuasion who would understand. The man had to come from forty miles away, reachable only by letter.

In Rhona's house, some tiles had come loose on the red roof on an equinoctial night. She hoped that the tarred roofing canvas beneath would survive, would not melt.

'Yes,' finalized Rhona. 'That is what I will do. I will be devious.'

'How? The Kane girls? Their campaign will come to something?'

'No,' said Rhona. 'They're not doing well. That march fiasco. All that fighting and vomiting.'

Cyril said, 'Aunt Rhona, everyone's laughing at them.'

'I need tea. Viva! Viva!'

No reply came. Viva lay in a deep sleep, legs apart in the sun. That night she wept with the pain of the sunburn on her long-shanked inner thighs.

14

llen accepted briskly, without question, their truce.
'The Engineer's coming for his tea,' she told Essie.

Preparations matched those for the Canon or an Inspector. Ellen baked her best cake. Four egg yolks; four ounces of dark melted chocolate; four ounces of caster sugar: two large tablespoons of flour: at the end, fold in the beaten-stiff egg whites meticulously.

He parked on the road, and bore a gift wrapped in damp brown paper.

'Where,' asked Thomas, 'did you get it?'

Dennis smiled. 'A friend of a friend who's a good fisherman, and he was out early this morning. For your breakfast tomorrow.'

Thomas showed Ellen the great trout, and she smiled formally.

The girls had been invited – Thomas's truce concession to Ellen. Grace resisted, close to rage when she read the note: Helena complied.

As they sat to table, she cycled through the gate. Dennis saw her arrive, and attempted to give Ellen a conspiratorial look: she focused on Helena. Who came uncertainly in. All watched Thomas. He moved to make room for her.

'Have you met our oldest, Dennis?' he asked. 'Helena. Born in 1926.'

Dennis, eyes like a falcon, said, 'Uh-huh, you mustn't reveal a lady's age. How do you do?' and he rose to shake Helena's hand.

Helena wore the lemon yellow dress, and her blonde hair curved under her chin. She moved nervously to sit by her father. Ellen watched Dennis's glances on Helena's thighs and waist. Thomas Kane's eyes watched nobody.

'Did you cycle?' asked Dennis Sykes of Helena.

'Yes.' She nodded.

'Strong wind today,' he said pleasantly. 'In that hot sun. Like France.'

'Does that ever interfere with your construction, Dennis?' asked Thomas. 'I mean, high wind?'

'It may later. When the men are working up on the dam wall.' Dennis Sykes turned to Helena. 'As a matter of interest, does it get hot where you are? I mean, deep within the valley?'

Helena said, 'Yes, I mean, no.'

She overcame her surprise at such open speech in so difficult a matter.

'No. Well, it does, yes. The sun comes at an angle, and it gets hotter for some reason.'

Once, at this very table, Leah and Ellen sat and observed Helena, then aged nineteen. She walked through the gate, head slightly tilted, unaware of the watching women.

'Do you see what I mean, Leah?'

Leah smiled with such affection. 'Yes, yes.'

'That innocence. I worry about her. Will she meet a nice man? Otherwise, how will she manage?'

'All that vul, vul – what's the word, she's very vul, oh drat it, I can't think of it.' Leah's bracelets clanged.

'But everybody likes her, that's the good thing. My heart hurts when I watch her.'

'Nerable!' Leah shot.

'Oh, *vulnerable*? Yes, that's a good word. Yes. The first-born.'

'The first-born,' echoed Leah. 'Yes, they're often vulnerable.'

Dennis Sykes praised things. He praised the strength of the tea, the pips in the jam, the dark moist sponginess at the heart of the cake.

'It's good and tense,' he said. 'A good chocolate cake should be tense.'

'Tense?' smiled Helena.

'You never married?' asked Ellen, determined to be polite, as Thomas had specifically requested.

'Nearly, once' – a master of the hint of eastern disappointment. In later life, he got his way at board meetings by knowing how never to overdo.

Against her wishes and her better judgement, Ellen's curiosity fizzed. 'Nearly? Once?'

'These things happen,' said Dennis. 'How many children have you, Mrs Kane?'

'I think you could call her Ellen,' smiled Thomas.

'Eight,' said Helena.

'Gosh! How lovely!' said Dennis the enthusiast, Dennis the wistful, Dennis the would-be family man, his brown eyes poignant.

Ellen asked, 'But do the English like large families? I thought they didn't.'

He smiled. 'A family of any kind would be welcome in my department.'

Thomas gave his rare, pleased nod. 'In my department,' he echoed, relishing.

And yet, the talk had some stiffness in it. Dennis, sensing this, visibly set out to warm the table. He told a long tale of an ancient hoard found in a Scottish site where he once surveyed. Ellen watched everyone listening to him. Believing him. Especially Helena: who, still a little wary of her father's looming bulk beside her, looked many times at Dennis's expressive hands. At the end of the tale Dennis rewarded himself.

'Is it rude to ask for more cake?'

Even Ellen dived to help.

'Did you like the things they found?' asked Helena, her first direct question.

Dennis held their attention yet further by not speaking with his mouth full. He brushed the crumbs away.

'I thought.' He used both his ring-fingers to scrabble crumbs from his lip-corners. 'That I had never.' Quick swallow. 'Seen anything so – so lustrous.'

Thomas echoed again. 'Lustrous.' He looked at Dennis with firm approval. 'Lustrous.'

'You could almost see,' said Dennis, 'the fingermarks of the goldsmiths on the wide bracelets.'

At this same table twenty-five years earlier, Ellen Kane, née Morris, had fought for her own composure. Three feet away, her husband, 'the Living Dead', lay stretched on his bed-chair. At every meal she argued silently with him, or talked to him as if he heard. Each night, with Helena in her cot, and Essie lumbering like an Indian cow on the floor above, Ellen had ranted at life and at her comatose man. Fists clenched, she cajoled and imprecated.

She hustled her husband, turned his face to the full moon silvering through the windows. Undressed before him. Painted his body from mouth to groin with her breasts. Called his name aloud, or whispered it. Drove at him with passionate confidences. Urged him back into his own life. Hauled him from his pallor and his oblivion. Cursed him. Now, at the same table, she sat with feet coiled around her chair-legs in tension. As she watched, the seeds of, to her, a worse tragedy were being planted – and beyond her reach.

Dennis Sykes's skill dominated the end of the night.

He turned to Helena and said, 'It is as good as dark now, why don't I give you a lift back to the Grey Valley, you can put the bike on the back of the car.' Precluding comment, he said to Thomas, 'That was a memorable thing for you to do. Bringing me into your family like this.'

Finally he turned to Ellen, whose hand he took. 'Mrs Kane, I can understand your suspicion of a man like me, coming in to a place he's bound to disrupt. The dam will change lives. I know that.'

Ellen, discomfited but courteous, said, but mainly to Helena, 'Mr Sykes it was very nice to have you for your tea. Helena, love, will you be cold without a coat? Take my light one.'

Helena peered forward into the night. She sniffed.

'Leather,' said Dennis Sykes. 'And wood. That's walnut, actually,' pointing to the trim in front of Helena's knees, 'the whole dashboard is walnut with leather.'

She drew a hand along it.

He remarked, 'I can see you understand these things.'

'Lovely smell.'

'How old are you exactly?' he asked.

'Just recently twenty-six.'

'Twenty-six. God! Talking about blushing unseen.'

'I don't blush!'

He said, 'No. I wasn't saying that. Don't you know the line?'

'What line?'

Dennis recited, 'Full many a gem of purest ray serene, The dark unfathom'd caves of ocean bear.'

Helena said, 'Oh? *That* line.'

'Finish it,' commanded Dennis.

Helena did so, without faltering. 'Full many a flower is born to blush unseen.'

Together they ended the quotation: 'And waste its sweetness on the desert air.'

One of Dennis's more reliable stock lines: he used it on Rose; he used it on Mona Nicolson; he used it on myriad others.

They had arrived at the Valley: trees hung over them in the dark. Dennis took Helena's hand as she stood by the car. He held her long fingers and said, 'I hope we meet again.'

She replied, 'We are certain to.'

'Certain to?'

'I mean – you and my father, and that.'

He asked, 'Can I meet you one night? I mean, as a secret?'

Helena could not see his face in the night.

He pressed on. 'Unless you have some boy or young man who wants to marry you?'

Helena said in amazement. 'Oh no, oh, no!'

'Whyever not?'

The girl shifted her feet on the earthen valley road. 'It – things – I mean, it doesn't go like that in our family. Or around here.'

He chuckled. 'You mean people don't marry?'

'No. They do. Oh, I mean – well, in my own life, I've sort of –' she paused, not having anything else to say.

Dennis remarked, 'I have the impression that your father likes me. Is that right, do you think?'

'Oh, yes, he does, I could tell.'

Dennis paused, allowing his implication to take root. Then he said, 'I must go now. And I am reluctant to. But – will you meet me again? I mean – as a secret to begin with? Given all the complications?'

Helena replied, 'But – my sister . . .'

'As a complete secret? Promise? Promise?'

'I promise.'

'Here? On this very spot? Next Wednesday evening? Late?'

'Yes. I will.'

'What excuse will you give your sister? You could say you were visiting your parents?'

229

Helena said, 'Yes, I suppose so.'

'In fact,' said Dennis, 'I have a better idea. Why don't you visit them anyway, and I'll call. By coincidence, as it were – and pick you up there.'

'By coincidence as it were,' echoed Helena. She so lacked self-esteem that her listeners frequently had to guess whether her inflection signified question or comment.

Mrs Stokes had gone to bed: Grace had not come in: when she did return from her night wanderings, Helena pretended sleep.

From early August, electricity fever had been rampaging. Perhaps the village had waited for any protests to die down; perhaps it took until then to subdue its wariness of that fierce blue flashing power. Slowly, it began to swing round. In due course, sceptics or recusants became figures of fun.

This new enthusiasm took two forms. Well-to-do neighbours conferred, pencilling remarks on brochures, gauging each other's finances according to the intended number of appliances. Even people with no carpets ordered vacuum cleaners. Housewives scoured their rooms, painted woodwork. Electricians came by, curly-haired men in blue overalls with urgent red flashes on their breasts. In thoughtful inspections they marked with great triangular pencils the places for power points on skirting-boards. Fire hazards became a topic: what to do with thatch? How far from the inside of a straw roof, now tinder-dry with age and the residue of smoke, might a light bulb be installed?

In the wiring enquiries, in the fumbling around under the roof, men found unknown things of their ancestry – old guns; pieces of ancient bacon; prayer-books hidden from the Penal Laws; money stored in the thatch. John Barron found a box full of three-pound notes. The bank told him they were called 'pig' notes, because 'one note could buy a pig back in 1880'. A new shop opened in Mooreville selling only 'Electrical Goods'. The ancient incumbent of the town, Joseph Comerford & Sons Hardware, had to hasten, and spoke indignantly of the upstart.

Many people began to pay visits to the dam site, as to a holy well. Dennis Sykes had wondered to Thomas if the Canon should come and bless the work. On the appointed day, Dennis provided more than one bottle of Jameson – and the Canon's beloved onion sandwiches. Nobody believed Jeremiah Williams would ever again make such a public appearance: they said he had had a stroke: why else would the Curate be saying both Masses at each end of the parish, Deanstown and Silverbridge, every Sunday?

Thomas drove Canon Williams, loading him into the car. The men, caps off, welcomed him at the site, steered him along the wooden walkway over the mud of recent rain. A senile Cortez on Darien, the Canon stood looking along the completed dam foundations, and the first rise of the wall. His lip had sagged a little: his left arm – did he hold it a little stiffly? That night the talkers could not agree.

He puffed as ever through his nostrils.

'Boys, boys. If I never saw the Hanging Gardens of Babylon, I'll see this. How many men?'

Thomas Kane, in all his authority, acted as aide-de-camp and said, 'All told there'll have been one thousand one hundred here for the completion of this bit, and then for the rest another one thousand two hundred and fifty will come in.'

Dennis Sykes, silent and respectful, nodded.

'All from the county?' said the Canon.

'Bar a few special workers,' agreed Thomas.

The Canon raised his right hand; a workman materialized with a glass bowl of Holy Water. 'In the name of the Father. And of the Son. And of the Holy Ghost.'

Thomas made Ellen laugh later.

'D'you know what he said? Dennis had this reception prepared for him, very well done really. Jeremiah took his usual two quick drinks, and settled down – and out he came with it, "D'you know what it is, boys? I'm as good a blesser as ever I was." You'd imagine there was some kind of championship for blessings.'

Grace watched the event from her vantage point. Hour after hour, she hid in these ferns and trees, observing.

'I feel like God. Or Gulliver,' she told Helena.

Her father's car had been arriving at the site every day. And every day she turned her head away briefly when it came – then forced herself to watch. For hours at a time she followed Dennis Sykes's movements far below, as he walked, walked. When Canon

Williams emerged, the sunshine lit the rain pools on the brown clay. Grace stood in anger.

Her mother used to say, 'Grace, you are too wilful. Too wilful.'

'I never quite understand the word, do you?' Grace asked Helena.

'It means following your own will without regard for the consequences,' said Helena.

'What else have we to follow?' asked Grace.

'Mama means your prayers and that.'

The aborted, drunken march, and the abuse of so many cottiers had sent Grace into temporary retreat. Worse than that, one or two of the valley families had begun to prepare for evacuation.

Treading water, she began to draw, and set out to note down every plant she could identify in the Grey Valley. She persuaded Helena to smuggle from home one of their favourite books, *The Wild Flora of the British Isles*. Day after day, Grace made an appointment with herself at four o'clock to match what growths she could find with the illustrations in the book.

Sometimes Helena disappeared, wandered off by herself. When Grace asked, she merely gave a diffident excuse: 'Thinking' – or, 'I needed to think.'

Watched by Mrs Stokes, Grace also sketched every view of the cottage interior. She noted down the colours within, each piece of fixed work, such as shutters, the wall-bed, the details of the iron crane from which the pots hung over the fire. The patterns in Mrs Stokes's lace bedspreads and curtains took ages; Grace counted the patches in the patchwork quilt. In morning light, she sat at the open door and named and sketched the trees she could see.

'What are you up to, girl?' the puzzled woman asked.

Grace, grinning, replied, 'I am a recording angel, Mrs Stokes, a recording angel, that's me. Here, Hellie, hold this' – and she fetched yet another pencil from her satchel.

Daily, Grace roamed the woods alone, looking, sketching – and always fetching up on the ridge, staring down at the works of the project. She rose near dawn and followed fixed habits, such as smelling the roasted apples of the briar by the door, and turning to watch the steam from her own morning urine rising in the thick, summer grass. The Grey Valley drew her deep into its grasp, and gave her ferocious purpose. By August she had begun to record every sound and mood of the place, the leaf, the branch, the fruit.

Each part of the day received colours from her. The morning began 'dove-grey', as she stood at the gable of the house and watched the other cottages materialize in the mist. Then it became 'mauve', as the sun tried to break through the high trees. On the many sunny days, she called mid-morning 'cinnamon'. She ordered Helena to find some cinnamon on a day-trip to Janesborough, so that Mrs Stokes could see what Grace meant by the colour. Mrs Stokes peered unknowingly at the cinnamon sticks in the long jar. Grace, impatient, took her to the front door and pointed.

'See,' said Grace, demanding as a child, 'that's cinnamon, that's cinnamon-coloured.' She held a stick of the spice to the light. 'Look! They say that's what Italy is like. Rome or Siena.'

Smiling, the old woman went along with it. By the Connaughtons' windows, the light had fallen on an old cart, making the derelict beautiful.

When Helena walked through the door, blinking and yawning into the early morning light, she found Grace on the wooden settle, paints open. Head on one side, Grace added grey weight to the wing-feathers of a wood-pigeon. She smiled at Helena.

'The sun shines straight through that nightdress, Hellie.'

Helena looked down, yawned again. 'Look at you fully dressed.' She leaned over Grace's shoulder. 'Oh, Gracey, that's lovely.'

Grace said, 'I wish I had all my things. I'm missing several crayons.'

Helena sat beside her. 'I can go home and get them for you.'

'Would you?'

Helen nodded – and deceived. 'I'll go, say, Wednesday.'

The girls sat easily side by side. Helena twirled her hair in one finger. They looked into the waxy shimmer of the morning's haze.

'Did you make Mrs Stokes any breakfast?' asked Helena.

Grace nodded. 'She said she didn't sleep. I think she's gone back to bed.'

Helena stretched her legs and looked down at them. 'Did you see that advertisement in the papers – for an ointment or a cream to take the hair off your legs?'

Grace laughed. 'Do men use it for shaving?'

Helena, in the middle of a yawn, laughed again.

'How was home last night?' Grace erased a line and blew the dust off the notebook page.

'All right. Mama was wearing that lovely cream silk blouse.'

'I told her,' grinned Grace, 'she's to leave it to me in her will.' Sobering, she asked, 'How was HE?'

'Oh – you know.' Helena said. 'Guests there.'

'So he was the perfect gentleman. Did he ask about me?' Grace busied herself.

'He couldn't have done, with all that was going on. What are you going to do today?'

Grace said, 'I don't know, yet. I thought of starting to count all the rare plants here, will you help me?'

Next afternoon, Thomas Kane arrived at the dam site. Dennis greeted him at the office door.

'Just in time.' To the office-girl he said, 'Tea, Mary? A cup and saucer for Mr Kane, I'll have my mug.'

They stood by the window. Dennis showed Thomas the latest workings; he verified for the teacher the next developments on the far end of the escarpment.

'Look at the birds,' he pointed. Overhead, they wheeled and drifted on the thermals above the valley. Some gulls had arrived, forty miles from the sea. 'We must be turning up a lot of worms.'

The tea arrived. Dennis said as they sat, 'I have to say – if it's not forward of me. Your daughter. Goodness, she's lovely.'

Thomas gave a small, embarrassed laugh.

'Does she have – is there a – a young man?'

'No, no.' Thomas shook his head. 'There really – there really aren't any – suitable. Any suitable *people* – around here. She'll probably have to go to a city if she wants to marry.'

Dennis smiled. 'Like her father did?'

Thomas laughed in surprise. 'Yes, yes. I never thought of that aspect.'

'Oh, by the way,' said Dennis, 'I want to drop in two new drawings to you. Will you be there on Wednesday evening?'

'Come for your tea,' said Thomas.

'I don't think I can. It'll be about nine before I get to you.'

=

234

Ellen cycled to see Rhona Ulverton. Munch, on his avenue patrol, saw her coming and ran alongside the bicycle, chattering like a guide. Ellen, untypically, answered in monosyllables. She handed him the bicycle carelessly; he grabbed it and began to cycle round and round in front of the house. Ellen pulled the brass handbell.

Rhona appeared, antennae waving.

'Come in immediately. What's the matter?'

Ellen asked, 'How did you know?'

'I watched you come up the avenue. You are agitated.'

'Yes, I am. I don't know what to do.'

The women faced each other in the hall.

'I think,' said Ellen, 'I think that fellow, that engineer, is after Helena. Rhona, am I wrong to be upset by that?'

'Tea. Immediately.'

'I brought some scones,' and Ellen handed over the parcel.

'How could you be wrong? Shall we kill him? I'm only half-joking.' Rhona took Ellen's hand. 'Calm down. Take off your coat. We have to plan. Tell me all.'

Ellen shook her head in worry, and draped her coat on a large cane chair. She followed Rhona into the kitchen, where she sat at the table and rubbed her face deeply. Rhona made tea.

'We have no butter, but here is some of your gooseberry jam.'

'He was in our house the other night for the first time. And then he gave Helena a lift back to the Grey Valley, put her bicycle on the car. I haven't seen her since. Although we had a note this morning to say she's coming for her supper tomorrow night. And now my husband tells me Sykes is dropping in as well. Rhona, am I imagining things?'

'No. An absolute no. No mother easily imagines something so fundamental as her daughter's danger.'

'Rhona, Helena's so impressionable.'

'I'm glad the girls are home again.'

'Grace isn't, only Helena.'

'Is she a virgin?' asked Rhona.

Ellen looked shocked. 'Of course she is!'

'Relax, my dear, relax, just measuring.'

Rhona poured the tea, put jam on her own scone and sat down.

'Now. Read it for me.'

'How do you mean?' asked Ellen.

'Spell out for me what you see as the problem.'
Ellen spoke with emphatic hands.

A She never trusted Sykes from the moment she saw him.
B He had her husband around his little finger.
C It would suit Sykes fine to pursue Helena and then he would
   surely drop her when the project was over.
D If, God forbid, he didn't, she could not imagine a more
   unsuitable husband.

'Because,' summarized Rhona, 'he is clearly an amoral little shit.
I've seen dozens of them. He's a user. He will use Helena. He
will do what he likes with her.'
   'Rhona, I saw him looking at her in the most, the most – *immodest*
way. Helena never noticed – but she wouldn't know what I was
talking about.'
   'I understand,' said Rhona, in her wild chiffon.
   'I mean – you may think I'm old-fashioned –'
   Rhona interjected again, 'But I understand your conventions.
And how safe you find them. Yes, you are right, and we must
fight. We shall have to see him off.'
   'But how?'

As Ellen walked around the kitchen, she muttered.
   Essie asked, 'What was that, Ma'am?'
   'No, nothing, Essie, I was talking to myself again.'
   'Couldn't be in better company, Ma'am.'
   The day dragged. Ellen did chores she had put off for months:
sorted, to repair or discard, blankets that the children had chewed
when small; counted the available preserving jars; wrote into her
ledger two recipes from wives. During each task she paused at
length, reflecting and muttering.
   'First things first,' Rhona said. 'Alert Helena. Warn her of such
men.'
   But the plan came adrift early. Thomas had accidentally met
Helena in the village as she cycled towards the house. Ellen saw
them arrive, saw, to her astonishment, Thomas smiling at his
daughter.
   Matters worsened. Thomas said as they walked to the door

236

together, 'I've just been telling Helena that she has an admirer.' The daughter blushed.

Ellen forced a smile. 'And who is the lucky man?'

'A distinguished man, no less,' said Thomas, smiling again. 'Look, she's still blushing.'

'How are you? Don't you look lovely?' said Ellen to her daughter.

The next occurrence completed the undoing of Ellen's and Rhona's scheme. All three Kanes perked at a car engine in the still, late afternoon.

Thomas took his watch from his top pocket. 'He's very early. He said he would not be able to call until nine o'clock or thereabouts.'

The car drew up.

'I'm sorry to intrude,' said the spry man, 'but I didn't expect to be passing.'

'Come in, come in, you're welcome anyway.' Thomas held the door.

Dennis in his perfect manners acknowledged Ellen first, then Helena.

'Now you will stay for your tea, won't you?' Thomas led the way.

Ellen rubbed her forearms vigorously when disturbed; nobody noticed.

'Isn't this a lovely room, I've been remembering it since the other night. I love parlours,' said Dennis Sykes. 'So that's the very same piano you played for John McCormack, Mrs Kane, well, well!'

How did he control it so easily? How did he command the whole evening so that Ellen never had an opportunity to speak to Helena alone? In the days to come she analysed and analysed.

'He simply made the assumption,' said Rhona, 'that the evening would run like that. Assumptions are very powerful medicine.'

Ellen did fire one salvo. Long after supper, as they prepared to depart, Helena said to Dennis Sykes, 'Oh, I've forgotten something,' and ran into the house to fetch the drawing materials Grace had requested. Thomas moved away from the group for a moment, to fix Helena's bicycle to the car. Ellen and Dennis stood alone. She peered into his face.

237

'Mr Sykes, what are you up to in my house?'

He stepped back. 'Up to? What does that mean?'

'Mr Sykes, you are up to something. I know it. Please leave my daughter alone!' Ellen had not meant to hiss. 'And you needn't bother giving me your pained look either.' (A warning of Rhona's, who had pulled the face to illustrate: 'He'll look pained, his sort always do.')

Thomas returned: Dennis won.

'Your wife,' he said it with such a smile, 'is attacking me.'

Ellen became confused and embarrassed.

Thomas asked, 'What is it?'

Helena returned before anything could develop. Thomas waved the car and the occupants away and stormed in. 'What was that all about?'

Essie left the kitchen too.

'Come on!' he snapped. 'What was that?!'

'I told him I didn't want him near Helena.'

'You what?!' Even Ellen had difficulty in not recoiling from Thomas in this anger. 'God in Heaven above, what are you doing? Are you gone blank-stupid, or something?'

'You've never spoken to me like this,' she said.

'That man!' said Thomas, pointing a crooked finger like a scythe in the direction of the departed car. 'That, that, that *excellent* man – he may want to marry Helena! He's already told me how much he likes her.'

'I don't trust him,' said Ellen quietly, hoping that by lowering her voice Thomas would follow suit.

'Well, I do! And I've taken the trouble to get to know him!' He thumped the table; the lamp jumped, and flickered violently. 'He is an educated and considerate man, and very successful. Where else will she get a husband like that? I mean – she's not the greatest catch in the ocean, is she?'

Ellen, stung, replied, 'Oh, Thomas, you're wrong. She's sweet-looking, and she has the loveliest nature, she's a very nice daughter to have.'

He snorted. 'She doesn't know her mind from one minute to the next.'

Ellen retorted, 'And look at what you do with a daughter who *has* firm opinions, you throw her out of the house.'

Thomas said, with as much force as Ellen had ever heard him use, 'If that man wants to marry one of my daughters I would feel privileged to have such a son-in-law. At least he's respectful towards *me*.'

At first, Helena Kane puzzled Dennis Sykes. She talked about the weather as if it lived and breathed, she discussed clouds and rain as if they had human life. Dennis's training as a listener paid off handsomely.

He asked only one question. 'Who is your closest friend?'

'Grace. My sister. I tell her everything. These are her drawing books, and things.' Helena indicated the pile in her lap.

A rabbit ran into the headlights: Dennis stopped the car, waited until the animal freed itself from the dazzle.

Helena said, 'That was kind.'

'God's creatures,' said Dennis matter-of-factly.

For the second time in that week, they reached the part beyond which no road existed, the entrance to the valley.

'I'll walk with you a little of the way,' said Dennis. As he carefully manhandled Helena's bicycle from the car his elbow touched her breast.

The night had not sufficient darkness to cloak them completely.

'Listen.'

Helena stood by her bicycle.

He whispered, 'Not a sound. I love silence.'

'Not even a dog barking,' she said.

'When do your summer holidays end?' he asked in a moment.

'Two weeks.'

'Look. I'd love to talk to you for ages and ages. If I meet you somewhere, can we spend an evening together? We could drive into Janesborough and have our supper in a hotel.'

'I don't know. What to say.' Helena fiddled with the handlebars of the bicycle.

'Say "yes", say it now,' he urged.

'The secret part, that worries me,' said Helena.

'What worries you about it?'

'I'd be lying to my sister.'

'But your parents wouldn't mind, would they?' asked Dennis. 'And – does she, your sister, does she know we arranged to meet this evening? Which we did. Remember? We arranged to meet without anyone knowing we had made an arrangement.'

'No. I didn't tell her, I was going to, later. I don't know, I mean – Grace and I, we've never –'

Dennis clinched it. 'Okay. I'll ask your father. All right?'

'Yes, yes.'

'And just for the moment, don't say anything to your sister, I mean if she's not at home – she won't know. So it will be all right.'

He held out his hand and Helena took it.

'Thank you,' she said.

'Oh, no, thank *you*.'

Rhona broke a twig from one of the trees and swished it.

'That whole swathe of behaviour suggests to me that he is really very practised. Very practised.'

'Explain that,' asked Ellen.

'He knows how to divide opinion. Divide and rule. If you have two people who obviously have had much to agree on – like a couple who have been married a long time. Then if you can split them – you have a power in you. He caused a row between you and your husband.'

'He did.' Ellen leaned against a tree, her skirt blowing in the warm late August wind. 'The worst ever. My husband never spoke to me like that before, even when times were really bad with him and the children.'

'Try this,' said Rhona. 'Try meeting Sykes on your own. Try having a conversation with him of a reasonable kind. Although I believe that he's a despicable and treacherous little shagabout, *you* must also satisfy yourself on the point. And at the same time you can get a better look at him. And you're a very good judge of character. Plus – you will disarm him.'

To begin with, Ellen had to disarm Thomas. When he said gruffly that 'Dennis' had asked permission to take Helena out, Ellen agreed.

'Of course. When?'

'Next Saturday evening. They will go to Janesborough. He will take her to supper.'

'Good,' said Ellen. 'Helena needs social experience.'

240

Thomas never even reflected surprise. She merely arranged further that Dennis should pick Helena up at Deanstown rather than the Grey Valley: a letter would be sent telling Helena.

Ellen sat in the chair facing Dennis Sykes. Thomas had gone upstairs to change from the garden; Helena had not yet arrived.

'Now, Mr Sykes. I believe I may owe you an apology.'

Dennis shook his head. He wore a navy polka-dot tie, small dots.

'No, Mrs Kane.' One of his hands lay mildly on the other, as if waiting to applaud.

She insisted. 'I was hasty with you, and I am sorry if I gave you offence. My girls are my pride and joy. I feel very protective of them.'

Dennis said, 'I understand. Mr Kane and I spoke about it.'

'Did you?' Ellen's eyes widened – and she regretted immediately having given away a position.

Dennis seized on it. 'Did he not say?'

Ellen, discommoded, began, 'He – we, sort of missed time spent –'

'Oh, yes, we had a long talk. I asked him for permission to take Helena out this evening. On reflection, and here I must apologize to you – I should also perhaps have asked you. So the apology due is mine, Mrs Kane.'

She recovered a little. 'We, I – know so little, we – we never met you, you're a stranger.'

Dennis replied, 'I've told your husband my life story.'

Ellen coped better. 'That is not what I mean. What I mean is – we run on very straight lines here, we –'

She stopped, then began again.

'Our lives are modest, Mr Sykes –'

'Call me "Dennis", please!' He laughed. 'I'm too young to be Mistered.'

This she would not yield.

'Our lives, Mr Sykes, are small. Our girls have their interests; they are careful girls; we brought them up carefully.'

'And beautifully, if I may say so.'

Ellen ignored the compliment. 'I brought them up to believe in their continuing life as it is here. As they know it. They are

241

innocent girls. You will notice that neither of them has moved too far away from home.'

He decided to engage with her. 'But, Mrs Kane, if I may say so. They are in their mid-twenties. I mean – many friends of mine that age have three children by now.'

Ellen fought back. 'I don't mean to give the impression that I don't want my daughters to marry.' Her voice ascended to a prissy note, usually a sign that she was confused.

'Well then?' Dennis sat back.

Ellen had no tact. 'I just don't want them to marry men I don't –' This time she did stop before the crucial, damning words – but too late anyway.

He pounced. 'Do you mean you don't want them to marry men you don't like?' In his concluding remark, he encircled her and took her prisoner. 'My dear Mrs Kane, if you don't know me – which is true, because I am a stranger here – how can you therefore know enough about me to dislike me?'

Ellen looked away, her cheeks reddening.

Dennis rose to go to the window, and broke the conversation. 'I think I see your daughter, do I, in the distance?' He looked at his watch. 'Punctual. Like her father.'

Thomas entered. Dennis repeated, 'Punctual, I was saying. Your daughter. Punctual like her father.'

Thomas laughed, and asked, 'Do you have a destination in mind?'

'Yes, Cruise's Hotel. I believe it is very good.'

'Oh, yes. And very famous.'

Ellen remained seated. The men left the room and met Helena on the driveway. Thomas took her bicycle, and Dennis held open the car door.

Thomas waved them good-bye and came to the door.

Ellen said, 'I'm going up to see Mrs Ulverton. I have some recipes she's tasting for me.'

In all the years Thomas never challenged the euphemism.

Rhona, alerted by Munch, walked to meet her. Ellen was cycling too fast, but responded to Rhona's police-raised hand.

'I can't, I can't!' Ellen flapped. 'Rhona, I can't have it! I'm worried. I'm so worried.'

'You're not worried, you're panicked. Now – stop!'

Rhona picked up the bicycle from where Ellen had pitched it. 'Come on,' said she. 'Talk.'

The words flurried out of Ellen's mouth.

'I did it. I did what you said. I sat him down and I looked at him. I looked into his eyes. I talked to him.'

'And?'

'And – I don't know what to say, I don't know what to SAY!'

'Come on, come on.' Rhona took Ellen's arm while trying with her other hand to steady the bicycle. She eventually let it fall again. 'Tell me. In your own words tell me. What is your impression of him?'

Ellen stood; Rhona held her arm.

Ellen gasped. 'He is worse than I thought. I hope I'm not exaggerating. Do you know what it is like when you think something or someone is really worrying, but I had this before, and I didn't act in time.'

'And?'

'And my husband got shot, that's what happened.'

'No, that's not what I meant. You looked in his eyes and what did you see?'

'I feel a fool even saying it.'

'Say it, Ellen.'

'Well, he's – filthy!'

'You can't mean unwashed.'

'No, he has a filthy soul. That's what I mean. He has a filthy spirit. He is unclean.'

Rhona said, 'If you genuinely feel that, then you must do all in your power to stop him.'

Ellen stamped her foot in frustration. 'I can't. That's what's wrong! Who will listen to me?'

'I'm listening to you,' said Rhona, and did something Ellen never knew before or expected: she reached down and embraced Ellen tight.

Ellen burst into tears.

'At last. At long last,' said Rhona. 'The number of times I've wished you would cry and let some of all that stuff in you out.'

When the embrace came to the end of its natural life, Ellen sniffed.

'He has everybody fooled, though. Rhona, nobody can see through him – and he's out with my beloved daughter tonight. What can I do?'

Rhona considered, then answered. 'My late husband had a saying. "To make good decisions you need good information." Therefore – we had better get some information.'

Dennis Sykes explained the etiquette.

'It feels ill-mannered, doesn't it? But think of it as coming down-stairs. The gentleman always goes down first, so that the lady will have something to fall on.' He smiled. 'Likewise, when walking to a table in a restaurant, the man leads the way so that he can pull the chair out for the lady. I like these details, don't you? Now – are you comfortable? You're not in a draught or anything?'

'No. Not at all.' Helena looked around.

He asked, 'Been here before?'

'Oh, no, no.'

'Like it?'

'Oh, yes. It is very – grand.'

'Oh, do you think so?' Dennis smiled. 'You should see the Ritz in London. They have gold statues. And a ceiling painted like the sky.'

She smiled. 'I read about it,' and Helena looked at Dennis's hands.

He said, 'Of course you read a great deal. Your father told me. By the way – are you nervous?'

'Yes. How did you know?'

'Because I am.'

'You are?' Her voice lifted in surprise.

'Yes. Why wouldn't I be? This is like my first ever date.'

'Date?' She seemed puzzled.

'Yes.' Dennis realized she did not know what the word meant. 'A "date" is what the Americans call, well this is, you know, an assignation.' It still did not get through. 'When a man and a girl go out for an evening to try and get to know each other. Or when they are what used to be called "courting". That's a date.'

Helena smiled. 'Around home they call it "coorting", they say a pair are "coorting". It's meant to be very –' She coloured a little.

Dennis waited.

'You know – very – private.'

He said, 'You'll hear the word "date" in songs. Don't you listen to the wireless?'

'Only the programmes my father and mother say we can hear. And there's no wireless in my lodgings.'

'I see.'

He changed the subject as the menu came. 'Does your sister know we're here?'

'No. You asked me not to tell her.'

'What's your sister like?' he asked. 'And as a main course? Something quite balanced after soup, don't you think?'

Helena worried.

He said, 'Why don't you have the chicken with breadcrumbs and I'll have the same?' Much relief on Helena's face.

'Now,' said Dennis, 'it is my intention to get to know all about you. What you want out of life, what you dream of, when you're happiest.'

'She's very – lively,' said Helena, 'she's a lot livelier than me.'

'Who's your favourite writer?'

Helena thought; always, she answered slowly. 'Oh, I don't know. That's like being asked your favourite food, or the nicest flower. Lewis Carroll intrigues me. And there are days when I think a lot of Charlotte Brontë. Mama, my mother, is reading *Adam Bede* at the moment, I finished it last year.'

'George Eliot.' Dennis merely placed the name in the air between them.

Helena looked at him in enthusiasm. 'Oh, you've read her.'

'You forget. I was educated in England.' He saw Helena looking into her soup. 'They're called croutons. French. Made of toast.'

She returned to the earlier subject. 'And Grace draws very well. That's what she likes, I think I told you that.'

At which point, Helena fetched from her handbag a newly-taken photograph.

15

The 'Ulverton Picture' (as Ellen now calls it) was taken by Viva in that summer of 1952. It shows how the two Kane daughters differed.

Both smile easily enough at the camera. As they stand next to each other, their affinity is plain. Beside the elaborate if decaying garden furniture, both look not a little international: aristocratic Italian, perhaps; Finzi-Continis. The old-fashionedness of their simple summer dresses, seen against the brick of the walled garden, suggests an earlier period, almost Edwardian. Notwithstanding the anachronism, both look well-kempt, blooming in health. The photograph is waist-high, and close on their faces: Helena is tentative; Grace's eyes are bolder without being forward; hers is the passionate mouth.

This is the photograph that, when shown to him by Helena that night at dinner in Cruise's Hotel, told Dennis how to pursue Grace Kane. No lines from Tennyson; no sweet reminiscences of Hans Christian Andersen; no cultural enquiries.

'Fears?' he echoed to Mr Quinlan's question. 'Should I have?'

'We got a whisper up here of two dirty words, just a hint we got. That Kane girl.'

'Grace Kane? Dirty words?'

'No,' Mr Quinlan chuckled at the misapprehension. 'The dirty words are "Public Enquiry". Someone's put her wise.'

'Could it happen?' Christ, Quinlan was maddeningly slow!

'We-ell, if she got influential people. Legal folks, especially. They stand to gain.'

Dennis asked, 'How long do Public Enquiries take in this country?'

'The last one lasted eighteen months.'

'Jesus!' swore Dennis, as he stepped from the phone booth.

=

Grace bustled.

'You'll have to move your feet, Mrs Stokes,' she chanted. 'Or I'll be washing them like Jesus washed the apostles' feet.'

Mrs Stokes laughed and lifted both ancient legs. Grace scrubbed furiously and quickly, then wiped the patch dry.

'Back now to *terra firma*!'

'What's that when it's at home?'

'You can put your legs back on the floor!' Grace looked up and smiled, then sat back on her hunkers and frowned.

'Tell me,' she said, 'have you noticed anything different about my sister? I mean – lately?'

Dennis Sykes and Helena had 'walked out' on four occasions in three weeks. Anything more frequent, reasoned Dennis, would be seen as 'fast'; any fewer – uninterested.

'She's out more, and she's quieter,' said Mrs Stokes. 'That can only mean one thing.'

'What?' asked Grace.

'A fella. A boy. A young man walking her out.'

'No! She'd have told me! Mama would have told me.'

Grace spoke more readily to men than Helena, had an easier welcome for them. Once or twice she came close to accepting invitations; each time she judged according to her liking for the man, rather than the idea of having an admirer. So far, nobody she had met proved attractive enough.

'You know when some of them shake hands, and you feel their hands and they're as hard as boards. I don't want that.'

She paused. 'Hellie, do you ever get the notion that we don't know a lot of things we should know?'

Helena answered with a vague, 'Yes.'

Grace warmed to the topic; they were sitting alone on the settle outside Mrs Stokes's.

'There was a girl in Teacher Training who was always in trouble. She was nearly denied a place in her finals when she told Mother Agatha our last Easter holiday that she used to go to dances. She showed me how to put on lipstick if I ever need to, and she wore slacks, I met her once in them.'

Helena laughed and said, 'Don't tell Mama you know someone who wears slacks.'

'Can't you see her face?' Grace mimicked. 'And hear her, "I bet

Our Lady never wore slacks." And the lips pursed. We ought to tease her about it.'

The girls enjoyed the joke: Grace continued.

'Anyway this girl, one night she began telling us about a boy she was walking out with. She showed us how he kissed her.' Grace stuck her tongue out, and Helena went, 'Yeeacchh!'

Grace laughed. 'Stoppit, Hellie. She said it was really exciting. She loved it. The French do it all the time.'

The sisters frequently discussed which of them would marry first. By and large they agreed on Grace.

Helena said, 'I'm not certain about the lying in bed together, smell of sweat,' and she shuddered, making Grace laugh.

'I'd just make sure I was just as sweaty,' she said. 'I'd work like a Trojan just before going to bed, and I'd give as good as I got.'

At which Helena laughed. 'No. I want to go to bed with perfume on.'

'And have him play a mandolin under your window,' said Grace, 'and send you flowers every seventh day. In case you forgot his name.'

Grace, a bitter tinge in her voice, said to Mrs Stokes, 'But we had an agreement. Hellie and I always agreed that whenever we met someone we'd tell each other immediately.'

Mrs Stokes replied, 'The only thing to do then, girl, is ask her.'

'I will,' said Grace. 'I will.' Her momentary dip had passed: her empowering cheerfulness returned.

Miss MacNamara said, 'You will do best campaigning against what most annoys you. Now – let's go through it. Point by point. One – you are not against the place getting electricity?'

Grace said, 'No.'

'Two – what you are against is the Grey Valley being flooded?'

Grace said, 'Yes.'

'Three – but you are not against the people there being re-housed and receiving compensation, and many of them would prefer that to living forever in the Grey Valley?'

'True,' said Grace.

'Four – so what is it that utterly sticks in your craw? Because that is the point on which you will have to fight. Truthfully now, Grace?'

'I can't bear the loss of my lovely place.'

Miss MacNamara said, 'No good. Although I sympathize with you, that won't help you. Try again.'

'How do you mean?'

'Grace, nobody is going to support a campaign because some exotic place that you like to browse in, is going to be destroyed. You have to give it public value.'

'Public value. Such as?' Grace frowned.

'How valuable is everything?'

Grace said, 'I went through that before. That's what the march was supposed to be for.'

'Forget the march,' said Miss MacNamara. 'Have you established what is the most valuable thing about the Valley?'

'The botany.'

'Not strong enough.'

'Well –' Grace reflected. 'Dr Elizabeth Miller from the Museum said that the built-in furniture in the Grey Valley was unique and that nowhere did such a perfect capsule of a European country's domestic past exist in the vernacular.'

Both paused and considered.

Miss MacNamara asked, 'How busy is the work-site these days?'

'Like an ant-hill.'

'Like they're in a hurry?'

'A big hurry.' Grace tapped a pencil against her teeth. 'Don't do that, child, it's irritating,' and Grace stopped.

The teacher continued, 'So – they're in a hurry. I see.'

She thought again, then asked, 'Grace, do you really believe you can stop the dam outright? I mean – truly?'

'I'd like to.'

'I know you'd like to – but do you truly believe you can? Answer me carefully.'

Grace pondered. She exhaled. 'I think. I think – that as long as he's going full tilt, it will go ahead.'

'But,' cut in the teacher, 'if you interrupt someone's momentum it's as good as stopping them forever. Did you know that?'

Grace said, 'Yes. Maybe.'

Said Miss MacNamara, 'Have you found out what the people themselves think of their furniture?'

'They're not pushed.'

'But it has value?'

'To the museum people, yes.'

Miss MacNamara said suddenly, 'Go for a Public Enquiry.'

'A what?'

'Get the historians behind you again, widen your net, do it with style. If you get a Public Enquiry, you'll make them consider an alternative scheme. On the grounds of the vernacular value.'

Grace began anew. Following the system Miss MacNamara outlined, she interviewed, without attempting to influence them, every person in the Valley who would speak to her. All their comments and observations, their feelings, their knowledge of the history of the furniture – all went into her notebook; and she made drawings of the pieces of furniture under discussion. Day and night she worked, and then, when she had a large collection, she began to compile a short document.

A printer in Janesborough went through it with her and Grace emerged with a five-page newsletter. Each page was headed with a drawing of a different piece of furniture: Mrs Stokes's Wall-Bed; the Carrolls' Paired Canopy Bed; John McCarthy's Fiddle-Fronted Dresser; the Hickeys' Sledge-Foot Dresser with Clevy for Hanging Utensils; Mrs Ryan's Carbery Settle.

Underneath Grace gave the quotations she had collected from the families who owned the furniture – statements of their esteem, affection and family history, simply expressed. All the vernacular pieces, she emphasized, had been created as part of each house: built into the walls, or fixed to stone floors – and therefore immovable. And therefore certain to be drowned.

She sent the first printer's pull to Dr Elizabeth Miller, and asked her for an observation she could use to complete her newsletter. Dr Miller wrote back: 'The Grey Valley has the single greatest concentration of Irish Vernacular Furniture in existence. It belongs in its own environment, and will lose much even if saved and housed in a museum. To place a cultural value on it, I would suggest that by virtue of its concentration in one locality, it has as much a place in the culture of the nation as a latter-day Book of Kells, or St Patrick's Bell.'

Grace whooped. She went back to Miss MacNamara, and showed her Dr Miller's letter.

'Now you have your campaign,' said the teacher. 'Now – this is what you do. You finish printing your newsletter with this as the front page, plus your own account of the Grey Valley. No emotion, Grace, just beautiful facts. Then, when it is all printed, you send it off to every political figure, every distinguished academic, everybody you can think of, and you ask them to write back to you. Most important, find a list of leading solicitors and barristers: you can get that from the Incorporated Law Society. Send the newsletter to each one. When you have all their letters, plus the signatures of the people in the Valley, then you give the editor of the *Nationalist* first crack at telling the world. At that point, you ask for a Public Enquiry. You can even talk about a National Park.'

In the car coming home from Cruise's Hotel, Dennis discussed at greater length the implications.

'I mean – I'm her greatest enemy, I'm the man drowning the Valley.'

Helena thought, and replied, 'But – I never had a secret from her.'

Grace sat up in bed drawing. When she heard the latch lifting and Helena's footsteps on the stone floor of Mrs Stokes's kitchen, she called out, 'Come in if you're good-looking.'

Helena smiled around the candlelit door. 'Hallo, artist.'

Grace said, 'Come here to me, have you a fella?'

'What?!' – but Grace misread Helena's alarmed reaction for a hint of outrage.

'I knew it, Mrs Stokes said you must have. I said she was wrong. How're they all at home?' asked Grace.

'Great. Mama sent this.' Helena, grateful for the diversion, handed over a small warm rug, and a bag of oatmeal scones. 'She says to tell you the autumn is coming on, so be careful to wrap.'

'Did she say anything about my not going back to work?'

'Not a word.'

'Great,' said Grace, 'because I have big plans' – which she conveyed in detail.

Helena's betrayal of Grace deepened. As she put her dilemma to her mother, her father listened.

'I don't know what to tell her if he asks me to go somewhere with him again. Or if Gracey asks me again if I have a – friend.'

Thomas butted in aggressively, 'He's a more decent man than you'll find around here. And you should be grateful that such a remarkable and successful figure takes an interest in you. Such a polished individual.'

Ellen opened her mouth to speak, but Thomas glared.

'Don't tell her yet,' butted in Thomas. 'And that's an order. Your sister is a troublemaker.'

Ellen soothed. 'I'll tell Grace,' she said, 'when the time is right,' and snapped the sewing thread with her teeth.

'By then,' said Thomas, 'her "campaign", that nonsense, that will all be a thing of the past.'

'I don't know,' said Helena, 'she now has very powerful material, and she's sending it to everybody.'

Ellen, gladdened, but not able to show it, asked, 'What do you mean?'

Helena pulled the newsletter from her bag and showed it to her mother.

'Grace is writing to nearly five hundred people asking for their support. When she gets their letters back, Mama, she feels she will have something valuable, and she's going to call for a Public Enquiry.'

'At this stage?' snapped Thomas.

'She'll then give all the letters to the *Nationalist*.'

Thomas fumed and ran from the room.

'Helena, love, keep out of it,' pleaded Ellen. 'And as for Mr Sykes –'

Thomas stormed back, in hat and coat.

'Helena, you are not to tell Grace you told us all this.'

Next week, having ascertained that Helena had still said nothing to Grace, Dennis praised her. 'There's such a thing as tact.'

The following week – 'And if she discovers that you and I have been walking out – as I hope we are?'

Helena, honest as ever, replied, 'I don't know what to say.'

'At least,' replied Dennis, 'you understand that Grace will be hurt. She will see you as having taken up with the enemy. That's why I always suggested that you say nothing to her. Time enough when all this is over.'

The work on the Deanstown hydro-electric project became a wider attraction. On Sundays, people from everywhere gathered on the high ridges to look down and marvel. They saw a deep scar in the ground, and, now, the gum of concrete rising well above the top. The curve fascinated the watchers – a perfect lateral arc, of grey, with an edge like a scimitar.

As his first line of defence against the new Grace Kane initiative, Dennis put in counterweights. Through an agency in Dublin, he engaged artists and writers to create a large storyboard. This was taken out of the construction huts every Sunday morning and erected in a prominent position. With Thomas, he arranged a school tour for the Deanstown children, at which he gave them an illustrated lecture on how such a project was undertaken. Thomas invited other schools, and led other parties of pupils.

Dennis Sykes understood the potential in the power of Grace's argument. Sure, he already had the overwhelming support of the community. Certainly, they looked forward eagerly to having electricity in their houses. Equally, they basked in the 'world-famousness' of the project. Yet, he had enough intelligence to understand that people from outside could be pressed into service emotionally – and financially.

He assessed his position. The Kanes, father and mother, were divided over his 'interest' in Helena. Thomas Kane made that clear.

'I think your wife doesn't like me.'

Thomas looked up from Dennis's project notes. 'Don't worry about that, my wife changes her mind about things.'

'So, about Helena.' Dennis held the pause. 'If my intentions ever became serious –?' He left the question unfinished.

Thomas actually blushed a little. He shook his head. 'Leave all that to me.'

Pressure. Pressure. Keep up the pressure. The phrase Helena had unwittingly reported haunted him: 'The Grey Valley – as important a national treasure as the Book of Kells': that could sink him.

'I was thinking,' said Dennis, 'of changing the work schedules. I was thinking of creating three teams, A, B, and C, and giving prizes for getting sections of work done quickest. You know these men. Would they like that?'

Once again he had rubbed Thomas's ego.

Thomas preened. 'Yes, yes. I believe they would.'

Thomas's next remark gave Dennis a brainwave. 'In fact,' said Thomas, 'they were saying in the Post Office this morning that the men said – they could work harder if they had to.'

'In the Post Office?' asked Dennis.

At which point he decided his next two moves.

The first depended upon his influence over Helena Kane. He began to make notes of every conversation he had with her. On the nights he returned from a meeting with her, he wrote down the key words of the evening: 'soft'; 'kind'; 'easy'; 'nervous'; 'gentle'; 'frightened'; 'afraid'; 'children'; 'mild'. He noted that she did not use these words as meanings in themselves, but as the paint in her ordinary language. Extrapolating, he wrote a short character sketch:

> Virginal: frightened: not unintelligent – but too meek to use her brain well. Obviously terrorized by her father, and in awe of her mother. Possible to speak to her unusually directly about sensitive matters; yet needs to be handled with kid gloves. If dealt with abruptly or hastily, she will fly away. Wants romance and tenderness and promises of a future which will have no hardship in it. Not much would push her into a nervous breakdown. For instance, she may only be kissed in the most chaste fashion. A devout girl, she will lie if asked to, so long as she can tell it in Confession. There will be nothing intimate of any kind in her life before marriage, and even within marriage only with difficulty.

He planned his strategy towards Helena accordingly.

Dennis the prude: 'I absolutely oppose any, you know – intimacy. Until people marry.'

Dennis the lover: 'I'm a romantic at heart – I like, well, poems.'

Dennis the companion: 'Isn't delicacy between people such an attractive, such a winsome thing?'

All the while he enquired subtly – usually by asking for comparisons – as to what her sister was like.

The sister sounds less patient, more passionate. This stands to reason, as the good quality of the relationship between H and G suggests that G is likely to be in contrast, and to have more of the mother's natural passion. Whereas H has the father's tendency to aloofness but without his innate violence.

He began to draw up an urgent timetable.

Rhona and Ellen met on the avenue. Ellen's anxiety had reached fever pitch.

'Any news?'

'Yes. Good news. I have had a letter,' said Rhona, and fished it out. 'Read it.'

Dear Rhona,

Odd that you should ask, not my usual line of country. But I did enquire, and I think I have come up with something.

Neville's brother in MacReady Armitage Bailey has a typist, a gossipy girl called Eileen or Eily. She has a friend who was 'wronged' by a well-off 'incomer', an engineer. Whether he left her in the family way, or whether she merely thought he was going to marry her and didn't, I cannot be clear, but if you like we can enquire who the girl was.

Apparently she was a laundress. Does that sound right? And what in the N. of G. are you up to?

Yours bemusedly,

Harriet.

Rhona asked, 'What do you think?'

Ellen said, 'Explain all that.'

Rhona took her time. 'My friend Harriet Armitage makes it her business to know as many people as she can. She's like that. If I ever want anyone found, you know, for mundane things, such as, well, polishing old ivory, that sort of thing – Harriet will know. She always knows someone. Who knows someone. Dublin is a small place. So – what do you think?'

255

'Enquire,' replied Ellen glumly. 'That's all we can do.'

'We can do more,' said Rhona, 'at least you can. If our enquiries work, you can go to Dublin. Gather evidence.'

'Oh, hardly!' said Ellen.

Rhona raised an eyebrow. 'My dear Ellen, it *is* your daughter. That little shagabout will be wanting to marry her next. I would go if I were you. Can I persuade you?'

Ellen said, 'Yes, but you'll have to come with me.'

16

Dennis set it out like this.

1 By October 7: begin 'approach' to GK.
2 By October 7: tighten up 'commitment' to HK.
3 By October 14: block all responses to GK's newsletter.
4 By October 14: Secure all TK's loyalties forever – at least until February 1.
5 By October 14: Compromise EK beyond recall.

He found her easily enough. From the site headquarters, his binoculars scanned the ridges each morning. Soon he divined that she had a pattern. At about ten o'clock, Grace climbed the eastern end of the ridge. From the top of the escarpment, with the sun behind her, she surveyed the progress of the site work. Sometimes she sketched into a large pad, then tucked it under her arm and descended into the trees and bushes, the fur of the Valley floor.

Three mornings in a row he watched, until he had verified her paths. When he climbed the ridge, he could see the cottage clearly: ironically, he had chosen that vantage point as the one from which the switches would be thrown to fill the Valley, and then light the village, on 1 February.

Rain delayed him for two days. On a morning of bright sunshine, he moved. As Grace scrabbled the last yards to the top of the escarpment, Dennis left the site and slipped down into the Valley. He had chosen a position that would directly place him in her returning path. The precise spot would enable her to see him first, and choose, should she wish, to avoid him. He would judge his next move from whether she acknowledged his presence – from which he would know immediately whether his hunches about her were right. In a conversation about the French, Helena had told

257

him Grace's kissing story: what matter if she had begun it in great embarrassment: as she had stopped and started, Dennis 'helped' her along with it.

He arrived at his chosen place, and stood, legs apart. The upwind breeze helped, bringing in advance the tune Grace hummed, and the noise of her brushing against the shrubs.

Timing, Dennis, timing.

About ten seconds from the moment when she could first see him, he faced in her oncoming direction, opened his trousers, took out his penis and began to urinate. He did so in an exaggerated fashion, hand on hip, stream flowing and steaming. He could be seen in detail – a flash of white underwear, a glimpse, even, of pubic hair.

If she fled, Dennis would have to re-think. If not –

He heard her stop: had positioned his head so that he could peer from under the lid of his hard-hat – without her seeing his eyes. The impression he gave was of a man completely unaware of any other creature. He finished and began to button his trousers, then she crashed forward and stopped. Yes! Yes! She *had* hidden. *And* stared!

He looked up and started. 'Oh, I'm – sorry.'

'For what?' Grace clearly intended pretence.

He changed tack. 'I mean – did I frighten you?'

She scorned, 'It would take more than you to frighten me.'

'I'm sure that's true, but what I mean is – you gave me a start.'

'A start? A start in what?'

'Aha!' Dennis laughed. 'A language barrier. I see. A "start" is what we call a fright. I mean – I didn't expect to meet anyone, and I thought perhaps you didn't either.'

Grace said, 'It's a free country.'

Like an admiring little satyr, Dennis looked at the trees, and the skies, and the ambience, and threw out his arms and said, 'Yes, and the old saying is true, the best things in life are free.'

'But you're trying to destroy them,' accused Grace.

'I'm only doing my job.'

She pounced as he meant her to. 'Ah, so you admit it, your job is to destroy this place?'

'Heavens, you are spirited,' he laughed. 'No, and you know perfectly well what I mean.' He stared at her breasts in her green

258

blouse. 'Anyway, I couldn't see you coming, you were wearing camouflage.'

Grace looked down.

He indicated. 'Lincoln green?'

'What?'

'Lincoln green. The colour. The colour of your blouse.'

'*Lincoln* green?'

'Yes. After Lincoln Forest, where Robin Hood was. He wore a suit of Lincoln green. Did you ever read about Robin Hood?'

'Yes. I did.'

'Oho!' He laughed.

Grace asked, 'What's so funny?'

'A girl reading boys' books. You must have been a tomboy.'

They stood facing each other. Neither moved. In a moment Grace gave way – she stepped back and fiddled with the branch of a tree.

'By the same token, how does a man know about colours? That's a woman's subject.'

'I studied painting.' Which he had not.

Grace hid most of her interest. 'What kind of painting – house-painting?'

Dennis smiled. 'No, but I'd probably make more money.' Now he relaxed. 'I studied all kinds of painting. Still life, you know, bowls of fruit. Life studies. Nude studies. Some landscapes. Animals.' He watched her closely.

Grace asked, still not entirely conversational, 'Animals seems a bit like your subject.'

He pretended not to see the irony. 'Yes, in fact. Shrewd of you. The anatomy is difficult to draw. That's why humans are interesting too.'

He looked at Grace and generated a silence. Then he turned and walked away.

Early in adult life, Dennis Sykes discovered what he called 'compartmentalization'. If he divided his mind and his activities into compartments, he could give his full attention to one issue at a time, and bring a burning focus to bear upon each. By fixing on it with all his concentration, like a magnifying glass held in the sun's rays, he could burn into that compartment, could achieve from it, or put upon it, exactly what he wanted and needed. This power gave him whatever firmness he had salvaged from his unstable, unfathered childhood.

He made Grace Kane a 'compartment'. After he turned away from her and appeared to head back to the dam project, Dennis looped in his tracks. Within about three minutes was abreast of her, up a slight slope – able to monitor her, but able to conceal himself if she suddenly turned to her right and saw him. She walked along briskly, head down, large sketch-pad clutched to her bosom. Like her mother, she talked to herself all the time; Dennis could see her lips moving and would have given his fortune to know what she said.

She stopped once, and stared into the distance ahead of her: he watched from behind a high and heavy briar-rose, saw her mouth move, her knuckles clench on the sketch-pad. As if having determined something, she shook her head and walked on. Dennis watched her out of sight, heard her call a greeting to the old woman.

Already as he walked back to the dam, he recognized his dilemma: how fast, how hard to move? Play her slowly? Should he dive in? Was there a middle course?

Thomas Kane said, 'You're going to have a visitor later today.'

'Who?'

'The new Minister.'

Beautiful. Beautiful. Another objective could be achieved at once.

'Are we neat and tidy?' Dennis asked Thomas. 'Is my face clean?'

Thomas, boyish only in the presence of Dennis Sykes, said, 'I'll have to inspect your fingernails.'

'Now,' said Dennis, 'you arranged this, didn't you?'

Thomas inclined his head. 'Well I did write to him to congratulate him on his appointment.'

'And,' said Dennis, taking up the story, 'you just simply suggested that he come and see the most advanced hydro-electric project in the world.' He gave an exasperated and puzzled exhalation. 'My goodness – your nous, that's the word for it, such nous!'

260

Thomas Kane did not appear displeased.

Rhona said, 'There are times, Ellen my dear, when a little judicious deception has a purpose, a greater purpose. This may be one of those times.'

'I hate telling lies.'

Rhona replied, 'Nobody likes them. That is to say, I don't like them either. There is a cause here, though. We have found our woman. And she will see us. And Sykes was the man in the case. The ruinous man. Your instincts were right.'

'How will we do it?'

Rhona thought. 'Tell your husband that you are coming to see the doctor with me in Dublin. If you do not elaborate, he will think it is a woman's complaint, and not ask questions, men do that.'

'I know.'

Rhona asked, 'Do you know where Terenure is?'

'I can afford a car to get us there from the station. Will you write to Miss Glacken, or will I?'

The Minister walked carefully, hands deep in the pocket of a raincoat. A man whose eyes moved all the time as if he had a kind of dancing myopia, he shook hands with everyone he saw. Thomas Kane and Dennis Sykes stood on the wooden walkway steps to greet him. The Minister snorted, put his head down, increased his pace and ran up the walkway.

'The man himself! And how are you?'

He held out his hand, and Thomas took it.

'This man,' said the Minister of Transport and Power to Dennis Sykes, 'without him I wouldn't be here.'

Dennis chimed in, 'Nor, Minister, would any of us on this site, I believe.'

'How are you? How are you?' insisted the Minister again.

'I'm well, Dan, and so are you, I think.'

'This man,' the Minister rapped Thomas's lapel softly with his knuckles, 'is one of this buckin' country's great heroes.' He turned to Thomas once again. 'But what are you doing here at all? Why aren't you in the school? A'course, 'tis Saturday, what am I saying?'

'Dan, this is Mr Sykes, the young genius who is in charge here.'

261

'And the wife, how is she herself, I heard you've lovely daughters. Hallo Mr Siki, Dan Cantrell, Minister for Transport and Power.'

'Sykes, Minister, how do you do?'

'Sykes, Dan,' Thomas Kane corrected gently, 'Dennis Sykes.'

'Sykes, ah, Sykes, a'course there used to be a boxer called Battling Siki, d'you remember him? Now where's this damn dam? Hallo girls, Dan Cantrell, Minister for Transport and Power. How are ye?'

The Minister walked forward and shook hands with the typists.

'But you didn't say? I know 'tis Saturday, but I'm still asking how did Thomas Kane, the man I know to be a schoolteacher and the best in the whole buckin' province too, how did he get to be a dam engineer?'

Dennis smiled. 'Minister, he's a kind of unpaid, unofficial adviser. Without whom we would not have managed. I assure you.'

'They say you're ahead of yourself?'

A civil servant behind the Minister nodded at Dennis.

'Just about, Minister. If it had not been for this man's help and understanding, we would not have advanced nearly as far.'

'My God,' said Dan Cantrell, Minister for Transport and Power, 'but I could tell you stories about this man, so I could. I remember one night, not two hundred thousand buckin' miles from here and lying with this man in a wet ditch –'

Thomas steadied himself. 'Now Dan, come on, the past is past.'

'See that!' cried Dan Cantrell, Minister for Transport and Power, 'this is not a man to boast. But I'll tell you one thing, there was never harder. What about them two Black and Tan officers? D'you remember staring them into the eyeballs –'

The civil servant intervened. 'Minister, the foreman here – he's a constituent of yours.'

The foreman came forward.

'Dan Cantrell, Minister for Transport and Power. What's your name now?'

'Paddy Prescott.'

'What Prescotts are you?'

'Ballingarry.'

'Ah sure listen, don't I know every chick and child in your whole

262

family, hadn't you an uncle died of TB two years ago up above in Peamount Sanatorium. I was at that funeral.'

Dan Cantrell, Minister for Transport and Power, had a pulse in his throat like a frog. It fascinated many.

'But come back here to me a minute,' he said to Dennis Sykes. 'How come this man here is acting unpaid?'

At this moment Dennis Sykes clinched his second objective.

'Minister,' he said, 'I have asked Mr Kane over and over to accept some kind of fee, some kind of consultancy payment, some sort of honorarium or stipend. He has refused, he says it is no more than his duty. A matter of honour. Now, I believe – and I can prove it to you, Minister, and to your advisers [Dennis had learned many years ago that civil servants liked being called 'advisers'] that without this man's help and advice we could not, as I indicated, we could not as quickly have progressed as far as we have done.'

The civil servant peered around the edge of the Minister.

'Minister, there is a precedent, for having local advisers on certain projects.'

'Right so.' Dan Cantrell took Thomas Kane's arm and addressed Dennis Sykes. 'He'll be an adviser to the Minister. And that's all there is to it. And why wouldn't he be?'

Like a thin gale, Dan Cantrell swept out of the office to inspect the dam earthworks and concrete, and in his wake Dennis Sykes lifted a pleased eye at Thomas Kane.

'Credit where credit is due,' Dennis said.

'This man,' mouthed Thomas silently, a mimicking echo of the Minister's oft-repeated phrase.

'I am being made an official adviser,' said Thomas to Ellen.

She stared and smiled. 'To the Minister?'

'Yes. For this. And he said "Who knows what else?" That's what he said.'

'Oh.' She clapped her hands. 'Well done. Well done. You can buy me a fur coat.'

He laughed. Then he said soberly, 'I should remark – it was at the recommendation of the Mr Sykes you don't like.'

Ellen recovered well. 'The important thing is that the Minister knows how seriously you take life around here.'

263

'Yes. Yes.' Thomas nodded gravely.

After some contemplation, Ellen said, 'Thomas. Next Saturday. This day week?'

'Yes?'

'Rhona Ulverton wants to go to Dublin. She asked me to go with her.'

'Why?' he asked, though not unamiably.

Ellen made a wavy gesture. 'A doctor. You know.'

'I see. Will you want a lift to the station?'

'Apparently Cyril has said he'll drive us. We'll go from the Junction.'

'Cyril?' Thomas laughed. 'You'll never get to the train, let alone Dublin.'

Next afternoon, Dennis said over and over, 'Third-Remember-that-thou-keep-Holy-the-Sabbath-Day.' He swished his way through the woods with a hazel stick he had cut, a long wand with a fork at the tip. Helena had arranged to meet him that night at her parents after Evening Devotions.

Dennis took a chance on the afternoon; but first, he stood on the ridge and checked Mrs Stokes's house with his binoculars. No sign of young life; the old lady came out once, threw a basin of white water away into the long late grasses and went back indoors.

Where was she? From the ridge he searched and searched: no sign of her. No bird life seemed disturbed. Other than occasional smoke from other, hidden chimneys, the Grey Valley was as still as the next world. All of autumn had come down to the valley floor, and he smelt it as clearly as he smelt women.

The ridge shelved a little under his feet, the undercarpet of shale yielding a possible fall. He stopped, picked up a curious stone, flung it away, then continued. The renowned valley blackberries had gone unpicked; a few remained as fat and black as sin. He plucked several, avoiding the long briars that reached for his sleeve. A sloe stung his tongue so bitterly that he spat it out. Two rabbits raced ahead, their scuts bobbing into the deep low hanging growth. He found a path, and stayed on it, with branches so low even he had to duck. Aloud he murmured the line of an old poem, 'I saw old Autumn in the misty morn, stand shadowless like Silence.' He stopped and listened – like a hunter. Which is what he meant to be.

In his notes last night he wrote:

Grace Kane: small and hot: legs like a Roman goddess: fat lips and strong eyes: would lead a husband a hard dance were she raised in a non-Catholic society: knows she has a body: is capable of telling lies quite easily: she saw me, I know she saw me. Don't wait. MOVE!

Now he went forward, on tiptoe, ear cocked. The humming – just ahead: a humming noise: a tune, but not recognizable. He saw her – she stood looking at a parasite on a tree, a growth of berries sprouting a red leprosy from the bark; she reached in and touched it, then returned to the sketch-pad, made some marks, then looked back. He stood. Unwatched, she groped back and pinched her grey skirt to ease underwear from a cleft somewhere.

Dennis strode forward.

'We meet again,' he called, his voice hard.

She spun. 'What are you doing here?'

'As we agreed. It's a free country.'

He stood right in front of her, 'Let me see.'

Grace made no effort to stop him, as he took the sketch-pad and stared. Only when he began to flick the pages did she attempt to prevent him.

He rapped, 'No!' and leaned back out of arm's reach.

Some pages earlier he found a rough sketch – of him, standing as he had been when he urinated while she looked. The sketch, full-length, had loose, fuzzy definition at the crotch.

Grace blushed bright-red as he handed it back.

'So – you saw? I thought you did.'

Her eyes defied his stare – but she was the first to look away.

He said, 'I dreamed about you last night.'

'A nightmare was it?'

He said, 'Maybe for you – but not for me.'

'Oh. Were you drowning me?'

He said, 'No. I was taking off your clothes. So that I could see you as you saw me.'

She turned back to look at him. He reached out, drew a hand softly along her face, from height of cheekbone down to mouth and down, down, quickly through her cleavage, down to her crotch, so quickly she hardly knew he did it. Then he turned and vanished into the trees.

Helena waited by the gate.

'My parents have visitors. Where are we going?'

'That hotel, that lovely old place I stayed in once.'

'Grabstown Manor.'

They drove. Helena said, 'Did you smell the autumn today?'

Dennis smiled and reached across for her hand. 'Isn't this the life,' he said. 'I may never leave this place. I think I've fallen in love with it.'

Over their drinks, both orange squash, they simply talked. He told her his invented life; she answered his questions about her family without seeing his motives.

That night, she had arranged to stay in Deanstown. In the darkness, he pressed his face to her cheek.

'Good-night, dear Helena. Can we meet next Saturday?'

'I don't know. I have to be here. Mama is going to Dublin.'

'Shopping?' asked Dennis. 'Why don't you go with her?'

'No. It – it is something odd. She said not to ask. Which is not like her at all. She and Mrs Ulverton have been writing to someone there.'

Dennis's antennae twanged.

In the car, as if writing in his notebook, Dennis assessed his orchestration so far. Thomas Kane flattered into abject loyalty. Time to ask for Helena's hand: but – next Saturday? Why was Kane's wife and that tall snotty bitch Ulverton, why were they going to Dublin? To dig up something? Bloody small country. Everyone knows someone who knows someone. Vital that the second Kane daughter fall utterly out with everybody – so that no one knows of my relationship with both. And those fucking letters? Had she now sent off all her Newsletters?

Move, Dennis, move! Now! Christ's sake! He braked, turned, changed direction.

Heavy, knee-high fog. He parked the car on the snout of the earthen path. One light showed; the old woman slept early, Helena had said. Only one other bedroom.

He walked straight to it. Curtains wide open: inside Grace sat up in bed; by her side on the floor a pile of letters, clearly ready for the postbox. She licked another and sealed it; she wore a cardigan over her white nightdress.

Dennis tapped on the window softly, softly enough to make her wonder if she had imagined it. He paused. She stopped and listened. In a moment he tapped again.

'Is that you, Hellie?' Grace had a rasping whisper, it came of her husky voice like her mother's.

Dennis tapped once more.

'Hellie, if that's you the door is open.'

Tap. Tap. Then a little scrape.

Grace climbed out: Dennis appreciated the thigh he saw. She came to the window, leaned across the wide sill, tried to peer out, hands either side of her eyes. Dennis stretched a hand in and tapped again. Grace wrestled the sash up.

Dennis spoke. 'It's me.'

'What?' Why did she not sound surprised?

'I have news for you.'

'What are you doing here?'

'Your father.' He knew all the most powerful introductory words.

'What's wrong with him?'

'Can I come in?'

Grace thought, then yielded. 'Be careful. Be quiet. I'll go to the door.' She took the candle. Dennis tiptoed in her wake through the dark kitchen to the room.

Grace never said, 'This is improper.'

Grace never said, 'I don't want to see you.'

Grace never said, 'Go away.'

Second draft of timetable: by Christmas all nuisance will have to be removed. G must be disarmed completely by then and – ideally – have gone from the area.

He sat uninvited on the bed, did not look around, behaved as a messenger.

'I'll come to the point. Did you know that your father has been made a special adviser to the Minister for Transport and Power?'

'When did this happen?' Grace looked at him.

Dennis looked her up and down, in her white lawn nightdress.

'It has been in preparation some time. Confirmation has just come through yesterday. Nothing to do with me.'

She sat on the rope-seat chair beside the bed. The candle flickered: Dennis took it from her, put it on the shelf. He said nothing, simply looked at her.

'Why did you come and tell me?'

He shrugged. 'Two reasons. One – fair's fair. There are now considerable powers ranged against you. Two – I wanted to see you again.'

'Why?'

'I like rebels. I'm one. You may not think so.'

In the silence that followed they heard Mrs Stokes snuffle-moaning in her sleep in the room across the kitchen.

'They never told me,' said Grace. 'Mama never told me. Why didn't she write?'

Dennis had figured accurately. In these circumstances Helena would have wept. With luck Grace would rage. She did.

Shaking her head, she clenched teeth and fists. 'All that talk about honour.' She said it over, and over, and over.

'I must go,' said Dennis. No reaction. After a moment or two, he said it again.

'I must go.'

If Grace had tears in her eyes, they shone with fury. She stood as he did. By the door he whispered, 'At least I got to seeing you again.'

He made to leave, then turned back. The psychological trick he had pulled on Rose Glacken was about to pay off again – associating intimacy with distress, affection with disappointment and fear. He took Grace's forearms and held her hands by her sides, then kissed her on the mouth. No movement on her lips, inexperience rather than lack of interest – so he moved her lips with his tongue. He stood back, and took both her hands: he spread them around her breasts. Like a child she looked down at her hands in his grasp; he dropped one hand and scraped his own fingernail lightly in her pubic hair as Betty had taught him in Lantern Street. Dennis scraped a second time; he reached in a little, pressed hard briefly – and left.

Next morning he saw Grace cycle from the Valley; on her pannier the bulk of several postal packets.

268

That night he called again. As she sat on the bed he tipped her very, very gently on her back and by way of a joke remarked, 'Never ask me again if I have a civil tongue in my head . . .'

He buried his face on hers. As he left, hours later, he remarked, 'Did you know that your sister's staying at home . . . ?'

17

O n the train, Ellen leaned over to Rhona and said, 'Now the next problem is how to get Grace back into the fold.'

'Has your husband eased any since he got that compliment from the Minister?'

'Not towards Grace.'

The women had dressed exquisitely. Ellen carried what Leah called 'her inevitable brown-paper parcel'.

'If Miss Glacken is a single girl living on her own, she may need some fresh baking, and a fruitcake lasts a while.' Sometimes Ellen had a self-satisfied air.

At the dam site later, Dennis Sykes said to Thomas, 'How does the postal system around here work?'

Thomas said drily, 'Slowly.'

'If, say, your daughter's campaign was to bring in a lot of letters – how long would it be before she got them?'

Thomas reflected and said, 'If there were a lot, the post-mistress'd prefer she collected them.'

'Are they stringent?'

'Stringent?'

Dennis clarified. 'Are they stringent in that only the addressee can collect? I mean – can one collect letters for a member of one's family?'

Thomas replied matter-of-factly, 'We open all the children's letters, not that there are many. My wife and I feel things are safer that way, there used to be a tradition around here of anonymous letters. We've always thought the children, especially the girls, should be protected from that sort of thing.'

The pathway's tiles gleamed as ever. Bright shone the brasses on the little hall-door.

'Which of you is which?' asked the large-faced girl gently.

'I'm Mrs Ulverton and this is Mrs Kane. Are you Miss Coleman or Miss Glacken?'

'I'm Rose.' She smiled tentatively, and led them in. Waiting by the little stairway stood Eily Coleman who introduced herself.

Rose said, 'Eily has to go, but she came around just to see that you'd arrived safely.'

Eily bobbed a little around the women and prepared to go. Ever since Man stood upright, no woman ever left a house as reluctantly as Eily Coleman left Rose Glacken's house that Saturday morning. Indeed, she even turned back, having forgotten her gloves. She admitted to Rhona's beady eye in the hallway that it was 'a bit early for gloves wasn't it' but she 'always had bad circulation'.

She called, 'Rose, d'you need tea made or anything?'

'We can probably manage,' said Rhona with a grin.

'A brighter set of colours on you would cheer you up,' said Rhona to Rose. 'But it is very good of you to see us.'

'I like maroon,' said Rose, 'but I thought this was a bit lighter when I bought it, until I put it on.'

'That can happen,' said Ellen.

They sat. Rose had prepared tea, sandwiches and cake. Ellen handed over the baking she had brought and Rose thanked her fulsomely. 'You shouldn't.'

Rhona led off immediately. 'Mrs Kane,' she said, 'will come to the point.'

'I gather,' said Ellen, still wearing her hat, 'that you know a Mr Dennis Sykes.'

Rose nodded.

'How well did you know him?'

Before Rose could speak, Ellen interrupted her with a blurt. 'You see, Miss Glacken, I'm worried sick. He's after my daughter and I don't think he's a sincere man.'

Rose gazed at the willow pattern on the teapot as if it were a crystal ball. The women waited for her answer.

'Sincere?' She said it softly. 'No. He isn't sincere. Does he still wear a watch with a light brown strap, a kind of tan colour?'

Ellen nodded.

'Well.' Rose continued her scrutiny of the teapot. 'He used to look at that watch behind my back when we were – if we were, if he was –' She struggled. 'You know – when he gave me a kiss or that.'

Rhona and Ellen had to lean forward to hear her. Rose drew her fingernail over and over across a little nep on the tablecloth. She had a small brown mole on her neck.

'Why should that be the thing I remember now?'

'Am I right to be worried?' insisted Ellen.

'There's a sweatstain on the watchstrap and that used to annoy him, and one evening here I asked him to take off the watch to see could the stain be polished away, and playing, like, I said to him, "Now you're not getting that watch back until you're leaving the house tonight." And d'you know what it is, I thought he was going to hit me. He snapped at me so hard that I gave it back to him in a fright.'

Rose looked up at the two women. 'What do you make of that?'

'He had to have control of everything,' said Rhona.

Ellen asked, 'How do you feel about him now?'

Rose's gaze returned to the teapot. She mumbled something.

Ellen said, 'Pardon?'

Rose said, 'Smeared. I feel smeared.' She made a dismissive gesture, as if washing herself down. 'I feel he dirtied me.'

Rhona and Ellen exchanged looks. Rose continued, 'I feel as if – as if, I don't know what. I didn't feel it for a while after he went, and then I began to feel as if, as if.' She paused. 'As if he came in here to, to – use me, like I was an old animal, a cow or something.'

She raised her face to look first at Rhona and then at Ellen, and then Rose's large placid and pleasing features collapsed. Her mouth arced downwards and her lower lip sank. No tears.

The three women sat there. A painter would have captured a woman as tall as a cossack's wife, her hand leaning on an ivory-handled cane; a small vivacious woman twisting her wedding ring; and Rose – a small hand fiddling with the nep of fabric on the tablecloth. Under the square rug, the lino on the floor had been waxed to local grandeur.

The visitors waited for Rose's words. She kept them waiting.

Rhona knew the uses of briskness.

'May I ask – where did you meet him?'

Rose began, 'He used to come and have coffee in the Oriental Café in South Great Georges Street.'

She told her story: of Dennis's slow build-up, of his attention, of his respect.

'How could I mind,' she asked rhetorically, 'even if I felt it was all a bit too perfect? All I ever had to say to myself was the truth – that I'd love to have a husband. He seemed nice to me.'

The gifts; the attentions; the Sunday papers; the 'taking of instruction'; the waiting for her outside Confession – all later came to dust when he vanished without explanation.

'I still don't know why he went.' Her monologue faltered. 'Maybe he guessed.'

Ellen pounced – but softly. 'Guessed what?'

'Well. I discovered I was expecting.'

Now Rhona pounced – on Ellen. Leaning out of Rose's range of vision she wagged a powerful finger when she saw the beginnings of disapproval on Ellen's face. She had to wag again before Ellen released the purse-strings of her mouth.

In a voice as kind as a grandmother's, Rhona asked, 'Was the baby – adopted?'

'No. I lost it. At four and a half months I felt a pain and I went into Holles Street by myself, and when I got there I asked the receptionist to take me to a bathroom, and the nurses just got to me. They were kindness personified.'

Rhona asked the question nobody else would have asked, and that Rose needed most to answer. 'Despite all, do you miss the baby?'

Rose nodded, as dumb as grief. 'I didn't care if it was a boy or a girl even. And now, even though 'twas probably too late for me anyway, even now, if I met somebody or even' – she hesitated – 'even if he came back, I can't have any children. They told me.'

On the homegoing train, the first chance they got to talk without being overheard, both women homed in on the same point and simultaneously quoted Rose: 'Even if he came back?!'

Rose talked and talked. Every detail materialized. She had forgotten nothing. They marvelled at her recall. She described specific occasions, told them where she and Dennis had gone, even what they ate. His clothes, her clothes, his views, her cooking for him.

273

Then came the questions she had never allowed herself to ask. Why she had never met his colleagues? The fact that he never wanted to meet her friends? How come he ran everything and she simply fell into his line of things?

Ellen and Rhona sat with Rose, as they had each sat with widows after a funeral. Each woman fed Rose from her own store of compassion – brusque, tender, turn and turn about. At the end, a silence.

Ellen broke it. 'Rose, I'm going to call you "Rose". My heart goes out to you. I've hardly ever met a nicer girl.'

Rose nodded.

Rhona said, 'Is there anything practical we can do – to stop this little, this little seducer ruining Helena's life?'

All considered.

'If he has any shame,' suggested Rose, 'the mention of my name, maybe. It might – it might tell him people know about him.'

'I can pretend,' said Rhona, 'that you're a friend of mine.'

As they left, Ellen shook Rose's hand warmly. 'I'll write to you,' she said.

Even as the women on the train planned, Dennis Sykes had moved ahead of them. He ticked off his objectives.

1 TK secured.
2 The *coup de grâce* about to be delivered on HK.
3 GK in hand (so to speak).
4 GK's effort about to be pre-empted on two fronts.

First, he approached the editor-owner of the *Nationalist* and bought the biggest advertising spread that newspaper had ever seen: 'To continue until April, all right?'

Said the editor, 'We support progress.'

Secondly, he had to make a small adjustment to Thomas's effort.

'But if you intercept *all* the letters,' said Dennis reasonably, 'then, if it were me – I would suspect. Shouldn't a few get through?'

Dennis looked forward to 'soothing' Grace's disappointment.

A problem remained, potentially – the Kane wife's trip to Dublin with that older of the two Ulverton bitches. For some unknown reason he felt persuaded that it concerned the girl, what was her name, in that funny little house with the cold lino floors?

Viva Ulverton moved his position from persuaded to convinced. Lately, she often unnerved Dennis by popping up: on the roadside; peering at him through the site fence; sitting on his car outside Hand's pub. She never said anything – just waved, or smiled, or skipped a little as if about to dance for him. On Monday morning, she sat on the saddle of a bicycle just by the site entrance.

He greeted her, pleasant as usual, his policy: 'Morning, Miss Ulverton.'

She pointed at him. 'Spoke in your wheel. Fly in your ointment.'

'What are you talking about?'

'Pebbles in your shoe, little man.'

Dennis grew cold: no effect.

'Wait and see, Dapper Dan.'

'Wait and see what? And who, may I ask, is Dapper Dan?'

Viva chortled. 'You are. Little fucker.' She wandered off.

Grace waited on the pathway down from the shale.

'You look nice.'

She shrugged. 'Easy words.'

'No.'

'Yes. You have a lot of words. They come easy to you.'

'Here.' He held out his hand. 'Give me your hand.'

Reluctantly, she agreed.

'Come for a walk.'

'I don't want to.'

He stopped and looked her in the eyes. 'Now what's wrong?'

She said, 'You made me sin. You made me commit a mortal sin.'

'How?'

'You touched me. Immorally.'

'I'm not a Catholic,' said hard and defiant Dennis.

'But you know about sin?'

'I don't see how a gesture of affection between two people can be a sin?'

She said, a little savagely, 'Affection? You don't know the meaning of the word.'

Dennis replied, equally aggressively, 'How do you know? You've hardly met me.'

275

'I know by your eyes.' She quoted him sarcastically. *'Gesture of affection.'*

'All right,' he said. 'Desire. Is that better?'

'A bit more honest, anyway.'

'So – you're so fucking perfect!' He watched carefully to gauge the effect of the expletive. She did not react. He took back the hand she had earlier snatched away.

'I've got the measure of you.'

'What do you mean?' she asked.

'One, you saw me on the pathway. I was pissing and you watched. You pretended you didn't. Two – you, with your Catholic sin and all that, you never batted an eyelid when I swore just now. Three, I felt your tongue move against mine.'

Grace repeated, 'You made me sin. I should not have let you – do. Do what you did.'

'What did I do?'

She replied, 'You know perfectly well.'

'Stand.' As she stopped he walked behind her, stood right against her back. 'And did you object?' he whispered in her ear. Grace did not answer. Dennis put a hand on her hip: shades of Audrey.

'And did you object?' he asked again: this time he spat the words.

No answer. With his other hand, Dennis reached around and smoothed a breast, then ran his fingernails in a circle until he found the nipple.

Grace said uncertainly, 'This isn't fair.'

Dennis dropped both hands to his sides. 'What isn't fair?'

'I have no one on my side.'

Dennis said, 'You have now. Let's walk on.'

She seemed near tears and he put an arm around her shoulder.

'Come on. I'm better than you think.'

They found a log and sat.

'Can't you make it up with your father?' asked Dennis.

'No. You don't know him,' objected Grace.

'He's very stern. Was he always like that?'

Grace, still avoiding Dennis's look, said, 'Mama said he wasn't. Until the accident.'

'Accident?'

'You must have heard.'

Dennis said, 'Only vaguely.'

276

'He was in a coma. Helena and I, when we were at school –
people used to say to us that my father was shot, and that my
mother afterwards –'

'Who shot him?'

'I don't know.'

'Your mother afterwards? What was it you were going to say?'

'I don't want to talk about it.'

'The man who shot him – was he caught?'

'He died.' Grace rose. 'I said! I don't want to talk about it.'

'All right, all right, keep your shirt on – or, rather, don't.'

Dennis's joke failed.

Grace said again, 'You made me sin.'

'Oh, for Jesus Christ's sake change the fucking tune, the band
is getting tired!'

Dennis tossed an angry little head. He pinned her arm, put a
hand roughly under her skirt and flicked. Grace tightened her
legs; they struggled; she parted her thighs briefly, soft flesh above
stocking-tops. He pressed two fingers right in, withdrew his hand,
rose and walked away, leaving Grace looking after him.

Ten yards off he turned and called, 'I'll see you later.'

In that village community, there are still no such things as secrets.
Nor do you ever hear what they say about you. But they know.
The unconsummated Hogan marriage. That John Shea and his
sister shared a bed. The small legacies. Or big debts. The death
of Dan Quinn.

When Thomas Kane recovered fully, there was one civic duty
he never again undertook: his wife successfully objected to it. In
the past he had been a Character Witness when the court circuit
came by. During the Hilary term of 1925, he testified on behalf
of Michael Quinn, a boy accused of stealing. But the court con-
victed the boy, and asked Thomas to carry out the birching.
Afterwards, the boy's father spoke vengefully to the righteous
schoolmaster, to his wife.

During the investigation of Thomas Kane's shooting, nobody
made allegations – and everybody knew. The police questioned
only one man, the bulky and dismissive Daniel Quinn. No proof.

In the succeeding months, Ellen Kane heard the flint of heavy
boots on the road near the house and on the gravel. Quinn came

into her garden once, and helped himself to a bucket of potatoes. In fright, but with presence of mind, she immediately invited the Canon to do likewise – very publicly. Quinn did not do so again.

On Christmas morning 1926, Daniel Quinn's body was found on the roadside, near the church. His horse grazed the winter verge nearby. Quinn died of head injuries, had drink taken, the heavy spirit of Christmas Eve. The vet's examination, to ascertain whether the horse might also have kicked the man, revealed a small but powerful, irrelevant wound on the horse's shank. When the Superintendent called upon Mrs Kane, he took away for examination a Tara brooch hatpin; it was returned two days later.

The inquest jury returned a verdict of 'death by misadventure': thrown by his horse. Deanstown still agreed on the natural justice of the outcome.

'We all said he had it coming to him.'

Dennis asked, 'The horse, Mrs Hand? Was it put down?'

Breege Hand said, 'No, no, the horse was harmless.'

'But it threw the man?'

Mrs Hand practised jovial malice. 'Ah, now sir! We do all get frantic if we're jabbed.'

'Jabbed?'

'Jabbed.'

'Jabbed with what?'

Mrs Hand laughed. 'Men knows nothing. There's many a man round here since wouldn't let his own wife own a hatpin.'

'Who had the hatpin, Mrs Hand?'

'Ah, now look, wasn't justice done? Didn't the hand of the Lord help?'

'But the hand of the Lord didn't push the hatpin, Mrs Hand?'

Mrs Hand eased herself out of the conversation. 'No, nor it didn't.'

Dennis Sykes had enough bait to go fishing.

Almost ready for bed, Ellen heard the Sykes car. It stopped outside; moments later the door slammed; the car drove away; she heard Helena's footsteps on the gravel, then around the house, then the girl came through the back door. Ellen went downstairs.

'Hello, Mama.'

'Hello, love, you look very nice. Did you have a pleasant outing?'

'He's very nice to me.'

Ellen smiled carefully at her daughter. 'Do you like him?'

'Well, I do. What I mean is. I know you don't like him, but Daddy does and since he, I mean Dennis, since he started to be interested in me, Daddy is very nice to me.'

'But is he the kind of man you would marry?'

Helena said, 'If he's going to be that nice to me – I mean, if, if –' She sighed. She considered. She began again. 'If he talks to me and tells me things, and if he doesn't bark at me. Tonight, for instance, he told me how much he likes children, he told me how much money he earns, he told me how much money he has saved. He said I was intelligent.'

Ellen protested, 'But you are intelligent, you are!'

Helena replied, 'He says that I say interesting things. He says that I know what I'm talking about. I don't feel afraid.' She took off her gloves. 'And tonight before Dennis called, Daddy actually showed me something to read from the paper and discussed it with me.'

Ellen said nothing, just nodded, then after a moment or two, asked, 'When are you seeing him again?'

Helena replied, 'He's taking me to the pictures in Mooreville on Tuesday night.'

'To the pictures?'

'Yes.'

'What's on? Is it suitable?'

'Yes, Mama, *Soldiers Three*. Stewart Granger is in it.'

'Oh, pity –' then Ellen bit her tongue.

'Pity about what?' asked Helena.

'Gracey loves Stewart Granger.' Ellen regrouped. 'Helena love – we have to *do* something. It is terrible that Gracey isn't speaking to us.'

'But Mama, it isn't my fault. And it isn't your fault.'

Ellen let the thought continue, then asked, 'And it isn't, I suppose, Gracey's fault?'

'No.'

'Then –' thinking aloud, 'whose fault is it?'

Helena said, 'It might be nobody's fault.'

Ellen rose. 'We have to think of something to do. I miss her terribly. I've written to her now three times and she won't write back to me, there's no reply.' At the kitchen door Ellen asked, 'Are you going to first or second Mass?'

Helena said, 'I'll go to first.'

'Goodnight, love.'

After Helena, he drove straight to the mouth of the Grey Valley. This time Grace heard him coming; the window stood raised. He whistled like a small animal or night bird. Grace pulled back the lace curtain.

'You?'

'Me.'

'What do you want?' All in whispers.

'You.'

'Stop it. Go away and leave me alone.' But she did not move the curtain.

'Why?'

'I have to get up for Mass. Tomorrow's Sunday. You upset me.'

'I did *not!*'

'Shhhh!'

'I did *not* upset you.'

She whispered, 'You did.'

'I didn't mean to. Can I come in?'

Grace defended briefly. 'The door is closed.'

Dennis indicated. 'The window is open.'

She made no attempt to prevent him hauling himself over the wide sill. He dusted down the flakes of whitewash from his black trousers. Grace stood there; the candle in her hand guttered a little in the breeze.

'A windy night was blowing on Rome,' Dennis quoted softly.

'What?'

'Nothing.'

He did not penetrate Grace that night. Nor did he take off his clothes and climb beneath the heavy blankets with her. He did kiss her repeatedly, stroked her, touched her bare skin, smoothed down her nightdress again; laid his face on her shoulderblades, kissed her neck under the hair, traced her lips with his fingers, then his tongue. He talked to her, or rather he listened, mostly about her father. She described the Christmas Day she called her father 'a bastard' and how her father had whipped her home like a small dog. When she grew distressed during a whispered memory, Dennis found an erotic means of distracting her, of making her halt the story for a moment or two.

Dawn raked the sky. As he slipped away, he whispered back through the window, 'Was all that sin?'

Grace shook her head, full of sadness and premonition.

The rabbits raced ahead; a distracted small bird whirred softly by Dennis's head. He walked, half-loped through the thick shrubbery of the valley floor. Stopping by one house, he heard the sleeping moan of an old person, the re-settling grunt; then silence. A cat ran home. No chimney smoke, no bark of a dog. In a clearing, Dennis checked the sky, and saw the sun coming up, its light unimpeded by the tails of long red-tinged cloud. He changed his mind, cut off to the east.

On the far ridge, he turned to face the Valley below. It looked like Africa. Man might have been born here, sixty-five million years ago. Dennis could see no houses, only the wavy, milky haze that softly clogged the upper strata of the greenery.

He spoke aloud. 'Grace is right! She's right to fight!'

His words had no echo – not in the valley, not across the empty space of that morning, nor in his heart. With his next breath he turned to view his beloved project.

The dam had now risen truly above the ground. That grey thick curve of wall had the sinister force of those submarines he saw in wartime newsreels. So compact! So – so *powerful*! Along the top, a column of twelve men could march abreast. Dennis's specifications to the builder resulted in a neat site, the work-in-progress always ordered and under control.

It all had a majesty; the wide young walls seemed an organic part of the planet itself. A week tomorrow, the workforce was about to double and in six weeks these walls would then reach their final height. When it began to curve in, the full beauty would appear. Nature did not have all the tricks, did She? A man could take Her on and tame Her to make something beautiful. In a little over two months, a new landscape would exist here, a shimmering lake of grey and silver satin held firm at one end by exquisite engineering. What a day was to come! The sluice at the far end, the last of the works that would be completed, would blast open and in would plough the rivers, spuming and ferocious. This valley bowl would fill in, what, six hours? At which point, the dam would begin its eternal work. Time it backwards: February the first: dusk falls at four o'clock: therefore, hold a ceremony to loose the waters at nine in the morning; then return for the switching-on of the lights at, say three? Return? Nobody would leave: the party would grow and grow as people came to watch the flooding of the valley.

To do all this: to change people's lives! To transform the face of the Earth itself! Not only that – this is the smallest, yet the most powerful piece of engineering work of its kind in the world, almost a toy, no bigger in its curved length across than a large battleship, no, perhaps an aircraft carrier. Small, like me! Powerful, like me! Elegant, like me! Came out of nothing, like me! No fear, no more. Fuck them!

Developments on Monday finally guaranteed Dennis Sykes absolute command. All had to do with the Kane family. They occurred between half-past two and half-past four.

The first took place on the hundred-yard stretch of road between Deanstown School and the Kane household. Ellen's day ended half an hour before Thomas closed the school at the statutory three o'clock. By twenty minutes to three, she had gathered her basket, donned her hat, smiled at Thomas through the partition and left. Autumn surrounded her, mild, warm and full of smoky thoughts. Carrie Egan filled a bucket from the green helmet of the old pump and waved a greeting. A hen stalked tediously in the thin-legged privet of Caseys' hedge. Ellen saw the black gleam before she heard the engine; inevitably he stopped.

'Hallo, there.' Until he died he would retain the habit of stroking his moustache as he greeted someone, a nervous reflex.

'Hallo, Mr Sykes.'

'Oh, look!' he sounded half-irritated, half-amused. 'You'll have to start calling me Dennis.'

He hauled on the ratcheting screech of the handbrake and got out. 'I knew there was something I've been meaning to say to you for weeks – that chocolate sponge cake.'

He made a circle with thumb and forefinger and punctuated the air between them.

'First-class.'

Then he looked Ellen's body up and down.

She attacked. 'Mr Sykes. I will not call you "Dennis". I will never call you by your first name. I will not have anything to do with you. You are ruining my family. And I know all about you.'

He recoiled but kept his head. 'All about me?'

'I know enough to make people suspicious of you, indeed to change their foolish view of you.'

'Now, Ellen.'

'I am "Mrs Kane" to you, Mr Sykes. Nor will I ever be more familiar. And if I have my way, you will be out of here as quick as your legs can carry you.'

'I believe you're mistaken, Ellen. I have a job to finish.'

'Believe what you like. Not that you believe in anything. No – I'm wrong. You do believe in something. You believe in wrecking people's lives.'

'Oh, come on! That's not on!'

Ellen played her card. 'Rose Glacken? 15 Mayhill Terrace, Terenure?' She puffed with triumph. Not for long.

He grinned. 'Oh, who's a snooper!' Dennis rubbed his hands with glee. 'Playing that game, are we? Nothing I like more. So – may I ask. Did you, in your snoopings, find out whether Miss Rose Glacken uses a hatpin? Or rides a horse?'

Ellen's mouth fell. He leaned back against the car, could afford to wait, no need to press. She began to come back at him, but – no words. He moved the matter forward, and not in the way she expected.

'Yes?' he said, in a jovial 'I'm waiting' tone.

Nothing. He had won.

Long pause. Reality. No pretence now, cold business: 'Here. We have to get on, you and me.'

'You and I.' Still she could not stop correcting people.

'All right. You and I. You're full of that sort of shit. But we have to get on.'

She tried once more, nothing if not courageous. 'You ruined that poor girl.'

'Love's labour's lost – Mrs Kane.'

'But you ruined her, she is – destroyed.'

Dennis smiled; he put on what Binnie used to call his 'glitter'. And stroked his moustache again. 'But she's alive.'

Ellen's shoulders conceded defeat.

Dennis said softly, 'Don't you know your Cicero. Very apposite in all this – *Mrs* Kane. "While the sick man has life there is hope." Must have been a time when that would have been a useful tag in your existence.'

Dennis opened the car door. He said over his shoulder, 'So in fact, we may now turn around and put to good use your earlier remark, what was it you said to me? "I know all about you." Yes, I believe that is what you said.'

He drove away, and was pleased to see that she stood watching him – probably, he hoped, in consternation – as he turned into the school playground fifty yards on.

Thomas Kane saw him arrive, released the school five minutes early. Dennis watched the motley children storm out.

'I must say,' he observed, 'it gives me deep satisfaction to think of the improvement electricity is going to make in their lives.'

Thomas smiled, 'Come in. Come in.'

'I won't stay. I just have two things I want to say. First of all, and most important. I met your wife on the road just now. Now – how can I put this to you?'

Thomas looked puzzled.

Dennis paused.

Thomas fixed the fireguard for the night, put a tall carboy of ink back in the cupboard.

Dennis began again. 'Your wife. Well – the conversation she and I had.' He pretended unease, then appeared to gather courage. 'Look, I don't know how to say this, I've never had to say this to a man before.'

Thomas now gave Dennis his full attention. The small man said, 'This is what I have to say. I would very much like, now that I've had a good look at both parents – I would very much like to marry your daughter, Helena.'

Thomas Kane laughed and rubbed his hands. 'Well, well, well. This is very good news. Very good news altogether.'

Dennis put out a hand: Thomas took it and shook it. 'It will be like having another son,' he said shyly.

'And it will be like having a father after all. We got on well, didn't we, from the moment we met?'

'We did indeed. We did indeed.'

Dennis said, 'I have such plans. If this entire project works out, I may even start my own engineering company, and to have your wisdom and advice. That would be just great.' He added anxiously, 'I hope your wife will be pleased.'

Thomas nodded, 'She will of course. She will of course. Every mother wants to see her daughters marry well.' He returned to his small, day-closing chores. 'Oh, this is excellent. Excellent.'

'Now, I have to go,' said Dennis.

'Indeed. Indeed.' The two men reflected for a moment.

Then Thomas said, 'You said there were two things?'

'Oh, yes. The postman told me this morning, there were what he called "several hundred" letters for your daughter – Grace.'

Thomas frowned. 'Leave that to me.'

Dennis contemplated. 'We have so much at stake now. Oh, by the way.' Dennis turned on his highly-polished shoe. 'Not a word to Helena yet. Please. I obviously want to –'

'Of course. Of course.' Thomas smiled again. 'And by the same token, I think I'll wait for a while to tell her mother.'

Dennis approved.

Effectively Grace Kane's protest ended that evening. She needed replies *en masse* by the middle of that last week in October. Had she received three hundred letters, she and Miss MacNamara gauged, a national newspaper would have taken up her cause. At the very least she would have persuaded some journalist to use the words, 'Public Enquiry'.

In her fantasy, all would have happened while the dam wall was still low enough to be covered in.

'What does the place look like?' asked Miss MacNamara.

'Well.' Grace hesitated. 'I have to say it doesn't look as bad as I thought. The thing is – the whole project is much more compact and neat.'

'How many letters?,' asked Miss MacNamara.

Grace blushed. 'Eleven.'

'How many did you send out?'

'Over six hundred.'

Miss MacNamara gazed out of the high window. Behind her desk hung a picture of Eugenio Pacelli, Pope Pius XII, thin nose, thinner spectacles.

'Eleven out of six hundred. That's what? One in sixty?' She sniffed her fingers. 'Of the eleven – anyone significant?'

Grace said, 'No. One museum-keeper, who wrote from home. The point is – there's no typewriting – all the letters I got are in handwriting, so –'

'So there's no *official* response?' asked Miss MacNamara finishing the thought.

'No.'

'That's funny. Oh, well. Perhaps they all felt – that it was too late or something, or often people in positions of authority, they often feel they can't, they can't – well, go against something so official. Does this mean you have no time left?'

Grace nodded.

Miss MacNamara said, 'That's a pity. A pity. And you fought so valiantly.' After a pause she asked, 'What do you want to do now?'

'I want to go on noting down and drawing everything,' said Grace. 'There are only three months left.'

'And when,' asked Miss MacNamara tenderly, 'do you want to come back to work?'

'The first of February.'

'Your job will be waiting. You will be very welcome. Have you enough money?'

Grace nodded. The Headmistress changed briskly, 'Now something else, Grace. You're not looking well. Are you all right?'

'I'm not sleeping.'

'Of course you're not.'

Grace said, 'I – I.' She stopped.

'Is there anything you want to talk about?'

When her staff smiled about Miss MacNamara and her beard, and her walk like a very fast bird, they also referred to her warmth. Yet, not even her heart could bring Grace to ask for help in the dilemma over Dennis Sykes, and the raids he made, and her awful compliance, and the guilt he caused her . . .

Last night he called again, very late. Last night he talked to her a little – and he listened, and listened, and listened. Last night he kissed the insides of her lips and she felt the skin stretch as her nipples rose. Last night he made her hot, and when he left in the small hours of the morning, slipping away through the rain, not even the breeze through the opened window could cool her cheeks.

Last night, when Mrs Stokes went to bed, long before Dennis the prince of darkness arrived, she sat by the fire and wept, now that she had failed and had nobody with whom she could share her failure. She wept because she missed Helena, who had not yet replied to the letters she sent – even though Grace wrote to Helena at her lodgings. She missed the jokes with her mother. And she wept because she had no words yet by which she could tell Mrs Stokes that she had failed, and that the Valley would be drowned after all.

'You're keeping me alive, girl,' the old woman said to her every morning. When it finally appeared as if no other letters would arrive, Grace feigned illness, left her room only to empty bladder and bowels.

Then, on the third morning, Mrs Stokes came into the room and said, softly, 'Child, I have a little bit of bad news. The big builders is in, they're in in force, there's hundreds and hundreds of them.'

The dam had reached the point where nobody could stop it now. All Grace had managed to do was raise a notional point-of-no-return, and that had passed and she had been virtually ineffectual. She and Mrs Stokes sat in silence.

18

Rhona Ulverton waited – for news of the *coup de grâce*.
    As she left the train, she said to Ellen, 'Go for him. Go straight for his jugular vein. It runs along here –' and she made a throat-cutting gesture with the flat edge of her hand.

No news – except from a surprised Viva, who said, 'Sykesy-Ikesy is livelier than ever. I thought you two were going to spike his guns?'

Rhona handed bread-bearing Essie a note.

> My dearest E,
> What happened? Did you beard the maggot in his den? I yearn to know.
> With affection,
> R.U.

Ellen replied,

> Dear Rhona,
> I'm afraid we have to let the hare sit a while. Things are complicated: I'll explain later.
> Hope the bread is fine.
> With affection,
> Ellen.

Rhona's inner questions tormented her. Three times in the next four days she walked in ways and places where she had been accustomed to meeting Ellen. No joy. Munch had not seen her. Viva had not seen her.

Essie arrived, laden again.

'How is the Mistress?' asked Rhona.

'Grand, Ma'am.'

'Is she very busy?'

'She is, Ma'am.'

'Can you ask her – very quietly, mind – to meet me tomorrow afternoon in the Bottom Field?'

'I know she can't do that, Ma'am, she've inspectors in the school like, and she've to be there, for their tea.'

'The day after?'

Life quickened as never before. Deanstown and Silverbridge became Klondike villages; Mooreville a Yukon town. The shops carried notices of delivery dates for appliances. Comerford's Hardware Stores ordered a hundred electric kettles: people flocked to see them, on the prime shelves, fat as copper duchesses; each had a pleased-with-itself spout, and a thick projecting stub of round plughole at the back. Customers lifted the lid, looked at the grey worm of element inside, asked about Brasso as the ideal cleaner. Lily Campion even came out from behind the counter and showed them by means of a measuring jug that each kettle held six pints.

In plain brown cardboard boxes the irons came, and each had a long coiling tail of thick speckled flex cord, ending in open wires awaiting a plug. Women hefted the weight and marvelled at the glass-smooth plate underneath.

The village of Silverbridge stole a march on the town of Mooreville. Hogan's Stores took delivery of six Belling cookers a full week early, on the second Thursday in November. Word went out, as if a travelling show or a fortune-teller had come. Wife after wife hurried over the humpy bridge; they tapped every plate, twisted every knob.

Ellen wrote to her daughter.

My dearest, lovely Gracey,

It seems as if the Grey Valley will turn into a lake after all. But maybe birds will nest on its banks, and maybe swans will come.

Are you well?

Will you come home? Please? Or, if you want to do things a different way, or if you want to talk first and can't face us all at once, could we meet?

I miss you, we all miss you. Hugh keeps asking for you, he

says he has new jokes for you. We can achieve almost anything by talking and your lovely friendly joy and intelligence are sorely missed by this house. Please reply.

Your loving,
Mama.

In the stillness of the night, Dennis listened.

Grace enumerated. 'They even say a silver fox used to come into this valley, all the way down from the Arctic Circle. There are gentians here we will never see again. And all the fossils. They will all disappear. That's the extent of the damage you're doing.'

He nodded. 'I know. I know.'

'These people. Mrs Stokes, she's heartbroken.'

He nodded.

'Compensation is only money,' Grace whispered.

Dennis whispered back, 'I have something to tell you.'

Grace listened now. Morning after morning she had met Dennis in the Valley floor, where they kissed on the edge of hostility. Before which she had climbed to the ridge in rain and hail and wind to see him leave the site and walk to meet her. When they parted, she grew anxious – and rushed up the shale again, to track him the whole way back to the construction hut. And day in day out, the grey wall of the dam rose and rose.

'Your newsletter.' Dennis watched her closely. He wore shiny, black riding-boots, his trousers tucked into them.

She looked askance and embarrassed.

'Two and a half weeks ago,' he said. 'Replies came.'

Grace said, 'I know. I got them. Eleven out of six hundred.'

Dennis shook his head. Grace leaned back against her pillows, as with a malady; Dennis, a hand on the patchwork counterpane, sat on the bedside.

'No.'

'What do you mean – "no"?'

Dennis traced a nipple idly through her nightdress. Grace wriggled away and asked, 'What are you saying?'

'I'm saying. There were several hundred.'

She frowned. 'No, I *sent* several hundred.'

'And – you got several hundred back.'

290

'I didn't.'

'You did. But you don't know it. Your father intercepted the letters. He collected them at the Post Office in Silverbridge, told the postmistress he would give them to you. I only found out yesterday.'

Dennis clamped a hand across Grace's lips. 'Shhhh! The old woman. Don't wake her.'

He held – until he felt her mouth ease; he took his hand away.

Grace swallowed and asked, 'How many letters?'

'He said, your father. He said. Well, he counted them.'

Grace hissed with ferocity. *'How many?'*

Dennis held up one hand, then the other. 'In hundreds.'

'Five hundred?'

'More. Five hundred and thirteen.'

'But? I got some?'

'Your father made a decision. He believed that if some replies reached you, you would not get suspicious.'

'Ooohhhnnnnhhhh!' It came out as a long whispered moan, true helplessness. Grace, since a child, when moved beyond endurance, put the heels of both her hands into her eyes. Perhaps in so doing she pressed ducts: in any event, tears never flowed until she pressed hard. She inhaled deeply and held her head back on the high pillows. From her under her closed eyes, tears began to seep.

Two weeks ago, he said to Helena, 'I would never want you to weep. I want to give you so much protection.' When Helena smiled, he whispered, 'Ohhh! Your lovely face.'

Dennis began to inch forward. Grace, drawn by his hands, allowed herself to fall towards him: he stroked the black abundant hair, buried his face in it. As each draft of weeping hit her, he drew her closer.

A week ago, 'Dearest, sweet Helena,' he told her in the car, 'I can't bear the thought of you ever needing anything. My role will be to provide for you, to let you sit, and be. To give you time and love. To make your dreams come true.'

=

291

With his toes and heels he eased off the black shiny boots, and slid up along the bed. And stroked, stroked. Soon, of her own volition, Grace pressed her face into his shoulder. Dennis slid her down from the pillows, until he and she lay parallel.

On Sunday, he offered Helena the mysterious package.

'This is for you. A gift. For no reason other than for your being you.'

'You call it "gift" – we call it "present". What is it?'

He played with her. 'I'm not going to tell you. You must open it.'

Helena said, 'Oh. Oh.'

He tapped the leather bindings. '*The Collected Works of Tennyson*. "On either side the river lie. Long fields of barley and of rye." Like it?'

He forced the bedding away until her legs lay exposed.

'Hallo,' he kept saying. 'Hallo.'

He slipped farther down, raised her knees and angled his pelvis under her. Much stroking, much, much stroking. Soon, and without ceremony or protest, he had gained careful entry. Patient, soft, holding her, not letting her raise her face; he stroked her hip; he stroked her hair with his other hand; he waited and waited. She never opened her eyes.

Last night, he said, 'Helena, darling – I want a special date with you one evening soon.'

'Why?'

'Nosey parker.' He tapped her nose.

With each half-thrust he whispered, 'Ease up, ease. Relax.'

He never hurt her, she never cried out; very little blood spilled. When he left, Grace had fallen asleep. She did not awaken until very late; an overcast morning had kept the sun hidden. For several moments she lay there, then she turned on one side, placed her head deep in her arm and began to sob without a sound or a tear.

Rhona and Ellen met in the Bottom Field.

'What happened? What happened?'

Ellen lied. 'I changed my mind.'

'You whaa-aat?'

'I changed my mind.' Set of lip, jut of jaw.

'But we said?'

'I know.'

'He will get away with murder if we don't stop him.'

Ellen said, 'We have to think of another way.' White of face; staring straight ahead.

Rhona turned, stopped in front of Ellen, causing her to halt.

'Ellen. Look at me! I'm an old fox. I know things. Something's gone wrong. What is it?'

Ellen stood, but not looking.

'Ellen, what *is* it?!'

'We have to think of something else.' Stubborn; head angled away.

'I know. Helena, isn't it?'

'Who told you?' Ellen seized the excuse.

'Viva said they were seen at the pictures. And at Cruise's Hotel in Janesborough. And over in Thurles.'

Ellen Kane could not have survived Thomas Kane's righteous depredations for so long without some inscrutability. His morality had been forged by the use of the gun. As he failed to grow, his morality never developed. Accordingly, she had to devise her own labyrinth and steer her family through it. An occasion such as this with Rhona Ulverton, however knowledgeable and worldly her opponent, posed few problems. By her silence she led Rhona. When assumptions tumbled from the older woman, Ellen chose the most suitable. Rhona reached it quite quickly.

'Your husband is encouraging Dennis Sykes to woo your daughter?'

Ellen nodded.

'In that case,' Rhona declared, 'I can easily use our new knowledge to discommode him.'

'I think we should wait. In any case, he will be gone in a few months.'

'But –'

'Look, Rhona. My best chance is to do nothing. Maybe it won't come to anything – him and Helena. Maybe he is only pretending to like her. In order to smooth his path while here.'

'That,' said Rhona, 'is almost certain.'

'In which case, let it blow over.'

Rhona said, 'It sticks in my gullet to have to do that.'

'Please. For Helena's sake.'

Rhona looked at her. 'If you wish. Nevertheless.' She raised a finger. 'I am going to say one last word. In all the years I have known you, I have never seen you so ashen. If you need me, you know I'm here.'

The final meeting of the electricity project for Deanstown & District took place in the schoolhouse on 20 November. In exceptionally mild weather, mist closed in early. Excitement ran high. Ellen did not appear.

Dennis addressed the meeting. 'Is everyone here from the Valley?' and a voice said, 'Only Mrs Stokes is missing.'

'Aah!' said Dennis sympathetically. 'Now – while Master Kane is doing his last calculations, I'll tell you exactly where we stand. Oh, by the way – the Department have informed me that all re-housing has now been agreed. Is that right?'

They nodded.

'Is there anyone here who feels worse off – I mean in terms of the house you've been given?'

No answer.

'All I hope,' said Dennis, 'is that the next community I work in, be it in Ireland or Iceland, will be as pleasant. I could not have done any of this without the help and co-operation you've all given me. The wall of the dam, as many of you have seen, is up to a great height. We are ahead of schedule. Thanks mainly to the quality of the workmen from around here. I have never worked with men who worked harder.'

Dennis clapped his hands, a one-man round of applause.

'Now. Let me tell you what will happen.'

He led them through each stage. On 1 January – 'what better day to start a new life?' – they would begin to evacuate. All transport and furniture removals would be provided. 'I know there has been some debate about the furniture you have, so if there's anything you want to bring – even if it is built-in to the wall, we will provide help.'

294

One voice said, 'Be glad to see the end of it.' Many cackled with the speaker.

'You can each have up to three trips to empty your house,' said Dennis. 'We want this to be as painless as possible.' They murmured their appreciation.

'By the last day of the month, all the work will be finished at both ends. Then the Great Day itself. We have photographers and reporters coming from abroad. As you know, the Archbishop is saying a special Mass at the site that morning at half-past seven. I know that's very early, but this is why. It will take only six hours, we calculate, for enough water to pour in. To activate the turbines. Those pumps are like atomic power.'

'Over Christmas, the last work at the far end will be done. On the morning itself, after he celebrates Mass, the Archbishop will bless the dam and then he will press the button that will blow the gelignite and unleash the rivers into the pumping mechanisms. And then into the Valley. No danger – but a lot of noise. Then you will see the greatest torrent you have ever seen in your life. Any questions so far?'

No, no questions.

'We will all go away and have breakfast. Or we can stay and watch; bring picnics if you like. To my sorrow we won't have enough to feed you all – unless the Archbishop brings enough loaves and fishes with him.' They laughed.

'Then.' Dennis got their attention again. 'At half-past three we will reconvene and observe the progress of the water. According to our estimates it should be three-quarter way up the wall of the dam; certainly it will have covered the tops of the trees by then, and a beautiful lake will have begun to form. I hope everyone'll be there. Because, all things being equal, we will turn on the electricity some time between four and five o'clock. As you know, if you choose the best spot up on the ridge, you will be able both to look into the Valley, and see down into the village. And you will see the lights of Deanstown being switched on.'

They applauded.

The schoolhouse door opened. Both lamps flickered. Dennis recognized her at once. Men standing at the back parted to let her walk through. Thomas Kane stood by the yellow lamplight and stared.

Grace, halfway up the classroom, turned to the people who had craned sideways towards her, and said with great calm, 'There is now one fewer house in the Grey Valley to be emptied. Mrs Stokes died this evening.'

'Go away!' Grace called from inside the locked house.

Ellen rapped on the door again and said, 'But Grace, Mrs Stokes has to be laid out.'

'We did all that last night. Mrs Allen helped. Now go away.'

'Oh, Grace, my love.' Ellen went to the window.

From behind the curtain, Grace said with perfect calm, 'I am not your love. I will not be your love again until you leave that man you are living with. Now go away and don't speak to me again.'

'But Grace, I'm married to him. He's my husband. Marriages can't break. He's your father.'

Grace said, 'He is not my father any more, not to me anyway. When all this is over, I am going to change my name legally. I do not want his name. He has betrayed me in every way.'

'Betrayed you? How?'

'Ask him. Now go away, Mother.'

Which gave Ellen no choice.

Dennis said, 'I wish there was a way in which I could help.'

Helena shook her head. 'If Mama can't talk her round, nobody can. Mama and Grace are very close.'

Dennis said, 'Are they very alike?'

'Yes.'

'Are you upset, Helena?'

'I miss her. And I feel guilty. Because I've been avoiding Grace.'

'On account of me?' Dennis chewed on his steak, turned his eyes on Helena.

She nodded. He laid a hand on her forearm. 'But, Helena – it will all blow over. In time. Yes,' said Dennis in his wise voice. 'Yes, it will.'

After dinner, they drove back by way of the dam. Dennis turned on the generator, trained the hand-spotlight on the far side of the curved dam wall. They stood in silence, Helena huddled in her coat.

'You know that I consider this beautiful, don't you, Helena?'

'I suppose so.'

He moved the spotlight again. 'Look at that curve. Look at the way the fog makes it seem like a kind of magic!'

Helena looked. Into the night, like a ghostly path to the future, stretched the high curve of the dam wall. The near levels had already been finished.

'We'll be able to walk along it next week,' said Dennis. 'Incidentally, will you give your mother a message from me?'

'What's that?' Helena's teeth began to chatter and she pulled the coat tighter.

'Tell her I met that Mrs Ulverton and I was able to do something about their getting a supply of electricity.'

'What?'

'Yes. I'm quite – pleased, really. Tell her Mrs Ulverton and I were able to work something out.'

'Oh,' said Helena, 'she'll be delighted.'

'She may be delighted too if you can answer the next question,' said Dennis.

Helena said in her mild way, 'Oh, yes?'

'This is the question. It is a very simple one. Will you marry me?'

'Oh!'

'I've asked your father.'

'What did he say?'

'He smiled like an angel. He is very fond of you.'

'Oh!'

'I thought we would announce our engagement at Christmas. Then we can take our time in deciding when to marry.'

Mrs Stokes had died in the afternoon. Word reached Ellen as to the manner of her death, and of Grace's involvement. Mrs Allen told Jack Hogan who told Miriam.

Grace came back from the Hanlons where she had been making drawings of their wall-bed. When the cat, hunched under the settle outside the cottage, ignored her friendship, Grace was alerted. The door was open; the fire almost out. She called. No reply. She called again. Odd. Mrs Stokes never went far.

Grace went to the old woman's bedroom door and listened.

Silence. She pushed through, saw the dark shape, half-kneeling, half-sprawling, as if she had tried to climb on the bed. Grace put down her sketch-pad and rushed over. The old woman said something Grace could not hear. With great strength she manipulated Mrs Stokes up and on to the bed, on her side, then rolled her over. Saliva came from her mouth corners.

Grace said, 'Are you all right, are you all right?'

Grace lit the candle, and rushed it to the bedside. She felt the woman's pulse, no sign.

'Are you all right, Mrs Stokes?'

Mrs Stokes tried to speak. The mouth gaped too much and as Grace bent to hear what she was saying, the eyes began to glaze.

Doubt never arises that someone has died. A force withers; new space becomes available in the air nearby. Grace sat on the chair beside the bed and gazed at the dead body. She never even knew she should close the eyes.

Grace's rejection sealed Ellen's feelings of despair, of isolation. Dennis Sykes had initiated the process by uncovering, and illuminating, the only foulness in her secret life. No good that she guessed he would never mention the feared and forbidden 'thing' again – in return, she presumed, for her own quiescence. No use, either, that she avoided him. Sykes even seemed to assist matters by calling to see Thomas at the school, but only in the afternoons, when Ellen had left. Nor did she see him much with Helena, whom he now met away from the home, collected her from her lodgings.

None of these facts contained any solace. All her resources seemed to be ebbing unstoppably down some dreadful tidal shelf. Such an impasse is often best dealt with by a degree of impassiveness. Ellen knew this from the year of Thomas's coma.

Which enabled her to judge carefully her response to Helena's agitated news: 'Oh, are you very excited?'

'Mama, I don't know what to say.'

'People in your position usually say either yes or no.' Ellen smiled.

'Daddy is nearly more excited than I am. Oh, Mama, do you think he'd be pleased? I mean do you think he'd like me more if – if I said, if I accepted?'

Ellen jumped in surprise. 'When did you tell him?'

'I didn't. Dennis asked him weeks ago. For my hand, I suppose.' Helena giggled in embarrassment.

'We must all talk it through,' Ellen stonewalled. 'We must talk through every detail. Did he give you, did the two of you, did you make any plans?'

'Just to get engaged at Christmas. And then he said,' Helena smiled – 'we could take our time, and decide slowly when to get married.'

'Have you said anything yet? I mean yes or no?' Both women laughed.

'No, Mama.'

Gravity never left Helena alone for long. Her face lengthened. 'I was thinking.'

'I know.' Her mother joined in. 'Grace.'

'Yes.' They paused.

On Monday morning, she watched Thomas teaching the senior classes. He had pinned three elm leaves to a piece of paper draped over the blackboard.

'The Elm,' he intoned, 'is one of the highest and most dignified trees in the wood. Its principle is to grow smaller leaves, but many of them. The Elm provides Man with spiritual and temporal sustenance. It is one of the first to flower in the Spring, and to many the fresh greenness of its foliage is the sign that Spring is only a few minutes away. Secondly, its wood, though not of a superior quality, proves equal to many fundamental situations. The inner bark of the Elm has been known to be capable of use in the brewing of beer. Thirdly, because it can endure moist circumstances, the timber of the Elm is used to make carts, mill-wheels and coffins.'

At morning break, she strolled into his classroom.

'Do they know yet,' she asked, 'of the holiday dates? The small ones were asking me.'

Thomas turned the calendar. 'The nineteenth to the twenty-sixth, that's one week, the twenty-sixth to the third, that's two weeks. If we say two weeks and two days, that brings them back on the fifth of January. That's good, that means the evacuation will be almost clear.'

Ellen said, 'By the way, I'm going up to see Mrs Ulverton this afternoon. And tomorrow, what are we going to do about Mrs Stokes's funeral?'

Thomas said, 'She's being buried during school hours, though. So there isn't much we can do.'

Ellen replied, 'I'll go.'

He replied, 'But it's at twelve o'clock.'

Ellen said quietly, 'I'll go anyway.'

'But what about –?'

Ellen interrupted, again speaking low, 'Grace will need some moral support, so I'll go. Now –' she rubbed her hands together; 'what would you like for your supper?'

He shook his head in irritation but made no comment.

In the Valley, Dennis shook the rain from his sou'wester hat.

'Don't you mind being alone in the house at night with a corpse?'

Grace shook her head. She pressed herself to the tree. 'Feel,' she said, patting the bole. 'The wood is warm, almost.'

Dennis wiped the rain from his face. 'You know the reason I didn't call is that it didn't seem right.'

'I know,' said Grace. She put her arms around his neck and kissed him.

Ellen said, 'I owe you an apology.'

'My dear, for what?'

'Well. I dragged you all the way to Dublin, we went to see that girl. I gave you to believe that I would then confront Mr Sykes with it. And I did nothing.'

'So is it true,' Rhona asked, 'that he wants to marry your daughter?'

Ellen nodded.

'Then you had good reason for doing nothing. But you can't be happy about it?'

'I'm not. But I have to think of Helena.'

'Is she happy?'

'Rhona, I don't know. This is her first experience of a man being nice to her. All I can do is watch.'

'You mean, Ellen dear, that is what you have decided to do.'

Ellen smiled. 'Yes.'

Rhona said, 'Let's go back into the house, I'm getting cold. By the way, I have a confession, too. Sykes and me. I never confronted him, either. Do you know why?'

'I think I can guess, I got a message. You did a deal with him.'

'I'm afraid so. I'm ashamed.'

'Because he offered to find a way of getting you the electricity without it costing you the earth.'

'Was I very wrong? It was Cyril's idea.'

'Oh, Rhona, no. You have to keep warm.'

'Yes, and anyway – we both have his measure. With two such women as ourselves we should be able to keep him under control.'

Ellen smiled thinly. Then she warmed and said, 'If you want me to talk to Joseph Comerford and Sons about appliances –'

Rhona said, 'I couldn't sleep last night, and I thought of something else. Your daughter Grace.'

'Yes?'

'Have you catered for her reaction if her sister marries that little man?'

Ellen said, 'I hope to see her tomorrow.'

Fewer than fifty people attended. Mud fouled the priest's white surplice. Intoning the prayers in raised voices above the wind, the daughter never looked in the mother's direction. Whereas the mother never took her eyes off the daughter.

In such a short time – what, ten, eleven months? – these women's existence had been polluted, faeces thrown in a crystal bowl. Up to then, in common with many families in their comfortable milieu, it was possible to think of life as a series of bridges to be crossed: or a wide-ish road, relatively clear up ahead; at worst, perhaps, a woodland path, full of easily moveable debris – Thomas Kane, father and husband, being the briar-thorns.

Such separation as had taken place between this girl, Grace Kane, and her family, cannot easily be bridged. The rift grows more troubled when parent and child feel so alike, seem so full of resemblance as these two women. Wind flayed the graveyard, driving the sleety rain before it, hammering it like small icy nails into people's clothes and bodies and cheeks.

Who else could have held Grace's pain safely, could have poured balm on it? She still had no language to encompass her father's abuse. The stolen letters became an emblem to her, a symbol of pillage, a tarring and feathering of her honourable efforts. In the many mad hurts of nocturnal fantasy, she assumed that Helena no longer wrote to her because of Thomas's intimidations. One person, and only one, had the capacity to ease Grace's soul: one person could even have listened and understood the rapine perpetrated by her night visitor.

That person stood a few yards away, unlooked-at, perhaps, by her daughter, but felt. Grace, so closely like her mother in body and mind, never had to raise her head to know it was Ellen who had entered a room. If not feeling guilty about her children of a day, if ever able on a random morning to acknowledge a difficult truth, Ellen would say to herself, unstoppably, 'I love Helena – but I adore Grace.'

When Grace turned away at the end of the graveside prayers, Ellen at last saw her daughter's eyes, puffy and red. The graveyard is a small one, rising to a hillock in the centre, where silvered railings mark the commemoration place for republican dead. Ellen halted beside a green-mottled headstone.

There are few descriptions which accurately capture the savage, shifting, lifelong jabs of parental anguish. There may be none which describe the primal desolation that a child – of any age – feels when it knows it has lost parents who go on living. Grace delayed and delayed, sheltering, talking to strangers.

Some years ago, the great hurricane blew down the giant macrocarpa trees at the western wall, and today the prevailing westerlies blow through here even more fiercely than they did on the morning Mrs Stokes was buried.

When Grace finally braved the pathway, she did not greet her mother. Ellen stepped out beside her.

'Gracey, can we talk?'

No answer.

'Grace!' Ellen tried authority.

No.

'Grace! Please!' Ellen took her daughter's arm. Grace glanced down coldly at the hand, then, standing motionless, looked into the distance, through the rain.

'Grace, it's Christmas the week after next. We want you home. That cottage is empty now, poor Mrs Stokes. I know how you liked her, God rest her dear bones. And soon the Valley won't exist at all. You have to come home, love. Please!'

So much rain had spilled on Grace's face that tears could not be measured. Dye from her scarf ran on her cheek, making a blue map. She dropped her purse and it fell open, spilled; Ellen bent to help; the women gathered coins from the mud, wiped them on their gloves. One by one, taking turns, they placed them in the purse, which Ellen snapped secure and handed back. Grace said, 'Thank you', bowed her head, raised her eyes again. She met her mother's gaze – and at that moment started the long journey back across their blood-bridge.

'Look, Mother.' Hesitant. Maybe tearful. 'This was all awful.' She chewed her lip, exactly like Ellen does.

'Oh, Gracey, the others miss you. I miss you, my dear, wilful daughter.'

'Wilful –?'

'No, I mean it as a joke. No, please.' Ellen took Grace's gloved hand and smiled a smile from long ago.

We do not always know the exact moment when we are making life-destroying errors: we only know the moment after we have made them.

'Do, love. Do come back. I give you my word. And I need you especially now. I need your life and soul for the party.'

Ellen smiled again, hoping her joke would land. She rattled on.

'Even though we're keeping it very quiet. Helena wants it that way. Although *he* – he would be happy, I think, with a pipe band playing.'

Grace turned, eyes like black-flamed lamps. 'Party?'

'Yes.' Ellen smiled in encouragement. 'Your father is very pleased with her. Imagine.' She half-giggled.

The punch of dread. Fear. The end of life.

Grace lost breath. She instantly knew everything, immediately recalled in vivid flashes the hard texture of his small-man's body, the shard of his fingernail, how it caught her askew, and she had to twist her hip to avoid the sting inside her.

'Hellie's getting engaged?' Desperate exhalation.

'There's no wedding date yet.'

'Aaaaa, hallo, ladies, there, I've to lock, like.' A man with keys

303

called them from the entrance to the graveyard. 'Aaaaa, the gates, like. Aaaa, sorry to disturb you.'

Grace did not ask the next question: Ellen answered it. But what can one do except speak on.

'Maybe late summer, we think. Depends on his, you know, Dennis's, his next position. Once the dam is completely finished.'

And nowhere to look, but up – to the sky and the rain. And nowhere to go, but away – forever and ever. One betrayal may break the heart; the second dismembers the soul.

19

Grace Kane disappeared. From the churchyard, Ellen, in distress, watched her daughter's retreating back: no point in even calling out. Steadily, the girl walked: not hurried, nor dogged.

At home, distressed to hysteria almost, Ellen wrote a letter. Or tried to.

'My dearest Grace.' Four times she began it. Four times she abandoned it. Splodges. Tears on the inky paper.

Helena arrived, and asked whether Grace had appeared at the funeral. Ellen replied ambiguously that it had not been possible to talk to her.

'Mama! What's wrong? Oh, Mama!'

Grace walked into Miss MacNamara's office at five o'clock that evening and asked for shelter. The headmistress looked at her and said, 'I will be finished here in half an hour. You can come home with me.'

Neither woman said a word on the cycle through Janesborough's suburbs to Miss MacNamara's neat and large brick house. Inside, she pointed Grace in the direction of bedroom and bathroom, and said, 'I will be down in the kitchen when you are ready.'

Grace did not appear that evening, nor the next. On the third morning, Miss MacNamara wrote to Ellen to tell her that Grace was safe and sound, if a little unwell; she advised no contact for the moment.

That night Miss MacNamara said to Grace, 'I don't know what has happened to you, and I only want to know if you want to tell me. This I do know. You are to call and see Dr MacMahon tomorrow at half-past eleven. I have made an appointment for you. I will accept no argument to the contrary. You will come back here and cook supper for me, which I will come home to eat at six o'clock. Thereafter, you will stay here until the first of February

305

when you will resume work as one of my teachers, part of our bargain, if you remember. I do not require you to speak to me until you are ready, and I have told Dr MacMahon – who is also my doctor – that you may wish to maintain your silence. He, too, understands.'

Grace lowered her head.

At Dr MacMahon's, she undressed piecemeal as he asked.

'Please nod your head if the answer is "yes", and shake it if the answer is "no". Have you been raped?'

Grace shook her head.

'Have you lost your virginity?'

Grace nodded.

'Have you had sexual intercourse more than five times?'

Grace nodded.

'More than ten times?'

Grace shook her head.

'Is your monthly period late do you think?'

Grace shook her head.

He looked in her eyes, and in her ears; he took her pulse and her blood pressure; he examined her hair and her nails.

'Dress, please.' She stood casually and put on her clothes.

As she sat in front of him he asked, 'Have you had a severe physical shock? Almost a bad accident, or anything like that?'

Grace shook her head.

'Have you had a bad experience, I mean a bad love affair.'

Grace stared straight ahead.

Dr MacMahon said, 'You know I must speak to Miss Mac-Namara, don't you?'

Grace nodded.

To Miss MacNamara that evening, as she called on her way home, he said. 'I have seen patients after the last war, and that was called "Shell-shock". You know what that's like. This seems not dissimilar.'

'What is your best guess, Doctor?'

'They also call it "catatonic". This is a mild version. Or it may be from choice. How and ever – something horrible has happened to her, some, I don't know – family trouble, something like that. Betrayal often produces it.'

Miss MacNamara asked, 'Will she come out of it?'

306

'Don't know. Don't honestly know. She should do, very fit. Very fit.'

'Anything I ought do – ?'

'Kindness and privacy. Nothing else.'

Grace missed the evacuation. Perhaps it was as well. It began at the farthest end, the point nearest the new pumping station, and how her heart would have caved in when the tractors came through with their trailers, crushing her beloved paths. Over the rise they came, like beasts stampeding methodically into the mouth of the Valley; they rolled regardless down the long line of hedgerow past Mrs Stokes's cottage. (No relatives had come forward to claim anything; the evacuators saw the heavy padlocks, made enquiries, shrugged: 'Their loss.')

Difficult right-angled turn: low, hard foliage brushed the smoke-stacks of the engines. One driver pointed out that those branches would have to be trimmed if any trailer came back piled high. Grace could have gone there, and sketched the trees before and after, howled at the barbarism of the sawmen.

They ravaged her earth, too: by the end of the day they were spreading gravel on that corner to try and ensure purchase – even for the bigger rubber wheels. The rain kept off.

In each house, the tractor driver and his helper asked, as they had been instructed by Dennis, 'Do you want to take anything built-in with you?' and they pointed to dressers, settles and wall-beds. Not one resident wished any of the vernacular furniture to be detached. All said something to the effect, 'Not at all, glad to be rid of it.' Grace could not have borne it; by then she was sleeping a dreamless broken sleep in her quiet city room.

For delicacy, it had been agreed to move one house at a time: two-hour intervals.

'They won't like their neighbours seeing everything they have,' advised Thomas. He and Dennis arranged to be at the entrance to the valley as each tractor emerged.

'Curious how little they actually have,' commented Dennis quietly, as the first load toiled past them. Thomas agreed.

'What's that?' Dennis pointed to a large wooden baulk on the second trailer.

Thomas peered. 'Good God!'

'What is it?'

'I'll tell you in a moment.' The cottier, his wife and their ageing, mentally infirm daughter walked past them behind the piled trailer: they acknowledged Dennis, ignored Thomas.

'What was it?' insisted Dennis.

'It was the roof-tree of the house,' said Thomas.

'What does that mean?'

'That's an old story. When people emigrated to America in the last century, they took the roof-tree with them, so that they would have some material with which to start building a new house.'

'But they're being rehoused,' said Dennis.

'It's in the blood,' said Thomas.

Grace could have recorded that incident: she could have made them stop for a moment, done one of her lightning sketches, thinking, 'Charcoal for the charred parts.'

Misty rain drifted in. The two men sat in Dennis Sykes's car. Another tractor noise drew them out again. This trailer had been piled high, high.

'Well-to-do?' asked Dennis.

Thomas nodded. 'All the children emigrated.' He called to the tractor driver, 'Is that everything out of that house?'

The man shouted back, 'Ah, 'tis, sir.'

'Where are they?'

'They've something hid they're waiting to get and they wouldn't look for it 'til I was gone,' said the driver, who crested the rise and reached the tarmacadam road in safety, then roared away down the hill-road towards Mooreville.

'What was that about?' asked Dennis.

Thomas smiled and said, 'We'll probably find out any minute now.'

He peered in the direction of the Valley mouth. Soon, two elderly men appeared. A small justice for Grace was at hand, a little crackle of retribution.

'Yes,' said Thomas grimly, 'I bet I know what this is.'

The men walked slowly towards him, one heavy on a walking-stick.

'Should we offer to drive them?' asked Dennis.

'No fear. Watch.'

Abreast, the men stopped. The one with the stick reached deep into the pocket of his greatcoat and drew out a large and obviously rusty Colt revolver. He pointed it at Thomas Kane. The trigger, he knew, would not pull.

'There you are, Kane. If this gun worked, I'd give you the contents. I'd empty it into your grey fuckin' oul' head, so I would. You fucker.'

His venom shook Dennis Sykes.

Thomas called back, 'A gun that wouldn't fire. Typical. You were a coward then, you're a coward now.'

The man threw the gun at Thomas; it landed several feet short.

'Pick it up, Kane. Put it to your head and pretend 'tis me. Fuck off to hell.'

'Big vocabulary as ever,' called Thomas Kane, and the men moved off.

'Whoooph!' said Dennis. 'Charming.'

Thomas stepped forward and picked up the handgun. He wiped the clay from it with a clump of grass.

'Now will you tell me?' demanded Dennis.

'Civil war,' said Thomas. 'We were on opposite sides.'

'But that was ages ago!'

'Thirty years precisely. But did you never hear the saying, "The English never remember and the Irish never forget." Look at this.' He displayed the gun to Dennis. 'No firing pin.'

Dennis took the gun. 'Whoo! Heavy!' He inspected it. 'Were you a good shot?' he asked. Thomas nodded.

Changing the subject he asked, 'Do you want to go and see those houses?'

Dennis said, 'No, I'll wait until they're all empty.'

Four more houses that day; four more tractors emerged from beneath the misty trees like creatures. On their trailers sat tables, chairs, bedding, cardboard boxes, tea-chests. These merry one-family processions looked like evacuees from some benign war, en route to the land they had been promised. One of the Valley's few children, a pal of Grace's, wore a saucepan on his head, and waved like a victor.

Tales had already begun leaking back to Deanstown of the Grey Valley people's ecstasy when they saw their new homes. Thomas Kane preened.

As the rain cleared, Dennis pointed. The curved wall of the dam could be seen through the glim. Some men walked along the top, seeing to things here and there.

'I am pleased,' said Dennis Sykes, 'at how compact it is.'

'And powerful,' chimed in Thomas Kane, 'like yourself, if you don't mind my saying so – compact and powerful.'

That night, Dennis Sykes went back into the Grey Valley to find Grace Kane. Christmas had been quiet and sombre. Helena said she wished to wear no ring just yet, not until Grace came home. Ellen Kane remained quiet, withdrawn even, but civil.

He shone his torch through the windows. In Grace's room, a white nightdress lay over the back of the chair. Her books remained stacked on their shelf. The cottage's back door had a heavier padlock than the one at the front: he drifted away.

The evacuated houses swung ajar. He wandered in and shone his torch all around. A settle had been opened down from the wall and left as if in use. He sat on it, caressing the timber with his hand. Grace had shown him her drawing of this piece. From his torchlight upon the chimney breast, he could see the cup-hooks on the rim of the high mantel, where they had not even taken away the oilcloth from the mantelshelf.

'Yes,' he said aloud, 'it could be Africa. Just as bloody primitive.' At the door something startled him. He flashed the torch at it: goddam barbarians – they had left without taking their cat!

Next morning, before Thomas Kane arrived at the observation point, Dennis stopped the first of that day's four tractors.

'Have you left any domestic animals behind?'

'Howja mean, like?'

'A cat or a dog?'

They shook their heads. The sun came out and the possessions on the trailers glowed in the watery light. One woman came over and shook Dennis's hand.

'God bless you sir, I hated that oul' house, so I did, and I asking the council to get me a new house with years now.'

=

310

By the middle of the following week, just before Thomas Kane reopened Deanstown School, the Grey Valley had been totally evacuated. The last tractor left at three in the afternoon.

'While there's still some light left?' suggested Dennis to Thomas. They walked in.

'I'd forgotten how small it is,' said Thomas. 'It's like a pocket, isn't it?'

'That's what makes it perfect for our purposes,' said Dennis. 'It will fill perfectly and at great speed, and then it will hold the force of that water forever. Wonderful idea, isn't it?'

He watched the elderly man carefully as they passed Mrs Stokes's house. Thomas looked neither to the right nor to the left. They visited seven of the empty houses.

'No interest, I see, in preserving "vernacular furniture", that's for sure,' said Thomas in a jeering tone.

As they returned, he again ignored the Stokes cottage.

'So – all set?' he said to Dennis, as they reached their separate cars.

'Went smoothly, didn't it?'

Thomas nodded.

'Thanks to you,' said Dennis. 'Look how you handled all that, all the persuasion, all the commonsense.'

In her note to Miss MacNamara, Grace said she had decided upon a short holiday, probably in Galway, a lot of walking, and she would be in touch. But Grace took the bus to Cork. On the same morning, Miss MacNamara took the bus to Deanstown, and conferred with Ellen.

'I am not an alarmist, am I?'

'No,' agreed Ellen. 'You are not an alarmist.'

'But she has not spoken a word. Not one word. In the afternoons she went for long walks and returned absolutely silently. We ate together; she never spoke a word. Nothing but silence.'

Ellen said, 'And she my most talkative child.'

'Yes.' The women sat in thought.

'Ellen, are you worried?'

'I am. Dreadfully.'

'That's the way I am.'

Ellen said, 'Should we put out an enquiry, I mean through official channels, a police notice on the wireless?'

Miss MacNamara said, 'I would.'

This did not happen. Thomas Kane said, 'Under no circumstances. This is just another means she has dreamt up of spoiling things. Of getting attention. How dare she?'

Ellen went for help. 'Rhona, Rhona, please! I know, I know, I feel it in my bones. I know.'

'I agree with you. Dear Ellen, I agree with you. Put the notice in yourself.'

'I can't – it has to go through the Sergeant and he won't do it without Thomas's signature, I can tell you that now.'

'Who do we know in Galway?' asked Rhona.

Ellen said, 'I don't know anyone.'

Rhona said, 'Nor do I.'

Ellen remembered. 'Miriam Hogan. Her brother's a Gardiner man, he's a doctor outside Galway. We'll ask her.'

But Miriam told Jack, and Jack told Thomas Kane.

On the twenty-ninth of January, Grace Kane came back to the Grey Valley. Via a roundabout, devious route, that began when she went to Cork, and deposited her from the bus almost twenty miles from the Valley. It rained heavily; Grace got to Mrs Stokes's house at one o'clock in the morning. In Cork she had bought a can of paraffin for the primus stove, several yards of strong thin rope and some sheets of thick oilcloth. The workmen had now closed the entrance to the valley, and she had to hike her bicycle over rocks and felled trees. The builders had begun the final sealing-off of that last remaining gap in the entrance.

She assembled a space like a bureau for herself at the table and wrote: to her mother, to the youngest Kane, Hugh, and, longest letter of all, to Helena. On the third morning she climbed the ridge at dawn and looked all around. Everything was in place. Nobody to be seen.

The dam waited, patient and firm. Smaller finally than Grace had expected; and she had to admit that the curve made it an object of great beauty. She ducked beneath the briars: far beyond her, Dennis Sykes appeared, walking like a game-cock on the wall of the dam, leaning over the railings, checking their strength.

'If I had a gun,' spat Grace aloud.

Her words made a bird fly screeching from the tree nearby, and Dennis looked up sharply. When nothing developed he continued his cocky stroll, the early sun shining on his yellow hard-hat. Under cover of the foliage all the way, Grace eventually went back to the cottage, and when she got there had again to hide. High above, and in full view, workmen had begun erecting the great opening-day platform.

For the next two days, Grace lived like a small animal. Mrs Stokes's stores of smoked bacon would satisfy her minimal food requirements; the stream had drinking water; the old primus stove would make tea – no smoke could she show until after dark. Heavy blankets sealed the windows: no firelight could shed a flickering message into the night.

Heavy in its frame, she bore Mrs Stokes's old mirror from the bedroom to the kitchen. By tilting the angle, Grace had a face to whom she could speak – her own. Only once did her resolve waver when, in an unguarded glance, she saw a face so like her mother's: she returned the mirror to the bedroom.

The house welcomed her; all its night-time noises crackled and sighed, and she recognized every voice. Pictures in the fire, again: flicks of blue flame, with orange; and the pillowy bed had no memory of the bad nights and the shames.

In the morning when she woke, she rose immediately, did not lie long abed. She washed carefully and all over: water taken in the previous night from the rain-barrels. No more prayers: they had stopped weeks ago.

All the time, she wrote her journal, pages and pages. When she heard the workmen leaving the sites, and their distant laughing gibes and farewell calls, and the lorries revving away in the distance, Grace slipped from the cottage and like a ghost toured the empty houses of the valley. From them, she gathered bric-a-brac: a pothook, a broken cup, a discarded fishing-rod.

On the evening of the thirtieth of January, she took down all Mrs Stokes's crockery and prepared to fill every vessel she could find with woodland decoration. Next morning early, she gathered a last few gentians, and broke branches from trees and shrubs. The stone-flagged old kitchen began to look like a cottage-garden. Later that day, Grace manhandled the wooden settle from the fire-nook into the middle of the floor, and surrounded it with lamps and candles.

One last flit. She knew the Valley floor so well. The foxes on the edge of the shale: they might have cubs. Grace slipped and slid upwards, a pale half-moon helping, the flashlamp to be used only when utterly needed.

Her heart thumped: a light came bobbling towards her. She stepped aside, ducked low, trying to be silent on a crop of loose, large stones. A long torch approached, in whose light the black boots glimmered. Grace's hand closed around a stone, and she hefted it into her hand. Feet from her, Dennis walked on, a last traverse of the heights before his triumph.

In darkness and strong wind, under floodlights, Mass began at half-past seven. From the canopied viewing platform, the Curate and the Archbishop could see the people's lights struggling up the ridge. Needless to remark, Thomas and Ellen Kane and their family had reached the site long before anyone else from the village.

'Wish me luck,' said Dennis.

'You don't need it,' whispered Thomas, and Helena pressed Dennis's hand secretly. Beneath them, the valley lay in hard, cold darkness. To their right, great lights played on the wall of the dam. One long searching lamp picked out the rock which at nine o'clock would be blasted to let the twin rivers merge and become glittering torrents.

The morning light began to spread. Mass ended with the Archbishop's blessing and a singing of 'Hail Glorious Saint Patrick'. A breakfast in the temporary hut rang with laughter and congratulations. The American news cameraman enthralled Hugh Kane with his stories of war and bullets.

'Do you smoke Camel cigarettes?' asked Hugh.

Ellen asked the cameraman to ensure that Hugh did not make a nuisance of himself. Other photographers snapped Dennis and Thomas and the Archbishop. The evacuated residents, Guests of Honour, told everyone of their fine new homes.

At three minutes to nine, Dennis led the Archbishop out into the open air again. On a podium, wires racing away from it, sat a large red button. The Archbishop, Edward Ahern, stood theatrically still. Beside him waited the Minister for Transport and Power,

Dan Cantrell, and Dennis Sykes – behind whom towered Thomas Kane.

All along the edge of the ridge, the villagers stood in lines. They leaned over, looking down; despite the raw February cold, they chattered and called as if at a garden party.

Ellen Kane remained impassive. Had Leah been there she would have felt alarm at the way Ellen's mouth worked in tiny, ceaseless movements.

'Thirty seconds to go, your Grace,' said Dennis Sykes. 'I checked my watch with the wireless last night.'

'I get my time from the BBC,' said the Archbishop, and smiled his pastor's buttered smile. 'They have the best time.' He folded his soft hands again.

'Get ready, your Grace.'

Archbishop Edward Ahern stepped forward.

'Now,' said Dennis Sykes.

Archbishop Edward Ahern plunged the button and at the far end of the valley there resounded a great crak-crak, then a boom. In the cottage below, Grace heard it, but did not see. Some said the flash was blue, some green; all saw the smoke and the flying rocks. Then the waters began to tumble – slower than they had expected.

Above the hubbub Dennis explained to the Archbishop, 'They have to move slowly at first. If the stream flowed too rapidly the pumping station would be overwhelmed. But when they hit the pumping station – watch, your Grace, look!' he cried. 'Now they'll begin to roll.'

Before all their eyes, the waters surged forward and as if kicked from behind rolled down into the early slopes of shale that led to the deeper valley. At first no wider than a mountain stream, the waters became a spate, then a torrent, then a wide cascade, sparkling and bounding down.

'How long, say, before these places down here will be covered?' asked the Archbishop.

'We calculate by about half-past two,' said Dennis. 'That is why we have timed the switching-on at three o'clock or just after it.'

'A work of genius,' said the Archbishop. 'Where do I switch on?'

'Same button, your Grace. The wonders of science,' smiled Dennis.

315

They clapped Dennis on the back; they photographed him again and again, and even the Archbishop agreed that a drink at this hour on a cold morning was acceptable in such remarkable circumstances.

The water found its way into the valley floor in directions nobody expected. As the sun appeared fitfully, the watchers on the ridge (none of whom had left) shouted, 'Over there', or 'Look, down here'. Soon that part of the valley floor directly beneath the platform resembled a field after several days of rain, a field with a tendency towards getting waterlogged, a field where curlews alight. Those who bought foreign-missions magazines were reminded of rice-paddies.

People who had not brought picnics mooched in the general direction of the large festivities tent, and were not disappointed. At eleven o'clock, Bill Prendergast and his sons arrived and set up a stall selling ice-cream and sausages.

'Ice-cream! On this day of the year, your Grace,' marvelled Thomas Kane to the Archbishop with whom he got on so well. 'And then,' he continued, telling the old tale, 'McCormack just opened his mouth –'

Edward Ahern, a fine, straight man for his eighty-five years of age, said when Thomas had finished, 'I love that story, Mr Kane.'

Ellen Kane smiled with her mouth but not with her eyes.

At one o'clock they began their wagers. At what time would it begin to go in under the nearest house door? Any minute now? Wasn't that where the old Stokes woman died? Yes, it was racing now, the water, out across the valley floor and rising. By twenty past one, it was lapping the foot of the dam wall, covering the last high winter grass over there.

As they had been told it would, the gap had opened wide by the pumping station, where the water was now hurtling down like a real big river in spate, spuming, bucking; powering down. Dennis appeared on the podium, peered down. They saw him and cheered him, and he acknowledged the cheers like a little *Duce*. And still the crowds gathered, streaming up the hill, hurried on by the cheers from up on the ridge.

=

Inside the tent, Dennis Sykes heard it first, heard the changed note. He held up a hand to halt the conversation he was having.

'Listen.' That was not a cheer. 'Shh, listen.'

A gabble. A moan. The door burst open and a man's face gasped, 'There's a woman down in the valley!'

Ellen screamed.

From the podium they all saw her. Grace came to the door of Mrs Stokes's house in her white nightdress. The silver water, now flowing flat, wide and fast as a tide, plucked and lapped at her calves. By opening the door she had let the water course into the house. She looked up, shading her eyes against the winter sun. People screamed, and the crowd released a moan of wonder and horror.

Ellen pushed forward. Every hand on the platform held her back. Thomas Kane crowded behind her. 'Who is it? Who is it?' he asked, and nobody told him – until he saw his wife's eyes on him. He covered his face with his hands.

Grace looked slowly along the ridge, scanning the long crowd standing on the lip behind the ropes. With no gesture, no acknowledgement, she walked back into the cottage and, with difficulty against the rushing waters, closed the door. With his binoculars Dennis saw light after light go on in the cottage.

People beleaguered him. The Archbishop commanded him.

'No, your Grace.' Dennis's voice rose in fright as he answered, explained. 'It takes nearly twenty minutes to get down. No, the pumping house cannot be switched off, there's nobody over there on account of the danger of the blasting. It would be – too late.'

The sun had begin to sink, and western light, Grace's favourite, flooded the kitchen. The candles and lamps now lit, she folded her last writings in the thick oilskin cloths, and bound them to her body. She had tied the settle to the iron fixings at the fireplace, and now she lay on the settle and tied herself to it. With her hair splayed out behind her, a dark Ophelia, she waited in peace for the waters to reach her.

The waters rose higher and higher; the watchers on the ridge saw the lights in the cottage flicker and go out, one by one.

Ellen never left the podium, never took her eyes off the cottage

317

windows, never blinked, never wept. Helena, her mouth frozen open, hugging herself in unspeakable dismay, had been led away by the Hogans. Thomas Kane could be seen alone in the catering tent, sitting upright on a chair, eyes closed. Of Dennis Sykes, no trace. In silence at half-past three, as the waters slapped the dam wall, the Archbishop pressed the great red button, and the lights of Deanstown in the distance were switched on, fireflies far away.

In the rare event that you have not enjoyed Frank Delaney's
A Stranger in Their Midst, return your copy, together with your
till receipt, giving the reasons for your disappointment, to the
following address before 5th July 1995 and we will give you a
full refund. HarperCollins*Publishers*, Trade Marketing,
77-85 Fulham Palace Road, London W6 8JB.